SEE THESE BONES

ALSO BY CHRIS TULLBANE

The Murder of Crows

See These Bones
Red Right Hand *
One Tin Soldier *

The Many Travails of John Smith

Investigation, Mediation, Vindication *
Blood is Thicker Than Lots of Stuff *
Ghost of a Chance *
The Italian Screwjob *
A Dead Man's Favor *
Godswar *
John Smith Doesn't Work Here Anymore *

*Forthcoming

See These Bones

Chris Tullbane

NEVADA

First published by Ghost Falls Press 2019

Publisher's Cataloging-in-Publication Data
provided by Five Rainbows Cataloging Services

Names: Tullbane, Chris, author.
Title: See these bones / Chris Tullbane.
Description: Henderson, NV : Ghost Falls Press, 2019. | Series: Murder of crows, bk. 1.
Identifiers: ISBN 978-1-7334824-1-7 (paperback) | ISBN 978-1-7334824-0-0 (ebook)
Subjects: LCSH: Superheroes--Fiction. | Heroes--Fiction. | Self-actualization (Psychology)--Fiction. | Fathers and sons--Fiction. | Bildungsromans. | Fantasy fiction. | Science fiction. | BISAC: FICTION / Superheroes. | FICTION / Coming of Age. | FICTION / Fantasy / General. | FICTION / Science Fiction / General. | GSAFD: Fantasy fiction. | Science fiction. | Bildungsromans.
Classification: LCC PS3620.U45 S44 2019 (print) | LCC PS3620.U45 (ebook) | DDC 813/.6--dc23.

Book cover design by ebooklaunch.com

FIRST EDITION

For Nami,
the reason for everything

ACKNOWLEDGMENTS

Writing is a solitary process, but I've found that everything after the initial draft is a hell of a lot easier when you have amazing people to rely on. I'd like to thank the following for their many contributions:

Nami, who reads everything I write, no matter how terrible. She is my wife, editor, agent, best friend, and narrative compass, all rolled into one.

Johanna, whose friendship keeps me going when the words run dry. This book's not a romance, I swear!

Jamie, who has been nudging me to get this book published since the day the first draft arrived in his inbox and who is both the best and the only brother I've ever had.

Shawn and Keith, my partners-in-crime during the eight month sabbatical that kick-started my writing career, who are quick to remind me that I should already be done with the sequel.

And last but not least, my parents, who didn't blink when I opted to pursue a degree in writing, (even if they did breathe a sigh of relief when I instead found a career in software development).

Thank you all.

CHAPTER 1

My mom was murdered when I was five.

The good news is they caught her killer. The bad news? It was my dad. Any shrink will tell you that's the sort of thing that can fuck a kid up.

By the time my sixth birthday rolled around, both parents were in the ground; Mom in a quiet cemetery on the other side of town and Dad in the considerably less quiet prison the Free States built for people like him.

And people like me, I guess.

Turns out dark hair and grey eyes aren't the only things that asshole and I have in common.

My mom was murdered when I was five. I didn't see her again until I turned nine, but ever since then, she's made a habit of following me around. Losing your virginity to the girl who works the slushy counter down the block is stressful enough without the ghost of your dead mother bearing witness.

Now, there was a time when even talking about ghosts earned someone a padded cell and a lifetime supply of medication. But that was before things went bad. Before Dr. Nowhere broke the world. These days, stories like mine divide neatly into two camps; the people who see the dead because they're batshit crazy and the people who are batshit crazy because they see the dead.

That second group? We call them Crows and they don't just *see* the dead. You've heard the stories. Lord Bone and his skeletal army.

Gravedigger's circle of elementary school sacrifices. The Crimson Death's march through the blood-soaked heart of Reno. And Sally Cemetery… well, everyone knows about Sally.

But those are just the big names. There are a dozen others that nobody has ever heard of, people whose body counts weren't high enough to merit a vid, whose atrocities failed to catch the nation's eye. Necromancers who only snuffed out a handful of souls. Or maybe just one.

Crows like my dad.

Crows like me.

We all go mad. That's just how it is. The weaker among us—the Ones, the Twos—end up in asylums with the everyday lunatics, one more flavor of crazy for the nuthouse. But the true Crows, the Threes and Fours who somehow survive to adulthood?

Villains. Black Hats. Murderers.

Every. Damn. One of us.

Which is what made my admittance to the Academy of Heroes so unexpected.

But my expulsion from that same institution?

Everyone saw *that* coming.

CHAPTER 2

I bounced between foster homes for a few years after Mom died, never staying with any family more than a couple of months. Not until the Jacobsens—Norm and Sue, because apparently it's a cosmic law that ordinary people have really stupid names.

For some reason, these two God-worshipping hero-vid junkies actually gave a damn. Wasn't like it had been with my real parents, but Norm didn't seem likely to up and murder Sue either, so I wasn't going to complain. Norm, Sue, and little Damian… the perfect pretend family.

Yeah, *Damian*. It's like Dad wanted to screw me over from the start.

Anyway, the Jacobsens spent six months tearing down my walls, six months sitting through night terrors and angry spells. Convincing me that they cared. That they'd be there for me through anything.

Then I turned nine.

Then Mom showed back up.

Then we all learned that Dad wasn't the only Crow in the family.

Just like that, I was back at Mama Rawlins' House of Unwanted Brats. Sue watched me go, peeking through her living room window from behind white, frilly curtains. I think she even cried. Which might have meant something if she and Norm hadn't been the ones who called the orphanage in the first place, the ones who decided I wasn't the son they'd been looking for after all.

I don't blame them. Not really.

I blame myself. Should have known better than to get attached.

The Jacobsens were my last ride on the foster family merry-go-round. Word gets around, I guess. I spent the next eight years as the orphanage's unofficial mascot, watching delighted little shits disappear into the arms of delighted older shits. And yeah, I bumped uglies with the slushy girl a couple times, so it wasn't all bad. Say what you will about her—or don't, unless you want an army of zombie rats crawling up your asshole—but she was warm, smelled better than I did, and didn't care what I might one day become.

Also? Free slushies! Compared to the synth-food the orphanage fed us, a cup of flavored ice was almost as good as sex.

She's dead now, of course. The slushy girl. I know what you're thinking, but I didn't do it. A year or so after we started seeing each other, she and her parents left Bakersfield. Went north to Palo Alto, to a sweet new job for her dad and an economy that hadn't spent the last four decades in the shitter.

That was five months before Scarlet's battle with the Capes from the North Star. In one afternoon, the Black Hat Pyromancer killed six hundred people and burned down half of Palo Alto. Everyone remembers the heroes Scarlet killed that day. Everyone remembers that Dominion responded by dropping a satellite on her head. Nobody remembers the people of Palo Alto.

I remember.

I remember the slushy girl.

Alicia. That was her name.

* * *

I was seventeen when Alicia left town. I was seventeen when she and six hundred other people died. I was *still* seventeen—if only barely—when my life changed yet again. Three days from my eighteenth birthday, when I'd become an adult in the eyes of the Free States and my free ride at the orphanage would end. To say I was worried about where I'd be sleeping, what I'd be eating, and how I'd pay for either was the understatement of the decade. There are a lot of words to describe Crows but employable isn't one of them.

I was trying to distract myself from impending doom by showing little Nyah—five years old, and a shoo-in to be adopted the next time a pair of needy parents wandered by—how to throw a punch, when the common room went dead quiet.

Mama Rawlins was standing at the orphanage door with a man.

He wasn't much to look at. Average height, average appearance, and average-length hair that was—you guessed it—a thoroughly average shade of brown. A grey suit hung loosely on a frame as remarkable as a clothes hanger. He was the sort of person that would fade into a crowd, who seemed to fade into the background even as the only stranger in the room.

That all changed when I saw his eyes. They were flat and cold, like pennies that had been worn down by time, leaving only smooth metal behind. They glittered in the common room's dim lighting.

Nyah shivered as those eyes focused on me.

Mama Rawlins escorted the penny-eyed man in my direction, a path through the common room appearing like it had been wished into existence. Ten of my fellow orphans, from Nyah all the way up to fifteen-year-old John, turned to watch the drama unfold.

The man's voice was quiet and empty of emotion. "This is he?"

"Yup." Mama Rawlins' voice, by contrast, was a scratchy baritone, courtesy of the two-pack habit her state salary and some truly creative bookkeeping afforded her. "Damian," she nodded to me, "meet Mr.—"

"Grey," the man filled in smoothly.

"Mr. Grey. From the government." Her eyes widened comically, as she added the words that would seal my fate. "He's a Finder."

I should have run. Young legs, not much meat on my bones… maybe I could have made it.

Instead, I let curiosity get the best of me.

Fucking moron.

CHAPTER 3

There aren't a lot of cars on the roads. I'm told they were everywhere before Dr. Nowhere broke the world, but these days, most people recognize them for the rolling death traps they are. Never know when another Pyro like Scarlet might show up or when that psycho Pele is going to surf in from the Pacific on a tidal wave of shit-you-not lava.

And that's before you even get to the Shifters or the Titans. Know what King Rex used to call cars? *Meals on wheels.* Dude had acres of style to go along with that skin condition and seventy-foot shadow.

Mr. Grey opened the passenger door of the rust-covered death trap parked at the curb, and waved me in.

After a moment's hesitation, I shrugged. Truth was, I'd always kind of wanted to ride in a car. I tossed my bag into the back seat, and climbed in.

The engine coughed and wheezed like an asthmatic choking on a bone. In a series of lurches, our car pulled into the empty street, noxious black smoke wafting out behind us.

The other reason nobody drives cars—especially in a town like Bakersfield—is that the roads are terrible; more pothole than surface. Or maybe the roads are terrible because nobody drives anymore. Hard to say which was the cause and which was the effect.

Anyway, it turns out that riding in a car really sucks. I'm talking *having-a-spring-shoved-up-your-ass-every-couple-seconds-while-the-whole-vehicle-shudders-around-you* sucks. And once we got up to top speed—slightly faster than your average non-Jitterbug could run—every scrape of metal against asphalt made me think the world was going to end in fire.

It will, of course… and sooner than anyone wants it to. But that's a story for another day.

Point is, in almost eighteen years of life, I'd done some stupid things, but nothing quite made my balls want to crawl up into my body like that car ride.

* * *

We'd traveled maybe a mile before I pulled myself together. I hugged my knees to my chest, shifted my ass so the damn spring—did you think I was being metaphorical?— poked something less delicate, and turned to the man who'd come for me.

"Are you really a Finder?"

Mr. Grey didn't give any sign that he'd heard me.

"Where are we going?"

Still nothing.

"Hello?"

Nothing. Guy made a stone wall seem talkative.

Yeah, I know some stone walls talk. You'll hear about one of those, if you stick around that long. But you get what I'm saying, right?

"I don't care what Mama Rawlins thinks," I finally said, "this is the Free States and you're not allowed to just kidnap me. Tell me where we're going or I'm sticking my head out this window and screaming bloody murder. I know all about *stranger danger*."

For those of you who *don't* know, that's pre-Break literature, something I'd found digging through the boxes of crap Mama Rawlins kept at the orphanage. They used to give these pamphlets to kids to teach them not to head off to strange places with people they didn't know.

Apparently, children were just as dumb back then as they are now. Seems hard to believe.

Not sure if it was the words, the threat, or my stunning display of pre-Break knowledge, but Mr. Grey finally responded. He pulled to the side of the empty road, killed the engine, and turned to me.

"I have a use for you, Mr. Banach, but you are not indispensable. Keep a civil tongue."

"Or what?" I challenged.

"Or you will be replaced." Those blank coins slipped just a tad, and behind them was something like white noise and hunger.

I know what you're thinking. *Damian Banach? Seriously? That's your name?* Well, you can fuck right off. Banach was Mom's maiden name. Think her side of the family came from Poland, way back when there was a Poland. I sure as hell wasn't keeping my dad's last name, on top of all the other shit he'd given me.

Could've been worse. I could've been Norm Jacobsen, Jr.

Or maybe you're thinking that Mama Rawlins' doublewide ass should be arrested for letting some psycho take her oldest orphan? Please. It's not like she was going to say no to the same government that kept her in cigarettes and synth-rations.

And I had even less choice in the matter. Nowhere to go, no skills to offer, no way to eat. Whatever the government wanted would beat starving in the street, right?

I swallowed my anger and shut the hell up.

He restarted the car and eased back out into the empty road.

CHAPTER 4

There's nothing to like about Bakersfield. Pretty sure that was true pre-Break, and it's sure as hell true now. Balls-hot in the summer, foggy and moist in the winter, boring as shit year-round. The city's a long way from the ocean, from L.A. or the Bay. It just sits in the middle of nowhere like a middle finger to the tumbleweeds.

No wonder Dad went nuts.

Not that it excuses what he did.

Anyway, Bakersfield; worst city in California, and probably the whole Free States. Used to be a lot of farms, I'm told, but it takes a full-fledged Weather Witch or Druid to grow much of anything these days, and Powers sure don't want to live out there. Used to be oil fields too, but there's not much need for the stuff anymore. Barely any cars and most of the country gets its juice from the grid, which is powered, in turn, by a few hundred Cat Two Sparks.

Powers; making the Free States better one lightbulb at a time.

Since the Break, Bakersfield's population has been nosediving like a Flyboy on a joy ride. Two different attempts to rebrand—first as a tourist destination, then as the country's new center for manufacturing—failed miserably way before my time, leaving behind only faded bulletin boards, looming over an increasingly empty skyline. The city is an old man getting older by the day, shrinking inward until there's nothing but skin and bones, surrounded by the rubble of its own decay.

Hell of a place to be born, abandoned, and then sort of raised.

Worst city in the Free States still makes it a damn sight better than the Badlands, mind you, let alone anywhere on the eastern side of the continent, where life expectancies are dipping into the low-thirties. Still, can't say I was sad to watch Bakersfield fall away in the passenger-side mirror.

I *was* pretty curious about where we were headed though.

I hadn't seen the sun in a week—because it was the tail-end of winter, and winter in the valley meant fog, mist, and more fog until you wanted to claw your eyes out just to see something different—so I had no clue if we were going north or south. We'd left behind the tiny slice of Bakersfield I knew after only a few minutes in the Finder's car. By the time we hit open highway, I was totally lost.

Got clued in about twenty minutes later, when we passed a couple of signs that hadn't been stomped flat, lit on fire, or transformed into cactuses.

Yeah, cactuses. Crows get all the bad press, but Druids are the worst.

The first sign said I-5 South.

The second? Ninety-seven miles to Los Angeles.

* * *

The road south of Bakersfield is where happy thoughts go to die.

I can't remember who said that, but they knew what they were talking about. Whole place is a wasteland; dirt, dust, and a scattering of scrub grass too dumb to know it's beaten. No ocean, no vid screens, no net access… just miles and miles of empty, until you wish the mist would roll back in just so you can pretend something interesting is hiding out there.

As near as I can figure, the road south has only two things going for it. The big one, of course, is that it's taking you away from Bakersfield. Almost as important is that it isn't the *north* road out of town. Take everything I said about the south route and triple it for the long, long ride up to the Bay.

Now *there's* a trip that can drive someone to murder.

* * *

We'd been rolling along for almost an hour when Mom decided to make one of her appearances. I glanced behind me to find her in the car's back seat next to my bag. She looked the same as ever, a dark-haired woman in a knee-length, floral print dress. In life, that dress had been yellow, the flowers on it red. Now, the dress was as faded as the rest of her, nothing but a vague hint of color to go along with the increasingly vague hint of personality.

Mom didn't speak. She never had, not since finding her way back to me. Given her murder, you'd have expected her ghost to be angry or haunted, but whenever I saw her, she was humming a silent, wordless tune, taking in the surroundings with a loopy smile on her see-through face. Was almost reassuring to see her always happy. Would have been better to have her alive, or at least aware of my presence, but you got to take what you can get.

"Who is it that you see?"

"How did…?" I stopped *that* question when it was only halfway out of my mouth, and went with one almost as stupid. "You know what I am?"

"Why else would I have come?" His voice remained absent of emotion. It was like he'd lost interest in the question even before he finished asking it, the last few words powered purely by inertia.

Yes, I know what inertia is. Fuck off with your whole *poor dumb orphan* bullshit.

"Since when do Finders bother with Crows?" A fraction of a percent of our country's population had powers, and it was the Finders' job to locate those individuals and make sure they were tested, trained, and employed. The bare handful who ranked higher than Cat Two made it into the pompously titled Academy of Heroes, where they were trained to be Capes.

Crows weren't a part of that. The government had no use for Necromancers and the Capes damn sure didn't want anything to do with us. So why had a Finder driven all the way out to Bakersfield to retrieve one?

The man's voice was quiet, but his eyes glowed as he spoke. "Times are changing and we must change with them. War is coming to the Free States."

CHAPTER 5

We'd traveled through another few miles of dust and dirt, the temperature rising steadily with the sun, before I finally replied.

"I don't know what you've heard about me, but all I do is see ghosts. Just one ghost, really. If you're looking for armies, I'm not your Crow."

"Not yet. With time and instruction… we will see."

I flinched as the car dodged a house-sized tumbleweed. "Are you saying the government has some sort of secret training facility for people like me?"

The Finder's smile flickered again. "It trains more than just Crows, and there is nothing at all secret about it."

I swallowed past the dry lump in my throat. "You mean the Academy."

"Yes."

"The Academy of fucking Superheroes."

"Fucking is not a part of the curriculum, but college-age men and women in close proximity with one another… I suspect it does occur, yes."

That was the closest thing to a joke I'd heard from Mr. Grey all day, but I wasn't in the mood for humor. "The Academy doesn't accept Crows!"

"Did not," he corrected me. "You may be the first."

"May?"

"We will find that out soon enough."

"And if I say to hell with the Academy?"

The man's eyes glittered again like copper pennies. He took both hands off the wheel and, for the second time, let our vehicle coast to a halt in the middle of the desolate freeway. The engine coughed, sputtered, and faded into silence.

"That would be... short-sighted." As I opened my mouth to demonstrate just how short-sighted I could be, he spoke again. "You have yet to answer my question."

"What question?"

"Who is it that you see in the backseat?"

I shrugged. "My mom."

"Ah." His voice remained mild. "Elora Jameson. Dead at thirty-two, at the hands of her husband, David. Your father."

"Don't talk about my parents." I felt my hands bunch into fists, knuckles cracking.

"I have little interest in your progenitors, given their respective fates. If anyone should pay them heed, it is you." Those copper eyes drifted down to my fists, and the empty smile widened.

"What's that supposed to mean?"

"The sins of the father, passed down to the son, repeated through history in an ever-spinning cycle of tragedy. How many decades before madness consumes you as it did him?" He nodded to Mom's ghost as if he could see her. "How many decades before your mother has company by your own hand?"

Mom met my gaze with a cheery smile and absolutely no recognition. I turned to look out the window, where a hundred miles of desolation stared back at me through bleak and empty eyes. "Everyone knows what happens to Crows."

"Untrained ones, yes. Poor, mad bastards like the father you do not wish to speak of."

I swallowed a second time. "Are you saying that training could keep me sane?"

He shrugged. "Power cannot be controlled through ignorance. No Crow has ever attended the Academy, but if its instructors can teach a Weather Witch to harness the lightning or a Shifter to hold their second form..."

"Then they might teach me how to keep from going nuts." I felt the first crack appear in my shell of well-honed pessimism. Since I was nine, I'd known my fate, known there was fuck-all I could do to stop it. It was hard to believe that there might be an alternative.

"However, if you prefer not to attend…" The Finder reached past me to push the passenger door open, letting in a blast of heat. "You are free to leave."

"We're in the middle of the desert," I reminded him.

"Yes."

"I'd die before I could make it to either Bakersfield *or* Los Angeles."

He shrugged again. "Every decision has its consequences."

I pulled the door shut before the hot air could cook my exposed skin. "Yeah. I think I'll go to the Academy."

"That choice will have consequences of its own," he warned.

I rolled my eyes and sank back into the uncomfortable seat as we began to move. No wonder everyone hated the government.

* * *

A half hour later, we encountered the first signs of life since leaving Bakersfield; a collection of sun-weathered, rust-covered buildings, huddled like hungry beggars around the cracked ribbon of highway. The Finder pulled our car onto a side street, driving past a handful of houses before coming to a stop in a parking lot. The building that bordered the lot was twice the size of its neighbors. A fresh coat of paint was busy peeling away from aluminum siding, and both front windows remained intact.

"This doesn't look like Los Angeles."

"Because it is not." He nodded to the mountains that rose above us just to the south. "The City of Angels lies beyond those hills. But this is a stop we must make first." He slipped out of the car and headed for the building.

With a shrug, I followed. If the place was on the grid, it might have air conditioning. And water. And hopefully some food. We were several hours past lunch, and I was already regretting not having swiped some of Mama Rawlins' synth-rations before we left.

* * *

As we passed through the doorway, the blessed hum of central air conditioning greeted us like the whispers of a benevolent god. I heard the room's other occupant before I saw him. He had his feet up on an oversized desk and his eyes were closed. His snores would have gotten him smothered in his sleep at the orphanage.

Mr. Grey made a beeline for the man, waited half a second to see if he would wake on his own, and then slammed an open palm against the desk's surface. The loud crack of flesh against wood was almost immediately followed by a startled scream, and an even louder thud, as the stranger toppled backwards out of his chair. A few moments later, he scrambled to his feet, reaching to pick up a pair of glasses from the desk.

"Uhm…" He squinted at us both. "Can I help you folks?"

"We are here for testing," the Finder told him evenly.

"Oh, right." The other man nodded sagely. "I'm going to need you to fill out…" He rustled through a stack of papers. "…forms 36A, 57B and 99." With a frown, he gave up his search and scanned the room. "Assuming I can find any of them."

"That will not be necessary," said Mr. Grey, leaning forward to flash the other man his identification. "The paperwork has been filed."

"Alrighty then. Which of you is being tested today?"

Something like emotion leaked into Mr. Grey's voice. Assuming irritation qualified as an emotion, anyway. "The boy."

"Right. Right." The other man looked over to me. "Well then, welcome to your testing. My name is Jeremy, and I'll be your operator today. Are you familiar with the process?"

Since I didn't have a clue what he was talking about, I shook my head.

"Sweet, I get to give the speech." Jeremy escorted us into the back room where two chairs—one of them slightly elevated and cushioned like an old barber's seat—had been set up next to a machine the size of Mama Rawlins' liquor cabinet. Atop that machine was a messy bundle of wires, each terminating in a white plastic pad. A set of bicycle handlebars had been grafted to the top of the machine and wrapped in copper wire. "Powers, you see," he began with obvious excitement, "come in all shapes, flavors and sizes, from the smallest trickle of ability to… well, someone like Dr. Nowhere, I guess. What this device does is…"

"Measure my power levels," I finished. The machine looked nothing like the gleaming devices I'd seen in hero-vids, but given that every Cape on those programs was both physically flawless and morally unassailable, I'd already suspected there were some serious liberties being taken with the truth.

The Finder's comment back in the car suddenly made sense. The Academy only opened its doors to those few Powers ranked Category Three or above. A Four was a shoe-in. A Five? They were so rare as to almost not exist. And if I was a One or a Two, I could kiss admission—and my only shot at staying sane—goodbye.

"So you *do* know." Jeremy looked disappointed for a moment, then shrugged. "Technically, it's your power level *potential*, but close enough. Grab a seat and take off your shirt."

I did as instructed, wadding my faded tee into a small ball and lowering myself into the indicated chair. The cracked vinyl cushioning made a rude noise beneath me.

I looked up to find Jeremy staring.

"That was the chair, not me." I scowled.

"Huh? Oh, the noise? Yeah, it's always like that." He turned and busied himself with the machine for a moment, before tossing a glance back over one shoulder. "So uh… can I get you something to eat, maybe? Like a sandwich? Or twelve?"

I looked down at my all-too prominent ribs and flushed. A sandwich sounded great, but I'd be damned if I accepted it with a side order of pity. I shot the older man a glare. "I'm good. Let's get on with this."

"Sure thing." Jeremy shrugged yet again, and began to sort through the bundle of wires. He slathered the plastic pads with some sort of cold, sticky gel and stuck them to my chest like mutated nipples. By the time, he was through, my torso was covered. "Grab the handles, please."

I leaned forward, causing the chair to fart a second time, and took hold of the copper-wrapped bike handles.

Nothing happened.

"Do you have to plug it in or something?"

"These don't work off garden-variety outlets." Jeremy winked. "That's what I'm here for." He rubbed his palms together for a moment, as if trying to warm them, and then reached forward and touched both hands to the machine. Moments later, a low hum told me it was active.

"You're a Spark?"

"Most testers are, for obvious reasons. And you are…" He paused, adjusted a couple of dials on his side of the box, and checked the readouts a second time. "Wait, you're…"

"A Necromancer," answered Mr. Grey mildly.

Jeremy mustered up a wan smile. "Never tested a Crow before. Alright now… keep a hold on the handles. This might tingle just a bit."

The world erupted in light.

CHAPTER 6

I was seven when Mama Rawlins finally decided to fork out the cash for a vid screen. Way she explained it, she was getting too damn old to be chasing us kids around and needed something to occupy our attention when she was off doing adult stuff.

Adult stuff, in this case, mostly meant smoking, though she did have a man come calling from time to time—even older than she was, with four long hairs pasted to an otherwise shiny bald scalp. That was a pairing designed to give you nightmares, let me tell you, even before I walked in on them in the moment. Or whatever passes for the moment, when you're a million years old.

Anyway, vid time became our entertainment of choice, and no matter how many times she programmed the box to stream educational programs, one of us would always switch to something a little bit more our speed.

Hero-vids, mainly.

A lot of it was crap, of course; pure kiddy stuff, where the Cape—someone like Captain Cosmo—was a noble stick in the mud, and the Black Hats were as dumb as they were dirty. Great for the little ones, but those of us creeping towards our teens knew bullshit when we saw it.

In the evenings, though, and every Saturday, they'd air vids based on real events. Paladin's year-long crusade into the Badlands. Aspen's awakening in the wreckage of San Diego. Even Tempest's battle with the Sea Reavers, where she sank their battleship and everyone on board with a storm of pure lightning.

The last one was my favorite. I must have seen it a dozen times—I could hum the musical score in my dreams—but I'd always focused on Tempest herself, long-limbed and gorgeous, ribbons streaming behind her in hurricane-force winds, eyes white and charged like the force of nature doing her bidding. I'd never once wondered what the Reavers must have felt like to have the electrical hammer of God crashing down on them.

Turns out it really sucks.

* * *

Sometime later—could have been minutes, could have been hours—I regained consciousness. I was slumped forward, head nestled in one arm, a cool surface under my cheek. My limbs were vibrating and my exposed skin felt hot and prickly, like I'd wrestled a thorn bush.

Pretty sure the thorn bush had won.

My eyes were open, but the world was blurry and indistinct. I focused on the closest blob, but it was the smell, more than anything, that told me what I was looking at.

A sandwich. Synth-meat—pork flavor, if my nose could be trusted—and a leaf of browned lettuce between two slabs of processed wheat. Behind it, carefully out of reach of my flailing hand, was a glass of water.

My mother—my real mother, not Mama Rawlins or Sue Jacobsen—had always joked about my appetite. She would know something was wrong, she told people with a grin, the day I passed up seconds at lunch… and if I skipped dessert, well, she was paying for a Flyboy to rush us to the hospital, and to seven hells with the cost.

After the asshole killed her, dessert became a thing of the past—along with seconds and a whole host of other happy family bullshit—but the basic point remained; few things motivated little Damian like food.

I flopped my second arm onto the table, and used both limbs to push myself into a seated position. Hell if I was going to just lie there with lunch waiting.

"Welcome back to the land of the living."

I looked up, mouth full of sandwich, to find Mr. Grey seated nearby, every bit as bland as the moment we'd met. We were back out in the front room of the testing facility.

"Whaddafugg habbnd?" I swallowed my food and tried again. "What happened?"

"An unfortunate blend of aging technology and poorly trained public servant." Copper eyes glittered in the dim light. "What matters is that you survived."

I shook my head. "That's *not* what matters."

"True enough." The Finder gave me a respectful nod. "Eat your sandwich. It is a long trip still to the Academy."

I felt the tension drain out of me in a rush. "You mean…?"

"Yes. Despite nearly killing you with his incompetence, Jeremy managed to complete your testing. Low-range Category Three. It appears this morning was not a waste of time after all."

I barely even heard his words through the rush of relief. Cat Three was the bare minimum for the Academy, and Low-Three meant I was about as weak as a Three could get, but it was enough. Admission meant training and training meant my descent into madness might not be so inevitable after all.

With apologies to dead Alicia, that moment of realization was better than anything I'd felt since Mom's murder.

* * *

I polished off my meal. "Where's Jeremy?"

Mr. Grey nodded to the back room. "Filing the results of your testing. Having served his purpose, it is unlikely that the two of you will meet again."

The words were innocuous, the tone even more so, but twelve years in an orphanage had left me a suspicious little shit, and Academy-bound or not, I wasn't ready to take the Finder's words at face value. I leveraged myself up onto still-wobbly legs. "I'm going to say goodbye."

This is the part where I tell you that the back room was a horror show, right? That pieces of Jeremy were strewn from wall to wall, leaving nothing but carnage across grey tiles?

Sounds like we've seen the same sort of vids. That or you've got a seriously fucked up imagination. Wonder if that's what got you killed?

The only sign of trouble I found was the small plume of smoke drifting lazily from the testing machine. In the chair next to it, Jeremy was bent over a net terminal, typing away, face downcast and pale except for two spots of color in his cheeks.

"You taking off?" All of the enthusiasm had drained from his voice, leaving it almost as flat as Mr. Grey's.

"Looks like it."

"Cool." He kept typing away, eyes down. "Sorry about the testing."

Maybe I should have held a grudge. Guy almost kills you, you don't forgive that shit, right? But Jeremy had played his part in potentially saving my sanity. Magnanimous near-adult that I was, I decided to let it go. "It's okay. Might want to get that thing fixed before the next kid comes through though."

"Still trying to figure out what went wrong," he mumbled, nodding in agreement.

"Well… thanks, I guess."

"Later." He still hadn't looked at me.

Asshole was even less social than I was. I turned to leave, but paused, that same little voice of suspicion whispering in my ear.

"What did I test out as, anyway?"

This time, Jeremy did look up, his expression odd. "Low-Three. Didn't the Finder tell you?"

"Right. Electrocution must be making me loopy." I gave a shrug, like I was just a forgetful idiot instead of a suspicious bastard, and made my exit.

Out front, Mr. Grey was waiting for me.

And this time, he had company.

CHAPTER 7

She had a body made for vids—legs a mile long, tits high and proud—every inch of her displayed to perfection by tight black leather, from low-heeled boots to painted-on-pants to a jacket of slightly heavier construction. But from the neck up…

I blinked, frowned, and blinked again. Her face was round and bright yellow, with two large black dots for eyes and a curved black line forming a smile.

"What the hell…?" The words slipped out, barely audible even to myself, but the woman glanced over anyway, and the glint of interior lights off her head was enough to correct my initial assumption. She was wearing a motorcycle helmet. The smiley face I'd seen was a decal wrapped across the helmet's visor.

"Meet your escort," said the Finder. "She will be taking you the rest of the way to the Academy."

My frown deepened. "You're not coming?"

"You are not the only individual on my list." His bland smile flickered into view then faded just as swiftly. He turned to look up at the woman at his side. "Deliver him to the Academy of Heroes no later than tomorrow evening. I leave the details to your discretion."

And just like that, Mr. Grey walked out of my life forever.

Well… not quite forever.

Life couldn't be *that* easy.

* * *

The wheeze of Mr. Grey's death trap had faded away before Smiley finally spoke.

"Let's go, kid." The voice didn't fit her body. It would barely have fit *Mama Rawlins*' body. It was deep, rough, and weirdly discordant, like razor blades scraping against one another on every syllable.

She was smoking hot—from the neck down, at least—but I wasn't a total fool. "I'm not going anywhere until you tell me who you are. Are you a Finder too?"

Her laughter was short and sharp, but it had actual humor in it in a way Mr. Grey hadn't managed even once since I'd met him. "You think *I'm* a Finder? Where the hell did he dig you up?"

"Bakersfield."

"My condolences." Again, that flicker of humor. I couldn't see a face beneath the decaled visor, but I could feel her studying me. "I'm a specialist, kid. Well-paid and well-armed, and that's all you need to know."

"Like hell it is."

She regarded me for a moment, then shrugged. "Come with me or don't." Those mile-long legs took her out into the brightly lit lot. The door slammed shut behind her, leaving me in near-darkness once again.

If the day was teaching me anything, it was that playing the hardass only worked if you had some actual leverage. Or a reputation. Or, at the very least, an alternate fucking means of getting to the Academy.

I rushed outside, where the nameless woman was carrying the half-filled bag that contained my every possession over to…

"Holy shit. Is that a motorcycle?"

I know what you're thinking: maybe the helmet should have been a clue? Thing is, in Bakersfield, bikes were almost as rare as cars. Less so by the coast, it turned out, but this was only the third or fourth one I'd ever seen.

Smiley paused in the act of shoving my belongings into the bike's saddlebags, and spun that yellow face back in my direction.

"Are you slow or something, Bakersfield?"

I felt my cheeks flame—and when you're as pale as I am, that sort of shit is visible from orbit—and tried to redeem myself. "What's it run on? The grid?"

"Battery… but that gets its juice from the grid," she acknowledged, turning back to the bike, and bending over to tie the saddlebags shut. "One charge can get me to the Bay and back."

I nodded, almost as impressed by that statistic as I was by the way the line of her legs led up to a truly spectacular ass. Before I could say something truly stupid, she spoke again.

"If you're coming, get over here. And stop staring at my ass."

Either Smiley had eyes in the back of her head or…

…or she knew how almost-eighteen-year-olds thought.

I'm guessing it was probably the latter. The flame in my cheeks now a bonfire, I joined her at the bike.

"It's a thing of beauty," I decided after a moment's pause.

"You'd better be talking about the bike."

I actually *had* been, but I bristled anyway. "And if I wasn't?"

Her voice clashed and sparked. "Then you're even dumber than I gave you credit for, Bakersfield. Boy like you…"

"I'll be eighteen in two and a half days," I corrected her, "and if you knew anything about my life—"

"*Boy like you*," she repeated, "needs to learn manners before some woman a whole lot less patient than me teaches you some. With a welding torch." She slid one leg over the bike and took her seat. "Now shut the fuck up and get on the bike."

I hadn't survived my early years in the orphanage by letting people push me around. But there was a time for defiance and a time for caution… and when people start talking welding torches, the time for defiance is well and truly over. I squashed down my anger, and tried for a more reasonable tone.

"Do I get a helmet?"

"Not unless you earn it, and the chances of that are lessening by the word."

"This is bullshit," I muttered to myself—one last pointless moment of defiance to salvage my pride—before climbing on behind her. "Do you at least have a name, or should I keep calling you Smiley?"

For a long while she was silent, the two of us frozen atop an immobile motorcycle, Mom's ghost standing just off to the side. Then she shrugged. Once again, I could hear the laughter in her voice. "Call me Your Majesty."

I rolled my eyes so hard I almost passed out.

It was enough to make me miss the Finder.

CHAPTER 8

Unlike Mr. Grey's car, the bike was practically silent; just a low hum of a motor and the sound of rubber on asphalt, both buried beneath the wind rushing past us. It was slower than the car—if that death trap had gone twenty-five, we were doing fifteen at best—but the open air made it a shit-ton more exhilarating. I held on tight, ducked my head into *Her Majesty's* shoulder to avoid bugs flying into my face, and concentrated on not falling off.

When we hit the incline, finally climbing into the mountains Mr. Grey had pointed out, our pace slowed further. We were still going faster than I could run—especially up a hill that steep—but it was a damn sight slower than the Finder's car. The sun slid down the sky in front of us and the hours crept by.

Two people, neither of them small, inching up an otherwise deserted road towards the rapidly setting sun?

Guess we made a pretty good target.

The sound reached my ears right after Smiley stiffened in front of me—a dull, echoing crack, that was swiftly followed by our bike spinning onto the shoulder. Somehow, she kept her hold on the handlebars.

I didn't keep my hold on her.

Guess it's good we were going so slow by then. And that the roads had turned to shit, leaving the shoulder mostly overgrown. All I know is that I didn't split my head open when I fell, even if the asphalt did chew right through my shirt and jeans to bite into the flesh beneath.

I landed on my side, which was probably the other reason my head didn't go splat. It left me in perfect position to see the bike careening wildly up the shoulder, to hear another two cracks of what must have been gunshots, and to see Her Majesty knocked out of her seat. Bike spun one way, she went the other. Both lay still.

All those nice things I said about the road south of Bakersfield?

I'm taking them back.

* * *

I lay on my bruised and bleeding side for all of a minute before my brain kicked back into activity. Maybe it was the sight of Mom, standing nearby, totally unconcerned. Or maybe it was the silhouettes of figures picking their way down the hill as the sun embraced the tree line.

I staggered to my feet. Between my earlier electrocution and the crash, I was barely mobile, but nothing seemed to be broken—nothing I needed right then anyway. I cradled one arm against my chest and looked up to where Smiley and the bike had been swallowed by darkness.

That's not some sort of fancy metaphor or anything, mind you; the sun was almost entirely gone, leaving the whole hill in deepening shadow. I couldn't see more than ten or so feet in either direction. Even so, I wanted to believe she'd made it. Badass hottie in leather? No doubt she was already up and ready to kick ass.

After being shot three times?

Alright; maybe not.

I could have checked to be sure, but that would have meant going toward the people who'd just shot at us.

Sorry, Your Majesty. At some point, it's every Crow for himself.

Not a Cape sort of thing to do, I guess, but I wasn't a Cape just yet. Wouldn't ever be one if I couldn't survive the next few minutes.

Live to run away and fight another day, am I right?

I'd made it all of ten feet off the road when something struck me in the head. No white light, like there'd been at the testing center. Just darkness.

Hurt almost as much though.

* * *

"This him?"

I don't how long I'd been out this time, but it couldn't have been more than a minute or two, because night was still in the process of falling. Against a backdrop of grainy twilight and a handful of cold stars, I made out the darker shapes of two figures standing over me.

"Better hope it is," answered the second guy, "since you shot the shit out of the other one."

"I don't got your special tricks, but my eyes work just fine. Boss man said get the *boy*, and that driver weren't no boy."

"Boss man also said to take the boy alive."

A hard boot caught me in the side, driving all the wind out of me and provoking a gasp.

"And he's alive. So why are you riding my ass?"

When the second man spoke, his voice had dropped to a low growl. "I'm riding your ass, Dale, because your dumb-fuck move could have cost us our cut. More importantly, I'm riding your ass because I'm the motherfucker in charge of this op. Unless this is you making a move?"

A bright light flared crimson and orange, illuminating the two men above me. Both unshaven, both dressed in layered clothing, both hard men with scarred faces and eyes that looked black as death in the night. One had a rifle in his hands, but he was the one backing away. And the other man… a snake of living fire was looping around his left hand, pulsing like a heartbeat.

"You're in charge, man," said Dale, still backing away. "All I was saying—"

We never got to find out what he was saying.

Smiley's motorcycle was quieter than a car, but it still made some noise; the hum of its motor, the squeal of tires against asphalt, and a half dozen other things that kept it from being entirely silent.

Except when it came flying through the air like a five-hundred-pound missile.

It hit Dale square in the back, taking him right off his feet and into the darkness. Judging by the sounds both he and the bike made hitting the ground, I didn't think either one was ever getting back up.

"What the fuck?" asked the other man, who had to be a Pyromancer. "Cole? Jackson? You guys up there?"

"Your men are dead, sweetling." Smiley stopped just short of the fire's light, glossy leather glistening amidst the greater darkness. "Time for you to join them."

"Fuck that shit." The Pyro crouched low, and a second snake ignited around his other hand. "Come and get it, puta." With a flick of his wrists, both snakes spat a torrent of orange fire at the woman.

Flames crackled, spit and eventually died, leaving nothing behind but darkness.

"Yeah, that's what I thought," he muttered.

Over the rush of blood in my ears, I heard something… the rasp of metal against metal, as if someone was running a crowbar over the teeth of a saw. Then I saw it.

It didn't snow much in Bakersfield—and when it did, all we got were small, dirty flakes that melted almost before they hit the ground—but I'd seen blizzards on vid; cold air thick with snow and a howling wind that sent the whole mess horizontal.

I'd never seen a blizzard quite like this though.

What came at us wasn't ice or snow or anything natural. It was shrapnel and steel and sharp, jagged edges, a cloud of gonna-fuck-you-up rocketing forward out of the windless dark. The Pyro's scream cut off in mid-crescendo as three rods pierced his chest and a half-dozen metal shards perforated his skull. The long, sinuous strands of barbed wire that followed—enveloping his body and twisting to shred exposed flesh—were a particularly gruesome bit of overkill.

The Pyro's flame died when he did, but the fires he'd set off on either side of the road gave enough light for me to watch the cyclone of shrapnel pull itself together, regaining the shape of a tall, leather-clad woman, a yellow smiley-face painted across her helmet's visor.

"Fucking hill trash never learn," growled Her Majesty.

CHAPTER 9

Our attackers were all very, very dead. That was the good news. The bad news was that the bike was a wreck, its frame bent out of shape, and its battery leaking something that smelled like farts and death.

Or maybe that last part was the corpses. Her Majesty had drafted me into moving the bodies into a pile down the hill, but I could still smell them on me; blood and piss and all the other foulness that comes spilling out of people at the end. With night well and truly fallen, I was now sitting by the road, trying hard not to smell myself, and watching Smiley stoke the dregs of the Pyro's last fire into something that might keep us warm through the night.

She tossed down her saddlebags on the far side of the fire and took a seat next to them, riding gear creaking noisily with the motion. She had yet to take off the helmet, and that giant yellow face—reflecting the flickering flames between us--wasn't doing a damn thing to calm my nerves.

It didn't help that we had company.

Mom stood nearby, smiling as usual, and taking very little notice of the fact that she was partially standing *in* the fire… but I was used to that much. The other ghost though? That was a new development. In fact, he'd been alive less than an hour earlier. Hell, it was *his* fire we using to warm ourselves.

Unlike Mom, the Pyro's ghost was plenty angry. He stomped soundlessly around Smiley, screaming silent imprecations. Naturally, she couldn't see him. More importantly, there wasn't a damn thing he could do to her. Ghosts couldn't touch the real world, couldn't do much of anything except annoy the fuck out of Crows like me. Thank god, that second bit never occurred to Mr. Recently Slaughtered. Instead, he focused his impotent rage on the woman who didn't know he was there. Eventually, he threw up his hands, mouthed what looked like a truly impressive chain of expletives, and stalked out of view.

I hoped that'd be the last time I saw him. One ghost following me around was bad enough.

"Get some sleep, Bakersfield. If we can't find the hill trash's transport when the sun's up tomorrow, it's going to be a long walk to the Academy."

"You mean you can't fly?"

I couldn't see her expression behind the visor, but her words communicated it just fine. "If I could, do you think we'd have putt-putt-putted up this hill for the last few hours?"

It was a good point. "You *are* a Power though, right?" Shifter, I was guessing, although I'd never heard of one quite like her before.

"More of one than *that* asshole was." The helmet nodded.

"Cool." Now that the episode was behind us, and the bodies—and the ghost—were safely out of view, I felt some of my equilibrium returning. It wasn't the first bit of violence I'd witnessed. The messiest, sure… but far from the first.

It wasn't the last one, either… but I guess that goes without saying.

"*Cool*, he says. Fucking teenagers." She shook her head. "Guess I should just be thankful you didn't try to help." I could barely see her, but apparently, she could read my expression just fine. "Don't get your panties in a knot, kid. Nothing worse than an amateur trying to contribute. Sort of thing that gets the wrong people dead."

"Instead, I just lay there like an asshole."

"Most assholes are too damn stupid to stay down." Another sound as she shrugged slim shoulders. "Anyway, you're not a Cape yet. Once you've swallowed their Kool-Aid and been molded into a proper…" She paused. "What kind of Power are you anyway?"

"Crow." I didn't know what Kool-Aid was, but it sounded illegal.

"Once you're molded into a …" She stopped a second time, and her voice went oddly soft. "You're a Necromancer? *And* you grew up in Bakersfield? Did Dr. Nowhere have something against your ancestors or were you just fucked over by complete random accident?"

I… wasn't quite sure how to respond to that.

"And since when does Cape University take Crows?" she continued.

"Since tomorrow, I guess. Mr. Grey says I'll be the first." I peered through the fire. "Shouldn't you already know all this, seeing as how you're such a *professional*?"

"In my line of work, there's a time for asking questions, and there's a time for taking the money and shutting up. This was definitely the latter."

"Oh yeah? Was there a welding torch involved?"

Her laugh was sharp and jagged. "There are scarier things than torches out there, kid. Scarier than me even." I heard as much as saw her shake her head. "If I'd known, I would have charged triple. I mean… a Crow Cape from Bakersfield? It's like a black cat spilling salt on a broken mirror. Or a unicorn's exact opposite."

"Am I supposed to know what any of that means?"

"It means you're bad news and even worse luck. No wonder that hill trash gang picked today of all days to claim the route."

"Luck had nothing to do with it. They were waiting for me." I told her what Dale and the Pyro had been saying when I first came to.

Her Majesty's silence was profound, eventually broken by a single, quiet word. "Motherfucker."

"What?"

"Don't worry about it," she eventually replied. "Nothing we can do about it and once I get you to the Academy, you'll be their problem, not mine. For now…" She scooted slightly away from the fire, and sprawled out, using her saddlebags as a lumpy pillow. "For now, get some sleep."

"Just like that?"

"Just like that. Way your life is going, you'd better learn to rest while you can."

The way my life was going, I wasn't sure I *could* sleep. Unfortunately, there wasn't a whole hell of a lot else to do, out in the middle of nowhere, with my only companion—only living one, anyway—already taking her own advice. I curled up, using my arm as a makeshift pillow, and closed my eyes.

Ten or so uncomfortable and not-at-all-restful minutes later, Smiley spoke again. "Cold, Bakersfield?"

"I thought you were asleep."

"Hard to sleep when I can hear your teeth chattering." Her rough voice went liquid for just a moment. "Want to come over here and… warm up?"

My mind flashed to the shredded pieces of the Pyro's skull, a skull I'd been forced to carry down the hill. "Thanks, but I think I'm good."

"You're gonna hurt a woman's feelings, kid. Don't you think I'm sexy anymore?"

Whatever I was going to say in reply was pre-empted by the long, strangely sensual sound of a zipper being pulled open. Might have been her jacket. Might have been her pants.

Come to think of it, the Pyro had gotten exactly what he deserved. Hell if I was going to let his memory get in the way of… *staying warm.*

I had just made it to my feet when the zipper was drowned out by another, now-familiar sound; the low scrape of razor blades, a saw grinding against a tire iron, or a thousand armored hornets having the world's most terrifying orgy.

On third thought… *fuck that shit.* I dropped back down to the ground, as close to the fire as I could get without actually getting anywhere near Her Majesty.

Mocking laughter serenaded me to sleep.

CHAPTER 10

I'd tell you about my dreams that night, but they were horrific… some in ways I still don't want to think about. So, let's take a bit of a breather instead. Most of you have probably kept up just fine so far, but I'm guessing a few of you lived your lives pre-Break, and wouldn't know a Cat One from a Five, a Shifter from a Spark, or even what I'm talking about when I say things like "pre-Break."

The story goes like this; eighty-some years ago, a guy had himself a dream. Less awful than mine, I'm guessing, but strange nonetheless; he dreamed of a world where people had powers like those he'd read about in comics, a world of bright and shiny possibilities far beyond the usual day-to-day rat race.

No idea why they raced rats back then, but it does seem like the sort of thing to drive a man to dream of something new.

Anyway, nothing too weird about any of that, right? Guy goes to sleep, guy has a dream, guy wakes up. Happens all the time. Thing is, when this guy woke up, *his* dream had become reality. Across the world, people—not all of them, just a percentage of a percentage—had been granted powers. Flight, strength, invulnerability, laser-fucking-eye-beams… you name it, it made an appearance, bestowed on a random sampling of strangers across the globe.

The aspect of his dream that *didn't* become reality was the bright and shiny part. Turns out, most people are dicks. Even the ones that don't have dicks. Give those people powers and… well, shit goes down.

The world changed forever in the course of a single man's dream… but the Break itself took longer. Can't speak for countries on the other five continents, but according to the history books, the United States of America tore itself apart over the course of several bloody years. The government fell. New regimes sprouted up like weeds, and all the while, new people kept developing powers, and everything kept getting worse.

Most people are dicks, sure enough… but the corollary to that rule is that some people aren't. None of us would be here if it weren't for one of the first Powers, a guy who won the metaphysical lottery and decided not to use it to shit all over his own species. He called himself Dominion, and as the rest of the world fell into chaos, he fought to save one small piece of it. Others came to join him, the handful of Powers who chose to protect rather than enslave. Collectively, they helped what was left of the military eke out a territory encompassing California, Oregon, Washington, and Arizona with pieces of Colorado, Nevada, Utah, and New Mexico. The new country called itself the Free States, and the Powers who chose to defend it became known as Capes.

East of us is the Badlands, a sort of free-for-all where nothing rules but chaos and fear. Past that, you start getting to the more established regimes; Steel and his fascists up in what used to be New England, Legion lording over Old Baltimore, and the procession of warlords that come and go in the dirty South. Places that make the Badlands look good. Places that make Bakersfield seem like paradise. A shithole, yeah, but still paradise.

In the early days, some scientist had the bright idea of grouping Powers by class and magnitude. Class is mostly self-explanatory; Flyboys fly, Druids grow stuff and obsess over trees like nature-loving stalkers, Necromancers do… whatever the fuck it is we do. Others are less obvious; Stalwarts and Titans both have combat gifts, but manifest them in different ways. Shifters… well, shift… sometimes into beasts, sometimes into minerals. Never heard of one that could do what Her Majesty did, but… we'll get to that, eventually.

As for magnitude? Even before the Break, there were legends of a Weather Witch named Mother Nature, the sort of bitch that loved to watch the world go pear-shaped. She got sad, rivers flooded. She got irritated, droughts and quakes happened. And when Mother Nature got well and truly pissed… well, then she unleashed holy hell in the form of earth-fucking storms. People called them hurricanes and scientists measured their strength from Category One to Category Five.

I can see some of you nodding your heads already. Yeah, the post-Break eggheads looked at those old-world rankings and decided what worked for hurricanes would work just as well for Powers.

It's an imperfect system—which is why those categories are further broken down into Highs, Mids, and Lows—but it stuck anyway. Don't blame me for that; I wasn't around when decisions were made, and nobody would've asked my opinion even if I had been. Likelihood is, I'd have been born somewhere else, and wouldn't have survived long enough to learn all the ways my life had been fucked by one man's dream.

As for the dreamer himself? He's the only Cat Six Power the scientists have ever classified… and nobody knows for sure who he was, if he's still among us, or what the hell he was thinking. All we have is a name—not his real name, but something the newspapers coined, back in the days before the world finished breaking.

They called him Dr. Nowhere.

CHAPTER 11

While I was asleep and dealing with dreams we still won't be discussing, Her Majesty was off looking for our attackers' car. My first clue that she'd found it was when she parked the fucker right next to my head and leaned on the horn like it was some kind of toy.

I was halfway to the other side of the road—and three quarters of the way to pissing myself—before I fully woke up.

"Up and at 'em, Bakersfield." The yellow smiley face across Her Majesty's visor looked a little bit more maniacal than I remembered… but it's possible I was projecting. "We've still got a drive ahead of us."

"Is that thing safe?"

The vehicle Smiley had found was *technically* a car, in that it had four wheels, belched black fumes, and didn't fly, but if Mr. Grey's vehicle had been a death trap, this thing redefined the word. It was little more than a frame and an engine. No doors, no roof, no windows, no chance of survival if we got in any sort of accident, and no guarantee it wouldn't explode the first time we hit a pothole.

Her Majesty shrugged. "It runs. And the brakes must work, or I'd have hit you. What more do you need?" Her rough, gravelly voice echoed from within the helmet, quietly mocking. "Now let's roll. Places to go, children to deliver, paychecks to earn."

My hesitation, surprisingly, had little to do with the car. I hadn't had much to eat or drink the previous day, but even so… "I have to take a leak."

"So what's stopping you?" That yellow face kept smiling away. "The world is your toilet."

I wasn't going to admit that I'd never been out of Bakersfield before and that the idea of finding a tree to piss on was as foreign as… well, sleeping around a campfire a few hundred feet away from fresh corpses. I was halfway convinced that the moment I took my dick out, some snake was going to leap out of nowhere and try to bite it.

Thankfully, we seemed to be in a snake-free zone that morning. Maybe Smiley had murdered them all before going to find the car. I zipped up my jeans and limped back to the road, feeling every ache and scrape I'd picked up the previous night.

Her Majesty nodded to the backseat, where she'd already loaded her saddlebags and the mangled remains of the electric motorcycle. "Grab a change of clothes from your bag while you're at it. Pretty sure your precious Academy has rules against showing up in bloody clothes."

"You didn't go there, I take it?" Anyone rated Cat Three or above was supposed to, but I had a hard time seeing Smiley in superhero school.

"Academy's for Capes. You see any Capes around here?"

I admitted that I didn't and climbed up to dig through the saddlebags for my own small pack. I pulled out one of my two remaining shirts and, conscious of her unseen gaze, swapped it for what I was wearing.

She pointed at my jeans, which had been torn in half a dozen places when I was thrown from the bike. "Pants too. Can't imagine the Academy wants to see your chicken legs any more than I do."

"Yeah, whatever." I felt my cheeks flush. It was bad enough that Jeremy had more or less counted my ribs, I didn't want Her Majesty knowing I only had the one pair of jeans. "You and the Academy can suck it up."

"Fair enough." That smile seemed amused now. "If you want to walk around school with your sweet little ass hanging out for the world to see, that's your business, kid."

Since leaving Mama Rawlins', I'd been out of my depth and mainly focused on not dying, but her vaguely condescending tone sparked some of the anger that had gotten me through all those years at the orphanage. I glared at her yellow, cheerful face. "I'm not a kid, *Your Majesty.*"

"Seems to me you passed up the chance to prove that last night." Her amusement seemed to have only deepened.

"*Seems to me*," I parroted, not wanting her to know that I'd been kicking myself over that very decision most of the night, "that you'd have murdered me if I did anything else."

"I guess that would have depended on your performance, kid." She didn't move at all, but I was suddenly uncomfortably aware of the way her pants clung to the twin curves of her hips and inner thighs. "Maybe I'd have eaten you alive," she added, "or maybe a whole different kind of eating would have taken place."

The good news is, I wasn't blushing anymore… but only because all my blood was elsewhere, and I was hard as a rock. I swallowed twice, my mouth suddenly dry, and tried for a casual tone. "I don't have to be at the Academy before tonight…"

Smiley's laugh was sharp, loud, and vaguely metallic. "You had your chance. Post-battle horniness is over, and with it any chance of me jumping your skinny bones. Now put some fresh-fucking-pants on. If I see even a hint of penis, I'm cutting it off."

The organ in question deflated like one of those balloons you see in birthday parties on vids. If it hadn't been attached to my body, it might have even made a desperate dash for safety. As blood fled to safer regions, I found myself embarrassed all over again.

"These are the only pants I have," I finally admitted.

Her Majesty stopped dead. After a very long and uncomfortable moment, she shook her head, muttering something under her breath. Then she shrugged. "Well, unless you're packing a peanut, nothing I have is gonna fit you. I guess you'll have to go as you are." Her voice regained its smile. "I always wanted to moon the Academy… just never thought I'd find a Crow to do it for me."

* * *

Los Angeles was exactly like it appeared in the vids… and nothing like it. The skyline was instantly recognizable—gleaming towers rising to dizzying heights as if they were trying to touch the sky—but the cameras hadn't captured the sprawl that lay beneath; concrete and metal and glass and dirt in every conceivable direction. It took us three hours to reach that mess, and then another two hours to get to our destination.

Part of that was the traffic. There still weren't many cars on the road, but bikes—from electric motorcycles to human-powered bicycles—were everywhere. Part of it was the fact that the tunnel we needed to take had been shut down as a result of some sort of battle the previous week. But most of it was just that the city was fucking huge.

Seen up close, Los Angeles was kind of a dump.

Still better than Bakersfield though.

As we drove west, pedestrians scrambling to get the hell out of Her Majesty's way, the urban sprawl started to fall away. Barred shop windows and curb-side parking gave way to franchise chains and outdoor malls and then finally to walled estates and the sort of lawns nobody managed without a Druid or a Weather Witch on staff. Even so, I remained unimpressed with the City of Angels. Right until we hit the top of the last hill, and the ocean spread out before us like a white-capped reminder of the planet's potential.

I'd seen the ocean in vids, of course. Even a painting once, though that had been of a stormy night, with the water black and hungry enough to swallow anyone who dared approach it. But nothing had prepared me for the real thing: deep blue waters, waves crashing toward shore, and just fucking open space and possibility, stretching as far as the eye could see.

Later, I would learn about the very many ways the Pacific could kill you, not even counting the Powers who called it home, and I would learn why the Free States had never been able to re-establish contact with places like Japan or Australia. I'd learn a lot of things, and the world being what it was, too damn few of them would be good, but for that moment, seen through almost-eighteen-year-old eyes… the ocean was the most beautiful thing I'd seen in years.

To be fair, Smiley's ass was a close second.

* * *

Another thing the vids had gotten wrong was the Academy itself. I recognized a handful of landmarks, the field where the Graduation Games took place among them, but there was so much more that the vids never showed; dozens of enormous buildings on multiple acres of green, the whole campus surrounded by an enormous wall.

Either there were a lot more Capes than I'd realized, or more than just Powers went to class here. Or every student got their own building.

We descended a steep hill toward the Academy grounds, but a block or two before we reached the gate, Smiley took a sharp right into a cross-street and brought our car to a shuddering stop.

"This is as far as I go, Bakersfield. Hop on out."

"Afraid to be seen with the man who moons the university?" I joked. If I put particular emphasis on the word man… well, I was only a day or so away from that being legally true, after all.

"Not interested in being seen at all," she corrected. "Capes tend to have a black and white view of the world. Don't take kindly to those of us who see it otherwise."

"Are you saying you're a bad, bad woman, Your Majesty?"

That smiley-face turned to regard me, the silence so profound that even I could hear my joke crash and burn. "I'm a professional. I take the jobs that pay. Some are good, some are bad. As for what that makes me?" She shrugged slim shoulders. "I'd say practical."

I met her shrug with one of my own. "Well, you saved my life. Maybe I'm just already going crazy, but that makes you good in my book. So thank you." I glanced in the direction of the Academy. "And nobody's going to hear about you from me."

When she said nothing in reply, I pulled my bag out of the back, and hopped down off of the car. "See you around, Your Majesty."

"Hold up a moment." Just like that, Smiley was standing between me and the Academy. "I don't know what sort of game you've gotten caught up in," she continued, her voice lacking its usual metallic snarl, "but odds are, it's going to get worse before it gets better. And if it does…" She offered me a small card.

It was as black and glossy as the glove that held it, blank except for a series of seventeen digits in silver.

"Is this your… number?" Just like pre-Break, communication was done via land lines, and telephone numbers had only six digits—seven including the city code—but I couldn't figure out what else it would be. Coordinates, maybe?

"It's a one-time net address for a drop box location I check daily. When you're in the shit, you might just need a bad, bad woman to bail that sweet little ass out." The humor re-entered her voice, and for a moment, the smile across her visor seemed sadistic. "Fair warning: if you use it for a booty call, I'll take your cock away with me as a souvenir afterward."

With statements like that, my dick was in real danger of becoming an innie rather than an outie, but the rest of me was oddly touched. I was about to enroll at the most secure institution in the country, and I couldn't see why I'd ever need protection, but the fact that she had offered…

Her Majesty was totally into me.

CHAPTER 12

Turns out that showing up to the Academy in blood-soaked clothes with no escort, school identification, or any sort of acceptance letter sets off a few alarm bells. Not just figurative ones either; before I could trot out my whole *stranger danger* speech, I'd been whisked off to some small, underground room to be run through half a dozen scanners under the watchful eyes of three guards and a fully automated turret. I was a breath away from having someone shove their gauntleted hand up my ass when word came down that the school dean wanted to see me.

Apparently, he and I had different definitions of *wanting to see someone* though. I spent thirty minutes sitting on my almost-violated ass outside the guy's office, under the watchful eye of a steel-haired matriarch who was both the dean's assistant and way scarier than any of the guards had been. My one attempt to enter the dean's office had been swiftly derailed by little more than a grim, bespectacled glare and a meaningful shake of her head.

It was like Mama Rawlins had a secret, long-lost, and fucking terrifying older sister.

There were four seats in a row along the wall, and I'd been deposited in the one furthest from the door to the dean's office. The next two chairs were unoccupied, while the last one…

"So what did you do to get sent here anyway?"

…held Mr. Fucking Talks-a-lot, who had come in halfway through my wait and seemed completely oblivious to my very obvious attempts to ignore him.

I was trying to be on my best behavior but there were limits.

"What?" I finally answered, infusing the single word with every bit of annoyance and irritation that I could muster.

"School hasn't even started and you've already been sent to the dean's office," he replied cheerfully. "That takes some skill. So what did you do? Dig a tunnel to the girls' dorm over the break? Hack a faculty net account? Have a wild orgy with the gardener's rose bushes?"

"*With* the bushes?"

"Not a Druid then, I take it?" He nodded pleasantly. "Probably for the best. Bush fucking is something the faculty takes pretty seriously here."

I cautiously upgraded him from clueless asshole to clueless-but-funny asshole.

"Are you a student?" He looked to be about ten years older than me, but the wrinkled tee, torn jeans, and sneakers pegged him as either a student or a writer.

"Nah, though I did run through the support curriculum a few years back."

"The what?"

"Support curriculum." He waved a hand dismissively. "It's one of the tracks the Academy offers to non-powered students."

"I thought this was a college for Capes?"

"It is," he agreed, "but it offers degrees to the rest of us too, mostly specializing in Cape-related sub-fields. You know; marketing, PR, product development, information technology…"

"And *support*." Whatever the hell that was.

"Yep. Everything a Cape team needs to run smoothly, and a half-dozen other related careers to keep the Free States plugging along." He eyed me, dark eyes curious. "But since this is news to you, I'm guessing you're here to become a Cape?"

"Yeah. A Finder picked me up yesterday and took me to a testing station. I passed."

"And then the two of you fought through a horde of screaming pygmies to reach Los Angeles?"

"What?"

"Just trying to explain what's left of your jeans."

I scowled. Funny was one thing. Nosy was something else entirely. "I don't think that's any business of yours. And what the fuck is a pygmy?"

"On second thought, *that* must be why you got sent to see the dean," he mused, ignoring my question. "What a shame. I was hoping it would be the bush thing."

"Look," I said, "I don't want to be a dick, but I've got a lot on my mind right now, this school's asshole dean has been keeping me waiting for no fucking reason, and answering *your* questions is way the hell down my list of priorities."

That little speech won me another arctic glare from the desk-bound assistant, but my cheerful interrogator just shrugged. "I guess that depends."

"Depends on what?" If I had any control over my necromancy, this guy would already be ass-deep in zombies.

"On whether you want to attend my school or not." He flashed a wide, shit-eating grin, and offered a handshake. "I'm the school's asshole dean. Pleased to meet you."

"Son of a bitch." I didn't realize I'd said the words aloud until the dean shrugged a second time.

"Truer than you know. But I'd prefer you call me Bard."

* * *

The dean's office was half again the size of the waiting room, but felt even bigger away from the assistant's sharp-eyed death stare. Bard took a seat behind the wooden desk that dominated the office and motioned me to one of the two chairs in front.

I eyed the chair he'd indicated, scowled, and dropped into the one next to it instead.

Bard raised one eyebrow, but said nothing. Leaning back, hands steepled in front of him, he watched me carefully, as if I was some sort of lab rat, or an equation gone surprisingly wrong.

I tried to match his casual indifference, but the truth was, I wasn't feeling particularly indifferent. I'd nearly died the night before—twice, if you included Her Majesty's sexual invitation, three times, if you added in my electrocution—and I badly needed some food, a shower, and an explanation, not a staring contest with a guy who, not five minutes earlier, had spoken to me about *bush-fucking.*

"Are you really Bard?"

"Last I checked."

"*The* Bard?" Even I had heard of him; the Academy's founder, and one of the Free States' richest and most powerful individuals.

"Well, no," he admitted. "He died three-hundred and sixty-odd years before the Break."

"Huh?"

"William Shakespeare?" He noted my confused look. "Never mind. If you were asking whether I founded this university, the answer is yes."

"Then what was the deal with all that… nonsense… in the waiting room?" With great—some might even say heroic—effort, I swallowed my usual assortment of expletives.

"I've found it easier to get a picture of who someone is when they are unaware of my identity."

I rolled my eyes. "Anal probes and lies. So far I'm not thrilled with orientation."

"Orientation isn't for another two days, Mr. Jameson."

"Banach."

"I'm sorry?"

"Damian Banach," I corrected. "I don't use my father's name."

"Duly noted." He flipped open the manila folder on his desk and made a correction. "As I was saying, this interview is not your orientation. This is where we decide whether or not you will attend the Academy at all."

That cut right through my sulk. "What are you talking about? I tested as a Cat Three!"

"So I read. But as I find myself having to tell one or two prospective students every year, there is more to attending the

Academy than your Test. Enrollment at the Academy is earned, not given."

"Earned how?"

"Through multiple years of education in high school, a battery of academic and psychological evaluations, and long-term observation," he replied.

None of which I'd had.

"The usual procedure," he continued, "is to funnel people like you back into the system. Assuming you then re-emerge as a candidate, you would be properly prepared."

"I'm eighteen. I have no family. I can't afford to do that!"

"It's a problem," he admitted, "as is your particular power, of course."

I frowned. "Mr. Grey seemed to think my admission was all but guaranteed."

"Mr. Grey?" Bard glanced down at the sheets of paper on his desk. "Ah yes, your Finder. While the Academy works in conjunction with the government, we are not under their authority. A Finder may designate a candidate for consideration—a right infrequently exercised, mind you—but I am the final arbiter when it comes to enrollment."

"Meaning?"

"Meaning that this is your opportunity to persuade me that you deserve an exemption to attend my school, that the potential gains outweigh the very real negatives, and that you are more than a foul-mouthed, poorly attired, obnoxious troll."

"Takes one to know one," I couldn't help but shoot back, proving his point.

"I suppose it does. But my future is secure, while yours is anything but. Now, do you want to continue trying to impress me with your attitude, or would you like to make an actual effort to convince me that you belong here?"

I winced. It was a week for getting my verbal ass handed to me. One word from Bard would doom me to a short and ugly life on the streets.

Or worse; turning into my dad.

"What do you want to know?"

"Where did the blood on your clothes come from?"

"We were attacked coming down from the north."

"You and Mr. Grey?"

"No. He and I parted ways at the testing station. Said he had more kids to find."

Bard picked up a pen, made a quick notation, and continued. "So who escorted you from there?"

I told him the story, sticking mostly to the truth, although—mindful of my promise—I replaced Her Majesty with a burly male mercenary who had taken down our attackers by more conventional means.

"And this mercenary left you before you reached the school?"

"He dropped me off around the block," I lied. "I thought if I showed up alone, then…"

"The other students would think you cooler than you are?"

I shrugged. I didn't give a shit what the other students thought, but if that worked for him… "I guess so. I didn't expect the guards to go nuts though."

"Security here is extensive because it too often needs to be. As for impressing your classmates, they won't be arriving for another day. Still, it wasn't the dumbest scheme I've heard." Bard shook his head. "That honor goes to the first-year who attempted to parachute into orientation, was nearly atomized by our automated defense systems, and still managed to break a leg crashing into the cafeteria."

"And this guy had already passed all your tests and screenings?"

"It was a woman, actually, but I'll admit that our screening remains a work in progress." He made another notation and then flipped to the next sheet. "Anyway, onto the standard intake form. I already have your name, of course, as well as date of birth—happy almost-birthday, by the way—and measurements."

"Measurements?"

"Height, weight, body mass, and other diagnostics, courtesy of one of the many scans you endured upon arrival," he replied absently, still working his way down the form. "And thanks to yesterday's testing, we know you are both a Crow and Category Three, so that piece of the puzzle is likewise taken care of. Which leaves only your basic psych profile and academic evaluations."

I didn't like the sound of *any* of that.

"Now, I've retrieved the records filed when you were a resident of the Bakersfield Home for Lost Children—"

"Already?" That was the official name of Mama Rawlins' orphanage, though there wasn't a kid there who called it that.

He nodded. "Not all of the scans you underwent were necessary, but security stalled until I had your paperwork in order. On the bright side, I can also inform you that you are not, and never have been, pregnant."

I was too pissed to even roll my eyes. Bard was damn lucky they hadn't gotten around to the anal cavity search.

"As for Mrs. Rawlins, she described you in her records as moody, withdrawn, and prone to violence."

Mama Rawlins had never been the sort to sugarcoat the truth, even when it hurt.

"I particularly liked this line," he continued. "Whenever there is any manner of confrontation, it is a given that Damian will be in the middle of it—"

But there was such a thing as taking honesty too far.

"—but although he does everything the hard way, his heart is in the right place. The little ones look to him as a leader and a protector, and he has stamped out the vast majority of bullying and abuse."

I swallowed past the sudden lump in my throat. Maybe the old woman had been paying more attention than I'd thought.

Bard nodded at whatever emotion he saw in my face. "That quote is the primary reason we're even having this interview, Mr. Banach."

I made a big show of shrugging. "People shouldn't pick on those who can't fight back."

"That's one way of putting it," he agreed. "I always preferred this one: 'What use strength, if not to defend those who have none? What use power, if not to promote peace?'"

"It's a bit wordy," I decided.

"Should you meet Dominion, you can tell him so." Bard made another notation. "As I said, what records we have of you suggest you might have the instincts to be a Cape. However, it takes more than just will to be a Cape… it takes power."

I winced and nodded.

"When did you first realize you were a Crow?"

"Nine."

"Weeks or months?"

I frowned. Who the fuck got their power nine weeks after they were born? "Years. But it wasn't until yesterday that the idea of being a Cape even seemed possible. While the other kids were talking about which power they wanted, and how they were going to be the next Paladin, I was busy hoping that the power I already had stayed small, so that I at least wouldn't cause too much damage when the madness took over."

Bard stared at me, eyes wide.

"Well, excuse me for oversharing," I said, suddenly embarrassed.

"*Nine years*?" At my nod, he frowned, and scanned the papers in front of him. "Are you certain?"

"My mom's ghost showed up when I turned nine. It's not the sort of thing you forget."

"The first official record of you having powers is yesterday afternoon, at your testing."

"Yeah, right." I waited for the punchline, but it didn't seem to be coming. "That's crazy. My foster parents kicked me out of their house when they found out!"

"This would be the Jacobsens?"

"Yes." I choked down the old, familiar hurt. After the Jacobsens, I'd been tainted goods. There hadn't been a set of foster parents out there willing to take me.

Bard shook his head. "I've looked at the paperwork. All it shows is that they canceled their bid for adoption. There is no mention of necromancy there or in Mrs. Rawlins' own notes."

"That doesn't make any sense."

"No, it doesn't. It does, however, explain how a Power in Bakersfield managed to avoid the government's notice."

"I thought you said you got one or two students like me a year."

"From the Badlands. From the Dirty South. Even a brave few smuggled out of the East, from under the local warlords' noses. But Bakersfield?"

Bard seemed to have a higher opinion of Bakersfield than the rest of us. Clearly, he'd never been there.

"So… what does that mean?"

"I don't know." Bard pinched the bridge of his nose, aging twenty years in an instant. "I will put in a request to speak with both your Finder and Mrs. Rawlins, but the government moves slowly in all things—and the present administration more than most. It is anyone's guess whether I ever hear back."

"Does it even matter?"

He sighed. "It's a mystery and I don't like mysteries. But as far as you're concerned, all it means is that you are very lucky that Mr. Grey found you when he did."

"That depends on whether you let me enroll."

"True enough." Bard put down his pen, and leaned further back in his chair, the very image of a thoughtful professor, if you could ignore his clothing. "People say that being a Cape is not just about who you are, it's also about what you are. By that logic, and given that there has never been a Necromancer hero, I'd be a fool to admit you."

I dropped my eyes.

"People also say," Bard continued, in that same considering voice, "that Dr. Nowhere broke the world. They're wrong about that. *We* broke the world. People. He handed us loaded weapons, but we were the ones who chose to pull the triggers."

"I think they're just as wrong about what makes a Cape. It all comes down to choice. We don't choose what ability we're given—if we're given one at all—but we can choose what to do with it. To the people who lived in those dark times, *every* Power was evil. No heroes, no Capes. Just the strong lording over the weak and the innocent suffering because of it."

"Until Dominion," I pointed out.

"Exactly. He chose to do something different with his gifts… and what was left of the government chose to believe in him, despite the examples of every Power before him. And because of those two choices, and the myriad of choices made since, we have a country. We have Capes. We have hope."

Dark eyes met mine for a long moment. "There has never been a Necromancer hero. And there never will be one… not unless we allow them that choice." He grinned suddenly. "My wife used to say I could turn a simple *I love you* into a twenty-page dissertation on flowers and rainbows, but this is my long-winded way of saying that what happens next is up to you. If you choose to become a Cape, then I will choose to believe in your ability to do so."

"Seriously?"

"Seriously." Bard's smile was wry. "But the first step is you making that choice."

The odd thing is that I had to stop to think about it. I didn't want to go crazy… that much was a given. And I didn't want to be a murdering asshole like my dad either, let alone a larger terror like the Crimson Death. But a Cape, with a code name and costume and endorsements? Baron Boner, Defender of Cemeteries? What the fuck sort of hero could a Necromancer even be?

I had no idea. But part of me wanted to find out.

I looked back at Bard. "I'm going to be the first Crow Cape."

"There will be conditions," he warned me.

"Anything except anal."

That knocked him off his game for just a moment, but he shook his head and pushed on. "We provide voluntary counseling to all our students, but for you, it would be mandatory. One hour every week, minimum. Miss a session and you're out. If your counselor red-flags you at any point, you're out."

"Got it." I'd had counseling following my mom's murder, and it had sucked, but after almost nine years of wondering if I was going crazy—and driving myself a little bit crazy in the process—there was something almost appealing about offloading that worry to a professional.

As long as they didn't ask about Mom. Especially on the days she came to therapy with me.

"Second, you will not leave the campus except under direct supervision."

That one kind of sucked, especially with the ocean so close by, but… "It's not like I have anywhere to go, right?"

He winced for some reason, but the truth was hard to deny. "Third, there will be no special treatment. You will be one of twenty-five incoming first-years, and will be subject to the same rules and regulations they are."

After all those years at the orphanage, that didn't even faze me. I nodded my acceptance.

"These conditions are iron clad," he warned me. "Break any of them and you're gone. As of tomorrow, you'll be an adult in the eyes of the government. You'll need to live with the choices you make."

"I get it," I said. "I don't have a problem with your rules."

By the end of that year, I'd have broken every one of them. But at the time, I meant it.

"I'll hold you to that," said Bard. "The only thing left is for you to pass your academic evaluations."

"Seriously?" Mama Rawlins had home schooled us, but my education had eventually taken a back seat to Alicia and her magical lady parts. "There's no wiggle room there at all?"

"What did I just say about special treatment?" Bard rolled his eyes and grinned, but his voice remained serious. "As a first-year and second-year, your curriculum includes regular schoolwork, in classes with the non-powered student population. The evaluations are designed to ensure that all of our students meet the same minimum academic standards."

"No problem. I've got this." I said, trying to convince myself as much as Bard. "So do I take the tests… now?"

"I think you've had enough excitement for the day," he decided, "especially given the presumably joyous news of your non-pregnancy. Agnes will schedule your examinations for tomorrow, and arrange a dorm room for you to stay in until orientation. Tonight, you should clean up, let one of our two resident Healers take a look at those scrapes, and get some rest."

Sleep sounded amazing, but passing my exams sounded even better. I'd take a shower and visit the Healer, as suggested, but after that? I was going to find some food, borrow a Glass, and study my ass off.

CHAPTER 13

"Do you want the good news or the bad news, Mr. Banach?"

I was back in Bard's office the following afternoon, officially regretting the two hours I'd spent sleeping and not studying. Not that the studying I *had* done had seemed to make any difference with the tests I'd taken.

"I'm kind of shocked there's *any* good news," I told him tiredly, for the first time wondering if learning to take off Alicia's bra one-handed had really been the best use of my time.

Which just went to show how tired I really was. I mean… *of course it had been.*

"Surprisingly, there were a few bright spots," said Bard.

"Seriously? Like what?" I'd left the testing convinced that I had not only failed, but done so in so spectacular a fashion that future generations would use me as an example for others.

"English."

"No fucking way."

Bard winced. "Despite all evidence to the contrary. You also eked out a score of 63% in Math."

Fucking-A. If the whole Cape thing didn't work out for me, I could become an accountant. An *insane* accountant, sure, but who would be able to tell the difference? "What about the other tests?"

"You bombed them all. Life Science, Physics, Geography, and both Pre-Break *and* Post-Break History—although you did somehow ace the Powers-related questions."

Some of you are probably wondering how anyone could fail Geography, given what little was left of the known world to be quizzed on. Let's just say I had a gift.

I sighed. "I'm guessing I know what the bad news is."

"That *was* the bad news. The good news is that you have friends in high places."

I risked a glance upward—when people can fly, you can't afford to assume someone is speaking figuratively—but there was nothing but ceiling above us. "Huh?"

"This morning, while you were singlehandedly disproving the merits of home schooling, I received a phone call from Mr. Isaac Clearwater. The Secretary of Superhuman Affairs," he clarified, when I gave him a blank stare.

"We have one of those?"

Bard shook his head slowly. "I guess it's a good thing political science isn't part of our academic screening. Yes, we have *one of those*. Despite being on his way to a budget meeting, Mr. Clearwater was taking the time out of his busy schedule to inquire about the promising Necromancer prospect his top Finder had personally delivered us."

I blinked. Since when did the government give a shit about me? Let alone this Secretary guy, who—from the way Bard had said his name—had to be at least somewhat important.

"I make the final decision on who attends my school," continued Bard, "but the Academy does not exist in a vacuum. When a member of the President's cabinet calls, even I have to listen."

"Meaning?"

"Meaning your life just got busy. I will not design a new curriculum to accommodate a single student, so you'll be taking the same classes as every other first-year. I'm assigning you tutors to help you actually pass those classes… although that depends on your willingness to put in the work, I suppose."

"You mean I'm in? I can stay?" After the awful morning of tests, I was having a hard time wrapping my brain around that fact.

The two hours of sleep probably didn't help either.

"It's not going to be easy," Bard warned me. "The life of a first-year is intentionally frenetic, but at least *they* get weekends off.

You'll be spending every weekend with your tutors. If you can't pass those classes… not even Sean Weatherly will be able to keep you here."

I wanted to ask who that was, but didn't want Bard to think…

"Sean Weatherly," he sighed. "President of the Free States."

Bard wasn't the only one glad we'd skipped the political science test.

INTERLUDE

Jonathan Bard sat at his desk for almost twenty minutes after Damian's departure, reviewing the many steps still needed to make the young Crow's enrollment a reality. Parent notifications, waiver agreements, and legal contingencies in the event that things went poorly… it was a mountain of paperwork, and he pitied whichever assistant ended up having to complete it on his behalf.

Before he could set those wheels in motion, however, there was one thing only *he* could do. Bard reached over to his desk phone and dialed a number he knew by heart. A number that very few other people in the country even had access to.

It rang for a few seconds then stopped. Whoever had picked up on the other end remained completely silent, but Bard was used to the security measures by now.

"It's Jonathan," he said into the silence. "Remember that student we talked about?"

"Yes." The voice was slow, smooth, and unmistakably female.

"Now there are two of them." He shook his head even though she couldn't see him. "The second one is a Crow, believe it or not."

"A Crow first-year?" Something like surprise leaked across the line. "How are the other families taking the news?"

"I haven't informed them yet. I wanted to make sure you were okay with the extra burden before I did anything else. I know I am asking a lot."

"It's okay, Jonathan. I can handle two patients as easily as one. I'll see you in a few days."

And then there was nothing but dial tone. Bard set the receiver back in its cradle and looked back at his notes.

One problem solved. A dozen to go.

CHAPTER 14

The dorm room I'd slept in before my exams turned out to be the room I'd be staying in as a first-year. Either someone had been confident I was going to stick around or it had been the only free space available.

According to the Academy handbook—which I had pulled up on my school-provided Glass and was presently reading, thanks to my newfound commitment to academic excellence—the majority of dorm buildings on campus were designated for the non-powered population, leaving only a handful of buildings for the first-year, second-year, and third-year Cape dorms. The last was frequently empty, as third-years spent a good portion of their school year off-campus, either interning with established teams—for those students who'd managed to win an invitation to do so—or doing mission work in the Badlands with the rest of the unwanted.

Students had begun pouring into campus shortly after my meeting with Bard, but none had made their way to the first-year dorm yet. I took the opportunity to pass out on one of the room's two beds, where my dreams mostly revolved around my new roommate being blonde, tan, and hugely stacked.

I ended up getting two out of three… just not the two I would have picked.

"How's it going? Looks like we'll be rooming together as first-years." Blonde and tan, sure, but given his gender, it was probably just as well that he wasn't stacked. He did have a mouthful of perfect teeth though, the sort of physique you saw in hero vids, and a hell of a grip.

"I'm Damian. Nice to meet you." I told him. At Mama Rawlins' place, that would have been the ideal time for one of us to sucker punch the other, but Blondie didn't seem concerned with asserting his dominance, and I didn't see the wisdom in starting something with a guy who outweighed me by at least thirty pounds of muscle.

"Likewise." After shaking my hand, he carried two enormous suitcases into the room—the lack of effort telling me he'd either packed feathers or had some sort of augmented strength—and then took a quick look around him. "You know, Dad talked about first-year dorms like they were prison cells, but this isn't bad at all."

It sure as hell beat the orphanage. Each dorm room had two full sets of furniture—bed, desk, dresser, bookshelf, and closet—with enough space left over to not make the whole thing feel crowded. No vid screens, but the common room I'd walked through to get here had one that was almost as big as I was, along with couches, chairs, and a ping pong table.

The blonde kid finished unloading his suitcases—which held a shit-ton of clothes, a personal Glass that was two generations newer than what the school provided, and a framed picture of other absurdly attractive people—before sitting lightly on the edge of his bed, and turning back to me with a smile.

"Sorry about that. If I'd waited to put everything away until after we chatted, I'd have spent the whole time worrying my mom was going to bust in here and stare disapprovingly at my suitcases."

My own mom was standing nearby and didn't seem to care at all that the only unpacking I'd done was to toss my bloody clothes into a laundry basket, while pulling on the Academy-logoed sweatpants I'd found in my top drawer.

"Anyway," he continued, still offering that easy smile, "I'm Matthew… Matthew Strich, but I prefer to go by—"

"Hey Paladin!" Another kid—almost as pale as I was, with spiky black hair and bushy eyebrows—stuck his head in our doorway, "They just posted our class roster in the commons. Come check it out!" Just as quickly, he was gone.

Matthew rolled his eyes and grinned. "Can you tell Caleb is part Jitterbug? Come on, roomie, let's go see who we'll be spending the next three years training with."

It was a bit early to be sure, but I was cautiously optimistic that my new roommate wasn't going to be a complete asshole.

Still would've preferred a girl though.

* * *

Despite Bard's joke about a tunnel to the girls' dorm, the Cape dormitories were co-ed. The girls' rooms and bathroom were in one wing, while ours were in the other, but at the center of the two wings was the common lounge we all shared.

That room was far from full—I never saw it full during my year there, no matter how many people flooded into it—but there were a handful of teenagers clustered about the two sheets of paper that had been pinned to an old-fashioned cork bulletin board.

Matthew and I joined the crowd, where Caleb was already reading through the class roster.

"Holy shit," he exclaimed, "We have a High-fucking-Four Pyro! Ish… Ish…"

"Ishmae, although she goes by Phoenix." The speaker was almost as skinny as I was, her most prominent features being large green eyes and black, curly hair.

"I think I've heard of her," said my own roommate. "Some kind of prodigy, right?"

As a High-Four, she kind of had to be. There were a handful of Cat Five Powers in the entire world, so a High-Four was the next best thing to royalty. It also made my Low-Three seem particularly puny by comparison.

"She must be," agreed the woman. "She looks like she's about fifteen." She sighed. "Out from under the parents' nose at last, and I get stuck with a child as a roommate. I bet she doesn't even drink."

"Don't worry, Tessa," said another woman, this one blonde, pale, and attractive. "London and I are next door to you two, so you'll always have a place to party."

"Where is your roommate anyway, Olympia?" asked Tessa.

"When I called this morning, she was still figuring out what to pack." When Olympia giggled, the whole room seemed to brighten.

Actually, the whole room *did* brighten. A Lightbringer then.

"What else do we have, Caleb?" asked the guy standing next to Matthew and I. He was about the same height as my roommate but olive-skinned and wiry, his shoulder-length brown hair pulled back into a ponytail. Like Tessa, he had green eyes, but his were pale, the color of sun-bleached grass.

I swallowed a curse. I was going to have a hard time getting any action at all if every first-year man ended up being prettier than I was.

"Let's see… most of us are Threes, of course." Caleb cocked an eye at Tessa. "Except for little Ms. Telekinetic here. Low-Four? Pretty sweet!"

She blushed prettily. "If you got it, flaunt it, right?" The second roster sheet peeled itself off the cork board and floated to her hand. "Ooo! We have a Healer too! High three!"

"Whoa." That was Ponytail again, but I think we all shared his sentiment. Given how rare Healers were, having one in our class—let alone a High-Three—was just as impressive as our High-Four Pyro. "I hope she's hot."

"Shane Stevenson? Sounds like a guy to me."

"Then I retract my last statement," grinned Ponytail. "Guy already has an unfair advantage. Everyone loves the unicorns."

Tessa's gaze was cool. "And who are you?"

"Santiago Tomayo." He executed a credible bow. "Santi to my friends, El Bosque to my admirers."

"And do you have a lot of admirers, *El Bosque*?"

"More and more all the time," he assured her, his grin widening.

"I guess there's no accounting for taste."

Santi's smile slipped slightly, but he shrugged. "Nothing for you to worry your little head about, regardless… I prefer flowers to weeds."

Leave it to a Druid to insult a woman using plant metaphors.

Tessa stiffened, her green eyes flashing dangerously, but before we could get into our very first student-on-student melee, the front door opened. The guy who stepped in was six and a half feet of hulking muscle, so wide that he almost looked short at first glance. He was tanned and dark-haired, but his most prominent features were the scars down one side of his face, and a pair of unblinking, golden eyes.

"How's it going?" My roommate was already walking over to the newcomer, hand outstretched. "Matthew Strich, but I go by—"

The other man brushed by him without a word, never slowing as he bypassed the rest of us and headed down the hall to the boys' dorm rooms. Matthew watched him go, his tan almost hiding the flush of embarrassment.

Holy hell. Someone even less social than me. Talk about unicorns…

"That must be Alan Jackson," whispered Caleb, still looking at his sheet. "Beast-shifter, Low-Four, and… get this… he's from the Badlands."

Santi whistled. "Fuck. That makes him my roommate. I sure hope he's housebroken."

Olympia shook her head. "Not everyone is a charmer like you, El Bosque. I'm sure if we give him time—" Her light flickered as a door slammed shut down the hall. "*Lots of time*," she corrected, "he'll come around."

"Or murder our resident Druid in his sleep." Tessa seemed in favor of that idea. "Alan's one of two Shifters, apparently. We also have a Titan and… ooooo a Switch. Low-Three, but still… that's pretty cool."

Switches were a bit of an oddity in the powered community. Unlike most Powers, they couldn't do anything by themselves. Instead, their abilities worked to amplify the talents of Powers around them or mute those same talents. They weren't as rare as Healers—or Crows, for that matter—but with every Team wanting at least one on their roster, demand far outstripped supply.

"Three Fours, a Healer, *and* a Switch." Matthew shook his head. "We've got one heck of a class, don't we?"

"Hell yeah," agreed Caleb with a grin, floating a few inches off the ground as he continued to read through the roster. "Class of 76 is going to be fucking legendary! We've got almost every element covered too, plus a secondary Stalwart, a Teleporter, and…" He frowned, his voice trailing off. "Hold up. This can't be right."

"You not the only Flyboy Jitterbug, dude?" drawled Santiago.

"Huh? No." Caleb shook his head, voice absent. "I'm one of a kind, Treefucker."

"Can you at least *try* not to swear every three words?" pleaded Olympia.

"What is it, Caleb?" asked Tessa.

"It's got to be a typo, but… this says we have a Crow."

Olympia's light went out.

* * *

"That has to be a mistake." Tessa snatched the second roster sheet page out of Caleb's hands—using her own hands this time instead of her telekinesis. "Or some sort of twisted joke." She scanned the sheet and frowned. "Low-Three, Damian Banach."

Any chance I'd had of delaying my reveal went out the window at that point. Matthew was already turning to me, eyes wide.

"Yeah, that's me."

It's said some Black Hats can clear a room just by walking into it. I didn't have that sort of mojo going for me, but a space had opened around me almost before I'd finished speaking.

"You're a Necromancer?!?" That was my roommate, who'd swapped out his easy smile for something stone-faced. "Seriously?"

I shrugged.

"Crows aren't heroes," protested Olympia. "They're insane, murdering assholes."

So much for her concerns about language. Or for me being welcomed with open arms. I looked at my fellow classmates, noted the horror, fear, and outright hate shining from their faces, and bared my teeth. "I haven't murdered anyone, but the day's not over yet."

Matthew positioned himself between me and the two ladies, but Olympia had gone even paler than normal at my words. A moment later, she fled down the hall toward her room.

I felt bad about that, actually. Nobody wants to make a Lightbringer sad. But she had no business calling me names.

Our strange little standoff had lasted for maybe ten seconds when a high, almost nasally, voice cut through the tension. "Don't everyone welcome me all at once or anything." A newcomer stood just inside the doorway, tall and thin, her hair pure white and waist-length, her nose only slightly less crooked than my own. "Penelope Von Pell," she announced. "I go by Winter." She frowned at the lack of response. "Am I missing something, or are you all just massive jerks?"

"We were saying hello to our new classmate, Penelope," said Caleb. He was the least imposing of any of the male first-years I'd met, but the menace in his voice almost made up for that fact. He gestured in my direction. "Meet Damian… the Crow."

"The… *Crow*? Oh to hell with that shit." She spun on one heel and stalked back the way she had come, her snow-white hair fanning out prettily behind her. At the door, she paused to address the rest of the class over one shoulder. "I'm going to complain to the dean and my father, in that order. If anyone wants to lodge a similar complaint, they are more than welcome to join me."

Apparently, I'd undersold my ability to clear a room. Within moments, I was the only one left. I picked up the class rosters from where they'd been dropped to the floor, glanced over the list of people I hadn't yet met, and then carefully tore both sheets of paper into tiny pieces.

So far, superhero school sucked.

CHAPTER 15

None of the others were back by the time dinner rolled around. Not that I wanted to eat with them or anything, but I'd have at least learned whether Bard had shut their protests down or not. If they all got their parents involved… well, I was pretty sure the Academy would rather have twenty-four first-years and no Crow than one Crow and no first-years.

Regardless, even a Necromancer had to eat, and I decided to head for the cafeteria. Unfortunately, when I hit the common room, I found Olympia doing the same thing. She froze in her tracks, pale eyes wide.

Murderous, insane asshole Crow I might be, but one thing nobody would ever accuse me of being was a bully. I stopped a good distance away. "I'm sorry if I scared you earlier. I'm not going to hurt you… or anyone else. I just don't like being called an asshole."

"You're a Crow," she told me quietly. "Your kind always hurts people, sooner or later."

"I'm here to prove otherwise." And to not go insane… but that didn't seem like the sort of thing that would help the conversation.

"Do whatever you want," she said. "Just stay away from me, please."

I choked down at least a half-dozen retorts and nodded. "I was going to the cafeteria to get something to eat, but if you're heading there too, go ahead. I'll wait. And don't worry, I'll eat at my own table."

She studied my face—presumably to see if I was lying and would murder her as soon as she turned her back—and then nodded, crossing the common room as fast as her long legs could carry her. In a moment, she too was gone.

* * *

One good thing about the cafeteria was that it served all students, not just Capes-in-training. It was easy enough to lose myself in the hundreds of people, many of them practically bouncing off the walls with excitement at being away from home. None of them knew a damn thing about me, or who and what I was, and I had no difficulty finding a seat in the chaos.

The second good thing about the cafeteria was the food. The night before, they'd made me an actual sandwich, with real salami and everything. This time around, I had a bowl of stew, the meat in it recognizably something other than synth-protein or rat, and a tall glass of cool water that *didn't* taste like it had been run through the recycler a dozen times.

It was good enough I went back for seconds. A few years of this and I might actually put on some weight for the first time ever.

Assuming the other first-years didn't get me tossed out.

That was the sort of thought that could kill even my appetite. I nodded a goodbye to the normals I'd shared the table with, deposited my bowl and glass on the wheeled table reserved for dirty dishes, and trudged back towards the dorm.

The sun had fallen by then, but the lights streaming from the building told me that more first-years had arrived, or the original group had returned, or—most likely of all—some combination of both. I paused outside the door, took a breath, wrapped myself in a cloak of don't-give-a-fuck, and entered the common room.

The conversation I'd been able to hear even from outside cut off instantly. There were a few new faces, but for the most part, I'd already met the people in the common room. They rose to their feet in silence, a dozen different faces made similar by hostility.

You know what? Fuck this being nice shit.

"Looks like we're all still here," I noted. "Sucks to be you."

I picked my way through the field of Super-assholes-in-training, and made my way down the hall to my room. Behind me, the conversation started up again, this time with a fresh undercurrent of anger. I slid one hand into my pocket to touch the reassuring weight of the steak knife I'd stolen from the cafeteria. So far, other than the crying-to-the-dean bits, this was playing out an awful lot like a day at Mama Rawlins'. That meant I could expect some sort of attack as soon as the lights went out. I'd be ready.

A small voice at the back of my head reminded me that—not even six hours earlier—I'd taken the huge step of deciding I actually *wanted* to be a Cape. Stabbing fellow first-years didn't really fit that mold, did it?

I told that little voice what it could do with its reminders. The other first-years had started it. Hell if I was going to just let someone jump me. Bard could expel my bony ass if he wanted.

I stalked into my room, and came to a halt. Matthew was almost done re-packing his suitcases.

"Going somewhere, *Paladin*?" Fucker didn't even have the brains to know that his codename was already taken by an active Cape. He'd be sued to an inch of his life if he tried to use the name after graduation.

Unlike the other first-years, his face didn't ooze hate, but his blue eyes were opaque. "I asked for and received dispensation to switch rooms."

"I didn't know they let cowards become Capes."

He started to say something, then swallowed it back down, tossing the last stack of perfectly folded clothes into his suitcase and zipping it closed. "You shouldn't be here. Maybe you're trying to make some sort of point, but there are twenty-plus other Powers in our class whose careers and *lives* will depend on what they learn over the next three years. It's bad enough that you might turn those years into a sideshow, but once we graduate? Whatever sort of distraction you were during our training will get some of us killed." His voice was matter-of-fact. That almost made it worse.

Before I could respond, he pulled both suitcases off the bed, and was out the door.

Possible upside: I had a huge dorm room to myself.

Unavoidable downside: The only first-year I'd met so far who didn't hate me was Alan Jackson. And it wasn't so much that he didn't hate me but that he seemed to hate everyone else just as much.

If the stew hadn't been so tasty… I'm pretty sure I'd have quit that very night.

Some people probably still wish I had.

* * *

While I heard the occasional first-year walking down the hall as the night went on—presumably coming back to dream their little Cape dreams of purity and perfect tans—nobody bothered me. By midnight, I'd gotten tired of re-reading the Academy handbook—I still hadn't found any rules against murdering your fellow classmates, so either it wasn't illegal, or they'd assumed the prohibition went without saying—and decided to go to sleep.

As if that had been a signal, the door opened. One glance told me I should have stolen a chainsaw instead of a steak knife.

He was almost as big as Alan Jackson, his skin so black that it blended into the thick, bushy beard that covered his face from cheeks to mid-chest. What kind of an eighteen-year-old had a full beard?

Maybe he was part bear. Tessa *had* said there was another Shifter.

Instead of decapitating me with a single paw, he brought in a large suitcase and gave me a level look. "You the Crow?" Even his voice was big, deep enough that I could feel it in my bones.

I nodded.

He tossed the suitcase onto his bed like it weighed nothing at all. "Touch my stuff and I'll tear your arms off."

At Mama Rawlins', I'd made a habit of sticking up for the little guy… but this was the first time in a long while that *I* was the little guy. I scowled. "You all need to get your stories straight. Either I'm a thief or I'm a murderer. I refuse to be both."

He shook his head. "Whatever. Warning stands."

Twenty minutes later, he was asleep.

I thought about stealing his suitcase and burying it somewhere even his bear nose wouldn't find it. The dumpsters behind the cafeteria, maybe? Instead, I tucked the steak knife under my pillow, wrapped one hand tightly around its fiberglass handle, and waited for sleep or my enemies to come.

Her Majesty would have approved.

CHAPTER 16

I'm not sure what Orientation was like for the regular students. From the brief glimpse I had of the field where it took place, it seemed to involve a lot of singing and laughing.

The twenty-four first-years of the Cape training program got an auditorium.

Those of you who've kept your brains functioning better than the rest might remember Bard saying there would be twenty-five of us, including me. Yeah, the school year hadn't even started yet, and we'd already lost a first-year. My fault, though I didn't know it at the time.

Anyway, while I'd have preferred the party the normals got, the auditorium we'd been herded into was nice enough; fifteen rows of comfortable, tiered seats like I'd seen in arena vids. There was a wide stage at the bottom with a podium and a row of empty chairs atop it, and the ceiling above us was vaulted and dotted with lights. Our class barely made a dent in a space that could have comfortably seated a hundred or more students—and frequently did during the school year.

Maybe other classes would have neatly filled the first few rows, leaving row upon row of empty seats behind them, but even at the start, our class was fracturing into cliques. There was a clump of students a few rows from the front, another clump in the back, a handful of women in the very first row, and then, all the way to the left, with three rows and multiple chairs between each of us, me, Alan Jackson, and the young woman I quickly identified as our High-Four Pyro, Ishmae Naser.

Whereas most of the students were dressed in normal streetwear, and I had on another set of school sweatpants along with one of the tees I'd brought from Bakersfield, Ishmae was draped in robes; multiple layers of crimson and golden cloth that concealed every inch of her small form. Only her head was bare, her brown skin smooth and hairless, her face dominated by enormous, almond-shaped eyes. Those eyes had examined each of us upon entry, dismissed us almost as quickly, and were now fixed upon the stage below. She looked exotic—like some sort of strange bird from one of the forgotten islands—and driven. She also looked more than a little self-conscious, and very, very young.

I had finished my own examination of the rest of the class—many of whom had arrived after I'd gone to bed or sometime between breakfast and Orientation—and was watching Mom's ghost slowly meander down the stairs, when one of the room's two doors swung open. Bard was almost unrecognizable; the messy hair now neatly combed and the casual clothing replaced by a sharp three-piece suit and a pair of glasses that added a decade to his appearance. Only his easy smile remained the same.

Ten adults trailed in after him, five men and five women, all of them way too old to be students. They settled into the chairs on stage, as Bard walked to the podium. He adjusted its microphone, cleared his throat once, and turned his smile on the rest of us like it was some kind of energy weapon.

"Ladies and Gentlemen of the Class of 76, I would like to welcome you to Orientation. For the few of you who I've yet to meet, my name is Jonathan Bard, and I am the dean and founder of this Academy."

The smile faded, the spotlight winked out, and Bard's next words were solemn.

"More than eighty years ago, Dr. Nowhere broke the world. We don't know exactly how it happened or why. What matters is that the world changed, and you are the direct result of that change. You are all here because you have gifts, and because you have shown a desire to use those gifts to defend the powerless. Lives are quite literally depending upon you. Every moment that passes, someone dies that you might have been able to save."

The speech had the air of words that were often repeated yet no less true for their repetition. I risked a glance at the other first-years and saw a variety of emotions parading across their faces.

"I know," Bard continued. "That's a hell of a burden to put on anyone, let alone a group of teenagers. It's a hard truth, but it is the truth. Because you're not the only ones with powers, and a great many of those other individuals, both in this country and outside of it, are using their abilities to steal, to maim, and to kill."

"Normals can't stop them. Neither can you." He offered a small smile in acknowledgement of the murmured protests. "Not yet, at least. It's our job to train you to do so. Equally importantly, it's our job to teach you *why* and *how* you should do so. How to save lives. How to inspire others."

"Some of you are legacies, and have heard this all before. Some of you have grown up on the stories of older Capes, and some of you—" I could swear his eyes landed on me. "—are entirely new to the idea of being a hero. But as of today, you are all first-years together, and if you make it through all three years at the Academy, you will graduate with the hopes of a nation resting on your actions. From that day onward, you will be more than just a person. You will be a symbol, a shield, and yes, a celebrity with endorsements, speaking engagements, and—God help you all—fan clubs."

He waited for the laughter to die down, and then his next words sliced through the air like razors.

"And then, one day, you will become a martyr for the cause. That's the secret that every Cape carries into battle, from Dominion to the freshest of Academy graduates. Some of you will die in your beds, bearing the scars of decades of battle. Some of you will die in the skies above the cities you've pledged to protect. The only certainty is that none of you will be getting out of this alive."

If I'd had a pin on me, and had chosen to drop it at that moment… well, let's just say every person in that auditorium would've heard it.

"That's a shocking thing to hear, I know, but as you age, you'll realize it holds true for everyone; Cape or Black Hat, Power or normal. Life is finite. Eventually, it will end. Of the Ten who first heard Dominion's call to arms, the Ten we honor and respect every Remembrance Day, three died within the first month. *Three!* None of the others lived long enough to see the Free States' first birthday. This country survived not just because of their sacrifice, but because, as they fell, others took up the mantle, fought, and fell in turn, in a passing of the torch that has occurred ever since, and will continue to occur as long as those with power seek to rain down death upon the innocent."

"The Academy is where that passing of the torch begins, for you and for your professors. Some of the individuals behind me are Powers themselves. Some fought and bled as Capes. Those without powers have been no less vital, dedicating years of their lives to helping me refine the Academy's training process. They are all here now to give you the benefit of their expertise; the skills, the training, and the foundational knowledge that you will need to make both your life *and* your death count." Bard's eyes scanned the auditorium, his words carrying easily in the dead silence. "Listen to them. Study as hard as you can, and train even harder. Remember why you wanted to be a hero, give everything you have to that pursuit, and when your time is over—whether that day is a week after graduation or fifty years down the road—you will be able to look back on your life, on the people you saved and the evil you stopped, and know that you made a difference."

With those words, Bard stepped out from behind the podium, breaking the spell he had cast over all of us. "That is the first and last speech you will hear from me until graduation, which I'm guessing comes as a relief to all of you." He waited for the chuckles to subside, and then continued. "Now then… before I introduce your professors, are there any questions?"

"Yeah." The speaker was in the cluster of students near the back; broad-shouldered and over-muscled, his long, blonde hair pulled back into braids. "Why the hell do we have a Crow in our class?"

Bard's eyes narrowed imperceptibly. "Mr. Banach qualified for admission, just as you did."

"Sure, but the rest of us aren't gonna go nuts and murder our classmates, are we?"

I clenched my fists, listening to the knuckles crack and pop, as murmurs of agreement rose up from the other first-years.

Bard's words were mild. "Mr. Thorsson, on the off-chance that your fellow first-years are unable to determine your power classification simply by looking at you, would you tell them what it is?"

The blonde kid rose to his feet. The seating made height difficult to judge, but I put him between six and a half and seven feet tall. He grinned easily, tossed his braids back, and flexed for the audience. "Titan. Strength, durability, and enough stamina to go all night long."

"Thank you, Mr. Thorsson. Please return to your seat before your display of masculinity overwhelms us all." Bard's smile faded as he turned back to the rest of us. "Dozer. Steel. Jackhammer. Carnage. The Anvil. What do they all have in common?"

"They're Black Hats," said a small woman with dark hair near the front.

"Half the story, Ms. Mandelhoff. What is the other half?"

"They're Titans." I couldn't see who made that comment, but Bard was nodding.

"Exactly. Every power group, from Titan to Stalwart and Flyboy to Jitterbug, has had its share of Black Hats. Many of those individuals have committed unspeakable atrocities. Should we deny all of you admission because of the actions of those villains who shared your power?"

A few—a very few—heads were nodding thoughtfully, but the tall, white-haired girl from the day before—Penelope-something-or-other—spoke up. "It's not the same thing at all."

"Are you sure, Ms. Von Pell?"

"I prefer Winter." She rose without being asked. "You said something similar yesterday… that it's not about the power, but instead the person who possesses that power. But that's not really true, is it?" She ticked off names on long, slender fingers. "Atlas. Incredible Ivan. The Iron Giant. Dominion himself. All Titans. All Capes."

"Are you certain you're not making my point for me?" Bard asked.

"That's just it," she said, her voice sharp. "Every power has its share of Capes and Black Hats… except one. Where are the Crow heroes?"

Silence greeted her words, and I felt a few hard eyes turn in my direction.

"Perhaps," Bard suggested gently, "you are now sitting with the first."

Judging by the expressions of the other first-years, and even a few of the teachers on stage, not everyone shared Bard's optimism.

* * *

Other questions quickly followed—most of them regarding basic information that had been covered in the Academy handbook—and then Bard provided a quick overview of what we could expect as students in the Academy. As first-years, our curriculum and schedules were set in stone; twenty weeks of introductory classes—Powers-related and otherwise—followed by mid-terms, a two week summer break, another twenty weeks of class and *more* exams. The school year ended in February with the Graduation Games and some sort of ultra-fancy Remembrance Day dance that a few of the first-year women were—impossibly enough—*already* excited about.

If we survived all of that *and* passed our exams—I didn't miss Bard's significant look in my direction on that last point—we'd be rewarded with another few weeks' break and the opportunity to do the whole thing again as second-years.

I wanted to be a Cape. I *really* wanted to stay sane. But forty weeks of classes? Not to mention the tests? It's like they were *hoping* I'd snap and murder someone.

That's not foreshadowing, for those of you who are wondering.

Unless it *is* foreshadowing, and I'm just lying to you. It's not like there's much you could do about it, if so. Time travel's not a power Dr. Nowhere felt fit to give us. Probably just as well, or someone would have used it to go back in time and kill his anonymous ass before this whole thing started.

By the time I'd finished freaking out about how much the next year was going to suck, Bard was introducing the instructors sitting behind him.

Isabel Ferra was tall, slender, and classically beautiful. For a lot of the other first-years, it was love at first sight, and her voice, melodic and smooth like some pre-Break jazz music, didn't hurt. However, she was one of the academics who had visibly disagreed with Bard's optimism regarding my future, so I hated her even *before* I found out she'd be teaching Ethics of Power.

My eyes were reserved for the woman next to her. Gabriella Stein was probably fifteen years older than Isabel, but barely looked it, with olive skin, sun-kissed golden hair, and curves that made me think of Alicia… or at least what Alicia might have grown up to be, had she gotten the chance. She introduced herself as Ms. Stein—meaning I still had a shot!—and would be teaching the classes on Control. Since I wasn't even sure what my powers could do yet, let alone how to control them, I was looking forward to a healthy bit of… personal instruction.

Yeah, I know… laugh it up. I bet you were all morons when you were eighteen too. Those of you who lived that long anyway. The rest of you are probably thinking *ew, girls!* Get used to that thought, kids; I didn't name myself Baron Boner just because it sounded cool.

No, I didn't end up naming myself Baron Boner. But you get my point, right?

Next was Nikolai Tsarnaev, he of the lantern jaw, crewcut, and muscles that made our own Titan look practically malnourished. To nobody's surprise, he'd be teaching Close Combat and Physical Education. I had him pegged as a sadist from the very first smile; a flash of teeth that was cold and mean.

Next was Amos Farshad, looking tiny next to Nikolai, his white hair and beard a sharp contrast to the deep brown of his heavily wrinkled skin. He would be our Professor of both Pre and Post-Break History. It was a subject he was uniquely qualified for given that he'd been born well *before* the Break. He'd been sixty-nine when Dr. Nowhere dreamed his little dream and now, so many decades later, he was *still* sixty-nine. Assuming nobody managed to kill his cantankerous, stodgy old ass, he would outlive us all, remaining that same age until his particular power burned out or the sun collapsed inward upon itself.

As our youngest professor, Jessica Strich had a lot going for her, all of it negated by the fact that she shared more than just a last name with my former roommate. She was dark-haired where Matthew was blonde, and sleek where he was built, but the family resemblance was still plenty obvious. She was only in her mid-twenties, but would be instructing us in tactics and weaponry. Maybe she'd teach Matthew how to wield the stick lodged up his own ass.

After that, the names and faces started to blur together. Robert Mance, also in his twenties, and the recipient of just as many lustful gazes as Isabel Ferra, would be teaching Philosophy to Powers and normals alike. Emery Goldstein, who hated me long before I told him he looked like a four-limbed penis, taught both Projection and Perception. Maria Curberas, late-thirties and plain as could be except for when the sunniest smiles you'd ever see transformed her into something angelic, was our Literature teacher. Professor Cade—no first name provided, leading to widespread speculation that his given name might actually be Professor—was pushing sixty in the worst of ways, taught mathematics, and didn't seem the tiniest bit concerned with who or what I was. Last but not least was our Mobility instructor, Macy Johnson. Black, slim, and small, she was also a world-class Jitterbug, something Caleb learned only after a particularly shameless round of his usual boasting.

The Powers class instructors would stick with us until graduation. That was less true for those who taught academic material. Curberas exclusively taught first-years. Cade taught lower and upper-level mathematics, but the latter was generally the domain of normals. Isabel Ferra, on the other hand… well, assuming I lasted until graduation, I'd be blessed with her instruction for all three years.

Apparently, ethics were considered important for would-be Capes. Who knew?

Anyway, those were the teachers we'd be studying under, arguing with, and—in a few particular cases—hating with fiery, all-consuming passion during our first year at the Academy. A lot of names, all at once, I know. Don't worry if you can't keep them all straight… God knows it took me time to do so, and *I* saw most of those fuckers on a weekly basis.

We'll come back to the ones that matter, soon enough. Maybe you'll learn to see them the way I did. Or maybe you'll decide even the worst of them were justified in their methods.

Now that? *That's* what we call foreshadowing. See the difference?

CHAPTER 17

After Orientation ended, I had the dubious pleasure of meeting my tutors, and they had the equally dubious pleasure of meeting me. I'm pretty sure it was mutual hatred at first sight, but I could have gotten past that if they hadn't promptly loaded me up with chapter readings from a half-dozen different texts on five different subjects.

Day one of school… no, *day zero* of school, and I already had fucking homework!

I swung by the cafeteria, grabbed another sandwich, and retreated to the dorm, trying to ignore the festivities that were still in full swing out on the field. We first-years got an hour-long speech on how we were all going to die, while the normal students got a party. The Academy's bullshit was already starting to stink.

Back in my room, I flopped onto the bed, waited to see if Mom's ghost was going to finally speak—she didn't, of course—and then picked up my Glass. Like my three sets of school-branded sweats, the tablet had been part of my enrollment package, and I couldn't deny the thrill of actually owning one for the first time in my life… even if I *was* being forced to use it for something as shitty as schoolwork. I thumbed it to life, loaded the first of the texts my tutors had assigned me, and got to work.

It sucked… and not the *good* kind of suck, if you know what I'm saying. This was mind-numbing drudgery, and it sucked in the least sexual way possible. But flunking out, going crazy, and ending up in the prison known as the Hole with my asshole dad? That would suck even more. So I read and I studied and eventually, sometime before my roommate or the rest of the class got back, I fell asleep.

And that was how I spent my birthday.

Eighteen years old.

Didn't feel much different from seventeen.

CHAPTER 18

Mondays as a first-year are always the same, a bucket of cold water in the face to shake you free of your weekend passivity (and heaven help the asshole who stayed out late Sunday night drinking). That's a *metaphorical* bucket of cold water, of course. Actual water would just make the first-year Hydros happy, and the Academy wasn't in the business of making any of us happy. Especially not on Mondays.

At six-forty-five A.M., every Glass in the dorm came to life, broadcasting a screaming noise like an air siren or a dozen children being sacrificed. I bolted upright in bed, grabbed the tablet from my dresser and hurled it across the room, where it dented the door, and kept on shrieking. Not sure what the devices were made of, but I only ever saw one get broken, and that took…well, let's just call it superhuman effort.

Anyway, nothing gets people out of bed quite like demon speakers shrieking in stereo. We poured out of our rooms and into the group showers, and were lined up in the common room, dressed in our school sweats, by twenty past the hour. The women came out of the opposite hall to line up next to us, most of them just as bleary-eyed as we were. One woman, brown-skinned, brown-haired, and built like a tree stump, was actually falling asleep on her feet. If she'd been any taller or even a little less wide, I think she'd have toppled right over. As it was, she kept catching herself and shaking herself back awake.

The last first-years to emerge were Olympia and Penelope 'Call me Winter' Von Pell. They both looked like they'd been up for an hour after getting the greatest sleep ever. Hell, they even had *makeup* on. Either the two of them had some new strain of superpower that the world had yet to classify or—and here, the demons in my head gibbered madly in terror—they were *morning people.*

And people call Crows evil!

I wasn't going to complain about Olympia in makeup though. Even if my very presence did scare the glow right out of her. She and a few other women almost made our shapeless grey Academy sweats look good.

We were all led across campus to the cafeteria by some second-year whose name I never caught, and who would end up dropping out before the year was up. Nobody was all that hungry but since our first block of classes stretched from eight to half past one, I was prepared to force myself to eat.

On the off chance that reincarnation is a thing and any of you come back one day to follow in little Damian's footsteps, take my advice: *eat lightly on Monday mornings.* Thursdays too, and occasionally Wednesdays, but *especially* Mondays. Especially that *first* Monday.

Not that you'll remember this. Or would listen, even if you did. You'll be eighteen, just like I was, convinced you know better than every other fucker around you. Hell, after I'd gotten over my groggy morning funk, I was so thrilled with the idea of eggs and real bacon that I went back for thirds.

Once we were fatted up like lambs for the slaughter, we were led across campus to our very first class at the Academy, marching past multi-story structures of glass and light—where the academic classes took place—to a short, windowless building that looked kind of like a concrete frog squatting to take a shit.

The inside wasn't any better. We filed through the wide doorway and then down a long stairway into a large room. Three of the four walls were unadorned concrete; one with three rows of benches set against it, the other two bare but for a set of closed doors. The wall opposite the benches was all glass, angled outward as if it was overlooking something, and in front of it stood Nikolai Tsarnaev, massive arms folded across his even more massive chest. As we entered, that same sadist's smile slowly stretched across his face.

"Officially, this class is known as *Physical Education & Introduction to Combat*," he said in a deep, slightly accented voice, "but the curriculum was written by administrators and pencil pushers. I prefer the name given by my very first students, more than ten years ago." That smile widened even further, exposing gleaming white teeth. "Welcome to Hell."

On cue, lights flooded the room beyond the glass wall. We crowded forward to look down upon an enormous cavern. A series of fixtures ringed the room's perimeter, glowing an electric blue, their hum audible even from where we stood. In the uneven floor of the cave were five pits, each maybe fifteen feet in diameter and at least that deep.

It didn't look like hell. It didn't look like much of anything.

Looks can be deceiving, I guess.

"On any other day," Nikolai continued, "you'd be out on the field, getting your laps in." Dark eyes glittered, taking careful note of the first-years groaning at the thought. "Then strength training, then drills, and then… if you somehow managed not to piss me off, maybe a little bit of fun. But today is different," he told us with great satisfaction. "Today is your first lesson on what it takes to be a Cape."

He unfolded one huge arm and motioned at the strange cave. "In the arena, the dampeners will keep your active powers suppressed. No fire, no shifting." Those eyes turned to me. "No corruption of the natural order. Just you, your hands and your feet. Over the next semester, you will learn to survive using those things."

He waited again for the confused murmurs to die down. "Five pairs at a time, one pair to each pit in the arena. When I call your names, you and your opponent will exit through the door in the left wall, proceed to the correct numbered door below, and enter, closing that door behind you. It will stay closed until your fight is over."

"Our… *what*?!" This was the dark-haired girl who'd been sitting in the front row during Orientation. Her grey eyes were wide, her voice soft.

Nikolai raised an eyebrow. "Which one are you again…?"

"Evelyn Mandelhoff," she told him.

"They don't pay me enough to memorize that mouthful," he decided, conveniently ignoring the fact that *his* last name was all consonants and impossible to pronounce. "What's your Cape name?"

"Wormhole."

"Better. So tell me, Wormhole," he said conversationally, taking a step closer to loom over her, "which part of *Introduction to Combat* did you *not* understand? Punch, kick, claw, or scratch… hell, you can bite if you think it will do any good. Each pair will fight until there is a victor, and you will all, winners and losers, be graded on your performance."

Tessa, our class Telekinetic, frowned and raised her hand. "I'm not a Titan or a Stalwart. Why would I ever stoop to *punching* someone?"

"Because someday you might care more about staying alive than your manicure," growled the tree stump of a woman who'd been asleep on her feet less than an hour earlier, "and powers don't solve everything."

"No shock that *you'd* want to go roll in the dirt, Sofia," shot back Tessa.

"Call me Silt, bitch."

Nikolai brought his hands together in a clap that sounded almost like a gunshot. "Enough. Silt's right, but if any of you children wish to skip this exercise, you may do so—" He waited for Tessa's satisfied nod before continuing. "—and accept an F in the class."

"For the day?" asked the Lightbringer, Olympia. "Because I'm actually okay with that—"

"For the year," roared Nikolai, "which means you leave the Academy, right now. There is no place here for cowards." He scanned the suddenly silent crowd, and nodded, his voice quieting to its usual rumble. "If there are no further questions?"

"What are the rules of engagement?" Matthew wanted to know.

"You're Paladin?"

"I will be."

Nikolai nodded. "See to it that you don't shame the name."

Matthew stood even straighter, blue eyes flashing. "Yes, sir."

"I've already given the rules," continued the teacher. "Fight until the other surrenders or is unable to continue. The school Healers will be standing by to attend to you after the fight, and the dampeners should prevent any fatalities."

"*Should* prevent them?" squeaked a small guy with pale skin, freckles, and carrot-colored hair.

Nikolai shrugged meaty shoulders. "Nothing in life is guaranteed."

* * *

I wasn't one of the first ten names called, so I found a good spot to watch the fights unfold. In addition to the glass window, five vid screens had lowered from the ceiling, each providing a high definition view of one of the pits.

On the first screen was Matthew, performing a handful of stretching exercises and looking calm and composed. Across from him was the class Titan, Erik Thorsson, who had told Nikolai to call him the Viking. He rolled his neck from side to side, and yawned, confident in his significant size advantage.

The pair in the second pit couldn't have been more different from the first. On one side was Ishmae, looking even smaller and younger out of her robes, her dark face expressionless. On the other side was the ginger who'd been worried about fatalities. Shane was two years older than Ishmae, but equally small, and the whites of his terrified eyes were clearly visible on the monitor above.

Next over were Tessa and Olympia. Neither woman looked happy to be there, but where Olympia was white-faced with fear, her silver eyes enormous on the large vid screen, Tessa looked angry enough to chew rocks.

After that was the outspoken Silt, facing down a woman I'd yet to meet… but badly wanted to. Her codename was Orca, and she moved like a vid dancer, all sleek muscle and controlled motion. I was almost positive she was our other Stalwart.

The final pair were Caleb the Jitterbug, looking more than a bit sluggish without his power, and Santiago the Druid. Neither looked happy to be there, but Santiago still had the presence of mind to toss a confident smile—and a wink—to his pit's camera.

I was kind of excited to watch those two beat each other senseless.

* * *

With five vid screens, it was impossible to keep up with all the action, but I did see Olympia immediately drop to her knees, throw up her hands, and surrender. For someone who hadn't wanted to even participate, Tessa seemed oddly irritated that she didn't get to throw a punch.

The second fight was over almost as quickly. In just under a minute, Ishmae had Shane flat on his belly and splayed out on the ground, her arm snaked under his chin. He waved his own pale arms ineffectually for about ten seconds, then dropped into unconsciousness.

Santiago didn't do anything fancy, but it was clear this wasn't his first fight. After a minute or two of circling, he sidestepped Caleb's charge, grabbed an arm, and swung the Jitterbug into the wall with a thud audible even from the observation room. Caleb staggered back to his feet just in time to receive a perfectly timed punch to the face, breaking his nose with a splatter of blood, and dropping him to the ground. This time, the Jitterbug didn't stand back up, curling in pain on the pit floor until the match was called.

Someone on the observation deck threw up. I wasn't particularly grossed out—the shit show I'd come through with Her Majesty on the way to the Academy had been way worse than a broken nose—but I wasn't thrilled either. I'd been in plenty of fights in the orphanage, but those had been *for* something. This was just violence for its own sake.

The other two fights were less one-sided. Silt appeared to have an edge in strength and weight over Orca, but the other woman was always two steps ahead, reacting to attacks almost like she could see them coming before they even happened. She moved a lot like the Stalwarts I'd seen in vids; the real Paladin or even The Scarlet Dynamo.

In fact, she moved *just like them.*

I frowned, suddenly suspicious, and looked to the other fight to see Matthew duck a wild punch from the Viking. The Titan's fist hit the wall with a crack that echoed through the room, but it was the stone that crumbled, not the big man's fingers. Meanwhile, Matthew landed three or four lightning-quick punches into the other man's midsection, hard enough to break a normal man's ribs. Neither fighter appeared winded yet, let alone injured.

Son of a bitch. Nikolai had said the dampeners would be high enough to cancel our *active* powers… but Stalwarts and Titans had passive power sets. Unless the dampeners were turned up all the way, the three of them would have some measure of their strength, speed and durability.

I was suddenly very glad my name hadn't been called yet.

* * *

Silt put on a good showing, but as the fight wore on, Orca just kept getting faster. The end came without warning, as she slipped past Silt's punch, and dropped the other woman with a flurry of blows too quick to see. Similarly, Matthew rode out the Viking's initial rush, returning multiple, pinpoint strikes for every one of the Titan's missed punches. When Thorsson finally fell, more than fifteen minutes into the match, I couldn't tell if it was from damage or simple exhaustion. Either way, the cavern shook as his massive body hit the ground.

The school's two on-site Healers had moved in to treat injuries as soon as each match concluded, and the pits were clear again just a few minutes later. Soon after, the ten combatants made their way back up the observation room, entering through the door in the opposite wall. Many showed signs of recent healing, though the front of Caleb's sweatshirt was wet with slowly drying blood, and Silt was leaning heavily on Orca's arm.

Nikolai ignored the returning combatants and read the next five pairs off his list. Once again, I hadn't been called. The four of us who had yet to fight stared each other down, paying very little attention as the next five matches kicked off.

Of my three possible opponents, Alan Jackson was by far the biggest threat. I watched his toaster-sized hands clench slowly into fists, release, and then clench again, the dull crunching sound audible despite the noise from the pits. Second on that list was my new roommate, every bit as large as Alan, but nowhere near as menacing, his bushy, black beard notwithstanding.

They each had a hundred pounds and six or more inches of reach on me, but based on the matchups we'd seen so far, I was pretty sure Nikolai would pair them against each other. That left me the fourth and final first-year; half a foot shorter than I was, pale-eyed and pudgy. He was the student who had thrown up when Santiago broke Caleb's nose.

Finally, life was throwing me a fucking bone.

* * *

As expected, Alan and Jeremiah were dispatched to the first pit. But after calling on the fat kid, who went by the awe-inspiring codename of Prince, Nikolai looked to the first-years who had already fought.

"Olympia, you're up."

"I already fought, Professor," she reminded him. "I shouldn't have to go again."

"You quit the moment the door closed," he growled, "which does absolutely fuck-all for you or any of us. Try again or get out of my class."

Whatever else you could say about the Lightbringer, it was clear she wanted to be a Cape. She swallowed her protests, shot the professor a silver-eyed glare, and followed Prince down into the pits, slamming the door shut behind her.

I coughed in the sudden silence. "So… do I just get an A or what?"

That cold smile flickered back across Nikolai's face. "Can't do that. Wouldn't be fair to the other first-years." Beady eyes met mine, and that smile widened as he raised his voice. "Paladin, you're up again."

Fucking hell.

I did my best to keep any reaction off my face as I turned and went through the designated door. A long hallway curved around and down to the next level, where five doors led to the individual pits. As I watched, the door to the last pit opened, and two stretchers exited, carrying the groaning forms of the women who'd been paired up. White hair identified one of them as Winter, but I hadn't been paying enough attention to her fight to know who her opponent had been, or even which of them had won. From the looks of it, neither was going to be feeling much like a victor any time soon.

The first two pits were occupied, but I ignored Nikolai's orders to enter the third, walking past its door without stopping. The fourth pit got the same treatment, but I stopped at the final pit—the one the stretchers had just left—and stepped in. The concrete floor was splattered with blood—some of it from Caleb's broken nose, and some of it from Winter and her opponent—and the gruesome décor fit my mood perfectly.

Teacher wanted to see my ass get kicked by a Stalwart?

Fuck if I was going down without a fight.

CHAPTER 19

The pits were bigger than they'd looked on the monitor. Fifteen, maybe twenty feet across, with walls that rose at least that high, making the arena's ceiling feel impossibly far away. Those walls were rough stone, empty of ornamentation, bare of anything other than the door we'd come through, the door that had shut and locked behind us.

Distant ceiling, locked door, stone walls… and blood. I could see it, dark pools on the floor and glistening geometric patterns across the closest arc of the wall. More than that, I could *smell* it. People say a lot of things about how blood smells; they say it's metallic, say it's coppery, say it's foul and polluted.

To me, it smells like home on that last day. Smells like the pie in the oven that's going to burn and burn and keep burning until only ash is left because she's not there to take it out, because she'll never be there to take it out, and because everyone else is too busy with why that's suddenly the case.

Mom's ghost hadn't followed me into the arena. I'm not sure if that was the dampeners at work or if she just wasn't in the mood. Maybe blood made her remember too. Maybe she didn't want to remember. That was the difference between us, I guess. I didn't ever want to forget.

I looked around one last time to make sure she was gone. Then I turned to Paladin.

Whatever he saw in my face had him taking a half-step back before he caught himself. Just that tiny flinch, and then he was stoic and unassailable again, but I took it as a victory. He had some portion of his powers; speed, strength, agility… all the shit that mixes together to make a perfect fighter. He had his skill and his training.

All I had was my memory and the thick smell of blood.

It wasn't going to be enough, couldn't be enough, but even a dumbass like Caleb had probably figured that much out when Paladin's name was called.

Can't doesn't always mean won't, and it sure as fuck doesn't mean don't.

When Nikolai's voice came, it rumbled like thunder from the speakers, more sound than words. I heard noise from the other pits; a choked cry; the meaty thud of flesh hitting flesh. The first sounded like Prince. The second could have been any of the four.

Before either sound had faded, Matthew was in motion.

He was fast. Too fast. I stepped away at an angle to avoid his first strike, but he caught me with the second, a punch that barely clipped me and still sent me skidding. I should've gone with the momentum of the punch, let it carry me out of range, but instead I fought to keep from going down. All that did was make me an easy target.

I didn't see the third punch; just felt the explosion of light, the sudden weightlessness of being, and the impact when I landed.

I spat blood, watched it mingle on the floor with all the rest. Paladin was already back across the pit where he'd started, watching to make sure I stayed down.

Fuck staying down.

I climbed back to my feet, mind racing. I had a slight reach advantage, but no way to use it without his speed and strength overwhelming me. The way he moved, first against the Viking, and now against me, spoke to his training. Real training, not the stuff I'd scraped together from late-night brawls, back-alley beatings and one close encounter with a screwdriver.

I couldn't win. I *definitely* couldn't win clean. So I needed to dirty this up.

This time, when Paladin came forward, I went to meet him. Wind whistled past my face as I slid under a punch that had *still* been almost too quick, and then I was inside his guard, far past the second punch that he threw towards where he'd expected me to be.

I spun like a corkscrew, dropping to one knee and throwing my elbow towards his kidney.

He blocked it. I don't fucking know how, but he did, twisting impossibly and diverting my hit to the side with his forearm. Elbow to forearm, advantage should've been elbow, but I felt something pop in my own arm, even before his other hand came down to exert pressure.

I exploded back to my feet, thrust my free hand at his face, thumb going for his baby blues, and he threw me into the air and over his shoulders with that single fucking hand. I renewed my acquaintance with the wall, reintroduced myself to the floor, and donated a little more blood to the pool.

This time, Paladin didn't wait. As I struggled to my feet, he was there, fist hammering into my right side like a steel wrecking ball. When I fell a third time, I donated more than just blood; half-digested remnants of eggs and bacon joined the gory stew.

Like I said, it doesn't pay to overeat at breakfast. Not on Mondays. Especially not that first Monday.

I could hear the disgust in Matthew's voice, as he looked toward the camera. "We're done, Professor."

Fuck being done too.

It was anger that got me back to my feet. Anger that drowned out the sharp pain in my side, and the harsh, strangled wheezing of my suddenly inadequate breath. Anger at the Academy, at this class, at Bard and his sanctimonious fucking speeches, at Matthew-fucking-Strich and his vid-star looks, at the fact that these sweats were practically the only clothes I fucking owned, and one set was now ruined for fucking forever.

"We are *not* fucking done," I growled.

Paladin's eyes widened, for just a moment, and then he came back in.

Anger got me through the first hit and the second.

Anger got me back off the floor the fourth time, the fifth time, even the sixth time, by which point Paladin's fists were dripping with my blood.

Anger got me a strike that *almost* landed, my extended fingers grazing his throat even as he hammered yet another fist into my stomach, sending me to the floor for the seventh fucking time in I didn't know how many fucking minutes.

That was when anger fled, taking with it the pain that it had almost hidden, leaving nothing behind but emptiness, cold and silent. I could feel the walls of the pit closing in on me, feel consciousness packing its bags as it prepared to follow anger right the fuck out that door in my mind. Try as I might, I couldn't find the words or the thoughts or the emotions to summon it back.

Nor could I find the energy to be surprised when my body gathered beneath me all on its own, and I stood back up for round eight.

CHAPTER 20

Regaining consciousness always sucks. First, there's the sense of confusion—*where am I, what am I doing here,* and on particularly fucked-up occasions, *who am I*? As the answers are just starting to make their way to the front of your brain, the questions cease to matter, wiped away by the world making itself known again through that sensation called pain.

This time was no different. My head was killing me, and every part of my body was rioting right along with it. Less pain than I'd have expected, less pain than I remembered from before I went out, but it sure didn't feel good. I cracked one eye open and immediately wished I hadn't. Regaining consciousness is bad enough, but waking up to find a ginger in your face? That's a whole new species of suck, even before you add in that this particular ginger was singing under his breath. Voice like his would have put Alicia's panties right back *on*, if you know what I'm saying.

If she hadn't already been dead, of course.

Fucking Scarlet.

Fucking parents who took Alicia out of Bakersfield.

Anyway, the ginger. I don't know what people thought of gingers before the Break. One theory holds that gingers didn't even exist pre-Break, that they're something Dr. Nowhere was in the midst of dreaming into existence when he woke up, leaving his last creation badly incomplete. And soulless. Totally soulless. I didn't buy that theory—and not just because I'd seen pre-Break comic books starring a Cape named Archie who was ginger as could be—but I didn't *totally* discount it either. Fuck knows pale skin, freckles, and carrot-colored hair are a combination too horrible to achieve on accident.

This particular ginger had eyes the color of a cloudless summer sky—the sort of sky too rarely seen in Bakersfield—set in a baby face above the aforementioned spattering of freckles. Those eyes widened as they met mine, and his song cut off in mid lyric.

"Shit!!"

I cocked an eyebrow, relieved to find that at least *that* didn't hurt. "Shit?"

"You're not supposed to be awake until I'm done."

"Done with what? Stealing my organs? Measuring my dick? Murdering that song?"

He went beet red. Not sure if it was my justified criticism of his singing or the comment about my dick, which was, given the cold steel beneath my all-too-bare ass, very much hanging out for the world to admire and possibly measure.

"Healing you," he finally managed. "We're supposed to keep patients asleep until everything's done, but that bit's way harder than the actual healing."

"Oh." I let my eyes flutter closed, as my brain finally woke up enough for me to place his face. Last I'd seen him, Ishmae had been choking him unconscious. "You're the first-year Healer. Shane something or other?"

"Shane Stevenson. Call me Balm."

I cracked one eye back open. "What the fuck sort of Healer name is Bomb?"

"Not Bomb… Balm. There's an l in there, and no b. Well, one b, I guess. It's a type of ointment that soothes pain."

I'd found a codename that made Baron Boner seem cool.

"So how come you're working on me instead of one of the professionals?"

"One second, please." Shane placed the palm of his right hand flat against my bare chest and concentrated. Moments later, warm spread outward from that point of contact, muffling the pain, if not killing it entirely. "This is part of my training," he said. "After Ishmae choked me out, they brought me back to help. Besides…" He flushed again.

"Besides?"

"I'm a High-Three," he shrugged self-consciously, "and they're Twos. I don't have their training yet, but in terms of raw power, I'm the only game in town. Given your condition when they carted you in, they decided to err on the side of caution." He paused again. "I've never gotten to fix internal bleeding before, let alone a collapsed lung. Your heart even stopped! Would it be weird if I said thank you?"

"It's weird that you even have to ask," I decided, taking my first big breath since waking up. Everything still hurt, but that sharp piercing I'd felt in my side was gone, as was the whistling that had accompanied my last gasps in the pit. "How long was I out?"

"More than an hour."

"Shit! I have class…"

"Me too," said Shane, "but it started like forty minutes ago and Ms. Stein already knows we won't make it to Control. Last year, only half the first-years were well enough to attend on the first day, so I guess three of us skipping is an improvement."

I was pretty sure the little guy and his powers were part of the reason for that. A High-Three Healer *and* a ginger? Unicorn didn't even begin to cover it.

"Wait… three of us?" After waking up to find Shane in my face, I'd very carefully *not* paid further attention to my surroundings. Or the fact that I was still fucking naked. Now, with every muscle complaining, I rolled to one side and took a careful look around.

I'd gone to the clinic when I first arrived at the Academy, but this wasn't it. The clinic had inspirational posters, comfortable couches and magazines, not to mention individual examination rooms. This room, which I would later learn was the on-campus medical ward—because what school is complete without its own surgical center?—was all off-white paint and sterile steel accessories. Long shelves spotted the wall to my left, near a row of oversized sinks with detachable shower heads. To my right were four gurneys just like the one I was lying on. Two were empty, one was partially occupied by the still-smiling figure of Mom's ghost, but the last held an actual patient; the mountainous, silent mass of my roommate, Jeremiah Jones.

"What happened to him?"

"Alan Jackson happened." Shane shivered, then visibly brightened. "Broken right clavicle, and a spiral fracture to the left ulna. Pretty straightforward to heal, it turns out, but still… kind of cool."

I flopped back down, clenching my teeth to keep the groan from slipping out. I'd been in my share of fights—and lost plenty of them, especially before puberty hit—but my match with Paladin was the first time in years I'd felt truly outclassed. It wasn't a feeling I cared for. "So we're all losers then? Might be the first thing my roommate and I have in common."

"What?" Balm's eyes widened again, and he shook his head, carrot hair flying about. "You didn't lose."

"You just spent an hour putting me back together. Of course I lost."

"You don't remember? Really?" He moved up and placed his palm on my forehead, concentrating. After a moment, he frowned. "No sign of brain damage that would suggest memory loss. Weird."

Healer or not, ginger or not, I was a breath away from kicking Shane's ass if he didn't tell me what he was talking about.

"I was down here working, but I watched the whole thing on vid," he explained. "*You wouldn't stop.* Sixteen fractures, a punctured lung, at least two heart attacks… and you just kept going."

"I thought you said my lung was *collapsed*."

"It's the same thing, medically speaking," he said absently. "Broken rib punctured the lung, the lung collapsed. Anyway, if Matthew hadn't surrendered—"

"He what?!?"

"Surrendered, ending the match. If he hadn't—" Shane's clear sky eyes were solemn. "—I think you might have died. Even *with* my help."

"Fuck."

"Yeah. The other Healers couldn't believe Professor Tsarnaev let things go that far."

My heartfelt expletive didn't have anything to do with almost dying. Maybe it's because I'd watched Her Majesty shred a Pyro just a few days earlier, or because Balm had already healed most of my injuries before I woke up, but I wasn't all that bothered by my latest near-death experience. I mean, it sucked, and would have sucked more if I'd actually kicked off, but I hadn't, so… whatever, right?

Of far greater concern was the revelation that my ex-roommate—who had quickly and effortlessly assumed the role of arch-nemesis—had just saved my life.

What the fuck was I supposed to say to that?

* * *

The Academy Healers may have trusted Balm—still the dumbest codename I'd ever heard—to patch me up, but that trust had its limits. I had to wait another twenty minutes for one of the pros to come and double-check the little ginger's work. Finally, after a lot of poking and prodding, mixed in with muttered comments about both the number of ribs I had showing and the boniness of my exposed ass, the older woman nodded in satisfaction.

I waited another half-minute, as the two of them reviewed what Balm had done, how, and why, before finally interrupting, waving one hand at my still-naked body. "Can I get my clothes back or should I just head outside like this? Not entirely sure how the Academy feels about dicks swinging in the breeze."

Shane went beet red again, but his counterpart, the same woman who had treated me on my arrival to the Academy, was made of sterner stuff. "I suppose that depends on the dick in question. As for your clothing, we had to cut it off of you … not that what remained would've been salvageable if we hadn't."

"So what am I supposed—?"

"Shockingly, you're not the first person to end up naked in the med ward. Usually, there's alcohol involved though." She nodded to the far wall. "Grab a set of fresh sweats from the third shelf before you blind us all."

I'm pretty sure that was a comment on my pallor and not the brilliant, awe-inspiring sight of my all-too-visible appendage. I swung my legs over the far side of the table, and scurried to the shelf in question. The sweats came in five sizes; small, medium, large, extra-large, and what-the-fuck-are-they-feeding-you. I grabbed a large and pulled on both the pants and long-sleeved top. Then, over one shoulder. "Do I need to bring these back when I'm done with them?"

"Do we look like a laundry service?" Despite the words, her voice was almost kind. Maybe naked Crow affected her more than she was letting on. If she hadn't been pushing sixty… nah, it had been a long time since Alicia, but there were still limits. "Keep them as a replacement."

I nodded in thanks, waited for her and Balm to head over to the still-unconscious Jeremiah… and then stole another set of sweats.

A few more near-death experiences and I might end up with a full week's worth of clothes.

CHAPTER 21

After all that time entombed in Nikolai's bunker of pain, the sun was painfully bright, hanging like an angry god in the crystal blue sky. The med ward was a few buildings from the arena, connected by little more than an underground hallway, and it took me a few moments to get my bearings. Once I did, I headed over to where Gabriella Stein taught Control. Limped over, if we're being truthful. The faculty felt we'd learn better if the Healers only *mostly* healed us, so even though nothing was broken, punctured, or collapsed anymore, I had bruises fucking everywhere.

I wasn't trying to make it *to* class, and not just because it was almost over. If nearly dying meant I got to skip school for a bit, I was good with that, even with Gabriella Stein being the embodiment of every teacher fantasy I'd never thought to have. Control was the one powers class we had five days a week, so there'd be plenty of opportunity for me to sweet talk my way into Ms. Stein's heart. Like Tuesday, for example.

So no; I didn't go because I wanted to attend class. I went because all of the other first-years would be there. More importantly, *Matthew* would be there.

Obligations are a bitch, but you can't just dream that shit away.

Most of the campus buildings held classes for both Powers and regular students. Nikolai's bunker was one exception. Ms. Stein's sunlit studio was another. The fewer people around the better when you're trying to teach first-years how *not* to crack the world in half. When the bell rang, and students poured out of every other classroom, the Control building stayed quiet at first. Simple law of numbers; five hundred shits in a building means some of them are pretty damn close to the door, and some of them are pretty damn anxious to get out. A mere twenty-one shits, half of whom were probably lusting after Ms. Stein as much as me? It took my fellow first-years a solid minute or two to emerge.

The first was Olympia—because *of course* it was—walking arm-in-arm with a raven-haired smoke show whose curves would put vid stars to shame. I'd noticed the brunette in Nikolai's class, of course—pretty sure her name was London—but she'd been part of the second pairings, and I hadn't paid any attention to her fight.

I was beating myself up over that little fact just then. She wore the same grey sweats as the rest of us, but like Olympia, she actually made them look good.

Both women saw me at the same time. Both stopped. Olympia's light went out, *again*, and London's pale skin went even paler.

"Ladies." I nodded.

Neither said a word, spines suddenly stiff like someone had insulted their mothers. Instead, they gave me a wide berth, eyes never leaving me, but never quite meeting mine. It wasn't until they were past me, merging back into the sea of humanity, that they began to speak again.

To each other, of course. Not me.

Made me miss Alicia, to be honest. Sappy shit, for sure, but also true. Girl never cared that I was a Crow. Girl never cared that I was an orphan either.

Girl's dead and buried, I reminded myself for the second time in less than an hour.

After London and Olympia came the rest of the first-years. The faces and names changed, but the reactions stayed the same. Apparently, getting the shit kicked out of me by Paladin hadn't convinced anyone I was harmless.

Weird thing was, I could swear some of them were *more* scared of me than they had been. What was *that* about?

Only four exceptions to that; Orca, Alan Jackson, the Viking, and Silt. First two paid no attention to me at all, each walking by themselves, each wrapped up in their own shit. The Viking swaggered by, giving me a shit-eating, superior grin, as if he hadn't been put down by Paladin just as hard as I had. And Silt…?

"Didn't know a skinny guy like you had so much blood in him," she told me in passing, her voice gruff. "Not sure they're ever getting those stains out."

She was gone before I could reply.

Last to leave—because *of course* he would be last—was Matthew Strich, not a bruise on him or a hair out of place to suggest that he'd fought both the Viking and me that morning. Like the other first-years, he went pale at the sight of me, but when I stepped in his path, those baby blues hardened. In the time it took me to take a step, he'd gone from post-meditation calm to fuck-you-up readiness.

Stalwarts… sometimes, I think they're even crazier than Crows.

"Paladin." It still wasn't his name, not with the real Paladin still running around, but for at least one day, I figured I owed him that much respect.

"Crow." His eyes stayed wary. "If this is about our match…"

"It is." I felt the snarl forming on my face, but forced the words out anyway. "I wanted to thank you."

For just a moment, his jaw stayed clenched. Then it dropped open. "Thank me? For what?!? Breaking every bone in your body?"

"For stopping when you did." I hated saying that. Hated admitting it, even to myself. "The Healers say if you hadn't, I would've died. Probably. I guess." He didn't say anything, and I watched his mouth swing shut again, his jaw clenching and unclenching like he was trying to chew through steel. I waited a moment longer and then shrugged. "Anyway, just wanted to say thanks."

I was five feet away, headed for the slowly shrinking river of people, when he finally spoke. "I didn't stop the match for *you*."

I looked back, stone grey eyes meeting vid star blue.

"I stopped because you wouldn't," he continued, forcing the words out, "because I couldn't figure out how to *make* you, and because that scared the hell out of me." Those eyes hardened again, and it was like the moment of vulnerability had never happened. "Next time will be different."

"Looking forward to it," I lied.

"I guess we'll see." He brushed past me and was gone.

Looked like that whole arch-nemesis thing was still on after all.

Fuck.

CHAPTER 22

I don't know what normal college is like, but the first week at the Academy is a shock to the system. Four-plus hours of powers classes every morning, then lunch, then regular classes, then homework, until your brain hurts just as much as your body. The only thing that makes it bearable is the weekend drawing closer and with it, that next chance to breathe.

By Thursday, most of us were feeling the strain. Three days of Control (two for those of us who missed Monday), a day of swinging sticks in Jessica Strich's weapons class, more schoolwork than I knew what to do with, and we *still* had two full days to go before it was over. There were a lot of tired faces and slumped shoulders as we exited the cafeteria and headed off to the first class of the day.

Our destination might have had something to do with it. Nikolai's concrete shithouse looked even more ominous than it had on Monday. Maybe because we all knew what was waiting for us inside. Three days later, I was still bruised and battered.

Down in the observation room, Nikolai was waiting for us, looming like a blocky, unfinished statue. He motioned us to the rows of benches set against the far wall, and waited until everyone was seated.

"You're all still here. Good. Becoming a Cape takes many things; ability, intelligence, ambition, and even creativity. But most of all, it takes perseverance and dedication. All the talent in the world can't teach heart. At least you have that much." His deep voice filled the chamber. "Every year, this class begins with battle. Why?"

"Sadism?" That was Caleb. His broken nose had been healed, but the black eyes resulting from it hadn't, making him look like a particularly feral breed of animal.

"Ha!" Nikolai shook his head. "Sadism would be letting you graduate untested, sending you off to join hero teams without knowing what it's like to be beaten or bloodied. That was what this school did the first few years. Rainbows up every student's ass, and a sequence of dance steps to be memorized. Step here. Dodge that. Strike there. And what happened when those newly graduated Capes found real battle?"

"They froze." That was Paladin, up in the front and looking as fresh as he had before the school week started.

"Damn right they froze. They froze and they died. Worse, they got their teammates killed, veteran Capes relying on them to cover their backs." This time, Nikolai's head shake was sharp and savage. "Not all of you will stand on the front lines when you leave this school. But combat doesn't obey rules, and it doesn't play nice. Whether you're a Healer or a Siren or a Gods-fucked Crow, you *will* someday find yourself in a position where you must fight. That is why I'm here." Beady eyes sought out Olympia, one row in front of me. "That is why I will not accept excuses or cowardice. If you make it through the Academy, lives will depend on you, and not just civilian lives, but those of your fellow Capes. No student of mine will meet that responsibility unprepared."

He paced back and forth in front of us. "You are all a very, very long way from that day. You aren't Capes. You aren't even Capes-in-training. Not yet. You're first-years, the lowest of the low, and judging by what I saw on Monday, we have our work cut out for us."

He stopped in front of Erik Thorsson. "A Titan who collapses after less than twenty minutes of combat. So much for *going all night long*." Next was Silt. "An Earthshaker who drops like a stone." Ishmae got a respectful nod and no commentary, and then he was in front of Paladin. "And a Stalwart who can't defeat a Crow in hand-to-hand combat."

Matthew sat stiff, cheeks flushed, and said nothing.

"Who here knows what Paladin did wrong?" Nikolai finally asked the class.

"He lost?" suggested Winter.

"Just like you did?" The teacher shook his head. "Everyone loses. No shame in that."

Winter scowled. I hadn't seen her match with Erin Pearson, a Wind Dancer who was only saved from ginger-ness by her less than pasty skin, but suddenly I really, really wanted to. With all that silky white hair, Winter could have been almost cute, even with the nose—after all, who I was to talk about noses?—but so far, she'd been every bit as cold as her namesake.

"Anyone else have an answer?" asked Nikolai.

"He quit." Those were the first words I'd heard Alan Jackson speak, his voice harsh and cold.

"Damn straight he quit." Nikolai let the words fall like an executioner's axe.

"Oh come on! You saw what happened!" protested London, who looked as good from behind and above as she had outside Control on Monday. "The Crow wasn't going to stop."

The Crow was getting sick of being called that. And of being treated like a fucking plague victim, for that matter. After four days of cold shoulders and silence from literally every attractive woman in my class—not to mention a surprising lack of progress in my campaign to win Ms. Stein's heart and body—that old Healer in the med ward was looking better and better.

The Academy was supposed to be keeping me sane, not driving me in the other direction.

"You're right. He *wasn't* going to stop," agreed Nikolai. "Sixteen fractures, and *the Crow* kept fighting. Why do you think that is?"

"Because he's a psycho zombie just pretending to be alive?" suggested Santiago.

"Could be, El Bosque," agreed Nikolai. "Maybe the dampeners don't work on his kind. Thing is… desperate, unwavering defiance is the sort of shit you'll be facing when you graduate, and not just from Crows. When it's life and death, some people choose not to roll over just because they're facing a Cape. And quitting sure as hell isn't an option then. So what should Mr. Strich have done?"

"Decapitate the fucker." Alan's word count had now reached five, and I was liking him less with every syllable.

"Surprisingly ineffective against Walkers," countered Nikolai, using the popular term for zombies, "and a quick pass to a lifetime stay in the Hole if it happens in my class, but not a bad suggestion otherwise. Anyone else?"

Shane raised his hand. "He could've choked him out, maybe?"

"Like Phoenix did to you, you mean?" Nikolai's grin widened as he looked from the little ginger to the even smaller Ishmae seated next to him. "After your little dirt nap, I guess it's no surprise that you'd think of it… but sure, that could work. No oxygen to the brain means no motor control means the opponent goes down. Unless he really is a Walker, of course. Anything else?"

The class gave a collective shrug, so Nikolai nodded and kept going. "Sometimes, killing is the best solution. Other times, you'll need to be use nonlethal means. Chokes. Immobilizations. Even the old stand-by of handcuffs and shackles."

"Sounds like some of my dates," laughed Caleb.

"Sounds like we have a volunteer when we get to those classes," responded Nikolai cheerfully. That humor vanished as he addressed us as a whole. "We don't hold these matches because I want to watch you bleed. Not even that mouthy Jitterbug over there. And I didn't call anyone out today to humiliate them." He dropped a massive hand onto Matthew's shoulder. "Fact is, Paladin ran into a situation he wasn't prepared for. That's what happens in this class. That's what this class is *about.* We fight and then, win or lose, we review what happened. We identify what went wrong, and we train to do better in the future."

"But all the fight experience in the world is useless if you lack the strength, the speed, or—" and here he looked directly at the Viking again, "—the endurance to capitalize on it. So now that I've gotten the measure of your class, we'll be tabling combat for a little while."

In front of me, Olympia not only perked up, she actually started glowing again.

"Instead, we're going to focus on conditioning. In a month or two, you'll be begging to hit someone and if you've trained hard enough, I may even let you. In the meantime, get ready for some real pain. We'll start with something simple before we get into strength training. A pleasant jog, for example." That sadistic smile reappeared. "I'm thinking five miles?"

Olympia's glow went right back out.

* * *

There's a special place in hell for people who schedule classes on Friday afternoon, when all anyone wants is an early end to the school week and a merciful start to the weekend. And at the center of that special place, deep within its disgusting, blood-soaked, shivering heart, there's an even *more* special place, reserved for people who schedule *Ethics* classes on Friday afternoons.

Not everyone minded, of course, because Isabel Ferra was young, pretty, and had a way of chewing on her pencil as she waited for answers that was borderline phallic. People like Paladin, Ishmae, and Winter even seemed to enjoy the discussion topics, which was enough to convince me that Crows weren't the only insane Powers in the world.

I hated it. Didn't care for Ms. Ferra, and she sure as fuck didn't care for me either, given the way she loved to bring up examples of Crow atrocities as models of *unethical behavior*. Because first-years really needed her expert instruction to understand that attacking someone with zombie rats was *bad*.

Even when the conversation wasn't Crow-related, Ethics class sucked. I'd never spent much time thinking about the subject growing up. Dad killing Mom was bad. Older kids picking on the little ones at Mama Rawlins? Also bad. Most everything else was a big fucking grey area and I was more than happy to leave it that way.

Turned out Ethics was all about digging into that grey area and carefully classifying it as good or bad, something that seemed to me to depend entirely on the situation, the people involved, and the end result. By the end of that first class, I had Her Majesty's words rattling around in my brain:

Capes tend to have a black and white view of the world. Don't take kindly to those of us who see it otherwise.

I was starting to think she might be right.

CHAPTER 23

On Saturday, while most of the class was sleeping in, I was up and heading to meet again with my tutors. By the time I made it back to the dorm, with a massive headache and a half-dozen new assignments to reinforce my regular schoolwork, Jeremiah was dressed to head out for the night. His dark pants and green button-down were a far cry from the sweats I was yet again wearing.

My roommate and I had barely spoken since that first night, but as I settled onto the bed with my Glass, a stylus, and way too much shit to do, he paused at the doorway. I thought for just a moment he was going to break the streak. Instead, he shook his head and then he and his beard both went out into the hall.

I didn't hear him come back that night, but he was hungover and miserable when I woke up on Sunday. Not sure if that made me feel better or not. I'd slept like shit, so it's not like I was feeling great either. I'd heard a few of my classmates complain about having to share rooms instead of having space to themselves, but I had the opposite problem. At Mama Rawlins' all the boys had slept in one room, and all the girls in another. Having only a single roommate, even one as oversized as mine, was weirdly hard to adjust to.

The persistent silence didn't help much either.

As a special treat, I swapped out Saturday's sweatshirt for one of my only remaining tees. Then I dumped the armful of dirty sweats into the basket we'd each been provided, and set out to look for the laundry room. I eventually found it on the far side of the same building that housed the cafeteria. Seemed kind of unsanitary to me, but what the hell did I know?

The campus was dead-quiet, with only a few people—most of them older students—out and about. I made it to the laundry building without anyone screaming or running in terror, pushed open the door, and came to a halt. "You've got to be fucking kidding me."

There were two people inside, folding clothes at one of the tables separating the giant rows of washing machines and dyers. The first was a slightly older Indian guy I'd never met… as big as my roommate and a shit-ton more muscular. But the second? *Matthew-mother-fucking-Strich.* Guy being my arch-nemesis was bad enough, but it felt like I was tripping over the asshole everywhere I went. And why would *he* have to do laundry anyway? Way most people treated him, even his shit smelled like roses… I couldn't imagine his sweat was any worse.

Both of them turned to the door, and Matthew's smile gave way to an immediate frown. The other guy looked at me and then back to Matthew. "Who's this?"

"Damian Banach," said Paladin, biting the words off. "Class of 76. Crow."

The other guy whistled. "*You're* the Crow? I've wondered where you were."

"Just been trying to get a handle on my homework."

"I wish I could say it gets easier," he said, "but *easy* isn't what this place is about." He clasped his hands in front of him and offered an odd little bow. "I'm a third-year. High-Three Stalwart. Call me WarChild."

"Damian. Low-Three devil spawn, looking for a better codename than Baron Boner."

WarChild winced. "Definitely keep looking."

"What the hell are you wearing *that* for?" That was Paladin, stomping all over what was only the second borderline-friendly conversation I'd had all week. He was pointing at my shirt.

"You've got something against t-shirts, *Matthew*?" I shot back.

"That one, I do."

I frowned for a moment, looking down at the logo and image of a Cape kicking Black Hat ass before it all clicked. "Right. Crow like me doesn't get to wear Cape merchandise, is that it? Or is it this particular Cape that bugs you? You have a problem with the *real* Paladin? Because I'm telling you, that fucker's three times the hero you could ever be, and you have no fucking right to steal his name."

The third-year winced again for some reason, and Matthew went quiet. When he spoke, his words were cold and sharp. "That *fucker* is my father. And it's his choice to gift me the name, not yours."

"Oh." Dominion was, without question, the strongest Cape in the Free States, but Paladin had once been my favorite. It wasn't until I hit puberty and started noticing women that he'd been nudged down to second place by Tempest. How had someone like *that* given birth to Matthew? "Well… your father's way cooler than mine," I finally managed.

"Whatever." He piled his folded laundry back into his own basket and turned to WarChild. "Thanks for the chat and the advice, Vikram. Talk to you later?"

"Sure thing. I start my internship next month, but while I'm still here, stop by if you need anything." The third-year waited for Matthew to leave, and then nodded to me. "That goes for you too, first-year, assuming you can keep your ass out of trouble."

"Have to get it out of trouble first before I can worry about keeping it out," I pointed out.

"True enough." He shook his head. "Baron Boner. What is this world coming to?"

Looking back, I probably should've taken WarChild up on his offer. A third-year who didn't automatically hate me? It was like finding a diamond in the Bakersfield mud. But part of me saw the offer as some kind of trap, and part of me saw it as nothing but pity, and I wasn't going to risk either possibility.

Wasn't the first time I screwed myself over out of pride. Wouldn't be the last either.

* * *

A few other people piled into the laundry room as I was waiting for my load to finish, but I don't think any were Capes-in-training… or, if they were, they didn't know who I was. I did recognize one of them from Amos' History of Powers class. Pretty damn cute too, or she might have been if she weren't wrapped around some guy, trying to send her tongue down his throat.

Anyway, nobody paid me much attention, but I got out as soon as my laundry was done, tossing the clothes back into the basket without bothering to fold them. It was a quick trip back to the dorm to dump the clothes on my bed, and then I was back out the door with my Glass, headed to the cafeteria for breakfast before the next round of tutoring and the one meeting I was really dreading.

Almost time to meet my counselor. The person tasked with making sure I stayed sane. Assuming I wasn't *already* nuts. Assuming he didn't hate me on sight and conspire to get my ass thrown out from the start.

So much potential for things to go to hell in a hurry.

But that's life in a nutshell, isn't it?

CHAPTER 24

Do you remember those Junior Cape vids they used to air for children? Not the good ones, like Paladin's fight with the Demonsouled or Tempest and the pirates… I'm talking about the early-morning vids, all fake and cheesy, starring made-up Capes in mock battles with absurdly incompetent Black Hats. Pretty sure I've mentioned them before. They only ran for a few years before they were replaced. Turned out the public wasn't buying the candy-colored, saccharine bullshit being peddled.

Anyway, after every episode, the Junior Cape of the day would look straight at the camera and offer some sort of lame fortune-cookie wisdom that had nothing to do with the plot of the actual vid. You know the sort: "An apple a day keeps Professor Inferno away", or "The early bird knows better than to stay out after dark", or my personal favorite: "What you don't know could possibly hurt you."

I don't think they ever had one about the danger of expectations. Maybe they should have.

After Mom's death, the government sent me to speak with a shrink… because that's the sort of thing a five-year old orphan should have to deal with. He was ancient; probably thirty or older, stuffed like a package of synth-meat into a threadbare suit and smelling vaguely of alcohol and moldy cheese. We went around in circles for a grand total of three sessions—slightly less than a month—before he pronounced me healthy, sane, and well on the way to recovery from my tragic event. I remember that phrase in particular; *tragic event.* Guess it beats *intentional de-parentification.*

Thirteen years and one ever-cheerful ghost later, I was more open to the idea of counseling, but I still went in expecting something similar to that guy from Bakersfield. Hopefully without the cheese smell, and maybe a bit younger—although at eighteen, thirty didn't seem quite so old anymore—but otherwise a white, wrinkled fucker, with wire-framed glasses and a protruding belly full of gin and superiority.

Expectations. They'll fuck with you every chance they get.

Kind of like people, I guess.

After a brief wait in a sitting room similar to the one outside Bard's office—minus Agnes and her weapon-grade death stare—I was called in. A low couch, wide enough to lie on, faced a wooden desk. A bronze nameplate on that desk read Dr. Gibbings, and a handful of degrees dotted one wall, with a landscape in pastels occupying another. Thick curtains covered the windows behind the desk, but the free-standing lamps that ringed the room gave it a homey feel.

All of that more or less fit what I remembered from Bakersfield though. Higher quality stuff, sure, but mostly the same.

It was the doctor herself who was different.

She sat behind the desk, quiet and tall, her pale skin the only thing about her that wasn't black. Black hair, black eyes, a crisp black blouse and—I was willing to believe, even if the desk made it impossible to know for sure—black pants and black shoes. Even the bracelet around one wrist was a circlet of black, unpolished stones.

"Who died?"

She cocked her head, like one of those seagulls Los Angeles was famous for. Her voice was slow and smooth, like caramelized sugar. "Most recently?"

I coughed. "It was a joke. Your clothes…"

She nodded thoughtfully. "Bard didn't say you had a sense of humor. That's a good sign."

"It is?"

"I'd like to think so. People who can't laugh at life… well, you just know those fuckers are going nuts."

I blinked and double-checked the diplomas on the wall. The doctor watched me do so, her smile a simple twist of the lips, gone before it had even fully formed.

"My name is Alexa, and as you're no doubt aware, I'm your school-appointed counselor. Given the number of years you spent in the system, I assume I'm not the first psychologist you've seen?"

"Second," I admitted.

"Then I'll start by telling you what I *won't* be doing in our sessions. I won't be sitting here taking notes in a little book—even a black one that matches my outfit." Again, that smile flashed. "I won't be asking about your mother or father, or what you saw or heard or felt on *that* day. You can tell me if you want, of course, but that's entirely up to you. I won't be showing you slides of inkblots and asking you what they look like, and I damn sure won't be playing word association games with you."

That pretty much eliminated everything the Bakersfield shrink had bothered with. "So what *will* you be doing?"

"Listening without judgement. Offering advice should you want it."

My scowl deepened. "Aren't you supposed to decide whether I'm batshit crazy or not?"

"Is that something you would like me to do?"

"It's what Bard said this whole thing was about."

"I'm well aware of the dean's thoughts." She regarded me steadily, as still as a painting, and somehow pretty without being at all attractive. "However, he isn't my patient. I'm asking what it is *you* want."

After a long moment, I shrugged. "To stay sane."

"And if that's not possible?" I'd been in the office for minutes now, and she hadn't blinked once.

"Then I want someone to recognize it, and to stop me if…"

I didn't finish the sentence, but she nodded as if I had. "I can do that."

"Cool." I swallowed past the lump in my throat and shrugged again. "So what now?"

"Now, you take a seat." She motioned to the couch. "You can stand if you'd rather, but after your first week at the Academy, I imagine you're even more exhausted than you look." She waited as I collapsed onto the couch. "Great. Now… just talk."

"About what?"

"Your classes, your fellow first-years, what you think of the city. Anything."

"Seriously?" This was so different from my Bakersfield shrink experience that I was still waiting for the other shoe to drop.

"Seriously. It's the talking that matters, not the subject. Silent, brooding guys make for great vid stars and reasonably good one-night-stands, but in real life, they're right there with the humorless assholes, waiting in line for their nervous breakdowns and prescription of crazy pills." Her black eyes met mine from across the room. "Just talk, Damian. We'll see how things go from there."

So I told her about Ethics class. Kind of funny; complaining about a teacher who saw everything as black and white to a woman who fit that same color scheme.

Probably should've made a joke out of it.

I'm pretty sure Alexa would've even smiled.

CHAPTER 25

In Bakersfield, winter stays late and summer comes early, meaning spring barely qualifies as a season. Hell, some years, it doesn't even qualify as a *week*; a few days of pleasant sunshine before the stifling heat comes rolling in to take up residence for the next four months, cooking vegetation and people alike until people are so fucked up they find themselves actually missing the fog.

Dad wanting to move to Bakersfield should have been Mom's first clue the asshole had gone nuts.

Los Angeles was different. Different when I'd arrived in early March, different in April and *still* different as we pushed into mid-May. Cool breezes blowing in from the ocean I'd only seen on that first trip into town. Temperatures hovering around the mid-seventies. Women in tank tops and mini-skirts or shorts, hanging around outside instead of scurrying for climate-controlled buildings. One hill just past the Graduation Games field had been converted into an impromptu "beach." Green grass instead of sand, but plenty of men and women in practically nothing, getting some sun, listening to music on their Glasses, and generally having a grand fucking time.

I *almost* wished the Academy was located in a place like Bakersfield. At least then, everyone would have been as miserable as us first-years. Eight hours of classes a day, plus homework and meals, didn't leave much time for relaxation. Or fun.

It didn't help that the Control classroom had floor-to-ceiling windows along one wall, or that Ms. Stein had us facing those windows during our daily exercises. I think she wanted us to feel like we were part of the world or nature or some sort of peace and balance shit, but all it meant to me was that I got to see what I was missing.

It *also* didn't help that, after two months of school, I still didn't have the faintest clue what my powers did, how to use them, or what exactly I was supposed to be learning to control. Other than my one fight against Paladin—which I was starting to think had been the result of a concussion rather than any kamikaze Crow abilities—the only evidence that I was a Necromancer at all was Mom's ghost… and nobody could see her other than me.

I swallowed a sigh and tried to regulate my breathing. Again.

Our class was split between two studios, each equipped with dampeners similar to those in Nikolai's pit. These dampeners were dialed down to be less restrictive, allowing the first-years with external powers to manifest their abilities without accidentally killing us all. Having half the class in a separate room, even if that room was only one door away, had its pluses and minuses. On the positive side, the wall between the two rooms muffled Tessa's constant bitching and kept us from getting frostbite from Winter's miniature ice storms. On the less positive side, they'd split up our Stalwarts and our Pyros, and the other room got *both* Orca and London—the two hottest women in our class, as far as I was concerned—leaving us Paladin and Ishmae.

Fucking Paladin. If anything was going to drive me crazy, it would be his constant presence. With a passive power set, he didn't have much to do in Control class, but seemed content to meditate the hours away, back straight and arms placed just right, no trace of irritation, impatience, or humanity disturbing his perfectly composed expression. In the other room, Orca was no doubt doing the exact same bit of nothing… but looking a hell of a lot better doing it.

Ishmae, on the other hand, had a wisp of fire hovering in the air above her and was leading that flame through increasingly complex loops and patterns. I'd seen her do the same with as many as ten wisps, each of them tightly braided, moving in their own patterns and burning steadily. Word was, London had only managed two wisps so far, and the second one had a tendency of drifting off of its own accord. Kind of like Winter's blizzards.

Seated next to Ishmae—always next to her—Shane spent most of his class time just watching the young Pyro. The only person in the class unaware of his painful, soul-devouring crush was the object of said crush. Ishmae had turned seventeen in April but showed no interest in anything beyond school and the cultivation of her power. Supposedly, a lot of High-Fours were like that.

To the left, Erin Pearson—our near-ginger Wind Dancer—was guiding a small cyclone about in a slow and stilted dance while Olympia used her own powers to shoot darts of light through the cyclone. Past those two, Prince was humming something under his breath, the chunky Siren's tones too quiet to affect the emotions of anyone around him. Caleb, one of a handful of first-years with dual powers, was hovering an inch or so off the floor, tossing a fistful of coins high into the air and then catching them again just before they could hit the ground, his angular features set in concentration and his hands alternating blurs. Silt had a handful of dirt in front of her and was glaring at it as it formed into a lopsided bowl, then a cylinder, and then something that was supposed to be a duck.

As for me, I sat, breathed, and waited for class to end, like I'd been doing every day for the last two months. Even my crush on Ms. Stein had faded under the relentless tedium. I'd known being a Crow would suck. I hadn't know it would mean I was going to be completely useless at *everything.*

I wasn't the only one losing patience. The Viking, as he'd loudly proclaimed on more than one occasion, thought meditation was for pussies. The two Shifters weren't loving Control either. Something about shifting being an all-or-nothing proposition and the dampeners being still set too high for them to transform. Alan Jackson was in the other room, intimidating the fuck out of everyone around him, but Jeremiah was in our room, doing his best not to fall asleep.

Then there were the stranger members of the class.

Freddy was our Switch, one of that rare breed who could affect the abilities of Powers around him. He was an Amplifier, which basically made him every first-year's favorite person. Nullifiers were significantly less appreciated… except when a Black Hat needed stopping. For Freddy, Control meant increasing the range and duration of his abilities, and one day being able to affect multiple targets.

With the way she blurred from one end of her mat to the other, Wormhole might have passed for a Jitterbug, but that was more a function of the dampeners and the enclosed space than anything. Whereas she and Caleb could both move from point A to point B in a flash, the button-nosed brunette was actually skipping everything in between. In their own way, Teleporters were even more badass than Flyboys or Wind Dancers.

What I couldn't figure out was why Wormhole ended every class noticeably heavier than she'd been at the start. It was like she was detouring to the donut dimension with each teleport. Even harder to understand was where that extra weight went; by the time History rolled around in the afternoon, Evelyn would be back to her petite self.

And then there was Kayleigh Watai. Five feet tall and golden skinned, I'd never heard her speak a word. She shunned the rest of the first-years every bit as much as they shunned me. In most classes, Kayleigh sat as far from the rest of us as she could, but in the tighter quarters of Control, there was nowhere to go. While everyone else was breathing or showing off, she was just twitching, head down, arms wrapped tightly around her bent knees until she was a small ball, rocking back and forth.

It reminded me of Nyah and how she would sometimes wake up after a nightmare at the orphanage. Maybe even of how I'd been in those first few months at Mama Rawlins', before Fat Joey taught me the value of staying quiet if I didn't want a love tap in the ribs from his size nine shoes.

I made it through all of four classes watching Kayleigh twitch before I went to Ms. Stein for help, but the lovely teacher had just tucked a strand of fabulously silky hair behind one equally fabulous ear and told me to focus on my own problems.

That might have been the moment my crush on Gabriella Stein started to fade.

A couple weeks later, I spoke to Alexa instead. First time I'd talked to her about anything that really mattered, anything that wasn't just a recap of my last few days of classes. She'd listened, fixed me with those unblinking black eyes of hers, and informed me that the faculty was well aware of Ms. Watai's difficulties, that those issues were related to her power, and that they would step in when and if it was necessary.

Didn't make me feel any better but it didn't leave me much recourse either—especially since I'd torn up the class roster that first day and had no idea what power Kayleigh even had. Some of the other first-years knew, no doubt, but it's not like I was on speaking terms with any of them except Shane, and the ginger Healer had an annoying habit of not spilling other people's secrets.

Shortly after my talk with Alexa, I'd watched Paladin try to speak to Kayleigh after class, but she'd shrunk away from him like he was Grannypocalypse or the Singer himself. If perfect-fucking-wonder-boy Matthew Strich provoked that kind of reaction, I didn't even want to think what someone like me trying to help might do. So instead, I sat and breathed, a little bit jealous of people like Ishmae, a little bit grateful that I wasn't like Kayleigh, but mostly just frustrated that I was utterly useless on two different fronts.

Should've gotten an A in that class just for not snapping, throwing a chair through the enormous window, and never coming back. Now *that's* real control for you.

Finally, our latest session came to an end. Kayleigh was off the floor and out the door before Jeremiah had even woken up, and long before the rest of the first-years filed in from the second room. I was still trying to rub feeling back into my legs and feet when Caleb spoke up.

"What's that, Gabriella?" Caleb and Santiago both insisted on addressing our teachers by their first names. Some teachers took it poorly, but Ms. Stein was one of the less prickly professors. The Jitterbug was pointing at the back of the room, where a door that was normally closed had been left partly open. Within, we could just vaguely see some sort of machinery.

"Oh, I didn't realize I'd left that open." Ms. Stein looked to the open door and then back to us. "I suppose there's no harm in showing you." She opened the door wide. "This is the Maze."

The Maze wasn't actually a maze. If anything, it reminded me of the machine used for my testing… only someone had fused the machine with a chair, so whoever sat in it would essentially be placing their head into the heart of the device. Two armrests terminated in copper-wrapped handles. A basket of copper and steel wire to the side was designed to be lowered over the occupant's head.

"The Maze," Ms. Stein continued, "is one of the challenges at the Graduation Games. Not as flashy as the more physical challenges, I suppose, but for those us who prize the perfection of control, it's by far the most exciting."

"How does it work?" That was Penelope, aka Winter, taking a rare break from the assumption that she knew everything.

"Well, in a way it's similar to the apparatus used for your initial testing—"

Ha! I'd totally nailed it.

"—but where that device simply measures the classification and magnitude of your power, the Maze evaluates your level of control by implanting challenges in your brain and measuring your attempts to meet those challenges."

"Can we try it?" That was Tessa.

"Oh heavens no!" Ms. Stein shooed us away from the door, then closed and locked it. "The Maze is intended for third-years, and even then, only for the top two or three in the class. It's not a toy, and it can be dangerous."

Anything that put shit directly in your brain was best avoided, in my opinion, but whatever Ms. Stein saw in the other first-years' faces had her concerned.

"As in *burn-your-powers-out-and-leave-you-a-vegetable* dangerous. Once you've made it to third-year, if any of you are interested in trying the Maze, you can come speak to me, but for now, you should all forget you even saw it."

That was easy enough for most of the class to do. A few stories circulated about past winners—and losers—and then everyone got on with their lives.

Almost everyone… but we didn't find that out until later.

Until it was way too late.

Someone should have fucking seen it coming.

CHAPTER 26

The sun was setting somewhere in the sky ahead of me as I picked my way through the small woods that filled the campus' western border. I still had homework to do—assigned by both my real teachers and my tutors—but for the moment, I was focused on a different kind of problem.

I still wasn't sure what to think of the monochromatic Dr. Gibbings—and I sure as hell didn't fully trust her—but I'd finally let go of my pride enough to mention my own failures in Control. Alexa had looked at me for a long moment in silence. Wasn't all that out of the ordinary for either of us. For a relationship that was supposed to be about talking, we spent an awful lot of time doing anything but.

Finally, she let those unblinking eyes drift off to the left and nodded. "There's not a lot we know about Necromancers, Damian, including whether Gabriella's techniques even apply to someone like you, but…"

"But?"

"Have you thought about practicing *outside* her classroom?"

"There aren't any dampeners outside the classroom."

"Exactly my point." She had her hands steepled in front of her on the desk, the black stone bangle on the right wrist today instead of the left. I was sure that meant something… but had no idea what.

I shook my head. "What if something goes wrong?"

"Wrong?"

"Walkers? Spirits of vengeance? A total fucking undead apocalypse?"

"Damian, you're eighteen, untrained, and a Low-Three. Apocalypses are a little beyond your reach. But I'm not suggesting you actually try to raise anything. Even with as many former Capes as we have on the faculty here, that's not the sort of excitement anyone wants."

"What are you suggesting then?"

"Practice your meditation. If you think it'll help, focus on that peace and balance mantra Gabriella gets her little silk panties in a knot over. But mainly, just spend time looking inward. See if you can find your power. Not use it; just find it. Maybe once you've done so, you'll have an easier time actually utilizing it under the safety of the dampeners."

I chewed that idea over. As frustrating as it was to be completely inept in Control, there was a part of me that was relieved when each hour of class ended without any sign of success. If I couldn't ever use my power, then maybe…

Alexa was already far too adept at reading my thoughts. "If there's one thing that history has shown us, it's that powers can't be ignored. Sooner or later, yours *will* emerge. When it does, do you want to control it or let it control you?" Something in her unblinking eyes softened. "If you'd prefer, I can set aside some time for you to try here, under my supervision."

I shook my head, reminding myself that I wasn't a little boy who needed to be looked after anymore… and that I hadn't been one for a long time. "It's okay. I'd rather practice on my own. Maybe someplace outside and away from everyone?"

She thought for a moment, and then that almost-smile flashed again. "I know just the place."

* * *

Just the place was, as I started to tell you earlier, somewhere on the west side of campus, through the thick forest of evergreens. There wasn't any sort of path to follow and Dr. Gibbings' directions had been unhelpfully vague. All I knew for sure was that *I'd know it when I saw it* and *if I reached the wall that encircled the campus, I'd have gone too far.*

I was willing to concede that Alexa might be a decent shrink—way easier to talk to than the fucker back in Bakersfield—but as far as navigators went, she kind of sucked. Next time, I'd request a map.

I thought about just taking a seat there in the woods. It was secluded enough, on the far side of campus from the so-called beach, and well away from the nearest buildings. The rough ground didn't scream *meditation* though, and for all I knew there were tigers hanging out in the dark trees above me, just waiting for an easy target.

Or was it jaguars that jumped out of trees?

I was still mulling over that question when I found the place.

Alexa was right; I knew it the moment I saw it.

A small clearing appeared before me, as if by a Druid's design. On three sides, it was bordered by the trees I'd been hiking through, but on the fourth was nothing but sky and darkness, the hill falling away in a deep slope down toward the campus wall. Above and beyond that wall, a thousand stars gleamed like a tapestry of light, reflected in the dark waters of an otherwise invisible ocean. The breeze from the Pacific was strong and cool, smelling of salt and age and something almost sad.

A stone bench sat maybe ten feet from the hill's edge, and I could see why the doctor had recommended the clearing. It was easy to imagine sitting on that bench, staring out toward the ocean, and letting the peace and quiet of the place guide my meditation.

Or it would have been, if the bench hadn't already been occupied.

Fuck my fucking life.

I was turning to leave, resigned to a hike back through the woods, when an all-too-recognizable sound stopped me. God knows I'd heard plenty of it over the years.

The person on the bench was crying.

* * *

Listen to enough tears in your life and you start to recognize the flavors they come in, kind of like how a connoisseur can blind-taste wine. That's not the Crow in me talking. That's the orphan. No place like an orphanage for tears, unless it's a cemetery. Abandonment and regret. Fear and grief. Loneliness and pitch-black despair. All of it just another word for pain, just one more expression of that particular tightness that twists away at your core, that squeezes sound from your chest and salt from your eyes.

Whoever was crying on the bench wasn't just homesick. She wasn't merely frustrated or angry. Her sobs were quiet, choked gasps that wracked her body. A boy at Mama Rawlins' had cried like that, three nights in a row, and we'd all let him be, each of us young and scared and maybe a little unwilling to risk caring about another human being. On the fourth night, he went silent, and it wasn't until the next morning, when someone found his body on the street, twenty feet below the upstairs balcony, that we knew why.

I'd been ten, still dealing with the Jacobsens' betrayal and the revelation of what I was going to become, but some part of me had looked down at that body, looked at the birds that kept trying to make away with the delicate pieces of what had been a boy, and wondered: *what if I could've stopped this?*

Took some of the older kids leaving. Took me gaining my height, more than a few pounds, and a shoebox of dirty tricks. Most of all, it took a lot of fights—scar tissue on my knuckles, bruises so regular they seemed like tattoos—but by the time I was thirteen, I had control. It was Mama Rawlins' place, but *I* took charge of the little ones as they came in. *I* did what was needed to keep the fighting reasonable, to keep the bullying to a minimum. And when someone cried tears like that dead boy had, I sure as fuck made sure one of us, or two of us, or the whole god damn bedroom was there and did what we could to help.

This wasn't Mama Rawlins', and I had no authority at the Academy. Less than none, given the way my fellow first-years saw me. Probably should've gone to get a teacher. Or Alexa, even—I was pretty sure she lived in her office; maybe even slept upside down, hanging from the ceiling like some sort of oddly analytical vampire. But I didn't know who the woman crying was, and I wasn't sure she'd still be there when I got back.

I don't like people. Not really. *That* might be the Crow in me talking. Might be the orphan too, I guess. But I like watching people suffer even less.

I stopped, turned around again, and headed for the bench.

* * *

Five steps away, and she was still crying like she hadn't heard me coming.

Three steps away, I stopped. "Are you okay?"

She launched off the bench, like Her Majesty being shot off the motorcycle, and spun to face me, small hands coming up in fists. "What the hell?!?!"

Those were the first three words Kayleigh Watai ever said to me. First three words I heard her say to anyone. With the sun gone from the sky, I couldn't see the electric blue streaks in her dark hair. Couldn't see her tear-stained face at all, really, but judging by her tone, she had gone from grief-stricken to pissed in the blink of an eye.

"Who do you think you are, sneaking up on people like that?!?"

I held my ground. "I wasn't sneaking. I just heard you—"

She cut me off, her voice suddenly puzzled. "You snuck up on me!"

"You said that already." Maybe I *should* have gotten Alexa. "I was trying to expla—"

"How is that possible?" she interrupted again.

"I… don't know how to answer that."

"I wasn't talking to you."

It was time to exit Crazytown. "I just wanted to make sure you're okay. Seems like you are—" Outside of being a total lunatic. "—so I'm going to—"

"Don't move."

Me not liking people? This sort of shit might be why.

Kayleigh came forward, closing in on me like personal space was something to be conquered. Even though her head barely came to my chest, I was the one fighting not to step back.

Badass Crow, and all it takes to freak him out is one crazy chick. Her Majesty would be laughing her leather-clad, inhumanly fine ass off.

"I can't feel you," she finally said, voice soft and full of wonder. "At all."

"Probably because you're not touching me," I pointed out helpfully. "Although I can feel you breathing on my shirt."

"I'm talking about your emotions, Necromancer."

"Oh." Everything clicked. "You're an Empath?"

"Unfortunately." Lightning-quick, she reached out and touched my hand. For a moment, she was stunned to silence. This time, her voice was outright awed. "Holy cow."

"Holy cow?"

"When I touch you, everything goes quiet." She started to cry again, small shoulders shaking, but I recognized these tears too, remembered them from the handful of kids who'd made it out of the system and into loving families and good homes. Not tears of joy so much as they were tears of relief.

"What does that mean?" I finally asked. "Everything goes quiet?"

"What do you know about Empaths?"

"You hear emotions." Like Bard had said, I'd aced the History of Powers section of my entrance exams.

"Yeah. *Everyone's* emotions. Except yours, apparently." She let go of my hand, and then quickly reached out and grabbed it again. "But when I touch you, I don't hear anything."

"You just said that—"

"I mean *anything*," she interrupted for what felt like the hundredth time. "The three guards down on the wall. The couple making out on the field. The janitors cleaning the nearest classrooms. When I'm touching you, I can't hear any of them."

"And that's… good?"

"It's kind of a miracle." She breathed out a little sigh and the tears finally stopped.

CHAPTER 27

"…so the scientific community—or what little of it survived the Break—worked feverishly to understand everything that had changed and to develop new theories to accommodate our very different new reality."

I haven't talked a lot about Amos to this point. Haven't talked at all about his class. Nothing too unusual about that; I haven't spent any time on Philosophy or Math or even Jessica Strich's weapons classes either. Life as a first-year was, as I may've mentioned, really busy, and if I was going to tell you every minor detail, we'd be here until I was as dead as you are. And what good would that do anyone? You're just going to have to trust that I'm hitting the high notes and the low notes, and that the rest of it is inconsequential.

Or don't. I'm not forcing you to listen, even though we know I could. Any of you can take off whenever you feel like it.

Say hi to hell for me when you go.

Anyway, Amos. He's the closest thing to proof that Dr. Nowhere had a sense of humor. Why else would you give immortality to someone who's already old, wrinkly, and as foul-tempered as a Beast-shifter during mating season? Any reasonable person would've granted that gift to someone young and hot. An eternally young Orca… just the idea makes me want to fall to my knees and give thanks.

But not Dr. Nowhere. No, he gave us old Amos. Eternally old Amos. Born before the Break, during what he calls the *first* World War, whatever that means. God knows the world's been at war the entire time the rest of us were alive. On the first day of class, Amos had joked that it was more His Story than History, since he'd actually lived the whole damn thing. Some people even laughed.

If you attend the Academy in your next life, do everyone a favor: don't laugh. It only encourages him.

"While physicists and chemists ran experiments to confirm that some of the universe's rules had stayed the same, biologists and zoologists focused on a different problem. People like me. People like some of you." Amos waved to the left side of the auditorium, where the first-years were seated. Twenty-four of us in total, outnumbered five-to-one by the regular students, but there wasn't a single non-Cape on the left side of the room, even if it left the other hundred-twenty students squashed together on the right.

I didn't have much of a handle on what Academy life was like for the regular students. They were there to major in careers that supported Capes or the industry we'd given rise to. More than a few hoped the connections they made would translate into job opportunities when they graduated, and no relationship was more valuable than a Cape who wanted you on their staff… but in the few mixed classes we had, this same pattern of division repeated over and over again. Maybe it was awe. Maybe it was fear. Maybe they just really hated the grey sweats that every first-year wore during the week. Whatever the reason, it was as much their doing as ours.

"I'm not sure how many sleepless nights it took," continued Amos, "but they went through a godawful amount of Jolt." He paused expectantly, but none of us had a clue what the hell Jolt was, what it had to do with zoology, or why he'd expected a laugh. He grumbled, and went on. "Eventually they emerged with what they called the Genus of Superpowers. They'd grouped powers into one of four general classes; Elementalism, Naturalism, Physicalism, and Mentalism. There's a long-running debate as to whether Elementalism and Naturalism should be separate at all, but that's a subject for the scientists, not us."

He tapped something on his Glass—a model that was older than I was—then tapped again, slightly harder, when that first tap didn't produce the desired result. On the vid screen behind him, the four classifications were listed out. "Each of these classifications contains one or more power sets, but there is no hard and fast rule about what that number should be. So Elementalism includes Hydromancers, Pyromancers, Wind Dancers, Sparks, and Earthshakers, while Mentalism includes only Empaths, Switches, Sirens, and Telekinetics."

I'd done the reading for the class, but had ended up with more questions than answers. In general, I tried to keep as low a profile as possible, but… I don't know. Maybe my sessions with Alexa were starting to rub off on me. I found myself raising one hand. "How do we know they got it right, Amos?"

He shaded his eyes and looked up at the seats until he located my raised hand. "Mr. Banach, is that you? And awake? I thought I might have grown so accustomed to the sound of your snoring that I just wasn't noticing it anymore."

One half of the auditorium laughed. *Not* the Cape side. Outside of Shane and maybe Kayleigh, the whole first-year class remained ice-cold and distant. Some of them hated me, some of them feared me, but none of them were comfortable laughing at me.

"When you say *got it right*, what are you referring to, Mr. Banach?"

"Everything, basically." More laughter, and I paused, trying to put the question into words. "Science is a guess that hasn't been disproven yet, right? And these classes and sets were just their best guess on how to organize things?"

"I'm sure you would have done a *much* better job," sniped Tessa. Poltergeist, as she now preferred to be called, most definitely belonged to the group that hated me.

"So far, so good, Mr. Banach," said Amos, ignoring Poltergeist's comment. "But I'm still not sure where the question is."

"Well, it's because of their guesses that we can label someone a Druid or a Stalwart, and that seems clear enough… but the system doesn't seem to account for people who bridge multiple categories or don't fit into any class at all. Like the Singer. Or Grannypocalypse. Or even you, for that matter. Hell, nobody can decide what class Dominion fits in, considering he has powers from so many of them!"

"It's a fair point," admitted Amos, "and one that makes me glad you chose to participate instead of sleep. For people with multiple power sets, we generally use their dominant power when classifying them. So Ms. Von Pell is a Weather Witch, despite her Wind Dancer abilities, and Mr. Mikkazi is more Jitterbug than Flyboy. However, as you noted, there are other individuals with a multitude of powers that all rank equally."

"So what do they get classified as?" That was a blonde guy on the regular student side.

"Extremely fortunate, Mr. Inglewood," answered Amos with a grin. "To be quite honest, beyond initial training methodologies, I'm not sure classification matters as much as we like to think it does."

It was easy for him to say that. As far as I could tell, everyone cared a hell of a lot about *my* classification.

"But what would you be considered, Professor?" the same blonde asked.

"Yeah, or the Singer? Or Tezcatlipoca, for that matter?"

Amos frowned, his wrinkles deepening. "I'll remind you all that the Voidsinger's existence has yet to be proven, despite the many tales circulating about him. As for myself, I would prefer *not* to be lumped into the same category as someone like Grannypocalypse or that murderous creature south of our border. However, it is true that the current system does not account for every power we're aware of, let alone all the powers that might exist around the globe. Does that mean the scientists got it wrong?"

He waited a moment for a reply.

"No," decided Winter.

"And why is that, Ms. Von Pell?"

"Because science isn't wrong."

"Oh, how I wish that were true! I could tell you stories about orange juice…" Amos shook his head. "But in a way, you're also correct. Science isn't static. The Genus was correct, given what information was available at the time, and for the most part, it remains correct even now. If a sufficient number of quasi-immortals show up one day, then maybe a new class will be added to the Genus. Until then, those few of us who don't fit are simply left unclassified. I like to think of myself as a Full-Five Amos, really."

"But what about Necromancers?" That was Poltergeist again, and I felt myself flush, even as Shane shifted uneasily next to me. I wasn't sure which of the regular students knew what I was, if any. I was kind of hoping none of them did. It would make getting dates a hell of a lot easier. God knew my chances with the first-year women were slim-to-none.

Not that I was giving up on Orca just yet.

Amos cleared his throat. "As rare as they are, their numbers are still sufficient to suggest they're not simply one-offs like myself. There is a proposal to add a new power class to the Genus." He carefully avoided glancing my way. "Both Crows and Summoners would be classified as Aberrants."

Of course we would.

"Once again," Amos continued with a grin, "we've somehow found ourselves on a tangent. That's the fun of history, I guess! It's as good a place as any to end my lecture for the day."

A few students exchanged puzzled looks. We had almost half an hour left and Amos never let us go early.

"The rest of today's class," he added, "will focus on what you'll be doing for the remainder of the semester in lieu of homework."

The number of puzzled looks increased dramatically. Amos loved homework even more than he loved his own weird jokes.

Amos tapped his Glass again. At the top of the vid screen appeared the two words every student eventually learns to fear:

Group Presentation.

The old bastard smiled as rustles of discontent filled the auditorium. "You will split into groups consisting of four to five individuals. I'm not going to determine those groups for you. The Free States has, in its infinite wisdom, decided you're all adults, so you can damn well form them without my help." He shook his head, grumbling again to himself. "By the end of today's class, I want each group to have chosen their name and a topic to present on. That topic must have *something* to do with post-Break History. Under your own direction and initiative, each group will meet over the next month outside of class to research the topic, design visual aids, and practice your presentation." His voice hardened momentarily. "When I say practice, I *mean* practice. If I feel any team has opted to *just wing it*, I will be giving that team a very carefully considered and well-practiced *F*."

Maybe sadism was a pre-requisite for faculty members.

CHAPTER 28

Groups formed quickly, especially on the Cape side, where there weren't that many of us to begin with. I'd had a feeling that Shane might stick with me—while we barely saw each other outside of class, he'd remained friendly since that first healing—but I was surprised when Kayleigh joined us.

The Empath had started to make a habit of seeking me out whenever the rush of other people's emotions became too much for her, but otherwise, she'd kept her distance. Even in History class, where the sheer number of students caused her serious problems, she sat behind me, in a row all by herself, rather than next to me. I was getting all too familiar with the feeling of her bare toes brushing the back of my neck.

Was she using me? Yeah, pretty much. But the deep lines under her eyes were starting to fade, and it felt kind of nice to be useful for once. Plus… it's not like any other first-year woman was in a hurry to touch me.

Even if her toes *were* cold as hell. Like little chips of ice.

Anyway, it was kind of a big deal when she came down to join Shane and me. Maybe our relationship wasn't all about me being used after all. Or maybe she was freaked out about having to do a group project without her favorite emotion nullifier.

Yeah, that sounded a bit more like it.

Unfortunately, we needed a minimum of four people in our group, and nobody else seemed interested. I'd given Orca a hopeful look—and not just because two months of Nikolai's training had somehow made Nadia even more stupendously hot—but the sleek Stalwart had already been heading in the other direction, descending the stairs to join a group consisting of Matthew, Santi, and London.

Flanked by two of the hottest women in our class, El Bosque was grinning like he'd just won the Graduation Games. Lucky fucking bastard. That smile slipped only slightly when Ishmae joined as their fifth.

I didn't have to be an Empath to feel Shane's disappointment in the Pyro's choice.

The next full group to form was Caleb, Jeremiah, Tessa, Freddy, and Olympia, but after that, the remaining groups started to all fall into place. I waited to see who would be the odd person out, forced to join our group by virtue of numbers and sheer necessity.

Somehow, it wasn't Alan Jackson. The Shifter ended up in a group with the Viking, Winter, Silt, and Erin Pearson. People choosing Alan-fucking-Jackson over me kind of hurt. Would've been different if this were Nikolai's class—Alan was a monster doing anything physical and any team would want him on their side—but for an academic project?

What was he going to do in a presentation besides terrify everyone?

When the dust had settled, and the other groups were fully formed, Wormhole found herself the odd first-year out. She glanced up toward our group, went pale, and looked away.

"On second thought, ladies and germs," Silt told her team in a loud voice, "I'm just not feeling our general Feng Shui." She stomped up the stairs toward Wormhole, like an avalanche with legs. "What do you say, roomie? Wanna help me make Boneboy do all the work?"

* * *

As the two women came closer, Silt nodded to each of us in turn. "Unicorn. Skeletor. Vibe."

"Vibe?" I looked to Kayleigh who nodded, tucking a wayward strand of electric-blue hair behind her ear.

"It seemed like a good name."

"It is," agreed Shane, "but I'm Balm, not Unicorn."

"Balm's a shitty codename," said the Earthshaker, "and you're the closest thing to a unicorn we've got. A ginger High-Three Healer? Come on, man."

"I *like* Balm," muttered Shane to himself.

Keeping everyone's codenames straight was kind of a pain in the ass. Some people went exclusively by codename; the Viking refused to answer to Erik or Mr. Thorsson, and I couldn't remember if I'd ever even heard Prince's real name. Some, like Matthew/Paladin and Nadia/Orca, didn't care what name people used, while others, like Alan Jackson and Erin, hadn't picked codenames at all.

"Not sure I get the Skeletor reference," I admitted. "Did you mean skeleton?"

"You people seriously don't get any pre-Break vids out here, do you?"

"I tried to tell you, Sofia," said Wormhole.

"I just didn't realize it was this bad. Fuck," said Silt, horrified realization dawning in her dark brown eyes. "I'm going to have to come up with an entirely new repertoire of insults!"

I couldn't figure the Earthshaker out. Of all the first-years, she and Alan Jackson were the only two who remained indifferent to me, but that seemed to be their general approach towards everyone. At least Silt was kind of funny on occasion. For a walking tree stump, anyway.

"Should we pick a team name?" asked Kayleigh, as Silt and Wormhole took their seats.

"How about Three Badass Bitches, a Unicorn, and a Little Birdie?" suggested Silt.

"Who are you calling little?" I asked. "I've seen children taller than you."

"And with dicks bigger than yours, no doubt," she retorted delightedly.

"Oh my God," murmured Wormhole. "This is a nightmare."

I don't know if Kayleigh agreed with Evelyn, or was just responding to the waves of embarrassment no doubt coming off of her, but the blue-haired Empath casually pressed her bare foot against my leg.

Toes like icicles, I'm telling you.

"Boneboy and I are just getting started, Evie," declared Silt, brown eyes gleaming. "Wait until we start hurling shit at each other like monkeys."

"You know," said the other girl, "with you joining this group, your old group only has four members… maybe I should pop down and join them?"

"Don't even think about it." Silt grinned. "I know where you sleep."

"What about *The Friendly Five*?" suggested Shane in desperation. His words prompted a moment of long, pained silence.

"I hereby move that Unicorn be stripped of all naming privileges," said Silt. "All those in favor?"

Shane's look of injured betrayal as everyone, even Vibe, voted in favor was a thing of rare beauty. Not unicorn-rare… but close.

"Now *Fearsome Five*, on the other hand," continued Silt. "That's got kind of a ring to it."

"If we were Black Hats," said Kayleigh, "but we're not."

"Black Hats… black sheep…" Silt shrugged. "I say we own it."

The Fearsome Five had a much easier time picking the topic for our project. Something Alexa had mentioned regarding the number of former Capes at the Academy had left me curious about our teachers. Nikolai was clearly a Titan, and Jessica a Stalwart, but what about the rest of them? Did they all have powers? Had they all been Capes? And if so, who? More importantly, what had Gabriella's costume looked like?

That flame might have gone dim, but it wasn't entirely out. Not yet anyway.

The other four came on board almost immediately. After three months of teachers forcing us to study, the idea of turning the tables and studying *them* had a definite appeal. It also meant we might be able to just interview our teachers and skip the more tedious research methods entirely. I don't think anyone minded that possibility.

The others headed off to the next class, while I went down to add our name and topic to the list. Amos had his feet on the desk, eyes closed, and the noises coming from his open mouth had to be heard to be believed. And the old man said *I* snored?

I rolled my eyes and started off.

"Mr. Banach." Amos' snores stopped before I could take a step, but his eyes stayed closed. "Good job. With today's discussion and the Empath both. Keep it up."

I was still shaking my head as I left and the snores rose again in volume. Curmudgeonly old fart or not, Amos was something else.

CHAPTER 29

Take your average first-year's schedule. Add in tutors on Saturday and Sunday, as well as a mandatory counseling session. Then pile on after-hours group meetings a couple times a week for History, not to mention the occasional drive-by sensory-deprivation request from the resident Empath…

Tired didn't even begin to cover how I felt. I could barely remember what simple tiredness was like. Sometimes, I dreamed of *just* being tired.

And then Nikolai decided we'd worked hard enough on conditioning, and that it was time to get back into actual combat. Two weeks of painful sparring later, I was one big walking bruise.

I shifted about on the hard soil, trying to find a position that *didn't* hurt. I was meeting with the other members of the so-called Fearsome Five out in the clearing where I'd first found Vibe, the Los Angeles sun still pleasant and cheerful despite our steady push toward summer.

"So Nikolai didn't tell you anything at all?" asked Shane.

"Afraid not, Unicorn." Silt shrugged. "I'm starting to think the guy just doesn't like me."

"Did you try to… you know… be nice?" That was Kayleigh.

"I'm *always* nice."

"We still have plenty of time," said Shane, the group's self-designated morale officer. "I'd say we're making pretty good progress."

"What about you, Boneboy? Any luck with Professor Strich?"

I'd pushed hard to have Gabriella Stein as my research subject, but for some reason, the others had voted me down. Given the way Isabel Ferra and Emery Goldstein felt about me, that had left me with a choice between Nikolai and Jessica Strich.

The choice had been pretty obvious.

"A little bit," I admitted, trying to straighten up without wincing. "Turns out Jessica is Matthew's older sister."

"Yeah, no kidding."

"I thought everyone knew that," added Evelyn. "What else would she have been?"

"Hell if I know. An aunt? A cousin?" I shrugged. "Anyway, she's a Stalwart, like we suspected. Graduated second in 69, and only became a teacher last year. She's also way, way cooler than her little brother."

Cute too, in a smile-with-you-flirt-with-you-drink-you-under-the-table-and-then-leave-you-chained-to-the-flagpole-in-nothing-but-your-underwear sort of way. Like Her Majesty, I guess… just without the fear-boner.

"Maybe we should change your codename," said Silt. "Captain Obvious is still available."

"Matthew's not that bad," protested Wormhole.

"Only because you're so busy checking out his cute little butt that you can't see the stick shoved right up it."

The Teleporter went bright red, but I think Shane blushed even harder. Silt had no filter between her mouth and her brain.

She was right about the stick up Paladin's ass though.

"*Anyway*, that leaves three years unaccounted for between graduation and her return to the Academy, but I'm not sure yet if she spent those years as a Cape… or what her codename was, if so."

"Clearly, daddy dearest decided not to make *her* the next Paladin."

I nodded. "I'm not sure what the story is there either."

"I know we're still just first-years, but have any of you thought about what *we'll* be doing once we graduate?" asked Wormhole.

"I think it depends on which Cape team we end up on," mused Shane.

"There isn't a team in the Free States who won't want a unicorn, Unicorn." Silt shrugged her wide shoulders. "You're going to have your pick."

"I'd like to stay here in Los Angeles," said Kayleigh, looking out at the endless waters of the Pacific. "Maybe join the older Paladin's Defenders. What about you, Damian?"

"Not sure," I admitted. "Graduation's a long way away. I'm more worried about making it out of this semester in one piece."

"I'm going home," said Silt.

"Back to Texas?" Evelyn frowned. "Why?"

It was a good question. Texas was part-Badlands, part-South, and entirely unpleasant.

Silt shrugged again. "I've got unfinished business in Brownsville."

Evelyn wrinkled her nose in thought. "By the time we graduate, I *might* be able to get you there in one hop."

"That would be helpful. Fuck knows walking would suck." Silt patted her roommate's knee. "I knew there was a reason I was keeping you around."

I must have winced or something as I shifted position yet again, because when I looked up, Shane was eyeing me worriedly. "Are you sure you're okay? I know Nikolai wanted us to taper down the healings even further, but maybe…"

"I'm fine." I shrugged, and then instantly wished I could go back in time to reconsider that gesture. Fucking hell. *Everything* hurt. "Nothing some ice, alcohol, and black-market stim-weed wouldn't fix."

Vibe looked only slightly less miserable than I felt. The Empath had been keeping even closer than usual over the past two weeks. Even out there in the clearing, her fingertips brushed against the exposed skin of my wrist. "I'm just glad to get a break from feeling everyone else's pain. My own bruises suck badly enough."

Silt, who'd been matched up in her most recent bout against Prince—still chubby, despite Nikolai's best efforts—and come through without a scratch, met my eyes and grinned. "Did we learn a little lesson yesterday about being careful what we wish for?"

"Do you think I *wanted* to fight Orca?" I'd heard the comments a handful of guys—normals, one and all—made when Nadia walked past. *Wouldn't mind getting taken down by her* and *Damn, five rounds wouldn't be enough, if you get what I'm saying.* Fucking morons. There's nothing sexy about getting your ass handed to you. The gorgeous Stalwart was stronger, faster, and more skilled than I was. The only advantage I had was my reach, and she'd gotten past that in about ten seconds.

She hit even harder than Paladin.

If I'd had any choice in the matter, I'd have been the one fighting Prince. Or maybe Shane. He was the closest thing to a friend I had at the Academy, but he still couldn't fight worth shit. Unfortunately, Nikolai was still choosing the pairings. In the past two weeks, I'd been matched up against the best fighters in our class. Alan Jackson. The Viking. El Bosque. Ishmae. And last but *far* from least, Orca.

"You might want to steer clear of Nadia for a bit," murmured Kayleigh. "From what I was sensing, she's super pissed off at you."

"Wait, *she's* pissed at *me*? I didn't even hit her once!"

"Exactly," said Silt. "Three months ago, you fought an epic, twenty-minute battle with Paladin, going full-Walker at the very end. Then yesterday, you let *her* win in a matter of seconds? That's not the way into a Stalwart's pants, Skeletor."

"I didn't let her win, any more than I did Alan-fucking-Jackson!" I protested. "Also, you've got to stop with this whole *full-Walker* thing. The arena's dampeners are clearly working or you'd be burying opponents in the dirt instead of just breaking their noses."

"And jaws."

"You broke Prince's jaw?"

Silt shrugged. "They healed it afterward."

"Damn." I was pretty sure I didn't want to face the stocky Earthshaker in the Pit either, dampeners or not. "Anyway, everything I've read about Crows says our powers are external, not internal. We *raise* Walkers… we don't become them."

On the bench next to Silt, Evelyn had gone pale. I kicked myself for letting Silt goad me. Wormhole still wasn't totally comfortable with my presence, and this topic was a fantastic fucking way to wipe out any progress I'd made.

"So how do *you* explain what happened with Paladin?" pressed Silt.

"First, he beat my face in, then I got angry, and then he beat my face in again?" I shrugged. "Everything after that can be blamed on the concussion."

"He *did* have one," admitted Shane, "although I'm not sure that explains—"

"There you have it," I said, cutting off the ginger. "Concussion-induced mania. It's a thing."

There was a moment of silence as everyone digested that possibility. Then, a slow smile spread across Silt's brown face. "So Nadia should've hit you *harder* if she wanted a real fight? Is that what you're saying?"

I frowned at the corner I'd backed myself into. "That wasn't my point. Just tell her she kicked my ass fair and square."

"And that you want a rematch on Monday?" Silt nodded, her dirt eyes sparkling. "Got it."

CHAPTER 30

The sleek Stalwart was still on my mind an hour or two later, as I lay on my bed, tabbing through my latest reading assignment. As much as I hated to admit it, the fight with Orca *had* gone differently than the one with Paladin, and it hadn't been just a matter of fighting styles. I'd done my best against Nadia, just as I had against every other opponent over the past few weeks, but I'd also been aware that it was only a training exercise. I'd kept my temper, I'd tried to utilize what Nikolai had taught us, and when she'd put me down, I'd stayed down.

I was certain I hadn't used my powers in the fight against Paladin. Hell, I'd been at the Academy for three months, and I still didn't know *how* to use my powers. But maybe Orca had a point. Anger had gotten me through thirteen years at Mama Rawlins'. It had gotten me through a good portion of the fight with Paladin. The combat techniques we were learning from Nikolai and Jessica were cool, but we were *all* learning those. Maybe anger was the only edge I had.

If Orca wanted a real fight, I'd give her one.

Weirdest way of flirting I'd ever heard of, but it'd been nine months since my last time with Alicia, and I was starting to get desperate.

On his side of the room, my roommate was getting ready for another Friday night, his deep black skin doing a stellar job of hiding the bruises he'd acquired in his match with Paladin. Like me, Nikolai had been pairing Jeremiah up with the better fighters, and he'd been losing more than he won. At this rate, neither of us was going to make it to second-year.

Jeremiah finished buttoning his dress shirt—this one a deep maroon, though the jeans beneath it were the same ones he usually wore out—combed his beard and cracked his neck. I waited for him to leave but he turned my way instead.

"The second-years are having a party tonight; normals and Powers. Do you want to come?"

I blinked. Those two sentences almost matched the total number of words Jeremiah had said to me since becoming my roommate. "Nah, I'm okay."

"Suit yourself." He shrugged, and then paused again, one hand on the doorknob. "Pretty sure Orca will be there though."

Maybe it was because she'd been on my mind since the fight. Maybe it's because my crush on Gabriella had mostly fizzled out. And maybe it's because my mind was suddenly conjuring an image of the sleek yet curvaceous Stalwart wearing something *other* than grey sweats…

Whatever the reason, I found myself on my feet before I even knew I'd changed my mind. I coughed. "Actually, maybe I'll go after all…"

Against the darkness of his skin and beard, Jeremiah's smile was brilliant.

First party I'd gone to all year. Hell, first party since I turned five and my parents invited some of the neighbors' kids over for cake and ice cream.

Could've gone better. But I guess if it had… well, maybe other things would've turned out worse.

* * *

"I did tell you that Orca would be there, didn't I? And other girls?"

I looked over—and up—at Jeremiah. "Other than Ishmae, they're all eighteen; it's okay to call them women. But yeah, you told me. Why?"

He waved a large hand at me. "Don't you want to wear something nicer?"

Dressed in my Paladin tee and the cleanest pair of grey sweatpants that I owned, I looked like a college student trying to sleep off his hangover, not one headed out for a party. Not that I had much choice in the matter. This was the nicest set of clothes I owned, but if Jeremiah hadn't realized that in three months of being my roommate, I sure as fuck wasn't going to tell him.

"Women hate it when guys try too hard," I said instead.

"I'll take your word for it," I barely heard him mutter.

The second-year dorms were next to ours, but we went in the opposite direction, heading to the south side of the campus, where one of the original Academy buildings had long ago been repurposed for student use. According to campus legend, it was the class of 59 that had pooled their money and paid to convert the place into a bar, The Liquid Hero. Since then, the responsibility for operating the bar had been passed down to each second-year Cape class.

"Why'd you invite me out tonight of all nights?" I asked my roommate, as we wove past students headed in the other direction.

"Dunno. Just seemed like an opportunity." He shrugged uncomfortably. "Truth is, after all this time as roommates, I don't know much about you."

It was my turn to shrug. "As far as most people are concerned, all that matters is what I am."

"Yeah. Don't know much about that either. Crows, I mean." We rounded the corner and our destination came into sight, along with the small crowd of people hanging around outside.

"I *am* a Crow, and I barely know anything." I wasn't sure why my roommate was being nice all of a sudden. Maybe Orca kicking my ass was helping break the ice? "As far as I know, I'm the only Crow in the city."

"Did you grow up here?" A small line of people was snaking through the crowd and into the bar, and we attached ourselves to the end of that line.

"No… Bakersfield."

The big man winced. "Ouch."

"Fucking tell me about it." As we neared the front of the line, I saw they had a Titan out front, taking money and handing out entry passes. "Oh uhm… I left my wallet back at the dorm." My empty wallet, but that didn't seem worth mentioning either.

"No worries. First-years get in free tonight. Guess it's the second-years' idea of a meet and greet."

The Titan was even bigger up close; Nikolai's size, if not larger. He turned to Jeremiah. "What's up, Stonewall? Who's this?"

"Hey Hektor, this is my roommate, Damian."

"The Crow?" Hektor brought his enormous fists in front of him and slowly cracked each knuckle. "We've heard about you."

"Half of it is lies," I told him.

"Sure, but which half?"

Since I didn't know what he'd heard about me, I just shrugged.

"As first-years, you both get in free tonight. Start any trouble though, and I can promise you'll pay plenty."

"No problem, man," Jeremiah said with a smile. "Stop by and have a drink when you're off shift?"

"Will do." Hektor turned to the next people in line, and my roommate and I headed inside to be greeted by a blast of music.

"Stonewall?"

"What?"

I raised my voice. "He called you Stonewall. That's your codename?"

"Yeah. Stone-shifter, so I figured… what the hell? No need to get overly creative or anything."

The Liquid Hero was larger than I'd expected it to be. Most of the floor was open space—or would have been if it weren't crowded by people—but a wooden bar stretched to our left, shelves of bottles behind it, and a handful of booths occupied the opposite wall. High tables at the far end of the room flanked a staircase leading up to the second floor.

There were people *everywhere*. The crowd was mixed; both normals and Capes, and I was surprised to realize that the latter were easy to spot… and not just the Titans who were half a foot taller than everyone else. I'd always assumed that the hyper-fit Capes in hero vids were simply propaganda, but after three months under Nikolai and

Jessica's tender mercies, many of the first-years were starting to trend in that direction. And the *second-years*? They made us look like children.

Most of the men, Capes or otherwise, were dressed like Jeremiah, in some variation of button-up shirt and jeans, but I caught a few in shorts, and a handful more in tees like me. I *was* the only one rocking Academy sweats though. As for the women…

"I've been spending way too much time doing homework," I breathed. One look around the bar told me that not making it to the so-called "beach" was just one of my many sins over the past three months on campus. There were a lot of women in the bar… an awful lot of those women were cute… and the vast majority were dressed to kill.

Not *literally* dressed to kill. That's a whole different sort of dress code, one that usually involves body armor, Kevlar or… well, skintight leather, in the case of Her Majesty.

There was no body armor in sight, although one woman had paired combat boots with the smallest and tightest miniskirt I'd ever seen. There was plenty of leather, a variety of skirts, an even more impressive mixture of tops, and—best of all—a fantastic amount of bare skin on display. After so many weeks with the same twelve first-year women, all of them dressed in dull grey sweats that even London and Nadia had to work at making sexy, a roomful of women in party clothes was enough to blow my mind.

If Orca really was wearing a dress, I was going to lose that mind entirely.

Jeremiah nodded to the stairs. "We're up top."

The second floor was basically an oversized balcony, wrapping around three walls of the bar and leaving open space in the middle so that you could look down on the dancers below. Two legs of the resulting U were too narrow for anything but stools and high tables, but the last leg was large enough for three long tables and a shitload of chairs. Sitting at one of those tables, the Viking was easy to pick out. I also spotted Winter's distinctive hair, and Olympia glowing like a fucking Christmas light.

For those of you from the distant, pre-Break past, Christmas is a day where adults get shit-faced, slobber about how much they love each other, and end up passed-out in a puddle of their own vomit. Remembrance Day without the presents, basically. No clue how or why colored lights got mixed into the tradition, but given that I was raised in a fucking orphanage, I'm guessing I missed out on the backstory.

Our arrival didn't cause as much of a stir as I'd expected. Olympia's light flickered a bit, but either those Control classes were paying off or the three empty beer bottles sitting in front of the Lightbringer had gone a long way to drowning out her usual terror. Winter had a single glass of white wine in her hand—because of course she fucking did—while the other first-years all had beers like Olympia.

It wasn't until she looked my way with a scowl that I even recognized Tessa. She'd pulled her curly black hair back and away from her face, and was wearing makeup that almost disguised the bruise she'd gotten from her own roommate, Ishmae, in Thursday's fight. Black, multi-layered skirts made her look a little bit like a witch—a real one, not a Weather Witch like Winter—but her burgundy halter top was low-cut.

Like… ridiculously low-cut.

Poltergeist had tits.

It's one thing to know it—I mean, she was technically female, so of course she had to have them—but it was another thing entirely to see them for myself.

"Looking at something, Crow?" At least her voice was the same, just the right combination of sarcasm and disdain to shake me free of my stupor.

"Yeah… I think it's your belly button." I was too busy pulling my eyes up and away to take any pleasure in her own hurried glance down and the resulting, equally hurried adjustment of her top.

Jeremiah cleared his throat—which, from a man his size, came out as a cross between a foghorn and an avalanche—and herded me over to a couple of free chairs on the very far side of the table from Poltergeist. I dropped into the suggested seat and took my first real look at who else was sitting around our table.

The Viking was half-naked—an all-too-common event in the guys' wing of the dorm—showing off an abundance of carefully flexed muscle, tanned skin, and golden hair. At least someone had made him put on pants. They weren't jeans, but something looser, dyed an incredibly bright Day-Glo yellow.

Erik-fucking-Thorsson had never lacked confidence.

In a little black dress, Olympia would've looked good next to anyone. Seated next to the Viking, she looked good *and* classy. She kept her silver-eyed gaze carefully fixed on something that wasn't me, and I returned the favor by not checking out her dress. The revelation of Tessa's tits had been enough of a mindfuck for one night.

London was chatting away with Santiago, the two of them a matched pair—and god I hoped *that* was purely coincidental—in deep green. Now *her* I could have stared at all night, but even I knew there was a line between appreciative and offensive. Plus, just because she lacked Ishmae's potential as a Pyro didn't mean she couldn't still light me on fire.

On the other side of Santiago was Paladin. Like the other guys not deluded enough to think themselves real-life Vikings, Matthew was in a button-down and jeans, his blonde hair perfectly parted. Unlike the other guys, he had a glass of something clear.

Anyone else, and I've have said it was vodka. Fucking Paladin though? Something told me it was water.

Next to Paladin was the aforementioned Tessa, and next to her was Winter, tall and thin and all in white to match her hair. Then Caleb—now going by Supersonic—followed by Erin, and Freddy.

I was the only one in sweats. Only one in a t-shirt too. Nobody said a word about it though, even if Paladin's jaw did go tight at the sight of the shirt. Try and pay respect to a guy's father, and he gets all pissy for some reason…

Anyway, nobody said anything about my bar clothes. Nobody said anything about anything, really… the whole lot of them working as hard as they could to ignore my presence. Most of them were less obvious about it than Olympia, but nine people not making eye contact tends to be a little bit obvious.

But Baron Boner, I can almost hear you say, *didn't you just describe ten people other than you and Stonewall at the table?* Right you are, oh anonymous ghost who should fucking know better than to interrupt me when I'm reminiscing… but I wasn't counting Freddy in the list of people ignoring me.

Guy wouldn't be making eye contact with *anyone,* given he was passed-out drunk.

CHAPTER 31

Hour or so later, and there was still no sign of Orca. I'd had a few sips of beer, decided I preferred the rotgut tequila Alicia had once smuggled out of her old man's liquor cabinet, and switched to water almost immediately after.

Two people drinking water in a bar. One of them in a Paladin t-shirt, one of them actually named Paladin. Has to be a joke in there somewhere.

But anyway, an hour later and still no Nadia. Still no eye contact from most of my beloved class members either, although Winter and Tessa occasionally pulled their shit together enough to shoot me grey and green eyed glares, respectively. No Nadia, no drunken flirtation, no real action—of any kind—and no alcohol worth drinking. As parties go, this one wasn't living up to the hype.

What I did have was conversation. Not with the nine first-years who were busy pretending I didn't exist, of course, or with the one first-year who remained passed out in his own drool. No, the person talking my ear off—the *only* person talking my ear off—was my usually stoic, frequently threatening, always-quiet roommate, Jeremiah.

On the one hand… not worrying that your Shifter roommate is going to come over and stomp you in your sleep is kind of a good thing. Wouldn't do a damn thing to help me sleep better—not after all those years on a cot in Mama Rawlins'—but still… kind of nice.

On the other hand, it was starting to feel more like an inquisition than a conversation.

"So when did you first realize you were a Crow?" the big man asked for the second time. The music was a lot quieter upstairs, but still loud enough that I'd been able to carry off pretending like I couldn't hear him on occasion. Since we'd sat down, he'd been peppering me with questions about my power, as if his curiosity had been building up over the past three months and he was now just letting it all go.

I shrugged. "I was fucking the cute redhead that lived next door to our house. Her parents and older brother were gone so the two of us were out back on a blanket. Neither of us knew the family that lived there before had buried their beloved dog in that yard. When I came… well, so did the dog."

"You mean…?"

"Yeah, burst right out of the ground, all dirt and bones and a few scraps of flesh. Hell of a way to ruin an orgasm."

Total bullshit, but you already know that. Norm and Sue. Jeremiah didn't get that truth. Didn't deserve it, far as I was concerned. My childhood had sucked, but it was *mine*, and fuck if I was going to give it away to anyone who asked.

Plus, making shit up was kind of fun.

"That's rough." He shook his head. "What did your parents say when they found out?"

And just like that, fun time was over. I waved Jeremiah off and went over to the balcony to look down at the first floor. If Nadia didn't show up in five minutes, I was going back to the dorm. Hell, maybe I'd even do homework or something.

There were still a lot of people down below, but no sign of a dirty-blonde Stalwart with ocean-colored eyes.

I started to turn away, then stopped and looked again.

A smaller woman with electric-blue streaks in her black hair was making her way through the crowd. Even from the balcony, I could see Vibe had her eyes scrunched shut, her face pinched as if she was trying to block out the madhouse of people around her. She took another step, then stumbled, half-collapsing to the floor before her legs firmed up beneath her. Whatever momentum had propelled her into the bar had already dwindled to almost nothing.

Can't think of many places worse for an Empath still learning to shut out emotions. Kayleigh was a lot of things, but dumb wasn't one of them. She wouldn't be here for no reason.

I left the other first-years sitting around the table and hurried downstairs.

* * *

By the time I made it down, one of the second-years—a Wind Dancer whose name started with an A, I think—had pulled Kayleigh over to the bar, and was doing his best to calm her down. Because nothing calms an Empath like having someone up in her space. She was still standing, if barely, curled in on herself like a ball or one of those armadillo things from Silt's homeland.

I cut between the two, ignoring A—'s barely audible squawk of surprise, and captured Vibe's hand in mine. Just like that, the pinched expression left her face, and strength returned to her legs.

"How did you do that?" A— asked over the music, looking me up and down in surprise. "I thought the first-year Healer was a ginger?"

I ignored him, focused on Vibe. "What are you doing here, Kayleigh?"

Even with my touch working as a buffer between her and the hundreds of teenage emotional roller coasters surrounding us, her voice was weak. If the bar music hadn't rolled over to a new song just then, I might not have heard her at all.

"I came looking for you." I waited for Kayleigh to continue, but even that limited and unhelpful sentence seemed to have exhausted her.

Oh well. It wasn't like I'd been having much fun anyway, between Orca's absence and Jeremiah's interrogation.

Not to mention Tessa and her sneak-attack cleavage. God help me.

"Well, you found me," I yelled back as the music returned to full volume. "Shall we get out of here?"

She nodded and held tightly to my hand as I led her through the crowd to the door.

A— never did find out what was going on.

* * *

Once we were outside, the combination of cold air, isolation, and a continued death-grip on my hand helped Vibe recover quickly. Even so, it took ten or so minutes of walking before she fully relaxed.

"Maybe you should wait to try that whole bar scene until—"

"My shielding's better?" she interrupted, dropping her eyes. "Yeah. I thought I could handle it for long enough to come get you."

"Next time, just set off a flare or something," I suggested. "Or find Orca and send her in. That would have totally worked."

"Gee, I wonder why?" She rolled her eyes.

"So what did you need me for, anyway? Not that I mind leaving the party-a-minute of Paladin, Winter, and Poltergeist."

"*Paladin* was at a bar?"

"Drinking water, but yeah. He probably read in his instruction manual that socialization is a vital component of team-building."

"He's not that bad, Damian."

First Wormhole, now Vibe. If Silt started singing Paladin's praises, I was going to scream.

"Anyway," she added, the smile falling from her face, "I came to warn you."

I would have asked her about what… but prior experience had taught me she would just interrupt me, mid-question. Instead, I just arched one eyebrow and waited.

"Patty overheard Caleb and Freddy talking about their group project for History."

Patty was Kayleigh's roommate, and one of our class' two Hydromancers. Don't think I've mentioned her yet. In a class of twenty-four, there are some kids you like, some you hate, and some you just never really run into. She belonged to that last group. Our two water-based Powers practically lived at the school's indoor pool, and while the image of first-years—or, God willing, *second-years*—in bikinis had its appeal, the reality was that the Hydros just swam to the floor of the pool's deep end and stayed there for hours, communing with their native element or some shit like that.

Pretty sure all that water was wrinkling more than just their fingers and toes.

"They're doing it on you," Vibe continued. "On Crows, I mean. They were saying it's in case any of us encounter a Necromancer after we graduate, but—"

"But really, they just want to embarrass me in front of a bigger audience," I finished with a scowl.

"I think so." She sighed, using her free hand to tuck a blue strand of hair behind one ear. "Some of them really do hate you. I don't know why."

I thought of my dad. "I do. But that doesn't give them the right—"

"No, it doesn't. Anyway, I was going to tell you tomorrow, but someone said you'd gone to the party, so I came to warn you." She paused, and looked up at me with a frown of her own. "Since when do *you* go to parties?"

"Staring at my dorm room wall every night is going to drive me nuts even faster than my powers. When Jeremiah invited me, I figured…" My voice trailed off. My roommate was in that same History group with Caleb, Freddy, Tessa and Olympia. "*That bearded motherfucker.*"

It wasn't until I felt Kayleigh's grip tighten on my wrist that I realized I'd spun around and was heading back toward the bar. "What are you doing?" she asked.

"I'm going to go teach someone a lesson about fucking with me."

"You can't fight him—"

"Yeah, I can." It was my turn to interrupt. "It would be different if Jeremiah walked around in stone form, but right now, he's just flesh and blood." And probably halfway to being drunk. I'd have time for at least one shot before he changed form.

"No… I mean you'll get kicked out of school!"

That stopped me, for just a moment. "There's no way they'd expel a Cape just for fighting."

"You're not a regular Cape," Kayleigh reminded me, "and it's not just first-years that are freaked out by that fact. If you go swinging your dick around like a monkey with something to prove, you're just going to make it easier for them to have you expelled."

"That's such fucking bullsh—" My voice trailed off. "*Swinging my dick around like a monkey?*"

Even with the dim light of the streetlamps and her naturally golden skin, Kayleigh's blush was noticeable. "It's a figure of speech. Why is it that boys always want to run off and make things worse?"

"You're the Empath," I reminded her. "You tell me."

"Well, I can't hear *your* emotions, but if you're anything like the others, I guess it's some combination of pride, insecurity, and raging testosterone."

I sighed and tucked my anger away. "Dating must suck for you."

"You have no idea. Anyway, I sort of figured you'd get pissed off. That's why I waited to tell you until we were on the far side of campus."

I glanced around. We'd traveled along one of the campus' many paths to its west-most extremity, the nearby woods a dark boundary just outside the last streetlamp's illumination. Mom's ghost was a pale figure on the periphery, but we were otherwise alone. "I thought *I* was getting *you* away from there."

"You were, at first," she admitted, "but it's been five minutes since we even saw anyone else." She scowled at whatever she saw in my face. "I don't *always* need saving, you know. I'm stronger than you all think."

With those words, she deliberately removed her hand from my wrist and stepped away, crossing her arms and staring up at me defiantly.

Then, her eyes rolled back in her head, and she collapsed to the ground.

I rushed over, but Kayleigh was already struggling back to her feet, almond-shaped eyes wide. She shied away from my extended hand with a hiss.

"What's—?"

"*Shh!*" She took another careful step away from me on wobbly legs, turning toward the woods behind us. After a long moment, she shuddered. The look she sent back at me was troubled.

"What is it?"

"Fear. Out there." Vibe's voice was strangled. "And strong."

"*How* strong?"

"Stronger than when Olympia looks at you. Thick enough to choke on." She frowned and cocked her head. "And almost lost beneath that, there's something else. Anger. Lust. Glee."

"You're getting all of that from one person?"

Kayleigh shook her head. "The fear is one person. A woman, I think. The rest is someone else. Maybe multiple someones. It's hard to hear beneath her terror." Her voice cracked slightly. "I think… I think she's in trouble."

This wasn't the sort of shit that was supposed to happen on the most securely guarded campus in the entire Free States. I scanned around us one more time. Still dark. Still empty. No Tempest. No Dominion. No faculty, for that matter. Just an Empath with barely any control and a Crow with no real powers *to* control.

And someone else, terrified for her life.

I'd barely found Alexa's clearing, even with directions. There was no chance I'd be able to find someone in the woods at night. But Vibe… "Can you track any of them by their emotions?"

"The woman. At least, I think so. She's drowning everything else out though."

"I won't be able to shield you." If I touched Kayleigh, she'd lose her ability to feel the other woman and we'd never find her. But that meant she'd have to weather all that fear on her own.

"I'll manage." The jury was still out on the rest of us, but those two words, uttered with weary, resigned determination, told me that Vibe was going to be one hell of a Cape.

Assuming either of us lived that long.

"Then let's go."

We headed into the darkness, Mom's ghost trailing behind.

CHAPTER 32

A minute into the woods was enough to confirm that I'd have been hopelessly lost without Kayleigh. The combination of a full moon and the city's ever-present glow kept things from being pitch black, but everything looked the same to me; nothing but trees, trees, and oh look, what's that? More fucking trees.

I knew Vibe had grown up in a city, like me, but she seemed comfortable in the dark woods. She led us ever deeper into the forest, pausing only occasionally to correct our path. The woods weren't huge, but we spent five minutes weaving back and forth before I heard anything beyond our own noisy passage.

Someone was rushing through the woods ahead of us.

Kayleigh changed course one last time. We broke out into another small clearing, maybe half the size of our group's meeting place, and without that space's phenomenal view. Several small trees had fallen, creating this brief break in the blanket of forest. A moment later, a woman burst into the clearing from the opposite direction, hair flowing behind her, the moonlight highlighting tear streaks down her face.

She saw us, let out a little shriek, and tried desperately to turn, but her feet slid out from under her, and she went down with a thump and a crack where she impacted another of the fallen trees.

"Crap." Kayleigh headed over to the fallen woman. "This is her."

With our help, the women was quickly upright again, but she was unsteady on her feet, the back of her head matted with blood from where she'd struck the tree trunk. Her clothes were torn and muddy, her eyes wide and terrified.

With the three of us motionless, I could hear other sounds now; low growls and a high-pitched cackle. Whoever they were… whatever they were…they were coming closer.

"Can you project fear as well as sense it, Kayleigh?"

The Empath shook her head. "You'd need a Siren for that, like Prince."

Fuck. I looked from Vibe to the woman she was supporting. "Can you get her to safety then?"

"I'm not going anywhere without you."

"We don't have a choice," I told her, conscious of the sounds of pursuit getting closer. "There's no way she can move fast enough to get away from whoever's hunting her."

"Then we'll stop them together," she insisted. "I'm a Cape-in-training, just like you."

"Kayleigh, there aren't any dampeners here, and fights—real fights—are nothing *but* emotion."

"You think I'm a liability?"

"I think we need someone to get her to safety and someone to stop what's coming. Let's play to our strengths."

She would have argued further—seemed prepared to do so, even—but we could both hear that the hunters were only moments away. With a scowl, Kayleigh helped the other woman hobble out of the clearing.

* * *

One thing Jessica Strich had always harped on was the value of picking our battlegrounds. I took advantage of the few seconds left to put the moon at my back and a fallen tree between me and whoever was coming.

They loped out of the darkness like feral nightmares, the one on the left giggling now instead of cackling, the larger shape on his right almost entirely silent. As they came to a sudden halt in the clearing, the moonlight was enough to tell me I was well and truly fucked.

The *small* one was close to my height and half again as wide, a sleeveless shirt exposing corded muscle and hairy arms. The other one was almost Titan-sized and similarly dressed. But that wasn't the part that had my balls climbing into my stomach. Size matters—no matter how the vids tried to pretend otherwise—and numbers *really* matter, but both can be overcome with enough skill and motivation.

I wasn't too sure about my skill, even after three months under Nikolai's harsh tutelage, but motivation I had in fucking spades.

The *real* problem lay with the other details the moon had revealed. The smaller man had high, triangular ears protruding from the top of his skull and a smattering of fur across his exposed flesh. The giant had a grey-furred snout in an otherwise human face. Worst of all, each of their hands ended in long-taloned claws.

Beast-shifters. Ones or Twos, given their limited transformations and the fact that I didn't recognize them as first-years or second-years, but still more than deadly enough to take care of one largely powerless Crow.

So I did what I always do when things go to shit; I went on the attack.

"Gentlemen." I spread my arms wide to make sure I had their attention, conscious that Kayleigh and the unnamed woman had less than a twenty second lead. "You've had your fun, but this hunt is over."

They had already started to spread out to circle me, but were hampered by the small clearing's layout. The smaller one paused. "Who the fuck are you?"

"One of the junior Capes," sneered the other, his words poorly formed because of the snout. "Thinks he's already a hero."

"Jury's still out on whether I end up Cape or Black Hat," I admitted. "Maybe that's why I'm willing to cut you two a break. Turn around now, and I'll let you walk out of here."

I was all the more glad I'd sent Vibe on her way. Having her present—or any woman, really—would've made the Shifters that much less likely to back down. More of the same stupid pride and insecurity she said all men suffered from, I guess.

Even with the Empath gone, I didn't expect the two Shifters to take me up on my offer, not when they were already drunk on the thrill of the chase. But it gave Kayleigh time to get away, and it gave me time to locate a loose branch—as long as my forearm and several inches thick—near where I was standing.

I'd have preferred a flamethrower. Or laser eye beams like some Lightbringers had. I'd have even settled for something as basic as the steak knife I'd stolen from the cafeteria, way back when. But a stick was better than nothing.

The larger Shifter paused, pretending to consider my proposal, but I'd seen the look he sent his companion. I was in motion even before the smaller Shifter leapt at me. Nikolai's footwork got me out of the way—if barely—and Jessica's training had me rotating my hips as I lashed out.

The stick cracked in half, but the way the Shifter squealed and clutched his arm told me my makeshift weapon wasn't the only thing that had broken. He took another step, stumbled over the fallen tree, and went down heavily.

Anyone who says you shouldn't kick an opponent when he's down has never been in a fight. I threw the branch fragments aside, and launched my foot into the fallen Shifter's side. This time, the crack I heard had everything to do with his ribs. He rolled back across the clearing with a groan, only to have the larger Shifter haul him to his feet with a single, massive paw.

The real problem with Beast-shifters isn't their heightened senses. It isn't even their claws. It's how fast they heal. Kodiak can lose a limb and grow it back before the day is out. Someone like Alan Jackson can recover from a broken bone in a matter of hours. These two were a long way from Kodiak, or even Alan, but they were still Beast-shifters; I watched as the lines of pain eased in the smaller one's face.

"That was your only warning shot, assholes."

The smaller one snarled, beyond human reason for just that moment, but the larger one remained unruffled. "You seem to have lost your stick, Crow."

"So you *do* know who I am."

"He's a... *what?*" asked the smaller one, suddenly looking uncertain.

"Someone that won't be missed," answered the giant. "Hell, the school would probably give us medals if they knew."

"Maybe so." I shrugged, the timer in my head continuing to count. Two minutes gone now, maybe three. It wasn't enough. "Assuming you had a chance in hell of taking me."

"You don't think we do?" That was the smaller one, whose ribs seemed fine again, even though his arm was still hanging limply.

"There are two of you and you seem to have some limited grasp of tactics." I shrugged a second time. "On the other hand, you're already halfway down the road to Fucked City, and neither of you is a Three. Hell, I'm not sure you're even Twos."

"Jake's a Two," snarled the little one, "and I'm High-One. Add those together—"

"And you don't have shit," I interrupted. "This isn't math class. But fuck it, why don't we find that out for ourselves. Maybe you two shitheads can manage what Paladin couldn't."

The little one went even paler at that. "Jake..."

"Shut up, Adam."

"Did he seriously take on Paladin...?"

"I said shut up!"

"Yeah, Adam," I agreed. "Shut up. Jake wants to see where this goes." I looked across the clearing at the two Shifters and twisted my lips into a smile. "By all means, make your play, so I can get on with killing you both."

"Threats don't scare us," growled Jake.

"After that," I continued, ignoring the larger Shifter's interruption, "I'm going to raise one of you as a Walker and send you back home to eat every fucking person who ever knew you." I glanced from the white-faced Adam to the suddenly uncertain Jake. "Which of you wants to come back? Should I just flip a coin?"

"You can't—"

"I'm a Crow." I let my smile grow. "What the fuck do I care about *can't*?"

Adam was terrified, and almost entirely back to human shape, but Jake was unconvinced, and he was the bigger threat by far. If he attacked…

The ground before me suddenly split open, sending both Shifters scrambling back. I had a moment to mask my own shock and then called out to them. "Oh look, here's a Walker now."

Neither man waited long enough to see what would crawl out of that pit.

Damn good thing too, since nothing ever did.

"Fucking hell, Boneboy. When you bluff, you bluff hard." Silt stepped out from the trees behind me.

"Don't play unless you believe you can win," I told her. "Where did you come from?"

"About two minutes that-a-way." She motioned in the direction Kayleigh had gone. "Our little bench clearing makes a fantastic make-out spot. Or it would have, if my date hadn't just been interrupted."

"*You* date?"

"Fuck you, Skeletor. Pretty sure I get more action than your crazy ass." She rolled her eyes. "Anyway, when Vibe came out of nowhere with some injured normal—"

"Are they okay?" I interrupted.

"Yeah, my date's taking them to the med center now. I promised Kayleigh I'd come find you and help." She looked in the direction the two Shifters had gone. "Who were they?"

"Students, I think. Regular ones, not Capes. Adam and Jake, both Beast-shifters. Shouldn't be hard for school security to track them down, especially with Adam's broken arm."

"What would you have done if I hadn't showed up?"

"Guess we'd have seen whether that full-Walker thing was just bullshit."

"And if it was?"

"Then I'd have done my best to at least take the fuckers down with me." I was a Crow. Silt and I were both training to be Capes. Wasn't like either of us expected to die of old age.

"You need a better name than Boneboy," Silt decided.

"Tell me about it." I took one last look back at the clearing before we left it behind. "Why didn't they smell you?"

"I'm an Earthshaker," she reminded me. "Nothing to smell here but good old natural dirt."

"You say that like it's a good thing." I paused. "Sorry about your date."

"They say anticipation just makes the final victory all the sweeter." Silt grinned. "Besides, there are worse things than having a Crow owe me a favor."

I thought that over as I followed her back into the woods. "Want backup when you head down to Texas?"

"If we both live that long, you mean? It's a deal. Fair warning though; Brownsville's a lot worse than Los Angeles." A few minutes later, she shook her head. "I think that was the first time I've ever seen you smile."

"When?"

"Back there. Staring down the Shifters."

"Oh." I frowned. "Might be the first time I *have* smiled since coming here."

"Please don't do it again." She shivered. "Scariest fucking thing I ever saw."

CHAPTER 33

It was a long time before we were allowed to leave the clinic, even though most of us had made it out of the woods unscathed. The girl we'd saved was named Sue, but I tried not to hold that against her. She'd gone into the woods to meet Jake for a moonlight stroll. Instead, she'd found both Jake *and* Adam, neither of whom had romance on the mind.

The good news was that, other than a concussion and numerous scrapes from sprinting through the woods, Sue was going to be fine. Bad news was that she had seriously shitty taste in men. You'd think guys like Jake would have signs around their necks: *will hunt for pleasure*. Nah. People like Jake blend right in with those around them. It's people like me that normals get all worried about.

Guess I can't blame them for that. Crows are a horror show waiting to happen, right?

When we were done at the clinic, it was on to campus security, where I got to tell the exact same story three separate times to four different people. I left out my threats, for the most part. Wasn't sure the real Capes would have approved. Was *positive* nobody wanted to think about me killing someone, raising them, and using them to murder a family.

As threats go though, that one had been fucking golden.

By the time we were done with security, they'd captured both Shifters. Adam had actually gone back to his dorm room like a moron. Jake had tried jumping the wall and getting the fuck out of town.

Neither succeeded. Wasn't sure what was going to happen to them, but I hoped it was something nasty.

It was somewhere around one or two in the morning by then, and everyone else headed back to the dorm. Not me. I was tired, yeah, but also kind of juiced from almost dying… and I wasn't sure yet what I'd do when I saw my roommate. The whole Shifter thing had pushed the rest of my night into the background, but I was still pissed off. So instead of going back, I found a bench—not the bench in the fucking woods, thank you very much—and laid down on it, looking up at a sky whose stars were mostly masked by the lights around me.

More than three months at the Academy, and things just kept getting more confusing, a big old ball of chaos spiraling in unexpected directions. Classmates that hated me. People digging into my past. Powers too weak to be Capes but still too much for a normal to handle. Tessa and her tits. And facing down two Beast-shifters… what the hell had I been thinking?

Life at Mama Rawlins' had been simple. Keep order. Protect the little ones. Fuck up anyone who got in the way. There was nothing simple about the Academy. Rescuing Sue had been a Cape thing to do, but it had been stupid too. I didn't know her. Didn't care about her. Yet I could have easily died trying to save her.

It wasn't the dying part that bothered me. Thing about meeting death when you're five is that you lose that feeling of invincibility early. Stench of blood, smell of apple pie, and nothing in front of you but mortality at its most unflinching, sprawled across the kitchen floor. I'd known from that day on that death was unavoidable. Wouldn't be many who cared when I was gone… the Beast-shifter had gotten that much right.

It wasn't the dying part that bothered me. It was why I'd done it. Was that what being a Cape was all about? Putting your life on the line for total strangers, for people you didn't know, and probably wouldn't like if you did know them? And then what? Suddenly, you're responsible for a city? A fucking country?

It was the first time I'd given much thought to Bard's Orientation speech. First time I really wondered whether I had it in me to be that sort of Cape. Vibe did. She'd shown that much tonight, walking head-on into a hurricane of emotions, not once but twice. Paladin probably did too, as much as I hated to admit it. Unicorn would never have to actually face combat, but his desire to just *help* people leaked out of every overly pale pore.

The rest of us? Fuck if I knew.

Eighteen years old and the world was suddenly bigger than just Mama Rawlins'. Bigger than Bakersfield. A great empty unknown waiting to fuck with me. And every day, the Academy was changing me. Friends were changing me. Even enemies were changing me.

Who the hell was I going to be when I graduated? *If* I graduated?

I shook myself and swung my legs over one side of the bench, pulling myself back upright. Mom sat on the other end of the bench in her faded sundress, smiling like she didn't have a care in the world. I studied her and for a moment—just a moment—I thought something close to recognition made its way into her empty eyes. Then it was gone, and she was looking past me, humming her soundless song.

I was too tired for this shit.

* * *

Should have known the day wouldn't just end like that. Shit day that turned into a shit night and had already gone on way too long?

Of course it couldn't stop there.

There was one person in the common room when I finally got in. Rest of the class was asleep—or banging each other silly in the privacy of their own rooms—but she couldn't pass up the chance to be a pain in my ass.

Of course Poltergeist was waiting for me.

She was drunk too. Jumped up way too quick when she saw me, spots of color in her cheeks, hair halfway between curly and bird's nest. She stalked over, green eyes flashing.

"Can this wait, Tessa? It's been—"

Never got to say what a shit night it had been because she was jabbing me in the chest with an overly long index finger and its equally long nail. No clue how those nails survived Nikolai's classes, but they weren't far from the claws the two Beast-shifters had been sporting.

"I don't care if my neckline is down around my ankles," she hissed. "If you *ever* look at my chest again, I'm going to pull out every one of your pubic hairs, one by one."

"With your teeth?"

"Excuse me?"

"It just seems like the kind of threat that should involve teeth," I told her.

My head snapped to one side, ears ringing from a slap that hadn't involved hands. In fact, Tessa hadn't moved at all.

"You know what I think?" she asked.

"It's hard not to, since you never shut up."

"I think that everyone's been giving you way too much credit, walking around on eggshells, worrying about what you might do. Other than bleeding all over Paladin's fists, what exactly *have* you accomplished? Failed at Control and slept through classes? I'm not sure you even *are* a Crow."

"Maybe I'm not."

"What?"

"Could be I was just added to this class as a test for you first-years, to see which of you would actually behave like Capes." I lowered my voice to a whisper. "Guess who's failing?"

"Funny." Tessa narrowed her green eyes. "When you flame out of here and end up on the streets or in an asylum where you belong, I just hope you don't bring anyone else down with you. Someone like Kayleigh."

"Yeah, because you sure gave a shit about her before all of this."

She shook her head. "Why am I even bothering? I don't understand how someone like you survives to adulthood. Let me guess… stim-weed addict for a mom and no clue which of three or four deadbeats was your real dad?"

I thought back to what Silt had said earlier that night, and let my smile slip out. The Telekinetic went pale and took a step back.

"Fuck your ignorance," I told her. "Fuck your theories about my parents and your sad attempts at superiority, but most of all, fuck you."

An invisible hand wrapped around my throat, lifting me easily into the air. "You're not a Cape, *Damian.* I'm not even sure you're a person. You're just some sort of thing, oozing along, not seeing how disgusting you really are."

I had a couple good comebacks to that, but they all required speech, and that was impossible with the telekinetic hand squeezing my throat.

"He's more of a Cape than you are, Tessa McShane." I couldn't see her, but I recognized Vibe's voice. "Capes don't go around choking people just because they're drunk."

The hand let me go and I dropped several inches to the floor, gasping for breath. Vibe was standing in the doorway to the girls' hall, skinny bare legs sticking out from under a voluminous sleep shirt.

"Capes save people," Kayleigh continued, "like Damian did tonight while you were busy getting drunk and making a fool of yourself at The Liquid Hero. Again."

Where my anger had just seemed to spark Tessa's, Vibe's had the opposite effect. Poltergeist winced and dropped her gaze. "What are you talking about?"

I was more interested in what exactly Tessa had done to make a fool of herself, but it didn't look like Kayleigh was in the mood to satisfy either of our curiosities.

"I'll tell you when you're sober," she decided before turning to me, her voice stern. "Good night, Damian."

I wasn't sure why *I* was in trouble… or when Kayleigh had transformed into a disciplinarian, for that matter, but I recognized the out and took it, fleeing for the boys' hall.

When I made it to my room, I barely even glanced at the still lump of Jeremiah. There was a time to fight and a time to sleep, and I was way too tired to fight.

Let that be a lesson to all of you on fucking with Telekinetics; just don't.

You'll never see their punches coming.

CHAPTER 34

I don't believe in God. If he or she exists at all, I think they're probably something like Dr. Nowhere, using the world as their toilet and then heading off into the great unknown while the rest of us drown in shit. But fuck if there isn't an occasional string of coincidences that pays off just right. If Vibe hadn't gotten me away from the bar before telling me about our classmates' project, if she hadn't felt the girl's terror, if we hadn't gone to confront the Shifters, if those Shifters hadn't both been caught shortly after, if Tessa hadn't gotten in my face when I returned to the dorms…

Probably would have done something rash. Probably would've gotten myself kicked out then and there, like Vibe had predicted.

But fact was, all those things *did* happen. What's more, by the time I woke up Sunday morning, Jeremiah was away; off to study, or exercise, or whatever the fuck the big bastard did when he wasn't snoring like an earthquake. He was gone, and the anger was a smaller thing, almost manageable, curled up in my chest like some sort of multi-clawed beast.

By the time I saw him again—later that night, and then the next morning when we all headed off for the food we'd probably vomit right back up in Nikolai's class—I had myself under control. Had myself almost convinced the whole thing had been a fair trade. Jeremiah had gotten the place of my birth along with a load of utter bullshit, and I'd gotten a reminder that the only thing free in this country was its name. Everything else—even a night at The Liquid Hero—had its cost, and that cost couldn't always be paid with coin.

Hard lesson to learn. One I'll keep learning until the day I die. Maybe even after that, when I'm one of you, and some shit-souled Crow pulls *me* into his orbit.

If you're not learning, you're dying. Not sure who said that. Was probably someone Pre-break.

Truth is, most of us are doing both.

* * *

It was several weeks before things went sideways again. Late June. Not long before presentations started, and only a few weeks more until mid-year exams. I wasn't looking forward to more tests, but I thought I had a fair chance at passing everything but Ethics.

And fuck Ethics anyway. Ms. Ferra was going to flunk me no matter what I did, oblivious to the irony of her actions.

Anyway, late June. I was flipped around on my bed, looking at the sunlit sky through our room's one window, when Jeremiah headed out for the day. I hadn't spoken to Stonewall since The Liquid Hero. Had worked my ass off to ignore him, in fact. I'd decided not to make something out of the whole class project thing, but I sure as fuck wasn't going to be friendly about it.

Might've stayed in that weird sort of status quo for weeks. Might've kept my anger nailed down all the way up to the presentation, maybe even further than that.

Might've done a lot of things, if Jeremiah hadn't left his Glass behind.

From my spot on the bed, I could see its screen, still online, still active. A minute or so of idle time before it would shut down, inaccessible to anyone but the big Shifter.

I don't remember deciding to move, but the next thing I knew, the Glass was in my hand. I tapped through the file system, found a folder helpfully labeled 'Crow research' and sent a copy of the entire folder over to my own Glass.

Didn't have a clue how to erase what I'd done from the logs. Didn't even think of it, to be honest. I'd gotten better with the tech since coming to school, but four months can only teach a guy so much.

Safely back on my side of the room, I turned to my own tablet, and started to dig through what I'd recovered.

The first sub-folder was all about Reno. Fucking Reno. The Crimson Death hadn't been the most powerful Crow ever—that was Lord Bone or Sally Cemetery—but his one very bad day in Nevada had sure as shit caught the public's attention. A whole city murdered on the sly while the Free States' Capes fought off a large-scale invasion from the Pacific. By the time even the fastest Flyboys had made it inland, there was nothing left to greet them but the Necromancer himself, elbow deep in carnage, a wide smile on his bone-white face.

Additional folders held information on the other big names and their atrocities. Pictures of the aftermaths. Accounts from the survivors, on the rare occasions where there were any. Page after page after page of the shit my fellow Necromancers had perpetrated, of the lives that had been ruined in their wake.

None of it was good. I mean… I'd known that, already—was living proof of the sort of damage Crows could wreak—but having it all laid out there like that—pools of black blood and wide, staring eyes—really brought the fucking point home.

Pretty soon, *I* was wondering what Bard had been thinking in letting me enroll.

Then I hit the last sub-folder in the directory. Its label was a single word.

Bakersfield.

Motherfuckers.

* * *

It was my fault. I'd woven a web of lies for my big bastard roommate, even before I knew why he was digging for information, but it hadn't occurred to me to lie about where I was from.

Turns out, that was all they'd needed to track me down.

I just stared at the folder for a long while. Bakersfield. Shit name for a shit town, but seeing it sent a cold chill down my spine. I stared at it, then stared some more, not wanting to click into the folder, not wanting to see what they'd uncovered.

Sad reality is, shit doesn't go away just because you want it to. Twenty minutes of staring, and that folder was still there waiting.

Fuck it. I'd lived through Mom's murder. It wasn't like reading about it could be any worse.

There's life again, lulling you in with expectations, and then kicking you in the balls as soon as your guard drops.

It was all there in excruciating detail; full-page articles about the murder, smaller stories detailing what had come after, even a follow-up piece on the fifth anniversary of Mom's murder, like it had been some sort of event to commemorate. Like there should've been balloons and cake and something other than a junior reporter trying to squeeze one more story out of a woman's death.

I didn't even remember the press covering Mom's murder. Sure as fuck didn't remember cameras, but they'd clearly been there; at the crime scene, at the funeral, and again at the trial, when Dad had been sentenced to the Hole.

The words were bad enough. Things about Mom I'd somehow forgotten. Things about Dad I was pretty sure I'd never known. Clinical descriptions of the wounds I'd watched appear like magic, the blood that sprayed when the enormous knife went in, and again when the knife came back out. Quotes from neighbors that my mind had erased and from multiple social workers that my memory had blurred into one faceless person.

As bad as the words were, the pictures were even worse. The tiny house. The courtroom. The cemetery. And in almost every image, a little boy; pale-faced with sharp cheekbones cutting upward beneath eyes more red than grey. Those eyes were open and empty, like tiny graves waiting to be filled.

I'd never seen a child Walker…wasn't sure they even existed, but if they did, I had to imagine they'd look a lot like my five-year-old self.

In the weeks and months that followed the trial, I'd found my anger. I'd built my walls. I'd buried that emptiness away, deep inside of me where no one could find it. But those pictures made me five all over again, every hard-won layer peeled away until I was left open and exposed, like a raw and bloody nerve.

I was on my feet and headed for the door before I knew it, hands clenched into fists so tight that the scar tissue across my knuckles pulled and creaked. Wasn't thinking about becoming a Cape, or proving my doubters wrong. Wasn't thinking about Alexa's words, or Bard's, or even Her Majesty's. All I was thinking about was Jeremiah and his group; Caleb, Freddy, Tessa and Olympia. The five of them had gone looking for my past and they'd found it. They *knew.* And if they knew, every first-year would too, soon enough. Twenty-three people reading these articles. Looking through these pictures. Digging into my past, into my body, into Mom's corpse, like vermin gorging themselves on rot and blood and pain.

Fuck fair trades.

Fuck the Academy and its rules.

Motherfuckers wanted pain?

It was time to share the fucking wealth.

* * *

Remember that God I don't believe in?

Remember those coincidences that miraculously piled up to save me from myself? Of course you do. We just talked about them, not too long ago.

Don't know if what came next was part of that same chain.

I really hope not.

If it was, if the world or a deity or Dr. Fucking Nowhere acted to put one last impediment in my path, one last deterrent to keep me from going Black Hat at eighteen…

…then it makes everything that followed my fault.

Not sure I could live with that knowledge.

Pretty sure I couldn't.

CHAPTER 35

The dorm hall was empty, every door shut tight as if the first-years could feel me coming. Didn't matter. Stonewall would be in the common room. Or Caleb would be, or one of the others. And if they weren't, I'd damn well find them anyway. Campus was big, but not *that* big. Fuckers couldn't hide for long.

I was three feet from the end of the hall when the door to the common room opened and one of the few people I *didn't* want bloody and beaten barreled through.

"Damian! Thank God! I need your help."

"Not now, Unicorn." I went to step around the small Healer. Somehow he got back in front of me, grabbing my arm and slowing me to a halt.

"Yes now! It's important!"

I looked down at the hand on my arm and over at the ginger. Whatever he saw in my face made him go even paler than usual, but he didn't let go. So I took the last step toward the common room, dragging Shane right along with me.

The room was empty. Because *of course* it was.

There were a half dozen other spots they might be, and I knew it wouldn't take much more than an hour to check them all. Hour-and-a-half, tops. But first I had to do something about the one-hundred-and-fifty-pound ginger hanging off my arm.

Problem was, when I looked down and met Shane's eyes, I found them full of stubborn determination, mixed in with fear and raw, desperate pleading. Hard to walk away from anyone looking at you like that. Harder still when it's one of your only friends in the world.

"Ishmae is missing," he said.

Fucking hell.

It wasn't like Jeremiah and his group were going anywhere, right? I tucked my anger back away, wrapping it like a blanket around the empty hole inside me, and blew out a long sigh.

"What do you mean she's missing?"

"We were supposed to meet half an hour ago." He blushed at the look I gave him. "To study! Her early admission to the Academy means she missed out on almost two years of high school math, so I've been helping her out."

Which was *such* a Unicorn thing to do. I could just picture the atmosphere of badly repressed feelings as he walked the younger Pyro through yet another Calculus proof.

"So your *emergency* is that she blew off studying for a day?" I scowled. "Fucking hell, Unicorn. She's probably in her room nursing a hangover or something."

"Ishmae doesn't drink," he argued. "And I already checked her room. Besides, there's no way she'd pass up a chance to get better…at anything. You have no idea how driven she is."

"So what's your explanation, Shane? Nobody's dumb enough to fuck with a High-Four. If she's missing, it's because she wants to be."

"For all her power, she's still just a person," he argued. "She could've fallen and hit her head, or been drugged or abducted or—"

"Alright, alright." I cut into the stream of increasingly unlikely explanations. "Fine. She's missing. How are we supposed to find her?"

He coughed, and stared at the tops of his sneakers. "I was hoping you'd have an idea."

I started to shake my head, then stopped. Truth was, *I did.*

* * *

Kayleigh opened her door, squeaked like a mouse being struck by lightning, and slammed the door back shut.

"What was that on her face?"

"No idea. Looked like mud or something." I shrugged and knocked on the door again. "Vibe, we need your help. *Unicorn* needs your help."

It was a full thirty seconds before the door cracked back open. Kayleigh's face made a reappearance, this time bright red, freshly scrubbed, and free of whatever had been smeared across it.

Mostly free, anyway. She'd missed a few streaks on one cheek, and a little more under the chin. Not that I was going to point that out, or the fact that one electric-blue strand of hair was sticking straight up in the air.

"What do you two want, and why couldn't it have waited like *five minutes* longer?"

"Ishmae is missing," said Shane. "I think something's happened to her."

"She's a High-Four," said Vibe, unconsciously reaching over to place one of her fingers on my bare arm. "What the hell *could* happen?"

"That's what *I* said," I muttered.

"I don't know," admitted the Healer, "but if something did…"

"We thought you might be able to find her," I finished. "Like you did with Sue."

She was shaking her head before I had finished. "It doesn't work like that. Not yet anyway. Ms. Ferra says every person has a distinctive signature, but I haven't learned how to read them yet. I can't hunt down a specific person; all I can do is listen for emotion."

"Well, could you try *that*, at least?" Shane's eyes were bright. "If something *has* happened, it might be enough to find her…"

I watched Vibe try her hardest not to wince. Picking up on the emotions of a scared woman at night and on the very edge of campus was one thing. Performing some sort of empathic sweep of the entire campus—an area containing thousands of individuals that Kayleigh spent every waking moment trying to block out—was something else entirely.

She swallowed once, tucked a strand of hair behind one ear with her free hand, and nodded. "I can try."

It's like I said earlier. Some people are Capes to the fucking core.

* * *

Three minutes later, Vibe reached blindly for my arm, her face pinched and drawn. She held on for a good twenty seconds, her breathing slowly steadying, and then released, going back under like a diver heading into the ocean.

That cycle repeated three more times. My wrist was starting to bruise when she surfaced for the last time, shaking her head.

"I'm sorry… there's so much out there. I can't…" Kayleigh shuddered again, her hand reflexively squeezing my wrist again and again. "I can't parse it all, but I didn't feel anything like the other night."

"So, maybe Ishmae is okay, after all—"

"Or she's out of my range. Or unconscious."

"Phoenix?" The three of us spun to find Winter peering out of her room one door down and across the hall. "She's fine. I saw her an hour or so ago."

"You did?" Unicorn pounced like he was some sort of cat, rather than a too-short ginger. "Where?"

Penelope paused to shoot Unicorn and I a suspicious glare. "Are you boys even supposed to be on this side of the dorm? Don't you need a pass or something?"

"For the love of God, Penelope," said Vibe, her voice still strained and weak. "Shut up and just answer his question."

Winter drew herself up to her full height, looking down that crooked nose at us, her smile every bit as cold as the season she'd taken for her name. "Which is it, *Kayleigh*? Should I shut up or answer his question?"

Before the Empath could respond, Shane was between the two women. "Please. It could be important. Seriously important."

"Oh fine." The taller woman rolled her eyes, and tossed her head, sending long, white hair in an arc over one shoulder. "I passed her on campus. Near the Control classroom, in fact. No doubt, she was headed to do some extra credit to ruin the curve even more for the rest of us."

"Like you care." I rolled my eyes. "You're acing everything anyway."

"Nobody asked for your opinion, Crow—" the Weather Witch shot back.

"Oh shit." Shane's natural state was pale, but now he was borderline translucent. "Shit fucking fuck shit."

Her other hand still clasped tightly around my arm, Kayleigh reached out to the little Healer. "What is it, Shane?"

"I know where Ishmae is." He glanced over at us, eyes wide. "We have to hurry."

"Hurry where?"

"To Control," he called over one shoulder, already running back toward the common room. "I think she's going to run the Maze."

* * *

If there was one positive that could be said for the four months we'd spent under Nikolai's tender mercies, it was that every first-year—from the tireless Orca to still-chubby Prince—could run. After twice-weekly, five-mile *warmups*, our sprint across campus to the Control building barely even registered.

Everything seemed quiet, the classroom's windows dark and still.

"I still don't get why you think Ishmae would've come here, Unicorn."

"Especially if Ms. Stein said the Maze was off-limits to first-years," agreed Kayleigh. She hadn't been there when the rest of us saw the device, but we'd filled her in on the way over.

"Ishmae's a High-Four," said Shane. "The first one in almost a decade, and she's known it since she was a child."

"And?"

"And the difference between a High-Four and the rest of us is like the difference between us and normals. Maybe even bigger."

"Yeah, everyone keeps saying that. So what?"

"So she thinks a High-Four should be able to do *everything* better than the rest of us, whether that's acing math classes she doesn't even have the foundational knowledge for, or—"

"Or running the Maze two years earlier than anyone else," I concluded.

"Exactly."

"Well, it makes sense, but…" I waved at the still-silent building. "…it doesn't seem like she's here."

"Well, we should make sure—"

"Actually, *someone* is here."

Shane looked from me to the blue-haired Empath. "You can sense someone inside? Is it Ishmae?"

"I'm not using my powers." She rolled her eyes and nodded to the side door. "The door is open."

* * *

At first, the interior was every bit as dark as it had seemed from the outside, but as we rounded the corner, a dim light split the gloom. At the back of the meditation studio, the door to the Maze's room was open, and in the chair, her bald head slick with sweat under the wire helmet, was Ishmae Naser.

I caught Shane before he could rush in. "If she's running the Maze, we don't know what interrupting her would do."

"We can't just leave her there, Damian!"

Again, it was Kayleigh who pointed out the obvious. "Do either of you smell smoke?"

Now that she'd mentioned it, we did. In fact, as we crept closer to the unconscious Pyro, we could see the smoke as well. It wasn't coming from her—always a concern with someone who could probably burn the whole city down—but from the device itself, slim threads wafting up from visibly blackened circuitry.

"I think she broke it," continued Vibe.

"Then why isn't she awake?" Shane shrugged free of my hand with one of the slick grip escapes Nikolai had taught us, and made it to Ishmae before I could react. He thumbed back one of the Pyro's eyelids and frowned. "No response to light stimuli. Irregular breathing."

"Meaning what?" I guessed.

"I don't think she's *just* unconscious… but there's only one way to be sure."

"Winter will be here any minute with one of the school Healers, Unicorn. We should just wait."

"Every second might matter, Kayleigh," he said absently, rolling up his sleeves, "and the school Healers can't fix much more than a simple break. If there's internal damage, let alone brain trauma, they'll need me to handle it."

Without another word, he placed one hand on the Pyro's forehead, and the other on her twitching bare arm.

* * *

A minute passed, then another, and nothing changed other than the amount of sweat beading on Shane's forehead. Then, as if a switch had been flipped, Ishmae's twitching limbs stilled. Color flooded back into her dark-skinned cheeks, and her breathing deepened from its shuddering rasp.

"It's working," whispered Vibe.

Which is, of course, when everything went to shit.

In his own way, Shane was every bit as unique as our High-Four Pyro. There was a reason Silt had named him Unicorn, and a reason that name had stuck. Healers like him came once a generation, if that. With the proper training, there was no telling what a High-Three Healer might accomplish.

But for all his power, Shane was just a first-year, like the rest of us. Partially trained. Still tripped up by the occasional bad habit.

Like forgetting to keep his patient sedated while he healed them.

Ishmae's eyes snapped open.

The world went white.

CHAPTER 36

I'm sorry, Shane.

Sorry I didn't stop you. Sorry you fell in love with a Pyro. Sorry it only took a single mistake to turn everything to ash.

In a better world, you'd still be here and I'd be gone.

In a better world, you'd be fixing this fucked-up life, one person at a time, like a ginger-haired promise of a future filled with something other than violence and death.

But this is Dr. Nowhere's world; cold and hard and bloody to the bone.

This is a world of Crows and monsters, of desperation and despair.

It has no time for hope or for healing.

It doesn't believe in unicorns.

CHAPTER 37

If there was any justice in the world, it would've rained at Shane's funeral; thick, fat drops exploding like liquid bombs against the hard earth, wind whipping between us with an almost-audible growl. Instead, the sky was cloudless, the sun was warm, and the clearing we'd gathered in behind the dean's office was fucking beautiful.

It was one of the few times since I'd left with Mr. Grey that I actually missed Bakersfield. *There's* a city fit for funerals.

There were twenty-one first-years present, arranged in uneven rows facing the casket the faculty had found for this occasion. The *empty* casket, because Phoenix hadn't left enough of Unicorn to even fill an urn.

Twenty-one students in the clearing because Ishmae herself was elsewhere, hidden away and drugged to her eyeballs.

Twenty-one because Vibe wasn't in any sort of state to be around people after experiencing Shane's dying emotions and the ensuing storm of Ishmae's own shock and mounting horror.

Twenty-one because Shane Stevenson was dead.

Twenty-one first-years and only three pairs of dry eyes among us.

The first belonged to Silt, who was busy comforting a sobbing Wormhole. The second belonged to Alan Jackson, who made a better stone wall than my roommate ever would.

And the last pair of dry eyes? They were mine. Because *of course* they fucking were.

Truth was, I hadn't cried since I was six. Spent a whole year after Mom's murder crying. Crying for her. Crying for myself. Crying whenever the older kids at Mama Rawlins' beat the shit out of me for crying.

By seven, I was all cried out. At eighteen, I could barely remember what it was like. I hadn't cried when they dug me out of the remnants of the Control class building, peeling me off of Vibe, who I'd shielded from some of the blast. Hadn't cried when they'd started treating my burns, when they'd ended up just slathering on ointments and wrapping me in bandages because Shane was right and some things really *were* beyond our school Healers' abilities. Hadn't even cried when I pulled myself off the med ward gurney and made the long, painful journey out to the clearing for Shane's funeral. Hadn't cried then, and wasn't going to cry now either.

That didn't mean I was happy or anything, standing there and looking at Shane's empty fucking casket. All it meant was that my eyes were dry. Conspicuously so.

As if I didn't already stand out enough.

I'd heard the whispers when I arrived. Twenty first-years in proper mourning colors, and here comes the Crow, wearing yet another pair of grey school sweats over his bandages. Asshole didn't bother to dress up for his own friend's funeral. Even Wormhole had given me a look halfway between outrage and dismay.

Wasn't like I had anything else to wear. Wasn't like I had any intention of telling them that either. They could go on assuming whatever the fuck they wanted.

Sometimes, I wonder how much shit I might've avoided if I hadn't been so concerned with my own pride.

It wasn't just first-years in the clearing, of course. Standing just past the casket was a row of faculty—Gabriella Stein conspicuous in her absence. And in front of his staff was the man himself, Jonathan Bard.

When I'd first met Bard outside his office, the dean had looked barely twenty—indistinguishable from any other graduate student at the Academy. Behind his desk, he'd looked closer to mid-thirties, baby face tempered by the mantle of authority.

Today, he looked almost as old as Amos, empty eyes fixed on the equally empty box in front of him.

"I met Shane when he was twelve," he finally said, his legendary voice scratched and worn. "He was in the hospital with his parents. Not because he was sick, but because other people were, and he wanted to help. His powers were barely active back then but he spent every weekend at L.A. General, doing what he could. Listening. Talking. Showing people that they weren't alone." He shook his head. "When his parents introduced us, he told me 'I'm going to make places like this unnecessary.' Just those words, from a twelve year old who looked even younger than his age, but I believed him. More importantly, I believed he would try. Not for glory. Not for endorsements, or money, or fame, but because he saw suffering and wanted to fix it. That's who Shane was. The man you called Unicorn."

Bard cleared his throat.

"During Orientation, I told you all that nobody makes it out of the Cape business alive. Over the past two decades, I've buried far too many former students. But they were all *former* students. The Academy is meant to be a place of safety, where you encounter nothing scarier than Nikolai's training sessions, or one of Amos' infamous pop quizzes. This is where you have the freedom to learn what it is to be a Cape without worrying that you'll pay that price prematurely. Yet here we are. Shane Stevenson is dead, and his dream is dead with him. That means we failed him. This school failed him. *I* failed him." He scanned the crowd of silent first-years, his gaze touching on each of us.

"Each of you is more than the power you've been gifted. You are young men and women, with hopes and dreams, fears and ambitions. You matter as individuals. Unicorn was a once-in-a-generation talent, but I urge you to remember who he was instead of what. There will be other Healers. There will be people similarly dedicated to removing suffering from the world. *There will never be another Shane.* Remember him. Honor him. In your own ways, try to emulate him." For the first time, Bard motioned to the faculty members behind him. "Your teachers will be having a remembrance ceremony tonight at Amos' house, here on campus. You are all welcome to attend. In the meantime, we will leave you to say your farewells in peace. Please use this time and space to honor his memory."

It was a good thought. Respectful. Appropriate.

Guess it won't shock any of you to hear that it all went to hell.

Or that I was at the center of the chaos, as fucking usual.

CHAPTER 38

I don't like graveyards. That's a weird thing for a Crow to say, but it's true. Never have, and probably never will. The clearing behind Bard's office wasn't a graveyard, the casket wasn't really a coffin, and Shane's body sure as hell wasn't anywhere inside of it, but even so, a part of me was back in the cemetery where Mom had been buried.

I looked down at the empty box and couldn't find any words to say.

I was the tenth or so first-year to visit the casket, but the others had gone in groups of two or three, clutching each other, crying, maybe even whispering some sort of goodbye or farewell, as if the little ginger was there and could hear them.

I was by myself, still dry-eyed, still silent, doing my best to ignore the eyes I could feel on me. Maybe if I'd had something to say, or if the weather *had* been shit, or if the other first-years hadn't happened to go still and quiet at that exact same moment, I wouldn't have heard her.

"It should have been him instead."

The words were whispered, but that whisper carried through the still air.

Olympia.

Two guesses who she was talking about.

I don't do grief well, but anger? Anger is my fucking kingdom. I spun away from Unicorn's empty coffin, and found her standing fifteen feet back with London, her silver eyes going wide with the realization that I'd heard.

"What did you say?"

Nine times out of ten, Olympia would've flinched just from me speaking to her. She'd have run away, I'd have felt like some sort of monster, and the standard cycle of Lightbringer-Crow bullshit would have kept on swirling.

This time, however, her eyes hardened, and her spine went stiff. "*I said it should have been you.* Shane is dead, Ishmae may have burned herself out, but somehow, we're still stuck with you."

"What the fuck is your problem?" I took two steps toward her, and this time, she *did* flinch. "Since the day I arrived, you've been pissing yourself every time we were even in the same room. Did we know each other in a past life or something? Or did your parents just not love you enough?"

She went bone-white, all the blood draining from her face, spun on one heeled foot, and fled the clearing. Just like that, the natural order of things had been restored.

Or it would've been, if London hadn't stepped forward instead. Like Olympia, she was all in black. Unlike Olympia, there was no fear whatsoever in her eyes.

"Fuck you, you asshole!"

"Your Lightbringer friend just told me she wished I had *died*, and *I'm* the asshole?"

"The asshole who brought up her family!"

What the hell did that even mean?

"Spectra's family were killed in Reno," said Santiago, strategically located near London, per usual. "Both parents and a little sister. Any surprise she's scared of Crows?"

"In Reno…" I scowled. "I'm not Crimson Death, for fuck's sake!"

"Are you sure about that?" Caleb left the crowd of first-years to meet me in the middle of the clearing. "The Academy's been here for eighteen years, and they've *never* had a student die. You show up, and just like that, we lose our Healer, and maybe even our High-Four." He sneered, playing to the crowd. "Only thing I can't figure out is how you did it."

For just one moment, everything was silent; a handful of first-years watching Caleb and I with wide eyes, Supersonic's sneer faltering as if he was only now realizing that he'd just accused me of murder.

In that moment, anything was possible. I could've swallowed my anger and walked away. I could've let someone—anyone—come to my defense. Hell, I could've even waited to see if Caleb would pull his head out of his own ass and apologize.

But the fucker had just accused me of murdering my friend. I leaned into that silence, met his blue eyes with mine, and bared my teeth. "Keep fucking with me and I promise you'll find out."

* * *

To hear Nikolai tell it, few Powers are more irritating in a fight than Flyboys and Jitterbugs. Their abilities mean they can come from almost anywhere, reach you before you know it, and be gone again before you can respond. Death by a thousand paper cuts.

But Nikolai was talking about veterans. Someone like Caleb—still a semester away from learning how to use his power in a fight—was entirely too predictable.

Doesn't matter how fast someone is going, even someone calling himself Supersonic, if they're traveling in a straight line. I didn't have to see him move to anticipate where he'd be, to slide out of his path and drive my knee into his midsection.

Flyboys and Jitterbugs are more durable than normal people. They have to be or their powers would kill them. But that's a long fucking way from the invulnerability of a Titan or even a Stalwart, and nobody is built to handle the air being blasted from their lungs.

Caleb went face-down and I was right on top of him, that same knee now planted in his back. I grabbed a handful of spiky black hair with one hand and pulled his head back and off the grass. Of its own accord, my other hand curled into a fist, and I drove it down toward the other first-year's head.

One thing I'd learned at Mama Rawlins' was how to throw a punch, but Nikolai's classes had taught me so much more—how to cork-screw my hips to increase the power of short strikes, how to add my own weight to downward blows, how to punch an inch or two through my target. I added every bit of what I'd learned to that punch.

That's probably not the sort of thing a Cape should admit to. Probably shouldn't tell you about the savage glee I felt either, as my fist shot downward. All I knew was that I'd lost my friend, and this asshole had picked the wrong fucking day to mess with me.

I know, I know; I've been saying that sort of shit for hours now, practically since the story began. I've been building up the tension and the angst and the fury and now that the moment I finally do *something* has arrived, here I am, *talking* again!

Get to the blood already, am I right?

Wish I could. Problem is, my whip-fast punch only made it about three inches before it stopped cold, an iron hand locked about my wrist. And before I could try one of those fancy escapes Nikolai had taught us, I was being pulled off of Caleb and tossed eight feet across the clearing.

So much for the bandages the Healers had wrapped my arm and back in. I could feel burnt skin tear as I hit, feel blisters pop, pus suddenly wet against the fire of my raw, still-forming layers of new skin. Not even the realization that my other hand held a clump of black hair, torn from Caleb's scalp, could outweigh that sudden rush of pain.

Paladin was there by the time I'd managed to stagger to my feet. Because *of course* it was Paladin who had stopped me. He slid past my punch—a punch that tore even more skin on my back—and got right up in my face. His blue eyes were blazing like tiny stars, but his voice was soft, the words meant only for me.

"Enough! I'm not letting either of you turn this memorial into a brawl."

Over Matthew's shoulder, I saw Caleb rolling to his feet, but Orca was there to stop him. Flyboys and Jitterbugs are a pain in the ass to fight, no doubt, but in the realm of close combat, nothing compares to a Stalwart. Other Powers have them beat on individual metrics—Titans are stronger, Jitterbugs are faster—but nobody blends everything together into *badass* quite like a Stalwart.

There's a reason Paladin—the real Paladin, not Matthew-fucking-Strich—had been one of my favorite Capes growing up. I had as much chance of getting past Matthew and Orca as Prince did of sprinting a five-minute mile. Shit just wasn't going to happen.

"He started it," I said instead, like a child.

"Maybe so… but you can finish it right now, by letting this go." His eyes bored into mine. "You didn't kill Unicorn and Caleb knows it. You're not going to kill Caleb, and *you* know that. Do you think this is what Shane would've wanted?"

"What the fuck do you know about Shane—?"

"Look around you, you jerk! Think about someone other than yourself for once in your life," he hissed. "We all knew Unicorn. We all *liked* him, Caleb included. You're not the only person who just lost a friend."

Against my better judgement, I took Paladin's advice and scanned the crowd. Wormhole was still weeping, clinging to Silt, who'd taken a step or two in my direction. Olympia was long gone, of course, but everyone else was still there. Most were watching the drama unfold with undisguised horror, but some of the class remained isolated in their own personal misery. Winter's long nose was bright red, dripping rivers of snot that mirrored the tears still streaming down her face. Tessa was kneeling in the grass, heedless of the stains it would leave on her ankle-length dress, her eyes closed and her hands clasped in front of her as her lips moved soundlessly through another prayer. Even Santiago—the always-slick, always-presentable El Bosque—was white-faced and red-eyed, holding onto London as much for his comfort as for hers.

Matthew was right. For all that Bard had said about Unicorn, maybe the biggest testament to the little ginger's character was that he'd somehow managed to befriend us all.

But that was the only thing Matthew was right about. Truth is, I didn't get the chance to finish anything. I was still looking at the circle of grieving first-years when I heard Orca cry out. I spun to see her stumble backwards. She came back to her feet in a smooth backwards somersault, but by then it was too late.

Rookie Jitterbugs are predictable. But that only matters if you're in a position to use that predictability against them.

Flat-footed and partially restrained, I never saw the punch that dropped me.

CHAPTER 39

There were times in that first year where the medical ward felt more like home than my actual dorm room. I sure as shit spent enough time there. Once again, I found myself waking up on a hard metal gurney, swaddled in bandages.

For a second, I wondered if the whole funeral had been a dream.

That question answered itself when I opened my eyes and saw Dean Bard seated in a chair next to me. He was still wearing the suit from Shane's service, and looked tired, old, and more than a little bit angry.

"You should see the other guy," I told him, wincing with each word. My jaw felt like it had been pounded with a sledgehammer. Given that I'd clearly been healed, Caleb's punch must have initially broken it.

"I *did* see the other guy, while you were being treated. Now it's your turn."

I'd never had a father figure in my life, since my biological dad was a murdering asshole monster and Mama Rawlins' wrinkled old booty call didn't want anything to do with us kids. Bard didn't qualify either, but there was something in the way he was looking at me—half-disappointed, half-resigned—that made me feel like a little boy being called to task.

Given what life as a little boy had been like, I can't say I enjoyed the feeling.

"You know Caleb started it, right? I didn't even punch him."

"Only because Mr. Strich was there to stop you."

"That's one way to look at it, I guess." I shrugged. They'd done what they could to fix my back again, but the new skin was tight under the many layers of fresh bandages. "Still, Supersonic attacked me. I just defended myself."

Bard's face hardened. When he finally spoke, there was nothing smooth about the words that came out. "I have multiple witnesses who will testify that you threatened Caleb's life. I have just as many who say that he blindsided you while Matthew was playing peacemaker. Truth be told, I don't particularly care about the details."

"Then what *do* you care about?" I shot back.

"Your future at my institution. I have neither the time nor the inclination to coddle you as if you were a child. You can either grow the fuck up or get the fuck out of my school."

I met the dean's cold-eyed glare with one of my own. "I'm betting Caleb didn't get that same ultimatum…"

"A bet you would lose. As I said, I saw him already."

"Oh." The thing about healing is that it takes a lot of its energy from the patient. I was exhausted, and that was making it hard to hold onto my anger. "So what did he say?"

"That is between Mr. Mikkazi and myself. At the moment, I am more interested in your response."

I turned my gaze to the ceiling. "You know I don't have anywhere else to go."

"Yes."

Bard could do more with a single word than most people could do with a monologue. I sighed.

"I wasn't trying to pick a fight. But Shane is… was… my friend. I'll be damned if I let anyone, from Caleb to Dominion himself, blame me for his death." I swallowed past the lump in my throat. "Or are you one of those people who think it was my fault?"

"I think there is ample blame to go around, but none of it falls upon you or Kayleigh Watai."

"Who then?"

"Ms. Stein for presenting the Maze to you first-years and then inadequately securing it. Ishmae for thinking that being a High-Four meant the rules did not apply to her. And last but not least, Shane himself."

That got my attention in a hurry. "*Shane?* How was any of this his fault?"

"He repeated young Ms. Naser's mistake. He overestimated his own training and proceeded recklessly. As great as his loss is, we are incredibly lucky that his actions didn't cause even more widespread tragedy."

My knuckles were white as I gripped the side of the metal gurney. "So all that crap you were saying about Shane earlier—"

"Was true," Bard finished, "if incomplete. Shane was a first-year. For all his power, he was still largely untrained. His decision to heal Ishmae rather than wait for assistance cost him his life. Even worse, it cost the world multiple decades of benefit from his gift."

"He didn't think she would survive long enough for us to wait for help."

"I know. I also know that he was in love with her, and there are few things less rational than a teenager in love." The hard lines of Bard's face softened. "But High-Four though she is, there is not a Cape in the Free States who would have willingly traded Shane's life for Ishmae's. And now, even that trade seems moot."

"What do you mean?"

He loosened his tie, and sank back into the chair. "Ishmae has chosen to leave the Academy."

"She *what*?"

"She just killed an innocent man, Mr. Banach. And not a stranger, but someone who cared for her, and who was himself destined for great things. That is the sort of weight that has broken older and stronger people than Ms. Naser."

"That's total bullshit," I growled. Bad enough that Shane had died because of her… now she was going to quit?!?

"It is also none of your concern," said Bard. "Particularly when you have problems of your own."

It was my turn to sigh. "What do you want from me, Bard? I'm doing my best. Hell, I even helped catch those two Shifters."

"Yes, you did. You've shown occasional flashes of potential. At the same time, I've received over a dozen complaints about you, the majority of them coming from your fellow first-years."

"That's bullshit too," I decided. "I haven't done a damn thing to any of them, unless you count bleeding all over Paladin and Orca. And the Viking. And Alan Jackson," I added after a moment's thought. Sometimes I thought the central theme of Nikolai's class was me getting my ass kicked. "Most of them hated me from the moment they found out what I was."

"True enough."

"That's all you have to say? *True enough*?"

"Hatred is something that *every* Cape must deal with, believe it or not. Powers are fundamentally different from the rest of us, and humanity has a long history of hating those who are different. Capes are the key to our nation's survival, but public sentiment is a fickle beast. It's the reason every Cape team has a public relations office, and it's the reason we pour funding into Cape vids and merchandising. It's also one of the core reasons this Academy even exists; to teach you control, so that you can fight without leaving a swath of death and destruction in your wake. It'll be years before we recover from what happened in Palo Alto last year. Another catastrophe and everything that has been built in this country over the last seven decades could slip away."

"I get all that. Amos has told us what it was like in the days after the Break."

"And you were actually awake to hear it?" Bard shook his head in mock astonishment. "Clearly, the rumors of your academic inattention have been exaggerated."

I rolled my eyes. "I know why normal people might fear or hate those of us with abilities. But the first-years are Powers too. So why do they hate *me*?"

"Of all people, you must understand why people would fear a Crow."

"Because we're insane, murdering assholes…. sure. But you saw what Ishmae did. She could've killed thousands of people when Shane woke her up—would have if her fire hadn't mostly gone vertical—but for some reason I'm the one everyone is terrified of. How does that make any sense? I see ghosts. She incinerates fucking cities!"

"A High-Four *is* terrifying, Mr. Banach. A Full-Five even more so. But Dominion and Grannypocalypse … in the end, they can only kill you."

"And that's a good thing?"

"It's a reality the world has adjusted to, post-Break. Life is precious, but it is also fleeting. There's a reason the concept of an afterlife holds such sway. Heaven, Valhalla, even the great wheel of karma; each suggests that physical death is not the end, but a gateway to something greater beyond this broken plane of existence."

"I have no idea where you're going with this," I admitted.

"What happened to the souls of those Lord Bone raised? What happens to the spirits that the Crimson Death consumed?"

"I don't know."

"Nobody does. That's the point. As awe-inspiring as other powers might be, they can only destroy the body. A Crow—and only a Crow—can do more."

"What about the Singer?"

"A Power who can literally sing someone out of existence?" Bard rolled his eyes. "The Voidsinger is a myth, Damian. Crows, on the other hand, are all too real."

"So the first-years are…what…? Worried that I'm going to snack on their souls like synth-rations? That's the dumbest thing I've ever heard!"

"Says the eighteen-year-old who threatened to kill someone, raise their corpse as a Walker, and send it home to murder their family."

I shifted uncomfortably on the gurney. How the hell had he heard about that? "If you know I'm sleeping through Amos' class, you also know that whole threat was a bluff. I can't do anything like that."

"Not yet."

"Even if I could, I wouldn't!"

"The two Shifters didn't know that."

"No shit! That's why the bluff worked!"

"And how many of the first-years do you think that same bluff would have worked on?"

I shrugged. "I don't know. A handful, maybe."

"I think you'd be surprised. We fear the unknown, Damian, and you remain an unknown to most of your classmates."

"Yeah, well… that's on them, not me."

"Is it? If it weren't for your history project, would you have spoken to any of your classmates other than Shane?"

I fixed my eyes on the ceiling. "If you have a point, please just say it. My head is killing me."

"When you graduate—if you graduate—you will join a team. You will need to trust the people on that team and they will need to trust you. For the next two and a half years, the class of 76 *is* your team. None of you have the luxury of remaining isolated. You're going to have to make the other first-years see you as more than just a Crow."

"That wasn't part of our deal."

"It is now." Bard rose to his feet. "You can start with the two first-years waiting outside."

He was halfway to the door when my voice stopped him.

"Was Olympia's family really in Reno?"

"Yes."

"Jesus. Why would you put me in her class?"

Bard's tone was almost wry. "You may recall that I had very little choice in the matter."

"You could've said no."

"And risked my funding when the budget comes up for renewal next year? True enough. If you hadn't convinced me otherwise, I might have done just that. But I chose to believe that you could be more than your power."

"I *am*."

"Prove it to your classmates. Prove it to Olympia Kennedy. Help her move past the blind hatred and fear that could derail her career before it even starts."

"That's a hell of a lot to ask."

"Welcome to life as a Cape, Damian. There are no easy missions."

CHAPTER 40

I was still chewing on the dean's parting words when my next visitor came in. When Bard had said there were first-years waiting to talk with me, I'd assumed one would be Vibe, looking for a little bit of emotion-deprivation time, and the other would be Silt. With Unicorn dead, they were the closest things to friends I had left on campus.

Instead, I looked up into the bearded face of my roommate, Jeremiah. "I brought a change of clothes," he said, waving the stack of grey sweats in his hands.

"What?"

"I figured you'd rather not walk back across campus half-naked." He nodded at my bandage-covered chest. Given the mess I'd made of my back—again—they'd had to cut my sweatshirt right off of me.

I eyed the fresh clothes warily. "Where did you get them?"

One bushy eyebrow went up. "From your closet, obviously." Stonewall shook his head. "I'm not sure where you put the rest of your clothes. All I saw in there were school sweats… and a couple of old t-shirts."

I pulled myself up to a seated position, ignoring the way the skin on my back pulled. "Stay out of my stuff. Stay out of my fucking *life*."

He tossed the neatly folded clothes down onto the foot of my gurney. "I guess gratitude was too much to ask for, huh?"

"You think I should be grateful?" Just that quickly, Bard's words of advice were forgotten. I gripped the edges of the gurney to keep from doing anything stupid, feeling the metal edges biting into my palms. "*To you?* After the shit you've pulled?"

"What the hell are you talking about, freak?" In six months, I'd never really seen Jeremiah angry, but from the way his voice had dropped to a low growl, that was about to change.

"I *know*, you asshole! All about your group project. That you've been fucking *researching* me!"

Someone as dark as Jeremiah Jones can't really go pale, but he took a half-step back. "How—?"

"Because I'm not a fucking idiot, that's how! I'm not an idiot, and I don't want your fucking charity."

"They're *your* fucking clothes, you asshole. This isn't charity."

"Then what is it?" I sneered.

"It's me protecting the campus from being blinded by your lily-white ass," he shot back. "And maybe letting you know that nobody thinks you had anything to do with Shane's death."

I rolled my eyes, but before I could say anything, he just kept on going.

"And sure, you're right about our project being on Crows, and that you were originally a part of it," he continued angrily, "but we decided a few days ago not to use you in our presentation."

That sucked some of the fire out of my anger. "Why?"

"Because we're training to be Capes, you asshole! Capes save people. They don't make things worse for them. Even when those people are dicks who really, really deserve it."

"*Capes save people?*" With all that had happened over the past few days, it took me a moment to place where I'd heard that before. "You've been talking to Kayleigh."

"Vibe? No. It was Poltergeist who put her foot down." Jeremiah shifted uneasily. "She was right though."

"Yeah, she was." If I lived to be one hundred, I was never going to figure Tessa out. "None of you had any right to dig up my past."

"It's public information," he began.

"It's *my life*! My family. My history."

"I know." When someone Jeremiah's size sighs, it's hard not to hear it. "I get it. I'm sorry."

For a long moment, the only sound came from the big man shifting his weight and shuffling his feet. It was my turn to sigh.

"Whatever. It happened and it's over with. It's not like killing your whole group will change that." I rolled my eyes again as he swallowed hard. "That's a joke. I'm pretty sure someone would stop me before I could get all of you." That was *also* a joke… but apparently he didn't see the humor in it. "So you're sticking with the project topic?"

"Yeah. There isn't time to find a new one—"

"Fine."

"—and we've already spent weeks on our presentation, and…" He trailed off. "Did you say *fine*? You?"

"My dad killed my mother." It was the first time I'd said those words aloud since arriving on campus, and they hurt. The fact that I was saying them to someone I didn't even consider a friend just made it worse. "And he's nothing compared to the real Black Hats. I'm here so I *won't* go nuts… so I can maybe even do some good, but nobody knows whether that is going to work. Likelihood is, any Crow you encounter in the wild is going to be a frothing-at-the-mouth, corpse-fucking asshole. Knowing how to spot them… knowing how to stop them, even…" I shrugged. "Why would I be against that?"

"It's not like we came up with some sort of guide to Crow-killing or anything," said Jeremiah. "They've all been different, and they've all been put down differently too. We're just trying to give a historical overview of the big names."

"As long as I'm left the fuck out of it."

"You will be. I already dumped the data we managed to dig up." He paused. "I know it's none of my business, but… I *am* sorry about your mom."

"Yeah." Off to the side, Mom's ghost was swaying back and forth, her faded sundress clipping in and out of the nearest gurney. "Everyone's sorry except the asshole himself."

He stood there awkwardly for a bit longer, then shrugged. "Anyway. See you around, Skeletor."

"It seems likely." Silt still hadn't explained that nickname to me. "Thanks for the clothes."

* * *

My second visitor wasn't Silt or Vibe either, but I was way happier to see Orca than I had been Jeremiah. It helped that she was still in the dress she'd worn to Shane's funeral.

I know I've talked a lot about Nadia. Some of you are probably sick of hearing about her by now, but considering that I'm the one telling this story, I'd say you're all shit out of luck. Drag your incorporeal asses back into the afterlife if it bothers you so much.

What's that? Still here? Imagine that. Must suck knowing that I'm the only show in town.

Anyway… Nadia Kahale, codename Orca. Flawless olive skin, dirty-blonde hair down to her waist, and eyes the color of sea foam. Seeing her poured into a little black dress made suitable for a funeral only by its color was enough to make me forget Caleb's sucker punch.

Almost.

"Nadia? What's up?"

"Not much." Her pale eyes flickered down my bandaged form for just a moment as she made her way over to the gurney. "I came to apologize."

I've always had good eyesight, but somehow Orca got prettier with every step she took. She walked like she fought; all smooth, flowing motion, like water rushing downhill. Up close, whatever perfume she had on cut right through the stale odor of dried blood and gauze.

By the time she'd reached me, I was starting to think I actually owed Caleb my thanks. First time Nadia had spoken to me all year, and she was in something other than Academy sweats. A (briefly) broken jaw was so worth it.

"Apologize? For what?"

"I misjudged the depths of Supersonic's motivation," she told me, the words slow and lightly accented, "and allowed him to break free as a result."

"Yeah. And…?"

A small vertical line appeared between her eyebrows. "And that's why he was able to hit you. That's why you're here."

"If it hadn't been Caleb's weak-ass punch, it would've been tomorrow's class with Nikolai." I shrugged. "Gladys says I spend so much time here, I should just move my stuff in and stay." As if I'd needed further confirmation that the old Healer had a thing for me.

"Gladys?"

"The head Healer?" I frowned. "Have you ever even been treated here?"

"Not yet." She shook her head, sending dirty blonde hair slithering over one shoulder. "I have high hopes for this week's match with Paladin though."

"Well, a trip to the medical ward isn't a big deal," I said. "Hell, the last time you and I sparred, I ended up here with way worse than just a busted jaw."

"That's different." She colored slightly under my incredulous look. "That was a fair fight. You had ample time to call on your power like you did against Matthew, but decided not to. You deserved your beating."

"I didn't *decide* not to. I seriously have no idea how to repeat whatever that was. Assuming it was something at all."

"If you say so. Anyway, we're straying from my point. I'm sorry for failing to subdue Supersonic, and for the damage you suffered as a result. Even though you did provoke him into action, my responsibility in the matter was clear."

I puzzled my way through that tightly packed apology before offering up a shrug. "Don't worry about it. Like I said, I'm fine."

"Okay." She nodded once, then spun on her heel, heading for the door.

"That's it?"

She stopped, looking back over one shoulder in an unconscious echo of Bard's pose fifteen minutes earlier. "That's all I wanted to say. Was there something more you wanted to talk about?"

"Not really. I just…" In that little dress, she looked even better leaving than she had coming in. Before I could catch myself, I heard the words slipping out. "Do you want to get some coffee and hang out sometime?"

She gave it less than a second's thought. "Not at all."

"Oh."

"But if you do remember how to trigger your power," she continued, "I'd be more than happy to spar again."

Stalwarts are their own special brand of crazy.

* * *

Between the fight with Caleb, Bard's unique combination of pep talk and lecture, and being completely shut down by Orca, it's fair to say my mind had managed to focus on pretty much anything *but* Shane's death for the better part of a day. But as I left the med center and made my way back across campus, all those other distractions fell away again.

Whatever the next few months held, whatever my roommate had done or would do, whatever my future as a Cape or Black Hat might be, there was one truth that was inescapable: Unicorn was gone, and despite the dozens of people currently crisscrossing the school grounds, the Academy felt empty as a result.

The faculty were having their own memorial service, attended, no doubt, by the majority of first-years, but I headed for my dorm room. Bard's advice could wait for another day. Improving relations with Olympia—however the fuck I was going to manage that—could wait for another day too. All I wanted to do was sleep—and grieve—in peace.

The common room was empty, like I'd expected. My dorm room was too, but I'd been on my bed for a minute at best when a knock came at the door.

I waited for whoever it was to go away, but another knock came shortly after, this time followed by Silt's voice.

"Damian?"

Unlike Nadia, Sofia had taken the time to change, and was now wearing a pair of plaid pajama bottoms under a long pink tank top. Her brown eyes were as dry as they'd been at Shane's funeral, but her face was pinched and drawn.

"Is everything okay?" I looked over her shoulder at the empty hall. "Is Wormhole—?"

"Evie's fine. Cried herself out and I tucked her in about ten minutes ago or so." Silt's voice was even gruffer than usual. "Glad to see they patched you back up already." She didn't wait for a reply, but slid past me into my dorm room, where she got the five second tour by virtue of heading to the center and slowly turning around.

I let the hallway door close, and leaned against it. "What can I do for you, Sofia?"

She didn't answer for a moment, face turned to our room's one window. Finally, she sighed. "If you tell anyone about this, I'll kill you."

A few things clicked into place. Her state of dress. The fact that she'd waited for everyone to be gone or asleep before coming to my bedroom. Maybe even why she'd bothered to be friends with me.

The problem was… I didn't feel that way about Sofia at all.

I wasn't a blushing virgin or anything—Alicia the slushy girl had seen to that—but it wasn't like I'd seen much other action at Mama Rawlins'. I certainly hadn't ever had to deal with letting someone down easily, outside of very young girls with puppy-dog crushes on the oldest orphan in the house.

"Sofia, I…"

I'd only made it through those two words when Silt finally turned around, took two steps and threw herself at me. I barely managed to catch her, but as soon as I did, she dropped her head against my chest and began to cry.

Oh.

This was something life at Mama Rawlins had taught me how to deal with. I wrapped my arms around the stocky Earthshaker and held her as she wept.

CHAPTER 41

I'd never woken up in bed with a woman I cared about before. Alicia and I had only ever fooled around at the shop; brief moments of pleasure that ended with her going back to her parents and me returning to Mama Rawlins'. Waking up next to a warm, curvy body showed me I'd been missing something. The soft, full boob under my hand didn't hurt at all.

It took my brain a handful of seconds to realize that it was *Silt's* boob that I was holding. I let go of it in a hurry, and scooted back to put some space between us… or at least as much space as the small bed allowed.

We were both still fully clothed, of course. Once Silt started crying, I'd finally realized she had come to me for comfort and not some hot Crow action. I'd held her on the bed until she cried herself out, much like she must have done for Wormhole earlier that day. Before I knew it, she was snoring against my chest. I'd thought about waking her, but sometime in the middle of that internal debate, I'd apparently dropped off as well.

There'd been nothing sexual at all about our night together. Which didn't save me from embarrassment when Jeremiah walked in that next morning.

"Shit!" His eyes were white craters in the darkness of his face as he took Silt and I in with a single glance. "Put a sock on the door or something in the future. Please!"

That was enough to wake up Silt as well, but while she was still fumbling towards full consciousness, I was springing out of bed. "This isn't what it looks like, Jeremiah."

"This is a judgement-free dorm room," he said. "If she wants to experiment…"

Wait. If *she* wanted to experiment? Even though nothing had happened, even though neither Silt nor I had wanted anything to happen, I found myself more than a little insulted. Since when did sleeping with me count as experimentation?

"I thought you were at Hektor's," said Silt, sleepily rolling out of bed to stretch like she didn't have a care in the world.

"Why would he have been at Hektor's?" I frowned.

"Why do you think?" Silt rolled her eyes, then turned back to my roommate. "Anyway, there wasn't any experimentation going on here, Stonebrain. I just badly needed a friend, and Boneboy gives good hugs."

"He does?"

"I do?" I asked, at almost the same time.

"Surprised me too," said Silt with a shrug. "Anyway, thanks for the best night of sleep I've had in a while, but I should go check on Evelyn and make sure she's doing better."

She was halfway out the door when I realized I had something to do as well. I followed her out.

"Hugs are all well and good, Boneboy, but I'm not going to let you follow me home."

"Shockingly," I said right back, "this isn't about you. I just remembered something Bard told me yesterday."

"And whatever this was means you need to go somewhere at the god-awful time Stonewall woke us up at?"

"The earlier I go, the more time I'll have to change her mind."

Silt's yawn was so wide I could actually hear her jaw pop. "Whose mind? What are you talking about?"

"Ishmae's." I felt Silt pause more than I saw it, but I kept going. When she'd caught back up to me, I added the rest. "Bard says she's quitting the Academy."

"And you want to stop her?"

"Not really." I held open the door to the common room and followed Sofia in. "But I think Shane would've wanted me to."

* * *

The first step was actually finding Ishmae. She hadn't returned to her and Tessa's room since Shane's death, and I knew for a fact that she wasn't in the medical ward, but where did that leave?

"Maybe we should just wait for Bard to get back and ask him?"

I shook my head. "We don't know how long he'll be away. The way he said it, Ishmae could leave at any time."

"Well, wandering the campus isn't getting us anywhere."

"You didn't have to come along. You can always go check on Wormhole like you'd planned."

"Cram it up your ass, Boneboy. Unicorn was my friend too. Evie will understand." Sofia dropped down onto one of the many benches that dotted the campus' walking paths. "I'm just saying we should walk smarter, not harder."

I gingerly lowered myself onto the same bench, mindful again of the torn skin on my back. Despite the healing I'd received, there was a dull ache in the right side of my face, and one glance in a mirror had shown the mottled yellow of a slowly healing bruise.

"So where do you think we should look then?"

Silt shrugged. "That's the question, isn't it? Unicorn healed her before she killed him, which is why she wasn't in the med ward. And they're probably worried she could be a danger to others, given her state of mind, which is why she never returned to her dorm room. But then where—"

It was the *state of mind* phrase that did it. I saw Silt's brown eyes widen as we both came to the same realization.

"Dr. Gibbings!"

"Alexa," I said, at the same time.

"Who's Alexa?"

Apparently, not all of us were on a first-name basis with the school counselor. But when I explained, Silt shook her head.

"Dr. Gibbings' first name is Stephanie."

"I go see her every week, Sofia. I think I know her name." I rolled my eyes. "Tall, slim, and monochromatic? Doesn't blink and curses almost as much as me?"

"Damian…" Silt's rough voice was confused. "Dr. Gibbings is pushing sixty, even wider than I am, and would probably faint if she heard the word *fuck*."

"That doesn't make any sense."

"Maybe they're sisters or something?"

I shook my head. "There are only diplomas for one doctor on the wall."

"Wow; you really *do* go there a lot."

"It's that or get my ass thrown out on the street."

"Well, either way, I think Dr. Gibbings is our best chance of finding Ishmae." Silt was built like a tree stump, but the majority of that was muscle; she bounced up from the bench with a grace that made me feel even clumsier than usual. "Shall we?"

* * *

Dr. Gibbings was exactly as Silt had described her, white-haired and maternal, seated behind the desk in the same office I'd been coming to for months. Even the diplomas, on careful re-examination, all said Stephanie Gibbings. With my mind going a thousand miles a second, I barely heard Silt trying to talk the older woman into giving up Ishmae's location. If this was Dr. Gibbings, then who the fuck had I been seeing all this time? Who was Alexa?

For the first time since my arrival at the Academy, I had to seriously question my own sanity. What if Alexa was someone I'd dreamed up, a mental projection of what I thought a shrink should be? What if I'd spent the last few months only *thinking* I was going to the counselor? If I was already that far gone, what chance did I have?

The only thing that kept me from truly freaking out was that I *knew* the office we were standing in. That meant I had to have seen it before… didn't it?

I'd missed a session with Alexa while I was being healed from Ishmae's fire, but I decided then and there that I was bringing someone else with me when I came for my next session. And if Alexa *was* here, and she *was* real, I was going to have some serious fucking questions for her.

In the periphery of my awareness, I saw the moment the real Dr. Gibbings finally gave in to Silt's arguments, learning—as those of us in the Fearsome Five already had—that the Earthshaker was an avalanche in motion; inescapable and unrelenting. The old counselor sighed and said something, waving a pudgy hand at the door.

"What did she say?" I asked, once Silt and I were both back in the hallway.

"Weren't you listening?"

"I was a little busy wondering who the fuck Alexa is, and whether or not she's a product of my Crow-given insanity."

That drew Sofia up short. "Do you think that's possible?"

"No clue, but if you or Vibe are willing to come along to my next session, I'm going to damn well find out."

"Deal." Silt was one of the few first-years who never seemed particularly concerned about either my power or my looming insanity. Even Shane, who saw my insanity as a new challenge for healing, had sometimes gotten freaked out. But Sofia just rolled on, and God help anyone who got in her way. "But first, let's go talk to the little Pyro." She frowned again. "Are you *sure* Shane would've wanted us to convince Ishmae to stay? She did kill him."

"This is Unicorn we're talking about," I reminded her. "Since when would he have held *that* against her?"

* * *

Ishmae wasn't all that far away. The same building that had the counselor's office also had a handful of visitors' suites, and the young Pyro was staying in the third one down the hall. The door was closed, but it opened within seconds of Silt's knock.

"Oh." Phoenix looked from Sofia to I and something in her wilted. She turned and stepped back into the room without another word, seemingly indifferent to whether the two of us followed her in or not.

Needless to say, we marched inside.

"How are you doing, Ishmae?" Sofia's voice was uncharacteristically kind.

"Fine." The Pyro slouched on the foot of her suite's bed, eyes downcast.

"You don't look fine." I shrugged when Silt shot me a look. "What? She doesn't."

It was true; Ishmae had always been young and small, but she'd had a sense of presence to her—part ego, part pride, part awareness of her power. All of that was gone, and without it, she looked even younger than her age, lost beneath her voluminous robes. The dark circles under her eyes didn't help, nor did the fingernails that she'd clearly been gnawing on.

I'd only come because it was what Shane would have wanted, but looking at the emotional wreckage perched on the bed in front of us, I couldn't help but feel sorry for her. As much death as I'd already seen, I'd at least never been responsible for it.

Directly responsible for it, anyway, I silently amended, thinking of the men Her Majesty had shredded north of Los Angeles.

"Did you two come to taunt me or to punish me?" Ishmae's voice was barely more than a breath.

"Neither." Silt traded a brief, troubled look with me, before continuing. "We heard that you were thinking of leaving—"

"Yes."

"Are you sure you want to do that? I know how much being a Cape means to you."

"I can't stay here." For just a moment, fire flickered deep in Ishmae's eyes. "And I'm not a Cape. Not now. Not ever."

"You can't let one accident…"

"Accident?!? *I murdered Shane!* A boy who was never anything but nice, who was our nation's best hope as a Healer, and I turned him to ash. What kind of a hero does that?"

"Someone who's still figuring this shit out, like the rest of us," I told her.

"That's easy for you to say."

"Right. Because fuck knows, being a Crow is a walk in the park."

Ishmae lifted bloodshot eyes to meet mine. "You were there, weren't you?"

It didn't take a genius to know what she was talking about. "Yeah. Kayleigh, Unicorn and I."

"Then I almost killed you and Vibe too. You should be happy that I'm leaving."

"Maybe I should be. Or maybe I should've kept Shane from trying to heal you until more help arrived. I could've done it, easily enough."

"So why didn't you?"

"Because he was an adult. Unicorn knew the risks, he knew what was at stake, and he thought you were worth the effort."

Large tears were cascading down the Pyro's dark cheeks. "He was wrong."

"I guess time will tell." I shrugged. "But the thing is… if you run away now, if you take all your power and bury it, what will he have died for?"

"Nothing," she said in a small voice. "He died for nothing at all."

"It doesn't have to be that way—" tried Silt.

"But it is. I appreciate all this, but I think you both should go now."

"That's it, then?"

"Go away. Please."

I don't know if it was the emotion in her plea that got us moving or if it was the way the tears streaming down her face had started to sizzle like butter on a hot pan. Either way, Sofia and I had retreated all the way to the door when Ishmae called my name. I turned back.

"Is it true that you see ghosts?"

"Sometimes, yeah."

"If you ever see Shane's ghost, could you… could you please tell him I'm sorry?"

My eyes drifted to a point above and behind her. "He knows, Ishmae. He knows, and he forgives you. Now, you just need to forgive yourself."

I waited for a reply, but she curled up on the bed, burying her head in a pillow and tangled mess of sheets.

* * *

Silt and I were silent until we left the building. Then the Earthshaker turned to me. "That was ballsy. I'm just sorry it didn't work."

"What was ballsy?"

She shook her head and sighed. "I still don't know you all that well, but I'm pretty sure I can tell when you're lying. You didn't actually see Shane's ghost, did you?"

I thought back to that moment in Phoenix's room, when the dead Healer had first appeared behind Ishmae. I thought of the snarl that twisted his pale, freckled face, the diamond hardness of his eyes and the way he'd stomped and raged in a circle around the seated Pyro, like an unseen storm trying to vent its fury upon unsuspecting passers-by.

"No," I agreed. "I didn't see him at all."

* * *

The next day, Ishmae was gone.

CHAPTER 42

A week without classes at the Academy should have been the next best thing to an all-day orgy, but the circumstances behind our mini-vacation made it feel almost like a punishment. The crying petered out after a day or two, but a dark cloud followed every first-year as we trudged back and forth to the cafeteria, or as individual students slipped out to meet with the counselor.

Which counselor they were meeting with was, of course, a question very much on my mind.

In that monotonous, seemingly endless week, two moments stood out.

First was round two with Caleb Mikkazi, aka Supersonic, aka Sergeant Sucker Punch. In a normal week, between the communal bathroom and the fact that we all had the exact same class schedule, a quick confrontation would have been all but inevitable.

On this particular week, we successfully avoided each other for almost a full day. But on Tuesday, I entered the common room from the boys' hall at the very same time that Supersonic was coming in from outside. I'm not sure which of us changed direction first, but a few steps later, we met just behind the main couch.

"Crow." Caleb couldn't help but glance at the still-healing bruise on my jaw and cheek, but he managed to keep his habitual smirk hidden.

"Fuck off."

"I'd be happy to, but I've been…" he paused, his scowl adding emphasis to the next word, "*instructed* to apologize for knocking you on your bony ass."

"Something you only managed because Paladin was holding me down," I shot back. "Before that, I seem to remember you eating dirt from a single knee."

Caleb's Adam's apple bobbed up and down, bright spots of color appearing in his cheeks. "Paladin or no Paladin, if you ever threaten me again, you'll see exactly what this Jitterbug can do."

"And if you accuse me of killing my friend again, I promise I won't stop with just a threat."

"Oh for the love of God, could you two give it a rest already?" That was Winter, who was sitting on the couch, her long white hair braided and twisted into one of the dumbest-looking hairstyles I'd ever seen.

"Or at least move on from this metaphoric dick-measuring contest to something a little more definitive." That was Tessa.

"Definitive how?" asked London, who had deigned to be cuddled by Santiago in one of the overstuffed chairs.

"Pants to the floor, whip out their cocks, and settle this bullshit once and for all." Tessa's smile was sharp. "Assuming anyone has a tape measure small enough?"

"Seriously, Poltergeist?" Caleb turned away from me to shoot the brunette a glare.

"Don't worry; I'm sure some woman out there still mistakenly believes that size doesn't matter."

"I don't know, Tessa… unless Skeletor sleeps with a billy club in his pants, you might need an *actual* ruler," mused Silt, who had manifested in the door to the girls' hall like some sort of avenging angel of humiliation. "Because something was sure squashed up against my ass the other night."

"Maybe it was his thumb?" mused London sweetly. Next to her, Santiago coughed and went beet red for some reason.

"Nah. Trust me… I know *exactly* where his hands were."

Fucking hell. Caleb and I traded glances, and then made for opposite doors as quickly and as quietly as possible. The Jitterbug may have won our first showdown, but I'm pretty sure we *both* lost the second.

* * *

The other event of note occurred the following weekend, a day before classes were to resume. Most of the first-years had slept in, tired and hungover from a night at The Liquid Hero. For only the second time ever, Jeremiah had invited me to join them, but I'd chosen not to attend. I wanted a clear head for Sunday's showdown.

I also wanted a reliable witness. Thankfully, Vibe was waiting in the common room as promised. The little Empath had come back to the dorms on Monday, and had stopped by my room every day since for some Crow-granted emotional deafness. During one of those visits, I'd broached the issue of my possibly non-existent counselor, and she'd agreed to come with me to my next session with Alexa.

She held my hand the entire way across the campus. As empty as the grounds were, I wasn't sure it was strictly necessary for her to maintain contact, but I wasn't going to complain. Since Shane's death, I'd been disconnected and weirdly distant. It felt like her cold hand was the only thing keeping me from floating away entirely.

I was also terrified and trying not to show it. If Alexa wasn't there… if Alexa didn't really exist… it would mean I'd already truly lost it, that none of this training had done a damn thing to fix me, and that I'd be out on my ass within minutes of Bard finding out. I'd have little choice but to check myself into an asylum and pray that they were equipped to keep me from hurting anyone.

The waiting room outside the office was the same as I remembered it from my sessions and the trip with Silt. I turned the knob on the office door, nudged it open with one toe, and risked a peek inside.

Alexa's black eyes moved from me to Vibe.

"Do you see her too?"

Vibe nodded, frowning. "That's not Dr. Gibbings."

"Very true," agreed Alexa pleasantly, long fingers steepled on the desk in front of her.

"Who are you then?" asked the Empath.

"I think that should be between my patient and me, Ms. Watai," the other woman answered smoothly, "although I am pleased to see you taking an interest in your classmates. Perhaps those Control lessons are paying off after all. Now, would you excuse us? Damian has already missed one session, and for the sake of his continued enrollment here, I'd prefer he not miss a second one."

I nodded when Kayleigh looked at me for confirmation. "It's fine. I really appreciate your coming all the way over, but now that I know she's real, *Alexa* is right. We have a whole fucking lot to talk about."

She gave a half-nod, let go of my hand, and then leaned in. "Be careful. She's not exactly like you, but I can't read her at all."

That was more than a little interesting. I waited for the door to close behind the departing Empath, and then I folded my arms across the chest, leaned against the nearby wall, and shot Alexa a look. "Who are you?"

She nodded to the couch. "Why don't you have a seat, and I'll tell you."

"I'm doing fine over here." I waved at Stephanie Gibbings' diplomas. "Are you even a real shrink?"

"According to Stanford University, yes." Her smile was razor sharp.

"But you're not Dr. Gibbings.... right?" I'd never heard of a Shifter that had different human forms, let alone one that was also a psychiatrist, but there was a first time for everything.

"As I told Ms. Watai, I am not."

"Funny how you didn't make that clear in a single one of our sessions over the past five fucking months."

"Did I *ever* claim to be Dr. Gibbings?"

"That's not the point."

"Isn't it? I gave you my name."

"Your first name."

"The only name I am at liberty to share with you, Damian. And, I might add, a name that quite clearly does not figure in any of the very many diplomas you keep waving at."

"So all I have is your word that you're even a professional. Why the hell should I trust you?"

"I would point to the sessions we've already had, and the good I believe those sessions have accomplished, but the truth is even simpler; I am the only person qualified to give you what you want."

I frowned again. "What I want?"

"In our very first session, you told me you wanted someone that could determine if you were going insane… and who could stop you if you did." Black eyes flickered with some emotion I couldn't decipher. "Having met Stephanie Gibbings, do you believe she would be able to do either of those two things?"

She had a point. I was pretty sure the grandmotherly Dr. Gibbings would have a heart attack the first time I even swore in her presence.

"And you could? Stop me, I mean?"

"Yes."

"And I should just… believe you?"

For the first time since I'd met her, the monochromatic psychiatrist rose from her chair, exposing long legs mostly hidden by an equally long skirt. She drummed her fingers on the desk's surface and then met my eyes.

"There are three people on this campus that even know I am here. Four, now that you've brought young Vibe into the fold."

"Is Bard one of them?"

"He is the one who asked me to come. I owed him—and his wife—a favor, and he called it in on your behalf."

"How did you know Bard?"

"A long time ago, and for a very brief time, I was a Cape."

Maybe if I'd had a normal childhood, one spent playing outside with other children or going to school or doing anything beyond watching hero vids—first to distract myself and later to distract the new kids at Mama Rawlins'—that admission wouldn't have meant anything. But for me, everything clicked.

"Holy shit! You're Midnight!"

After almost five months, the slight flutter of one eyelid was the closest I'd seen Alexa come to showing her surprise. "What makes you say that?"

"I saw the fight with Professor Inferno." The vid had focused primarily on Rocket, the chiseled Flyboy who'd first broken the speed of sound, but in the background had been the other members of his team; Blue Shock, Talon, and—most distant of all—the tall, slim figure known only as Midnight. "It was Midnight's only broadcast appearance, and she was masked, but you move like she did… and have the same color scheme, for that matter."

Alexa shook her head. "Jonathan said you were barely passing History. I'll let him know that Amos may simply not be challenging you enough."

"So you *are* her? Midnight, I mean?"

"I was."

Midnight had been a Shadecaster, although the exact extent of her powers had been as mysterious as the woman herself. That was before the advent of sponsorship money and marketing opportunities… when secret identities were still a thing. If Alexa was Midnight, I was pretty sure she was more than capable of stopping me, as promised.

Alexa leaned over the desk, her voice intent. "That information cannot leave this room, Damian. Even one more person knowing my identity puts the lives of those I know and love at risk."

"But you're not a Cape anymore."

"There are other ways for a Power to serve the Free States than by being a Cape."

That threw me for a bit of a loop. As far as I know, the only alternative was to join the government's mundane workforce, but that didn't sound like what she was talking about. And it certainly wouldn't have required secrecy.

"I won't tell anyone," I promised. "But if my knowing puts you in danger, why did you even let me guess?"

She shrugged. "Therapy relies on trust between patient and doctor. I can either try to repair that trust or vacate the position Jonathan asked me to fill."

"What happens if you do leave?"

"I don't know. He'll find someone else, I suppose."

"*Another* psychiatrist who's also a Power, and ready and capable of putting down a Cat Three Crow?"

"I didn't say it would be easy." Her lips twitched in that almost-smile. "But Bard will do what he must. He always does." She nodded to the couch I had yet to sit in. "The decision is yours. Is my Cape identity sufficient coin to repurchase your trust, or should I tell Jonathan to begin his search?"

"I meant what I said about needing someone to stop me." I pushed off the wall, took two long steps to the couch, and dropped down into it. After almost a week, my back barely even hurt. "It might as well be you."

"May that day never come." Alexa returned to her own chair, and regarded me for a long moment. "When you met Dr. Gibbings and realized I was not her, you were worried that I was a hallucination."

"Yeah. Can you blame me? Between that and Unicorn's death…" I swallowed. "Shitty fucking week."

"If you'd like, we can talk about that today." Those black eyes sharpened as she read something in my expression. "Unless there's something *else* on your mind?"

I very carefully didn't look at Mom's ghost perched on one corner of the desk, while Shane stomped in an angry circle around the room.

I also didn't look at the three unnamed ghosts that had joined me on Wednesday, the child-sized ghost that I'd found in my dorm room closet on Friday, or the spectral woman who had been sitting on my dresser when I woke up that very morning.

"No," I said instead, "there's nothing else to talk about."

CHAPTER 43

There's a saying you hear sometimes, mostly from old people like Amos or Bard: *time heals all wounds.* I'm pretty sure it comes from before the Break, when Healers weren't a thing, and when doctors spent less time trying to save lives than they did sleeping around, faking their own deaths, and blaming one-armed men for murder.

Sometimes I wonder if Dr. Nowhere really broke the world. From what I know, it was pretty broken even before his dream.

But even in a world of Capes and Black Hats, there's something to be said for time. After a few weeks of classes, the dark clouds that had followed the first-years since Shane's death began to fade. In some cases, they blew away entirely. Even Vibe regained her smile, though at first it was a small and fragile thing, easily banished by a stray thought or memory.

Maybe it was the comforting familiarity of the Academy's rigid schedule. Maybe it was because that same schedule left us too tired to do much beyond eat, sleep, and—for the particularly brave—drink at The Liquid Hero. Or maybe those pre-Break philosophers had gotten *something* right, and time itself was a sort of Power. Either way, it took far less than a month for the class to recover from Unicorn's death, for gossip and competition and drunken one-night-stands to again be the order of the day.

Guess it won't surprise any of you that, once again, I was the lone man out.

You'd think someone whose power was rooted in death—who'd seen as much of it as I had even at that age—would be the first to recover. Normally, you might even have been right.

But what the fuck did normal ever have to do with my life?

I don't talk much about Mom's ghost. After nine years, she sometimes just felt like part of the fucked-up scenery of my life; a faded, silent, specter that floated through each day without affecting it or being affected by it. When she first came back, I'd thought I was going nuts, but the revelation of my powers had ended up hitting me way harder than Mom's ghostly presence. By then, I'd had years to get over her dying. I'd done my grieving, such as it was. I'd taken my bruises and shed my tears, and there was a part of me that her ghost no longer knew and couldn't reach.

It was different with Shane. I'd barely begun to mourn my friend when his ghost showed up. How was I supposed to move on, to *find my center* as the still-absent Ms. Stein had called it, when Shane was always there, always angry, always prowling about the confines of my perspective like some kind of pale predator?

Gingers weren't even supposed to have souls. How was I being haunted by one? More importantly, why was he mad at me and how the fuck was I supposed to get him to go away?

I'd tried talking to the dead Healer, but that was one of the few things his ghost and Mom's had in common; neither made a sound or reacted to my voice. Each seemed content to remain isolated in their own private dramas.

Even Shane's unwanted addition might have been something I adjusted to… the same way I'd adjusted to the Academy's hellish schedule or the unspoken rules at Mama Rawlins' house. Maybe Shane would've faded into the background like Mom, and I'd have found a way to move on through my life with two ghosts trailing behind me instead of just one.

But as you already know, it wasn't just two ghosts.

Every day, another few specters appeared, like I had become one of those giant whirlpools Tempest had created in the Pacific, except pulling in spirits instead of boats. Three weeks in and there were dozens of them; sitting in my bed when I woke up, huddled in the communal showers, even spread through the common room. They were young and old, tall and small, some with features so faded that their faces were barely hints of a nose and eyes or the downturned corner of a mouth, others as sharply defined as the first-years that walked through them unknowingly.

Like Shane, like Mom, the ghosts didn't make any noise—even the ones whose mouths were perpetually open, screaming or shouting—but I felt them, like a silent breeze on the back of my neck, or the sort of prickling you get across your skin when your mind conjures up visions of insects, creeping and crawling on your exposed flesh. I felt them when my eyes were closed, when I slept or tried to meditate, even on the rare occasions when I snuck away to the bathroom for a quick and unsatisfying date with my hand.

A month after Shane's death and the other first-years were healing, just like that old adage had predicted they would.

But me? I was heading full-speed in the opposite fucking direction.

* * *

"Where's Wormhole?"

Silt shrugged as she dropped down onto the bench. "No clue. I'm sure she'll be along soon."

"I hope she hurries. Our presentation is next week and we still have a ton of work to do." Vibe turned to me. "What do you think, Damian? Should we get started now or wait for Evelyn?"

The clearing should have seemed empty without Shane and Wormhole, but the dozens of ghosts ringing us had me feeling claustrophobic instead. Four ghosts crowded onto the bench, and it had taken every shred of control I had left not to react when Silt sat directly on top of one of them.

"Damian?" Kayleigh prompted again.

"Sorry, Vibe," I finally managed. "What was the question?"

"What's up with you lately, Skeletor? You've been spacier than Prince after a hit of stim-weed."

I looked at Silt, trying not to let my eyes slide to the ghostly head that was sprouting out of her left shoulder. This ghost was one of the less faded ones; with a beak of a nose that put mine and Winter's to shame, and a few strands of hair clinging to an otherwise bald and spotted skull. His mouth was opening and closing, again and again, but I couldn't tell if he was trying to speak or thought he was in mid-meal. Every time his mouth contracted, ghostly teeth cut down and through Silt's bare flesh.

"She's right," agreed Vibe. "Are you feeling okay?"

I shrugged. "Yeah, just… you know. Tired. And sore."

"Maybe you should stop sparring with Nadia, just for a bit?" said Kayleigh.

"I'll second that. I don't think this strategy of letting her beat you up is working out quite like you wanted."

"I don't have a strategy…"

"Really? You're sparring twice as often as the rest of us, Boneboy. Seems like every time I see you, someone's just scraped you off the floor with a spatula."

"A what?"

"Fucking shit. Do they seriously not have spatulas over here?"

"Of course we do," answered Vibe. "We're not barbarians."

"Oh. Good. Anyway, I don't think pity's the way to Orca's heart," said Silt. "Although you're doing a good job of convincing the rest of the class that you're borderline harmless." Her voice trailed off. "If *that* was your plan, you might be more subtle than I gave you credit for."

The truth was, I didn't have a plan. I'd been spending as much time down in Nikolai's pits as I could because they were the one place on campus with dampeners running anywhere close to full-bore. Which meant they were also the one place on campus I could be free of the steadily growing legion of ghosts that traveled in my wake.

The fact that I got my ass kicked every time I went down seemed like a small price to pay. Even Nadia's ever-increasing disappointment barely registered, which was saying something.

"Anyway, Evie will be here soon enough. Girl hates to be late… not that she'd ever have to be, if she would just *use* her power. I vote we wait. A day like today is meant to be enjoyed, not wasted talking about school." Silt sighed happily. "Shit. A day like today is almost enough to make me reconsider heading inland for summer break."

"I'm sure Phoenix is nice…" Even I could hear the doubt in Kayleigh's voice. Vibe was one of several first-years who had grown up in Los Angeles, and to her, every other town in the Free States was a shithole by comparison.

Which might have been true; I only had Bakersfield to go by, and God knew *that* city was a dumpster fire.

"Phoenix sucks," countered Sofia, "but I've got a cousin there. It'll be nice to get away from the usual Academy bullshit, even if it's only for a few weeks." She lay down length-wise on the bench, short, thick legs cropping through the ghosts seated next to her. "You're welcome to come along if you want, Skeletor. Might do you some good to get away."

"I already offered," said Vibe. "Two weeks by the beach… amazing home-cooked meals, courtesy of my family's chef… maybe even our first shared glimpse of a *real* night life." Seated next to me as she was, I couldn't see her expression, but I could feel the frown. "He said no."

As far as I knew, Stonewall and his team had held firm to their promise not to share what they'd discovered about my past, but some pieces had made it out into the wild anyway. Like the fact that I didn't have any family, if not the why and the how of it. Silt's offer was actually the third I'd fielded, behind Vibe and—of all people—Jeremiah himself.

If I hadn't been so distracted by the ghost-ridden mess that my life had become, I might have been annoyed by my classmates' blatant pity.

"What I said was that I *couldn't.*" I looked at both women, as new ghosts continued to file into the clearing. "I'm not allowed to leave campus."

"Like… ever?"

"Until graduation, maybe. Bard wants me here, under supervision."

"Well that's bullshit."

"According to some, it's bullshit that I'm even allowed to be here."

"So what are you going to *do* for two weeks?"

"See if I can grow a beard. Sleep in every morning. Watch vids in the common room in my underwear…"

"I really didn't need to hear that last part," said Vibe.

"That actually sounds better than Phoenix. Maybe I should—"

"Stick around and be bored out of your mind?" I shook my head. "Go get drunk in Arizona. Don't worry about me."

"Me? Worry? About some skinny-ass, broken-nosed Crow?" Silt's smile took the sting out of her words. "Perish the thought. But if you're sure…"

"I am."

Any other year, and I would've probably liked the company. I'd gotten kind of used to it over the past few months. But I had plans for my summer vacation, and those plans didn't have space for an Earthshaker, no matter how foul-mouthed and entertaining she was.

Don't worry; we'll get to those plans eventually. What they were and how they fell apart. How I took that first unknowing step down the road to forever.

That shit's coming.

* * *

It was another ten minutes before Wormhole arrived, pushing through a wall of ghosts that she couldn't even see. The sheen of sweat on her forehead told us that she'd once again decided to walk instead of teleport. Evelyn and I still weren't what I'd describe as friendly, but I'd picked up from Sofia that the Teleporter rarely, if ever, chose to use her power.

Just goes to show how screwed up this world is. If *I'd* been able to teleport, I'd have done that shit constantly. I mean… *fuck walking*, am I right?

"There you are, roomie. I was starting to wonder if you—"

"Can we skip the small talk and get started? Please?" Vibe colored under the other women's scrutiny. "I don't mean to be rude, but we're running out of practice time."

"It's just a *history* project, Kayleigh. What gives?" Silt made room for Evelyn to sit on the bench, which now held four ghosts and two live women in a nightmarish mishmash of bodies and limbs.

"I'm an Empath, Sofia. Public speaking is…" Vibe shivered. "Let's just say it's not my favorite thing ever."

"I thought you were doing better with that stuff?"

Vibe risked a quick glance in my direction. "I am… sort of… but control takes concentration, and that's going to be hard to manage if I'm improvising my way through the presentation!"

"You can always grab a handful of Skeletor if it comes to that," said Silt.

"It won't. Come to that, I mean." Wormhole didn't register as attractive on my stupid, eighteen-year-old scale, but her smile lit up the whole clearing. "That's why I was late. I ran into Amos on campus."

"What did the old fart have to say?"

"That we've been excused from next week's presentation, on account of…" Here, her smile dimmed. "You know, Shane being in our group and everything."

"Seriously?" Vibe frowned. "Why didn't he just tell us so in class yesterday?"

"I don't know."

"Knowing Amos, he waited until the last minute to tell us so we wouldn't spend all this time slacking off," said Silt.

"Because God knows, free time is such a horrible thing." I felt more than saw Wormhole gesture at me. "Is he spacing out again?"

"Says he's tired," replied Silt.

"He'll be fine." Once again, I could hear the doubt that shaded Kayleigh's words.

I knew I should say something… anything… but I couldn't find the energy to respond, or a voice to respond with. When Evelyn's smile had faded, it had taken the light from the clearing with it. In the sudden darkness, all I could see were ghosts, pouring through the trees. Dozens of them, more than dozens, layered so heavily atop one another that I couldn't see through them to the live people beneath.

The inaudible sound of the dead rose higher and higher until my bones were vibrating, and it was all I could do to wrap my arms around my legs and shrink away from the noise.

CHAPTER 44

That day in the clearing wasn't the start of the downward spiral—that had been Shane's death, or maybe Ishmae's departure—but it *was* a breaking point. We had only a few weeks left until summer break, but I remember lying awake in the small hours of the night, surrounded by the silent, demanding dead, wondering how I could possibly make it that long.

I could have told my friends what was going on—fuck knows they must have noticed *something* was wrong, no matter how I tried to pretend otherwise—but what would any of them have been able to do? None of them even saw the ghosts. They sure as hell couldn't help me banish them.

Alexa would have been a better choice as confidante, but she'd happily let me believe she was someone else for a whole semester. Maybe we'd find our way back to the trust that she was so fond of talking about, but that day was still a long fucking way off.

That left me alone with my problems. I did what I could to soldier on, but the greater the number of ghosts crowding in around me, the harder it was to look past them to the reality that lay underneath. I remember stopping on one of the long, winding paths through campus to yell at a pair of ghosts who seemed intent upon barreling into me. It was only when they both shied away, with muttered words and wary glances, that I realized they hadn't been ghosts at all, but students. Normals, I'm guessing. First-years or second-years would've gone straight to Bard.

I'm sure Silt and Vibe tried to talk with me at various points, and I must have said or done the right things because life kept on going, but I don't remember those conversations. I barely even remember exams; all my mind can conjure is the image of myself walking into the lecture halls and then walking back out again a few hours later, as if *I'd* been a ghost, watching my own body from a distance.

Finally, just when my mind was ready to snap with the strain of pretending that everything was normal, the semester ended. Students, both Powers and normals, fled the campus in a series of waves, rushing back into the outside world for a few weeks of relaxation and family-time. When the noise had died down, I wandered the first-year dorm. I made certain that everyone had left, and then I returned to my room. I took a seat on my bed and waited and watched as the dead gathered around me in disorderly ranks.

I looked from Mom to Shane to the legions of strangers, and gave them all the smile that still made Silt shiver.

"Okay, you fuckers. Let's get it on."

* * *

There isn't much information out there on Crows. Biographies and such, sure enough—as Stonewall and the others had found out—but that's about it. Other Powers have it easy. There are dozens of books on the developmental paths a Pyromancer's powers might take. There's years of study on the multiple types of Shifters and how their transformations affect them biologically, and on the way some Powers work to oppose each other, like Shadecasters and Lightbringers, while others work in harmony, like Empaths and Sirens. But Crows? Nobody knows exactly what we do, let alone how, and the scientific community sure as shit isn't interested in teaching us how to develop those powers.

In my more lucid moments over the past month, I'd gathered what data I could from the Academy's digital library. Most of it was worse than useless; a combination of folk lore and superstition, all heavily flavored with fear. The only thing that had made any sense at all came from a philosopher in the early decades post-Break. He'd theorized that necromancy, by its very nature, was a struggle between the Crow's will and the dead he was trying to control. If mind control had been a thing—and thank God it fucking wasn't—he reasoned it would have functioned the same way.

Since the ghosts showed no signs of wanting to leave, it was clear I was going to have to *make* them go. If that took a battle of wills, then so be it.

* * *

Problem was… seated on my bed and surrounded by the dead, I had no clue how to start the war I so badly needed to win. The ghosts took my declaration of battle the same way they took everything I said; with a complete lack of reaction. Those who were screaming kept on screaming. Those who were weeping kept on doing so. The angry ones, like Shane, didn't even pause in their silent rage.

And in the middle of it all was Mom, beaming and humming her soundless tune.

A full semester at the Academy and I knew as little about my power as when I'd started. Five months, and I'd never even managed to actively use it.

Mr. Grey should've just left me in Bakersfield.

After a wasted hour, I found myself thinking back to that first fight with Matthew. The first-years were still split on whether I'd used my powers then or not. I'd come down firmly on the side that chalked the whole thing up to a concussion… but what if I was wrong? What if I *had* used my power? How the hell had I managed it?

Paladin was off having happy home-time with his famous father and perfect family, so I couldn't rely on the Stalwart to beat me into unconsciousness again. Nor could that have been the key anyway, seeing as how a dozen-plus beatings since had failed to trigger a similar reaction. So if it wasn't the physical pain that had sparked my power… what was it?

I tried to remember my mindset during that first battle in the pit; the realization that I couldn't win, my hatred of Matthew's casual superiority, even my burning resentment that Nikolai had knowingly sent me down to get battered for his own amusement.

Beneath all of those thoughts and emotions had been anger, black and thick like Bakersfield mud after the driving fall rains, the anger that had been with me from those first years after Mom's murder, giving me the strength I needed, helping me weather the blows that came again and again.

Anger? *That* I could do.

I closed my eyes and took a long breath. I reached deep for the anger I carried everywhere and let it bubble to the surface, I let it rise within me until it had flooded every part of me, until my fingers twitched with the need to scratch and claw. Then I opened my eyes, looking at a dorm room tinged red with a haze like blood, and I unleashed that anger at the ghosts around me, chasing it with every scrap of will I could bring to bear, all tied up into a single word.

Leave.

The red haze thickened and darkened until my vision was totally obscured. I collapsed back onto the bed, my pulse a loud drumbeat in my skull. Minutes passed before I was able to catch my breath, before I was able to do more than simply lie there and twitch. Eventually, I pushed myself back up to a seated position with one shaking hand, feeling as old as Amos. I swallowed once, then twice, and finally opened my eyes to see what I had wrought.

Absolutely nothing had changed.

God fucking damn it.

* * *

After that, things got a little incoherent. I remember conversations that couldn't have happened and encounters that were almost definitely dreams. At various times, the asshole who murdered my mom showed up, and I drove him away by hurling pieces of furniture at him, but each time, that same furniture was whole and in its usual place moments later.

Somewhere in there, I must have gotten food at the cafeteria, but I can't recall doing so, and none of the staff copped to ever seeing me come in. I don't remember leaving the dorm room at all, even once, but at some point, I found myself back in that clearing on the west edge of campus. It was night, but I could still see, the world around me lit with the harsh light of the dead.

I tore my eyes from the ghosts rushing in from the tree line. The sky was full of stars that were not stars but spirits, drifting down out of the darkness like spiders on invisible threads of silk. I turned my eyes to the ocean, and found it disgorging waves of glowing forms onto the shoreline, miles away, forms that slithered their way towards me as if distance was just an abstract concept. As they neared, I realized they too were ghosts, many of them bloated and misshapen, swaying forward on staggering spectral limbs.

Where once there had been a single ghost, then two, then a few dozen, now there were hundreds. Maybe thousands. The silent, skin-crawling buzz filled me, drowning out every last shred of the world around me. I felt the rings of ghosts around me tighten. I felt the last remnants of space between me and that very first and smallest circle—the one that held Mom and Shane and two of the bandits Her Majesty had killed on the road—shrink until there was nothing left, until the air was not air, but the forms of the dead, and my lungs began to seize from the lack of oxygen.

And then I felt something new.

The endless, soundless hum stuttered, then stopped. The ranks of ghosts furthest from me shivered and broke apart, that pattern repeated again and again as a path slowly opened to where I huddled. Down that path came a woman, taking small, mincing steps forward as a thousand ghosts made way before her with reverent haste.

She was wearing a simple black dress straight out of old-time vids; little black buttons from the ankle-length hem all the way up the long column of her neck, every one of them securely fastened. Hair as dark as the dress was pulled back into a bun that added a decade to her appearance, but her pale face was young and unlined. A doll's mouth curved insouciantly below a button nose, and high cheekbones made her look fancy rather than just underfed.

It wasn't until she was within arm's reach, when the last ring of ghosts had scattered rather than stand in her way, that I saw her eyes. Mud brown and empty, like freshly dug graves, they were eyes that every person in the country would have recognized and feared.

"Hello there," she finally said, with a quiet smile that died somewhere in the abyss of those eyes, "My name is Sally."

CHAPTER 45

Everyone knows about Sally Cemetery.

Everyone knows the things she did.

I should have been terrified when she walked out of the forest, spirits bowing before her like she was some sort of queen of the underworld. Instead, I remember only relief. I remember the way thousands of ghosts went silent, and the sweetness of the breath I took in that stillness; nothing but cool air filling my lungs. I remember feeling free for the first time since Shane's death.

Even now, with everything that's happened since, with the terrible things I've learned and the equally terrible things I've done, there's a part of me that loves Sally for that singular moment of release.

And the rest of me?

Well, that's a little bit more complicated, isn't it?

* * *

"How did you find me?"

Sally had arranged herself primly on a suddenly vacant bench, her delicate face turned up to the night sky, small mouth barely open as if silently laughing at a joke I couldn't hear. At my words, she turned those cavernous eyes in my direction.

"The same way they did." The endless ranks of ghosts around us shivered as if a stiff wind had blown through them. "I heard the call, and came to see who was making it."

I frowned as her meaning hit me.

"You're saying *I'm* the reason they're here? I called them?"

"It certainly wasn't me." She patted the bench next to her with a lace-covered hand. "Take a seat and tell me your name."

Her words were quiet, the voice almost sweet, but when Sally Cemetery tells you to do something, you do it. I sat next to her, far enough away to avoid the folds of her black skirt, and stuck out my hand. "Damian Banach."

She looked down at my outstretched hand and something cold and dark crept into her smile. "You don't want me to touch you."

I let my hand fall away.

"Which is just as well," she continued in that same empty voice, "as I don't wish to be touched."

"I'm sorry."

"Men always are."

It was my turn to shiver, though there was nothing cold about August in Los Angeles.

* * *

I don't know how much time passed before she spoke again. The moon seemed fixed in place, like the ghosts ringed about us, like Sally herself, on the far side of the bench.

Finally, she stirred, a porcelain statue coming back to life.

"Someone died recently."

"Yeah." Shane's ghost was still in the front ranks of the dead, but Mom was nowhere to be found. "How did you know?"

"It's how these things go." Sally regarded Shane's ghost for a long moment. "Necromancy isn't like other powers. It takes more than control or practice for a Crow to tap their potential. It takes death."

"Death?"

Sally's eyes, mud-brown and torn, met mine, and she cupped her hands together in front of her to form a bowl. "This is the power you were born with. Each death fills the vessel a little more, turning potential into ability. Sometimes, that progression is small, almost unnoticeable. Other times," she nodded at the ghosts surrounding us, "it is less small."

I thought of Shane and the men Her Majesty had killed on the road to Los Angeles. I thought of the suicide at Mama Rawlins'. Most of all, I thought of Mom.

"How many deaths?"

"As many as it takes. Your strength is fixed. Only the ability to wield it changes."

"I'm just a Low-Three."

"Lucky you." Her smile twisted.

* * *

"Is that why Shane is angry? Because I used his death as some sort of power boost?"

The moon was still fixed in the sky and refusing to move, but it felt like I'd been on that hill for days already, like I'd been born there and would be there until the day I died.

"*Is* he angry?"

I followed her gaze to the motionless ginger. "Not right now… not with you here, but yeah. I thought it was because of how he died, or that I wasn't able to convince Ishmae to stay, but—"

Sally was already shaking her head.

"The dead have life within them, but they are not living. They are here only because you called them."

"I don't understand."

"If the boy is angry, it's because you think he should be. If he will not leave you alone, it is because you don't want him to go."

"That's impossible." I gripped the edge of the bench so tightly the stone bit into my palms. "I don't even know how to use my power."

"And yet here we are."

It was my turn to shake my head. "You don't understand. I've *tried* to use it. I tried to send them all away, but it didn't fucking work!"

Sally's smile was cold and quiet and sharp as razor. "Show me."

* * *

I'd drawn so heavily on my anger back in the dorm room that at first it failed to come at all. I sat there in silence, struggling to grasp the tattered shreds of the rage I carried with me. I could feel Sally's eyes on me; her gaze both weight and whirlpool, pinning me to the stone bench even as it threatened to pull me under.

I wasn't sure if she had come to help me or to kill me, but disappointing her seemed unwise.

I turned to the memories I usually kept locked away, to limbs splayed wide across the tiles, to carnage that smelled like blood and apple pie, and the way Mom's eyes went flat as I fumbled uselessly at one of her many gaping wounds. People say there's a light that leaves the eyes with death, but I'd seen only darkness, spilling out in waterfalls and streams, staining whatever it touched.

I thought of Mom and her murder and felt my anger reignite. I fed that flickering spark the last memory I had of the man who killed her, hands chained behind him, his own grey eyes red-rimmed as if he'd dared to shed tears for the woman he'd stabbed eleven times. I added in everything that had happened since that day; the Jacobsens and Mama Rawlins, the first-years and the Academy. And when I could feel the anger roaring again inside me, like a fire scorching my organs, I took hold of it, I gathered my will, and—

"No."

One word, delivered by the quiet voice of Sally Cemetery, and all my gathered rage fell away, slipping through my grasp like water, to leave me shuddering and spent on the bench.

It took a minute, or maybe ten, but eventually, I cracked one eye open, and looked at the Crow who shared my bench.

"No?" Even my voice was cracked and hoarse, as if I'd spent the past hour screaming, and not focused inward, stoking the anger I needed to call my power.

The power she had just blown away with a single word.

"Anger is a crutch. It will not help you."

I sighed, too tired to even ponder that statement. "Why not?"

"Passion is for the living." For the first time, Sally looked almost sad. "The dead do not feel it. Nor do they answer to it."

"Then what *do* they answer to?"

"They answer to you."

Which was no answer at all.

It was her turn to sigh. She held out her skinny arms in front of her, lace-covered palms facing the sky. "The world sees life and death as two separate things." She nodded to the left hand. "You are alive—" She nodded to the right. "—or you are dead."

I frowned, annoyed by the tangent, but afraid to show it. "Are you saying that's not true?"

"I'm saying it's not so simple. Life isn't the beginning any more than death is the end. More importantly, neither stands in opposition to the other."

I gave that a few moments thought, but it still didn't make any sense. "I don't understand."

"I know." Sally shook her head, empty eyes distant. "I've never had to explain this before. Usually, I come for other reasons."

Another shudder swept through the assembled dead.

"There is no such thing as a person who is wholly alive," she finally said. "From the moment of birth, we are dying, from our skin to our hair to the building blocks of our bodies. Nor is there such a thing as a person who is wholly dead. Each spirit carries within it a fragment of their former life. By the time that fragment has faded, their discarded body has given rise to life in new forms, from the creatures that feed upon it to the plants that take root in its soil."

"You're talking about the conservation of energy?" Science wasn't my strong suit, but I wasn't completely ignorant either.

"I'm talking about the cycle." She wove bony fingers together. "Life and death woven together to form the fabric of existence."

"What does any of that have to do with me? Or *them*?"

"For most living creatures, the death they carry with them is inaccessible. Only a Crow can find the void and draw upon it."

I started to protest, yet again, that I didn't have a fucking clue what she was talking about, but the words died unspoken, as I realized that I kind of did.

"You're talking about the emptiness. That space at the heart of everything."

"Yes."

"But… I thought you said death *filled* the cup?"

Her eyes were torn, her smile absent. "What would death fill you with, if not emptiness?"

After a moment's pause, I nodded.

"Then I say again, Damian Banach, Low-Three Crow," said Sally Cemetery, dropping each word onto the stone bench between us like it was a threat, "show me your power."

I dove back into my sub-conscious, down past the noise of my still-shaky breathing, past the staccato drumbeat of my heart, past the anger I'd wrapped around myself for protection and the five-year-old boy who was beyond all hopes of protection. Down past everything that was me, to the bone-gnawing emptiness I'd carried with me since that day, the void I'd never been able to banish from my soul.

I couldn't touch it, because it had no form. Couldn't channel it, because it wasn't there. Instead, I peeled away everything that life had wrapped around it. I set it free.

I opened my eyes and felt nothing. No fear. No pain. I looked to the ghosts gathered about me, and said, in a voice so empty of inflection that the words vanished as I spoke them, "Go away."

They scattered like dry leaves before the wind, rank after rank after rank of ghosts streaking into the darkness, their glow fading as they departed. Within moments, the clearing was empty.

Almost empty.

I frowned at Shane's ghost and turned to Sally. "Why is he still here?"

Sally's face was pinched and tight, but when she spoke, her voice was as quiet as ever. "Perhaps some part of you doesn't want him gone. Is he still angry?"

"I don't think so." I frowned. "Is that because *I'm* not angry?"

"Every Crow is different, Damian. Who we are and what we do. But one truth is unavoidable; the dead do not feel. They merely respond to the will of the Crow who calls them."

I puzzled through that, as emotions started to seep back into me, as all the pieces that combined to be Damian Banach re-assembled around the pool of emptiness at my core.

"So this isn't really Shane."

"It's a piece of who he was, a remnant of the life he possessed, now wrapped in the trappings of death."

I nodded slowly. I'd spent almost a month thinking that Shane was haunting me for something I'd done or failed to do. Instead, *I'd* been the one holding on, projecting my own emotions onto a shell that only resembled my friend.

If it wasn't so sad, it would almost have been funny.

"Then I guess I should let him go."

CHAPTER 46

We'd been talking so long that my voice had gone hoarse again, though I couldn't remember even a fraction of what we'd said, Sally and I on the bench, each far enough away to prevent even accidental contact. One thing I do remember was asking her about my fight with Paladin and if that had been me using my power. Her empty eyes were turned away towards the sea, but she shrugged, narrow shoulders jerking up and down in an almost violent twitch.

"As I said, every Crow is different. Only the source of our power remains consistent."

"And the madness?"

She smiled, still looking toward the ocean. "Ah. The madness."

"Can it be avoided?"

Finally, she turned back toward me. "Because this is a night for sharing, I will let you in on a little secret."

I leaned in to catch her next words.

"This world is more insane than you or I will ever be."

"So Crows *don't* go crazy?"

"Of course we do. The question is why you'd wish to be sane in a world that isn't."

I frowned. "I don't want to hurt anyone."

Her smile sharpened. "That ship sailed long ago."

I wasn't sure how she knew that. "I mean I want to be in control of when and if I hurt someone."

She waved a lace-covered hand. "So be in control."

"But if I go crazy—"

"You are a Crow with dreams of becoming a Cape, speaking to Sally Cemetery on a night that will not end." Vacant eyes met mine. "What makes you think you're not already crazy?"

"I'd know."

"Perhaps." She folded her hands into her lap and turned back to the ocean. The pale moon lit her profile, casting her eyes in bottomless shadow. "And perhaps sanity and madness are no different than life and death; eternally intertwined until it's impossible to know where one starts and the other stops."

"Are you saying you're *not* crazy?"

It was the only time in that too-long night that I heard Sally Cemetery laugh, a hollow, aching sound that restlessly roamed the clearing as if searching for an exit. "I am as mad as the proverbial hatter, yet the actions I've taken were by my choice and mine alone."

I thought of all the stories she played a brutal part in and swallowed. "Every action?"

"Every grisly and terrible feat. Or did you think I was some sort of lost sheep in need of saving?"

"No. I just—"

Sally's voice dropped to a whisper, so low that I could barely hear the words that every child knows by heart.

"Sally Jenkins, pale and wary
seems to be so ordinary
yet all the bodies she could bury
would fill the whole world's cemetery."

As she spoke, the moon came unmoored, sinking like a stone towards the horizon, leaving her unlined face in darkness, leaving her figure a dark and narrow silhouette on the far end of the bench.

Despite myself, despite everything I knew, I reached toward that darkness. Toward Sally.

* * *

The morning light was too strong to bear, the August sun reflecting off the Pacific far below to drive bright spikes through my closed eyelids. I shaded my face with one hand and blinked tears from my eyes. I squinted against the mirrored glare and looked to the far end of the bench, hoping for a glimpse of black skirts and too-white skin.

There was nothing to see but pock-marked stone.

Sally Cemetery was gone.

INTERLUDE

The first indication that Jonathan Bard was not alone in his office was when the woman on the couch noisily cleared her throat. To his credit, Bard didn't spill the mug of coffee in his hands. Instead, he placed it down on a coaster, if a bit more heavily than necessary, and raised an eyebrow.

"Somehow, I missed hearing Agnes announce you, Alexa."

Midnight smiled. "You said you wanted to see me. You didn't say I should make an event of it."

"I'll never hear the end of it if she finds out."

"You do remember that she's your assistant, and not your mother?"

"There are times I think she's a little bit of both." He grinned. "Can I get you anything?"

"Chai, if you have any leaves left." As Bard went to a table at the back of his office, her voice softened. "You look tired, Jonathan."

"It's been a difficult semester."

"And Marissa? Any change?"

"None." He sprinkled tea leaves into a small china cup, added in a spoonful of spices, and then poured the hot water. "As far as the doctors are concerned, she's the picture of health, but…"

"But she still hasn't woken up."

"Not in over a year."

"And the Stevenson boy—?"

"Was years away from attempting a healing."

Alexa sighed. "I'm sorry."

He crossed the office and handed her the tea. "I'm not giving up."

"Nor would I expect you to. It's one of the reasons Mari loves you so much."

The smile Bard sent her was grateful, as much for her usage of the present tense as for the reminder of his wife's devotion. "She's lucky to have a friend like you."

"When she wakes up, I suspect she'll disagree vehemently. As usual." Alexa's lips quirked in her usual half-smile. "But you didn't invite me here to talk about Marissa."

"No, although I always appreciate the opportunity." Bard sighed. "With a semester behind us, I wanted to check in with you on your patient."

"Which one?"

"Let's start with Mr. Jackson."

"Meaning that this impromptu interrogation is really about Damian." Alexa smirked. "As for Alan Jackson, I believe he's adjusting as well as could be expected."

"To life in the Free States?"

"To being around people. For years, it was just he and his father, traipsing through what's left of the Dakotas. The dorms, the classes… even the limited socialization… every facet of life at the Academy requires an adjustment. But he's making progress."

"It's nice to have some good news for a change. Nikolai is raving about his combat potential. The last time I saw the old warhorse this excited was when the Scarlet Dynamo was a first-year." Bard stared into his coffee for a long moment. "And Mr. Banach?"

"He's hurting over Shane's death… like a lot of first-years, I imagine."

"*Hurting* I can accept. It's the other rumors I'm worried about. Is he still sane?"

"I suppose that depends on your definition of sanity."

"Alexa…"

She shook her head. "I'm not being difficult, Jonathan. You've known hundreds of Capes in your time. How many of them would you consider entirely sane?"

"Well, there *was* one woman, if you could ignore her propensity for all-black clothing… but I'm told she quit the business for other pursuits." Bard's smile was gentle, almost teasing. "Let me rephrase; is he a danger to those around him?"

"I don't believe so."

He gave a short nod. "Then he stays… for now, at least. I'll keep running interference with the other parents."

"How is that going?"

"It's going. I just remind them that this is my school, not theirs, and that Damian's enrollment was my decision to make. So far, they've either swallowed that lie or are too polite to call me on it."

"Have you had any luck on finding out why the government was so focused on his admission?"

"No. I lost most of my contacts when President Weatherly took office. The few who remain have only been able to confirm that the order came from his cabinet." He eyed Midnight. "Do you think someone in your agency might know?"

"I can check, but it's unlikely. Very few people in the present administration even know we exist, and our handlers would prefer to keep it that way." She paused. "What about the Finder?"

"The mysterious Mr. Grey?"

"Yes. Given that he located Damian, despite the lack of records on the boy's existence as a Crow, someone must have told him something. I'd be curious to know exactly what."

"You're not the only one. Unfortunately, Mr. Grey is in the wind. You know how Finders are. In all likelihood, we won't hear from him until the next student shows up on our doorstep… or until someone stumbles across his corpse."

"If you need him located sooner than that…" Her lips twisted into that half-smile. "I know a woman."

"I appreciate the offer, but I need you here, keeping tabs on our young Crow. For as long as he remains a student at least."

"There's every chance he makes it to graduation."

"Really? You think he *could* become a Cape?"

"It's a possibility. Some of the basics are there. He has a well-developed protective instinct, and a selfless streak I'm not sure he even recognizes. But…"

"But?"

"He's eighteen, stubborn, slow to trust, and proud. Worse, he's carrying a lot of anger around with him. Not unlike my other patient, if we're drawing parallels. But where Alan's issues are purely psychological, there is the ever-present unknown of how Damian's power will affect him. This is new territory, even for me."

"Don't let the professors at Stanford hear you say that. You'll tarnish the reputation of our alma mater forever." Bard's grin quickly fell away. "If he did graduate, what team would choose to add a Crow to their roster? The public relations cost alone…"

"Not every Power who serves does so as a Cape." Alexa's voice was quiet.

"Your agency would have him?"

"Provided his nature doesn't consume him, I think he deserves the opportunity."

Bard paused, dark eyes scanning the woman on the far side of the office. "You actually *like* him."

"Oh Jonathan." She laughed softly. "I like everyone. It's one of the reasons I am so good at what I do."

"Therapy?"

She shrugged. "That too."

CHAPTER 47

"You're looking better today, Damian."

"Am I?" I rolled my shoulders and tried to relax, but the couch in Dr. Gibbings' office was somehow less comfortable than usual.

"Yes." Alexa was all in black, as always, although she had draped her suit jacket over the back of her chair in acknowledgement of the August heat. "I'd like to spend today's session discussing whatever it was that has been troubling you for the past few weeks."

"I thought whatever we talked about was supposed to be up to me?"

"Normally, yes. But let's not pretend that your behavior lately has been normal." There was no humor at all in Alexa's black eyes. "I don't need to know every aspect of your life, but when it comes to your power—and your mental health—there cannot be secrets between us." When I continued to hesitate, the corners of her mouth turned downward. "I chose not to make an issue of you missing last week's session because of the way the semester ended, but that grace period is over, Damian. This isn't baseball; you don't get three strikes."

For those of you who were born post-Break, baseball was an archaic sport from Dr. Nowhere's time, involving three teams armed with bats, each trying to capture the other teams' bases. In the absence of Healers, the only thing preventing mass casualties was the 'three strikes' rule, which defined a limit on how many times a given player could be hit. I'm still not sure how *balls* figured into the whole thing, but given that my own testicles want to crawl up into my body just thinking about it, I'm okay with remaining ignorant.

All of which is a tangent, of course; a distraction from the fact that, even now, I'm not sure how to describe the thoughts and emotions that filled me when Alexa pushed for details. Part of me wanted to refuse, of course… as much because I didn't like being told what to do as because I was worried on how she would react to the truth. Part of me was angry at being backed into a corner, part of me was still hung up on the counselor's own lie of omission, and yet another part of me thought I should have told her everything back when all the shit had started.

I don't know which of those emotions made sense—or if any of them did—but it was the last one that ended up resonating. I didn't think Alexa could have done anything to help with my ghost problem, but if I was really, truly going to trust her with my sanity, then lying was just about the dumbest possible thing I could do.

So I looked across the room into Alexa's coal-black eyes and told her about Shane and the other ghosts. I told her about my last month of classes and of the way it all had come to a head that past week.

I told her about Sally.

* * *

I don't know how long the story took to tell. It had been four days since I'd met Sally in the clearing, but only a day since I'd reached out and found her gone, and I still wasn't sure exactly what had happened to all the time in between, or why I hadn't been hungry or thirsty despite losing a half-week to a single conversation. With all of that so fresh in my mind, my grasp on time was a little bit shaky, but I'm pretty sure we'd exceeded our session's designated hour by the time I finally trailed off.

Alexa hadn't moved once during my recitation—she hadn't even blinked—but just as the silence between us reached maddening proportions, she stirred. One slender eyebrow, black as night against her pale face, slowly crept upward.

"You spoke with *Sally Cemetery* on Academy grounds last Wednesday?"

"Yeah. And for most of Thursday and Friday, I think. Some of it gets a little hazy."

She shook her head slowly. "Damian, I'm not sure how to say this, but—"

"I know," I said. "Sally's been dead for years."

* * *

Most of you already knew that, of course. Some of you probably remember when Sally's death became national news, when men all across the Free States breathed a sigh of relief. And those who *didn't* know were no doubt wondering how a Crow as infamous as Sally had just waltzed past the Academy's defenses. Maybe you put two and two together, and got an incredibly-fucked-up-but-no-less-accurate-for-that-fact four.

But here's the part that's really going to fry your brain. Sally Cemetery had told me that ghosts weren't people at all, that they were just mindless shells whose sparks of life had yet to fully fade. But Sally had been dead nineteen years, which meant Sally herself was a ghost. So how had she spoken? How had she taught me to access my power? How the fuck did anything from the past few days add up?

* * *

Over the next half-hour, Alexa and I talked through some of those same inconsistencies. She was hard to read, her professional mask every bit as effective as her Cape mask had been, but the questions she asked were thoughtful and detailed. Either she believed me or she was doing a spectacular job of faking it while waiting for security… and I was pretty sure the woman formerly known as Midnight didn't need security's help to deal with one baby Crow.

"So what do you think? Am I crazy?"

"Do you feel crazy?"

"Not really," I admitted. "Mostly, I'm just confused. But I'm not a therapist either."

"Despite what some of the tremendous assholes in my profession would prefer everyone think, a doctoral degree doesn't grant omniscience," said Alexa. "I can't tell you whether you actually met with Sally Jenkins, or if that whole encounter was something your mind created internally to help you deal with a traumatic situation. Post-

Break, such things are less cut and dried than they used to be. What I can say is that the Damian I saw two weeks ago was clearly struggling, and that is not the case today."

"You could tell?"

Alexa's right eyebrow crept back up. "It's my job."

"Did you tell Bard?"

"No. Jonathan is a gifted man and a brilliant orator, but he is not a trained psychoanalyst. He doesn't understand that therapy is a process, with peaks and valleys, and that sometimes those valleys are where the greatest progress is made." She shrugged. "The mind goes through struggles, just like the rest of us. Sometimes, those struggles are what make the mind even stronger."

"And if they break it instead?"

"Then I will honor my promise to you, and ensure that no one else suffers." For just a moment, the shadows seemed to spill from her eyes. "And then, and only then, will I inform Bard."

CHAPTER 48

"Sally Fucking Cemetery?!? Are you serious?"

I nodded absently at Silt before turning to Vibe and pointing to the sandwich I was in the process of demolishing. "I thought the cafeteria food was good, but this…this is fantastic."

"It's the marinade. That and high-quality, actual beef. I told you my family's chef is amazing." The Empath had brought sandwiches back to school for all of us, and was eating hers one-handed, her other hand resting atop my bare arm.

"If I'd known food could taste like this, I would've been a lot less happy with the synth-rations back in Bakersfield." I took another bite and let the multitude of flavors roll around in my mouth.

"I'm all for listening to the two of you talk about how much you love having meat in your mouths, but could we get back to the bomb that Skeletor just dropped?" asked Silt. "You seriously saw Sally Cemetery?"

"Yeah."

"Sally Jenkins, pale and wary… *the* Sally Cemetery?"

"Yeah." I nodded to the bench Silt was perched on. "She was sitting about three feet to your right."

Unconsciously, Silt shifted to the left. "But she died before any of us were even born!"

"I know." I'd decided I owed it to Vibe and Silt to tell them everything, starting with my parents, and ending with what I'd gone through over the break, but the story wasn't any less confusing on its second telling. "It was her ghost, I think. And before you ask, I have no fucking idea what that means."

"What did Shrink Spooky think?"

"Alexa? She's reserving judgement. Waiting to see if this was the final push needed to send me over the edge."

"What was Sally like?" Kayleigh wanted to know.

I chewed on my sandwich for a few moments while considering the question. "Scary. Alone. Kind of sad. Scary."

"You said scary twice," pointed out Silt.

"Yeah, I did."

"Was she pretty?" pressed Vibe.

"Yes?" I frowned. "Maybe? Sort of. I'm not sure."

"I'll take Evasive Answers for six-hundred bucks, Alex." Silt scowled when Vibe and I turned confused looks in her direction. "Come on… *Jeopardy? Alex Trebek?* Did the Free States purge *all* of its Pre-Break pop culture?"

"I'm not being evasive." I shrugged. "I thought I was losing my mind. I'm still not totally sure I didn't. Why would I care if Sally was hot?"

"Because you're eighteen and unless you're some sort of sex-ninja, you haven't gotten any action since you arrived at the Academy?"

"Sofia!" Vibe's hand tightened like a vise around my arm as she stared at the stocky Earthshaker.

"What, Kayleigh?" The look Silt sent back was pure innocence and all the less believable for it. "Men have needs, just like we do. Or so I've been told."

"*Sally's a ghost,*" I reminded her, "and even if she wasn't …"

Both women leaned in as I trailed off.

"You guys know the stories. She doesn't want to be touched."

My words brought silence to the small clearing, and wiped the grin off of Silt's broad face. For a while, the three of us just sat there, sandwiches in hand, as the first September winds rustled the leaves on the trees around us.

"Well, I'm no shrink, spooky or otherwise, but I know two things for sure. First, you seem way less crazy now than you did before break."

Next to me, I felt more than saw Vibe nod vigorously. Apparently, Alexa hadn't been the only one to notice something was wrong.

"And second?"

"Next time they give us a few weeks off, I'm staying here on campus where the action is."

"You didn't have fun in Phoenix?"

"Have we met?!? I have fun everywhere I go. But who would choose cheap beer over a showdown with an army of ghosts and a long-dead, ultra-infamous Crow?"

"Is everyone from Texas insane or just you?"

"Depends on who you ask." Silt's wide grin made a triumphant return.

"You're not a Necromancer, Sofia," said Vibe. "You wouldn't have been able to see any of them."

"Oh. Right." Silt shrugged heavy shoulders. "Sounds like a nut that Boneboy will have to crack before next time."

"There won't *be* a next time," I said. "Everything's good now."

"Sure it is." Silt's smile was oddly gentle. "But next time it isn't, you're going to make sure we're in a position to help, right?"

I took another bite of my sandwich and nodded. "I'll do what I can."

Of all the promises I ended up breaking that year, that's one of the very few I take no responsibility for. None of us—Crows or otherwise—have as much control over our lives as we want to believe.

Sometimes, the world spins, and all we can do is hold on for the ride.

CHAPTER 49

The first semester at the Academy is kind of like sparring a Stalwart. Orientation hits you before you're ready for it, like a jab to the face that leaves you reeling. The weeks that follow are a barrage of body blows and by the time you've regained your footing, your wind is shot, your limbs are heavy, and the faint hope of victory has been replaced by the inescapable reality of your defeat.

The second semester is different. For most first-years, the second semester feels like the prize earned for making it that far.

Most first-years.

See, that first semester is all about making sure every Cape has a basic foundation in certain skills; self-defense, weapons-work, even meditation. Winter or Poltergeist having to punch their way out of a fight seemed every bit as unlikely as me dating either of them, but there's a big difference between unlikely and never-fucking-happening. As Nikolai says, *it pays to be sure, because if you're not sure, you're gonna pay.*

It sounds better when he says it.

Anyway, that's the first semester. In the second semester, we're assigned classes according to our respective powers. In addition to continued classes in Control, Close Combat, and Weapons Training, there's Mobility, taught by Macy Johnson. If your life totally sucks, you might wind up in one of Emery Goldstein's courses; Projection or Perception. Every first-year has to take at least two powers classes—Control and one other—but nobody takes more than four.

That's what the handbook says anyway. Turned out that part was bullshit too. Six powers classes, and every one of them was on my curriculum.

Every.

Single.

One.

* * *

"Why is *he* here, Nikolai?" asked Orca, nodding in my direction. Wherever she'd gone over the break, her dirty blonde hair was now a shade or two lighter than usual, and set off even more spectacularly by olive skin that was a an equal number of shades darker.

In addition to looking amazing, she sort of had a point.

Six of us had made it into second-semester Combat, informally known as Hell's Second Coming. Me, the Viking, Paladin, Orca, Alan-fucking-Jackson, and my roommate, Stonewall. Five had enhanced strength, durability, and/or speed. The two Shifters even had accelerated healing.

I could see ghosts. And maybe talk to them, in the case of Sally Cemetery.

You do the fucking math.

"Discounting powers, Damian is one of the best hand-to-hand fighters in your class," answered Nikolai in a baritone rumble.

"Discounting powers? Does that mean we're *not* reducing the dampeners?" That was my roommate, who'd spent most of the first semester getting his ass kicked because of those same dampeners.

"The dampeners will still be active, to keep some of you from accidentally destroying my classroom, but they'll be turned down sufficiently to allow both you and Alan to shift."

Five sets of first-year eyes turned back to me, but I kept my face a mask. Low dampeners didn't just mean Alan Jackson and Jeremiah would be able to turn into their secondary forms. It meant Paladin and Orca would be that much faster and more agile. It meant Erik would be that much stronger and more durable.

Four of the five had kicked my ass back when the dampeners were at full power. Now, even Jeremiah was going to be a nightmare.

What chance did I have of survival with the playing field *completely* uneven?

Surprisingly, it was Alan who spoke. "How do we keep from accidentally killing him?"

"The same way you'll do it in the field," said Nikolai. "Control. Anyone who tells you Capes never kill is a fool or a liar, but *we* make the choice. We don't allow our powers to choose for us. The dampeners are down so you can learn to utilize your gifts in combat, and so you get experience fighting against powered opponents, but I've never lost a student in the arena, and I don't intend to change that now. Training will be done at reduced speed and intensity until you understand and can control the movements you are making."

My roommate nodded, but it was Nadia's turn to frown. "We still get to spar though, right?"

"I was getting to that, Orca. Starting with today's class, you will each spar once every two weeks. All matches will be full speed and full intensity, but lethal blows will not be permitted and combat will end at *my* discretion. Any more questions?" Nikolai waited for half a breath, then nodded. "Good. First up, the Viking and—" He paused, beady eyes fixed on me. "Have you picked a codename yet, Crow?"

"Not yet." Vibe and Silt had convinced me that Baron Boner was a non-starter, but I wasn't sold on either of the two nicknames Sofia had suggested.

"Figure one out before second-year, or one of the image consultants will choose for you." The big man gave a mock shiver. "Not something you want, believe me. Anyway, let's see how you fare today against our resident Titan."

"I'm going to break you like a twig, Crow," said Erik, as we headed down the tunnel to the arena.

"Keep telling yourself that," I shot back. "All I have to do is dodge for half a minute until your fat ass keels over."

Turns out, his prediction was a shit-ton more accurate than mine.

* * *

I'm not going to give you a blow-by-blow of the whole fight. I'm sure there's a vid of it somewhere in the Academy records, if you're really curious. Maybe you can find some other Crow and convince her to get that vid and play it for you.

Let's just say that five months of training had done the Viking's stamina a world of good. Let's say that I dodged his first punch easily, then made the mistake of driving my own fist into his ribs, where regular bones—mine—met superhumanly dense bones—his—with predictable results.

Let's also say that ducking under a follow-up blow, climbing the slab-like wall of your opponent's back, and choking him out is way harder than it might seem in theory, especially when one of your two hands is already shattered.

As soon as I'd pulled myself onto his back, I realized something else; leaving the ground negated any advantage I'd had in terms of speed and mobility. I was halfway up, my good arm reaching for Erik's throat, when an enormous hand reached around, peeled me off like I was a wet towel, and swung me right into the wall.

If you want to know more, go find the fucking vid. I still ache just thinking about it.

* * *

After Combat came Control… still the only class we had five days a week, even if it had been moved to a new building on campus. More than a month after Shane's death and Ishmae's departure, Ms. Stein remained a shadow of her formerly cheerful self. Part of me was glad about that. She'd played a role in what had gone down with Unicorn and Phoenix, just like I had. Neither of us got to just shrug that shit off and pretend it hadn't happened.

That first Monday, I missed Control, courtesy of another extended stay at the med ward. By the time I peeled myself off the gurney and stole yet another pair of sweats, it was time to head over to Projection.

Fucking Projection.

I've told you about Emery, right? Guy with a stick the size of one of those archaic baseball bats wedged up his ass? Only good thing I can say about him was that he made Isabel's Ethics class almost enjoyable by comparison. I mean… the willowy professor hated me as much as Emery did, and Ethics was one of the dumbest courses in the history of academics, but at least she was halfway decent to look at. A damn sight better than the four-limbed, walking cock known as Emery Goldsmith.

It didn't help that I had to see him four times a week—twice for Projection and twice for Perception. It also didn't help that I had no idea what I was doing in either class. At least in Combat, I could throw a punch. But Projection? I wasn't an Earthshaker. I couldn't wave my hand and cause a rockslide.

Perception was just as dumb, except that—to the naked eye—the other first-years seemed every bit as useless as I was. More than half the first-years were in Projection, but there were only three of us in Perception. I spent each class kneeling in a circle with Vibe and Freddy—our Switch, now going by Muse—as Emery droned on about opening ourselves to the flow of energy of the world around us. While the other two closed their eyes and tried to open their chakras or whatever the professor was saying, I spent my time focused inward, trying to repeat what I'd managed in the clearing with Sally, digging down for the empty space at my core.

There were a few times in that first month where I thought I almost had it, only to have something intrude; irritation, annoyance, even the occasional cramp in my quads from the stupid kneeling pose Emery insisted we maintain for the entirety of his class. Each time, I found myself back at square one, an entire living world somehow separating me from my power.

Emery Goldstein hated me from the moment we met. After a single day in his classes, that feeling was mutual.

* * *

If Mondays and Wednesdays—where I had Combat, Control, *and* the two P's—were my worst days, Tuesdays and Thursdays were my best.

Just after breakfast was Weapons Training. Even in a world of Powers, it seemed like the sort of thing that would be useful to every first-year, but there were surprisingly few of us in attendance. The two Stalwarts were a given, of course; the irritation of spending more time with Matthew-fucking-Strich far outweighed by the opportunity to spend that same time with Nadia. My surprise at Tessa's inclusion ended the first time she used her telekinesis to pick up a half-dozen weapons off the nearby wall. She damn near cut my head off three times in our first minute of sparring. Last in the group were Kayleigh and Evelyn. Neither Vibe nor Wormhole's powers were offensive in nature, so weapons offered them another way to contribute.

The best part about Weapons Training wasn't my classmates though. It wasn't even Jessica Strich, who was surprisingly funny and light-hearted, and would have been devastatingly sexy if she hadn't reminded me so much of her little brother. The best part about Weapons Training was that it was the one class where I *didn't* totally suck. I was lousy with any gun larger than a pistol—Jessica said it had to do with the way I was sighting down the barrel—but everything else, from daggers to staves, just made sense.

That's not to say I became some sort of master or anything in the span of a few weeks. Jessica put me on my ass nine times out of ten, and Orca wasn't far behind. But I didn't feel utterly useless either. As much as part of me enjoyed the raw, combative nature of Nikolai's class, Weapons Training was flat-out *fun*.

* * *

Weapons Training was succeeded by another boring hour of Control, but after *that* came Mobility. Macy Johnson was bald and whip-thin, with skin the same soft brown as Ishmae's, but without the Pyro's almond-shaped eyes. She was always smiling and always in motion, her individual movements frequently too fast for the naked eye to see.

Like Emery, Macy had been surprised to be sent a student who didn't have powers suited for her class. I couldn't fly or teleport, I didn't have super speed, and what agility I possessed paled to that of Paladin and Orca, making me by default the worst student in her class. Unlike Emery, the older Jitterbug didn't care. She'd left for a fraction of a second and come back with a scaled-down set of agility drills for me to participate in. Before I knew it, I was dodging around obstacles and learning how to incorporate Jessica and Nikolai's lessons in falling while running at full speed.

We both knew I'd never make it to the higher-level Mobility classes, but Macy worked her nonexistent ass off anyway to ensure I learned something as her student.

We were never friends. I was only in her class for the one semester, but I can still remember Macy Johnson's smiling face. I remember the way her dark eyes sparkled when Supersonic challenged her to a race, and the arch look she gave him when he stumbled across the finish line forty seconds later, having been lapped twice by the older woman.

We were never friends, but I miss her.

CHAPTER 50

The upside of owning nothing but sweats is that you don't have to worry about hanging them… or even folding them. The downside is that it can take weeks before you notice that someone *did* hang something in your closet.

"What the fuck is this?" I'd just come back from doing laundry to initiate a room-wide search for the one sock that somehow always went missing when I realized that the only hanger in my closet was no longer bare.

On his side of the room, my roommate cracked one eye open, saw where I was pointing, and let that eye drift shut again. "It's called a suit."

"I know that. Where did it come from?" In addition to the black jacket and matching pants, there was a synth-leather belt and a dark red button-up shirt.

Jeremiah sighed and swung his legs over the edge of the bed, slowly hoisting himself to his feet in the way only big men ever have to. "I brought it from home. Figured you might appreciate having something other than sweats the next time a formal occasion comes up."

"Did I *ask* you to buy me clothes, Stonewall?"

"I knew this was going to go to shit," the other man muttered. "I didn't *buy* the suit. My little brother outgrew it, and my parents were going to donate it since he's the last one left in high school. I figured you could use it instead."

"You figured wrong." I threw the suit, hangar and all, across the room, where Jeremiah plucked it out of the air.

"Are you kidding me?" He stocked past me to gesture at my empty closet. "You've got nothing, Damian! Are you going to wear sweats to the Remembrance Day dance?"

"That's my problem," I growled. "I don't need your charity."

Stonewall threw his hands up in the air, suit, hanger and all. "What is it with you and charity?"

Three months earlier, I would have just sneered and stalked off. But that was before Shane's death and Bard's lecture. That was before Sally Cemetery's visit and Alexa's baseball reference. Instead, I dropped back onto my bed and, for the first time that I could remember, tried to put the feeling into words.

Before I could, there was a knock at the door, and Paladin's blonde head peeked in.

"Everything okay in here?"

"What the fuck business is it of yours, Matthew?"

Blue eyes turned on me and he motioned to the wall by my bed. "Supersonic has the hangover from hell. Normally, I'd be all for him being taught the error of his drunken ways, but I've had to empty the bucket twice already, and he just finally dropped back off to sleep. If you guys want to rage at each other and wake him up, you can deal with the next bucket."

I opened my mouth to tell Paladin what he could do with Supersonic and his vomit bucket, but Jeremiah cut me off.

"Sorry, Paladin. We're hashing some shit out, but I'll try to keep it down."

"I'd appreciate it." He nodded to the big man. "Hektor was looking for you last night at The Liquid Hero."

"Yeah." Jeremiah sighed. "I know. I'm going to find him this afternoon." He waited for the door to close and then turned back to me. "I know you and I aren't ever going to be friends, but could you at least try to stop assuming every little thing I do is an attack?"

"The first time we met, you called me a thief and threatened me."

"And how many times have you beaten the crap out of me in Combat class since then?"

"A bunch, although I guess that's over now that powers are in play."

"Maybe." He shook his enormous head. "Keep the suit or toss it. I was trying to do something nice, as an apology for sticking our noses in your business last semester, but if you don't want it, that's fine too."

I looked at the suit in his hands. "You really want to know why I don't like charity?"

Jeremiah's tone was wary. "Maybe."

"Everything I've ever been *given* was taken away again." I waved off the question I could see forming. "My parents… the Jacobsens… even my time at Mama Rawlins' came with a built-in expiration date. My enrollment at the Academy lasts exactly as long as I remain sane. Whenever they decide I'm nuts, I'll be out on my ass, and the only thing I'll be taking with me *is* me. What I've learned, what I've done, and who I am. Everything else is just temporary bullshit."

"What does that have to do with my brother's suit? I'm not going to ask for it back if you get kicked out."

"When the only constant in your life is you, you can't afford to rely on anyone else."

"That's dumb." Despite the words, Stonewall's voice was a quiet rumble. "Everyone ends up alone, but that doesn't mean you go through life that way. And how many pairs of sweats have you stolen from the Academy med ward now? Fifteen?"

"I lost count somewhere around ten," I admitted.

"Do you really think Gladys doesn't know you're taking them?" He shook his head. "This isn't about self-reliance. It's about pride."

I swallowed the first three expletive-laden retorts that came to mind. "Maybe. Pride's something I can take with me."

"You know what else you can take with you?" He shook the hanger at me. "A fucking suit! You could be the best dressed asshole at the nuthouse. How's that for pride?"

"Fuck you," I said half-heartedly, my mind suddenly filled with images of me parading around an asylum in formal wear.

"I can throw in a top hat too," he added, teeth flashing white against his dark skin and darker beard. "Maybe a cane. *There goes Damian*, they'll say, *fanciest damn honky we ever did see.*"

"Honky?"

"My grandpa used to call our neighbors that. Not sure what it means. Asshole, maybe." He shrugged. "You can't eat pride. You can't wear it, and it sure as shit won't cuddle you at night. So maybe you should put pride aside every now and then and let people help you?"

For some reason, my thoughts turned to Her Majesty and her moment of almost-compassion outside the Academy. She'd been paid to get me there, sure, but everything else… had that been kindness or pity? And did it matter? Had Shane been less of a friend because he wanted to see if he could heal Crow insanity? Was Vibe less of one because she was using me as an emotional shield? Was Silt…

I stopped myself and shook my head. Silt was even crazier than I was. There was no point trying to guess her motives.

Stonewall misinterpreted my head shake. "Fine. Then don't think of the suit as charity. Think of it as… an exchange."

"For what?"

"I need your help." He laid the suit down on top of his dresser, and sank down onto his own bed, face turned to the small window. "You saw my match with Orca, right?"

I winced.

"My first sparring match in full stone form, and it didn't help at all. She wiped the floor with me."

"How am I supposed to help with that? I'm the worst fighter left in Combat."

"No, you're not. You're the weakest one."

I frowned. "What's the difference?"

"The difference is that you do the right things. You make the right moves. You only lose because you don't have the power to actually hurt any of us."

I fought unsuccessfully not to clench my jaw. "And?"

"And I've got the power, but I'm never in position to use it. If you had my power, you'd have shattered the Viking's ribs instead of your hand. Me? I'm going to be pawing at nothing but air."

"You want me to teach you to fight?"

"I want you to show me what I'm doing wrong. I feel like I get the moves in practice, but when it comes to sparring…" He shook his head. "I'm a Shifter. If I can't win a close-quarters fight, I'm useless."

As someone whose power still remained a total mystery, I knew all about being useless. The problem was, I had six powers classes, four non-powers classes, multiple tutors, and weekly sessions with Alexa. What I didn't have was free time.

Much free time, anyway.

"Fine. Friday nights."

My roommate's smile vanished almost as soon as it appeared. "Seriously? Friday *nights*?"

"Do you have any idea what my schedule is like?"

"This is the longest conversation we've ever had, so… no." He sighed and shook his head. "Friday nights it is. And this," he added, picking the suit back up by its hanger, "is yours."

I took the suit and returned it to my closet. "If I can help you win a match or two, I'll expect something more."

"Like what, exactly?"

"Like a top hat," I said, "and a cane."

Jeremiah's laugh was just loud enough to wake Caleb back up next door. For some reason, Paladin didn't carry through on his threat about the bucket.

CHAPTER 51

"Let's try that again."

"Are you serious?" Stonewall pushed himself back to his feet. His grey sweatshirt was dark with sweat, and his beard was matted with the same.

"You wanted my help," I reminded him.

"Yeah," he huffed. "Starting to regret that, to be honest. Three weeks and all I've gotten are more bruises. And Paladin *still* handed me my ass last week."

"Which gives you tonight's session to prepare for Alan Jackson." I shook out my right hand behind my back, hiding a wince. I was pretty sure I'd cracked a knuckle in that last exchange. Even in human form, Jeremiah was solid.

Across the pit, he continued like he hadn't heard me. "I think Gladys is starting to wonder what's going on."

"Don't worry about her. She's seen worse."

"Yeah… like you, every other Monday." Jeremiah paused. "I can't believe I'm giving up my Friday nights for this."

"And I can't believe you still have the energy to bitch about it," I shot back.

"Cardio's not my problem." Stonewall cracked his neck, rolled his shoulders, and raised his fists, but it was my turn to stop the fight before it could begin. Something in his last statement had set my mind buzzing.

"No, it's not. And your problem isn't size or strength either, even if the Viking has you beat in those two areas." I frowned. After three weeks training together, my roommate hadn't improved at all. Teaching wasn't my strong suit, but the extra practice should have been helping. "So how is it that I'm still kicking your ass?"

"The dampeners are on, and I can't use my powers," he rumbled. "Pretty sure it's going to be different when we face each other in class."

As if on cue, my injured hand twitched. If I'd cracked a knuckle—and broken at least one finger—hitting Jeremiah while he was flesh and bone, I didn't even want to think about what it would feel like trying to take him down when he was stone.

Even so, his answer rang false. "You've got six inches on me, at least that much of a reach advantage, and fifty-plus pounds. Even with the dampeners on, that should be enough."

"Except I suck. I know that already. Isn't that why we're here?"

"You don't suck. You do as well in training as the rest of us. It's just the actual fighting where you fall apart."

"Great. That's going to look fantastic on my Cape resume."

"At first, I thought it was just a question of experience. Some people freeze up when the adrenaline starts to flow. Hell, I did the same in my first few fights."

Jeremiah gave me an odd look. "You didn't freeze at all when you were fighting Paladin. Even after you were unconscious."

"I'm not talking about at the Academy." I sighed and leaned back against the curved wall of the pit. "How many fights did you get in growing up?"

"I have a sister and three brothers, all but one of them older—"

"*Real* fights. Where you were worried the other guy was going to put you in the hospital or the ground."

"Uhm… none? I was big before my powers hit, and my brothers are even bigger. Besides, this is the Free States, not the Badlands." He frowned. "You think that's my problem? I had too nice a childhood?"

"Paladin's been training since he could walk. Orca's never seen a fight she'd walk away from. Erik doesn't have enough brain to get in the way of instinct. And Alan…" I shrugged, feeling something pop in one shoulder. "Well, he's a fucking monster."

"And you? When was *your* first fight?"

"I was six."

"You were getting punched when you were *six*?"

"No, I was getting punched when I was five. I started punching back when I was six."

"Fucking hell, man."

"Put two dozen kids in a small space, most of them angry, all of them alone, and shit happens." I shook my head. "Didn't know what the fuck I was doing, of course, but at that age, aggression goes a long way."

"I don't think aggression is my problem. After three weeks of this, I'd be more than happy to tear your arm off."

Something in his words struck me.

"Okay… maybe I wouldn't tear your arm off," he relented, as my silence grew, "but I'd be happy to send *you* to Gladys for a change."

"I'm sure she'd love that," I murmured, still lost in thought. "Old woman has a major thing for baby Crow."

"What?"

"Actually, I think maybe aggression *is* your problem."

"I just told you—"

"Shut up and listen. In Mobility class last week—"

"Why are *you* in Mobility?"

"I haven't been able to use my power, and nobody knows what good it will be in a fight," I pointed out. "Least they can do is teach me how to run away. Now do you want to go another round, or do you want to listen to what I'm trying to say?"

Stonewall waved a large hand. "Yes sir, teacher sir."

I let the sarcasm slide, more because my hand hurt like a motherfucker than because of any generosity or patience on my part. If the rest of the first-years were anything like Jeremiah, it was a wonder our teachers hadn't murdered us in our sleep.

"In Mobility class last week, Macy was talking about flow. We all move differently, based on our body types, our powers, and even who we are as individuals." I paused expectantly, but my roommate stayed blessedly silent. "So Winter, Supersonic, and Erin Pearson—"

"Cyclone."

"Say what?"

"Erin goes by Cyclone now."

"I don't care. Point is, they all fly, but the way they fly—not just the mechanics, but the motion of it—is different. Supersonic is a bullet. Winter goes straight up in the air then mostly hovers, so she can rain down shit and attitude on everyone, and Erin—sorry, *Cyclone*—kind of flits around like a butterfly."

"And?"

"And it just occurred to me that that's true for Combat class too. We all have our flow. Orca moves like water. Paladin's a robot programmed with a thousand ways to kill you. Erik's a big-ass tank rolling forward, and Alan and I…"

"Yeah?"

"We're full-on aggression. Only he's way better at it than I am."

"Where does that leave me?"

"Trying too damn hard to be like Alan. Or me, for that matter." I shook my head, annoyed that it had taken me so long to see it. "I thought you were just inexperienced, but that's not the problem. You're going against your own flow."

Jeremiah's sigh was impossibly loud in the confines of the pit. "Either I have a concussion or you're talking pure bullshit. Maybe both."

"It goes back to my original question. Why do I keep kicking your ass? And don't blame the dampeners this time."

He paused, visibly swallowing the words. After a moment's consideration, he shrugged. "You're too fast. Speed kills."

"Paladin's fast. Orca's fucking magic." I shook my head. "I'm a bit faster than you, but it's not enough to make up for the difference in reach. At least it shouldn't be."

"Then what's going on?"

"I told you; you're trying to be someone you're not. You're trying to be Alan Jackson, but you aren't him. Offense like an avalanche isn't who you are, and every time you try to be that person, you're fighting your own instincts. *That's* what's slowing you down. That's why I'm beating you. In your stone form, it's even worse."

Jeremiah frowned. "So you're saying I'm fucked."

"That's not—"

"A Shifter who can't fight isn't worth shit," he reminded me.

"I didn't say you couldn't fight. I said you couldn't fight like Alan. If it's not in your nature to attack, maybe you should try defending instead?"

"But…" His words trailed off. "Like a counter-puncher?"

"Yeah. Seems to me any Cape team out there would be happy to have some huge fucker who can turn into solid stone and defend a position. Combat class is about one-on-one combat, but in the real world, your team is going to have Lightbringers or Sparks or, if you're really unlucky, pain-in-the-ass Telekinetics like Poltergeist."

Almost against his will, Jeremiah grinned. "Tessa doesn't like you either. You should hear some of the things she says."

I didn't let myself get distracted by the tangent, but it was a close thing. "Point is, they can all do way more damage than you can, and from a distance, but they're just flesh and blood. On a team, they're going to need someone durable to hide behind."

"And I could be that someone."

"Some part of you must have already known that," I pointed out. "It's in your codename."

* * *

Two weeks later, Jeremiah faced off with Alan Jackson. He lost… but the fight lasted five minutes, and for the first time ever, it was almost competitive. As he was carted off to the med ward with a broken collarbone and a knee that squished every time he bent it, his bloody smile was victorious.

At the end of class, Nikolai summoned me to his office.

* * *

It says something about Nikolai that none of us even knew he had an office. I'd pretty much just figured his place was right there in the observation room, gleefully watching his students knock the shit out of each other.

Truth is, I could have happily gone through all three years at the Academy without ever seeing that office. Some professors have open door policies where students can come, eat cookies, and ask questions about the material. Others turn their offices into makeshift lounges for teaching assistants and a few exalted students. But with Nikolai, there's only one reason you'll see his office's bland, grey walls, and it sure as shit doesn't involve cookies.

Not that I knew any of that when I first walked in. Not sure knowing would've made a difference, but I'd have had an easier time not laughing at the sight of the enormous professor wedged in behind a regulation-sized desk.

"You wanted to see me?"

"Take a seat, Banach." He nodded to the single chair that had been positioned in front of his grossly inadequate desk. "I understand you had something to do with Stonewall's performance today?"

I shrugged as I dropped into the chair. "He just needed a nudge in the right direction. Anyone could have done it. In fact…" I trailed off.

"Say it."

"You're our Combat instructor. Why didn't *you* see what was going on?"

"I've been doing this for more than ten years. What makes you think I didn't?"

"The fact that you sat on your ass and said nothing?"

Nikolai's nasty smile made a reappearance. "You've got balls, which is why I like you. But if you've got a problem with me or the way I teach, we can settle it in the pit."

"Dampeners on or off?"

"It wouldn't matter either way." His massive hands clenched slowly into even more massive fists, knuckles popping like tiny bombs.

"Maybe some other time," I finally managed.

"My door's always open." The smile faded and Nikolai leaned back in a chair that creaked alarmingly under his weight. "Of course I saw where Stonewall was going wrong. Hard to miss it, really. But being a Cape is about more than just following orders and punching things. It's about understanding your own strengths and weaknesses. Even more importantly, it's about teamwork."

"You were waiting for one of us to help him?"

"Got it on the first try." Nikolai sneered. "Guess you're not quite as dim as the other professors say."

I ignored the dig. I'd passed all my classes first semester—even Ethics, although a D was nothing to cheer about—so my professors could say whatever the hell they wanted. "But what if none of us had?"

"Then I'd have brought Stonewall into my office for a little chat."

I paused, glanced around, and swallowed. "Oh."

"Yeah."

"I'm not here because I helped Jeremiah, am I?"

"Afraid not, kid." It was the closest I'd seen Nikolai's smile come to kindness. "It's a shame, because you're one of our best natural fighters, but combat isn't fair. All the ability in the world doesn't mean shit if you lack the power to back it up. And whatever it was you showed in that first fight against Paladin, we haven't seen even a glimmer of it since."

"What are you saying?"

"I'm saying this isn't the right path for you. Maybe you'll do better in one of the other powers classes."

Clearly, he hadn't spoken to my other teachers. "Come on, Nikolai. Give me a chance here."

"I've given you more chances than I should have. I've also had my ass reamed twice now by Gladys for the state you keep showing up in, and let me tell you, kid, that old bat has *never* squawked about my students before."

I should have known my overpowering attractiveness to older women would come back to haunt me. "I'll deal with Gladys. Just give me some more time."

Nikolai was silent, lantern jaw tight as he studied my face.

"I'm close to being able to use my power," I continued, drawing on thirteen years as an orphan to make that lie believable. "I just need a little bit longer. Please. This is the one thing I'm good at."

That part wasn't a lie. Given my complete uselessness in the two Ps, Combat was my only shot at making it to second-year.

"One month, baby Crow," he said at last. "If you haven't shown anything by then, then you're going to quit instead of making me kick you out." He shrugged massive shoulders at my unspoken question. "Less paperwork for me."

"One month." I nodded. "Not a problem."

I was so fucked.

CHAPTER 52

"It's not fair!"

"Life's not fair—" I started to say.

"We're not talking about *life*! We're talking about *your* life!" interrupted Kayleigh. "They can't kick you out of college just because you're still trying to figure out your power!"

I shrugged. "Nobody's said anything about kicking me out of the Academy yet… just Nikolai's class. But if I can't hold my own in a fight, what sort of Cape would I make?"

"The same sort as me, I suppose." Vibe's voice had gone quiet, her cold fingers barely brushing against my arm.

"Not even on my best day. Unlike necromancy, your power has plenty of applications outside of combat."

"Like what, exactly?"

"Like being able to sense if anyone is in a building before you leave it? Or picking out the handful of people in a crowd that mean your team harm? Or even figuring out the best way to avoid a fight entirely! Any team would be lucky to have an Empath."

"Then the same should be true for you."

I shook my head. Vibe was one of the closest things I had to a friend, but she seemed hopelessly naïve sometimes. "The only productive thing I've done with my power since coming here was that first fight with Paladin."

"So you *do* think that was your power at work?"

"I guess so. Everything I've read says necromancy is an external power, but maybe I'm different. It felt almost identical to when Sally had me use my powers to dismiss the ghosts."

"Sally!" Vibe sat straight up on the bench. "You should bring her back and ask for help!"

"I don't think it works like that."

"She said it was your power that called the ghosts. That called her."

"She came because of my power, but I'm not so sure she was summoned by it." I looked down at the small Empath's confused expression. "When has Sally Cemetery ever answered to anyone?"

"She's dead. And she said herself that—"

"She also said that ghosts can't talk and that they don't have wills or personalities of their own." I shook my head again. "I don't know how much of what she said was true or why she'd lie about the rest of it, but something tells me I've gotten all the help from her I can expect."

"Then what are you going to do?"

"The same thing you've been doing since school started, I guess." I shrugged and looked to the ocean. Early November in Los Angeles was only marginally colder than September had been, but the sunlight on the water lacked its usual brilliance. "Anything I can."

* * *

"Are we boring you, Mr. Banach?"

For the tenth time in as many minutes—and the thousandth time in the past week—I felt the emptiness slip right through my mental grasp, frustration pouring in to replace it, like water filling a basin. I cracked open eyes that had drifted shut somewhere in the process and glared across the room at Isabel Ferra. "Pretty much, yeah."

"Perhaps we can make the subject matter more interesting for you then." The words themselves were almost pleasant, the tone anything but. Ms. Ferra's smile was all sharp edges, her bared teeth so white they practically glowed.

"Why start now?" Eight months since I'd started this dance with the slender Ethics professor and we disliked each other more than ever.

Ignoring my retort, Isabel turned to the rest of the class. "Who can remind your inattentive classmate what it is we've been discussing for the past half hour?"

Around me, almost every male first-year raised their hand, but the teacher pointed instead to the student at the front of the class. "Go ahead, Penelope."

Winter—because *of course* it would be Winter—rose from her chair. "We were talking about situational ethics in Cape life. Specifically, the needs of the many versus the needs of the few."

"Thank you, my dear." Isabel refocused on me. "And what does that topic mean to you, Mr. Banach?"

As far as I was concerned, it meant we had another half-hour of total boredom ahead of us… but there were limits to the amount of shit I could give the teacher before our cold war went nuclear. "I guess it depends on the situation."

"Obviously. That *is* why it's called situational ethics." More than a few of the first-years snickered, although Silt—several seats away and carefully out of Isabel's view—rolled her eyes and yawned. "If you're having difficulties grasping the abstract principles at work, we can always focus on specific examples."

I shrugged away the implied insult. "Whatever you want, *Isabel*."

"Those may be the first intelligent words you've managed all year." More laughs, but there was no humor in the teacher's pretty eyes. "Gather around, first-years. This may be your only opportunity to hear a Crow's enlightened take on ethics."

"That seems overly optimistic," I said. "We're all stuck attending your class until we graduate."

"Only those who actually make it past first-year." Her smile could have drawn blood. "I'm told that's unlikely to happen in some cases."

I met her gaze, tombstone grey eyes clashing with morning sky blue, determined not to let her know the words had struck home. "You were saying something about examples?"

"Let's start with a hypothetical. Major Disaster has hidden an explosive device somewhere in the city, but the Black Hat himself is nowhere to be found. However, intelligence has located an individual who reportedly has that information locked deep within his mind. The only way to retrieve the information is through telepathy that will lobotomize the individual in question… a man who is, as far as you or anyone can tell, entirely innocent. Do you shatter one mind to potentially save hundreds?"

I shook my head. "Of course not."

"You'd let all those people die?"

"I wouldn't have to. Major Disaster doesn't use bombs." I waited for the obviousness of that statement to sink in. "If there's no bomb, there's no threat. And mind reading doesn't exist, so it wouldn't be an option anyway."

"This is a *hypothetical*, Mr. Banach."

"Then I'd *hypothetically* dream up a pretend-Telepath powerful enough to scan the man without hurting him."

It was Winter's turn to roll her eyes. "You can't change the hypothetical, *Damian*."

"Nobody asked you, Penelope."

"Just answer the question, Skeletor." That was Santiago, barely visible past the dual bulks of Jeremiah and Alan Jackson. "Some of us actually have plans tonight."

"Fine. In this magical world where Major Disaster bothers to use bombs and telepathy is a real thing… "I gave it a moment's thought and then shrugged. "My answer would still be no."

"So you *would* condemn hundreds to death?"

"*Potentially* hundreds. You said yourself that we don't know where the bomb is located. We don't know how many people are at risk. We don't even know for sure that the person being held has the information." I shook my head. "I'm not lobotomizing someone just because it *might* save people."

A couple of the other first-years were nodding their heads, Tessa and pale Erin Pearson among them.

"So you'd just sit on your ass then?" That was Caleb, tearing his eyes away from Isabel's own rear end for just long enough to join the debate.

"No. I'd get Jitterbugs like you to canvas the city while Earthshakers and Druids used their powers to sense for locations the device might have been stashed. And I'd have Sirens like Prince help evacuate public centers to minimize casualties in the event that we couldn't find the bomb."

"That's… not a bad plan," admitted Paladin.

"It's also irrelevant," said Ms. Ferra. "This is Ethics of Power 102, not Disaster Preparedness." She focused back in on me. "Let's modify the hypothetical. What if you knew for a fact that this person had information on the bomb?"

"How would I know that?"

Winter started to babble something about hypotheticals again, but Isabel cut her off with one upraised hand. "Let's say that the person in question is Major Disaster himself."

"So he went through the trouble of planting this bomb, and then somehow managed to get caught?" I frowned. "Sounds to me like he's already been lobotomized, but whatever. Fuck him. He deserves what he gets."

She narrowed her eyes but let the expletive go by unchallenged. "So your concerns about an individual's rights and freedoms are contingent upon that individual's innocence?"

"He's the one who placed the bomb," I reminded her. "That makes his brain fair game."

"Even a Black Hat has rights, Damian."

I turned to Paladin. "Does he? Nikolai's been literally beating it into our heads that we need to be prepared to kill should it come to that."

"Yeah, *in combat*. This is different. You can't lobotomize someone in cold blood."

"If you say so." I turned back to Isabel. "Are we done?"

"Not quite. Let's add one final wrinkle. After setting the bomb, Major Disaster was killed in action. However, you know with complete certainty that he was able to telepathically embed the information about that bomb in a single person's head. You also know that you have a fifty percent chance of retrieving that information from the individual's brain without causing any damage. However," and here she paused to smile yet again, "that person is not some random individual, but instead a friend."

"That might be pushing the hypothetical too far, Ms. Ferra," complained the Viking. "Damian doesn't have friends."

"No?" Isabel's eyes landed on Kayleigh, seated next to me. "For the sake of argument, let's say the individual in question was Ms. Watai. Would you risk destroying her mind?"

"No." I wasn't sure what she was driving at. I just knew her end goal was to make me look bad in front of the class.

Her smile widened triumphantly. "You'd put the needs of one over the needs of a hundred?"

"Depends on the one, I guess." Kayleigh. Dead Alicia. Little Nyah back at Mama Rawlins'. Even Silt. Can't say the list of names was all that long, but I guess it didn't have to be. "But yeah."

"How about a thousand innocent people? Ten thousand? Exactly how far are you willing to go?"

"As far as I need to," I growled back, my words seeming to echo in a classroom that had suddenly gone quiet.

"One person's life over the rest of the nation? Over the world?"

"Fuck the world," I told her. "What's it ever done for me?"

* * *

See what I mean about Ethics?

Total bullshit, every fucking time.

CHAPTER 53

Ethics wasn't the only class where my lack of focus was noticed, and Isabel Ferra wasn't the only teacher I got into it with over the ensuing weeks. Even got reamed by Amos once, which was an experience. When you live forever, I guess you learn all there is to know about verbally tearing someone a new asshole.

It's not like I didn't realize pissing off my professors was stupid. It's not like I was going out of my way to do so either… with the possible exceptions of Isabel and Emery-fucking-Goldstein. Mostly, I was just stuck in a loop; fixating on Nikolai's ultimatum and my own lack of progress in that area.

I was eighteen and scared. Can you blame me?

If you're the sort of asshole who answered yes to that, you're going to have some serious problems with my actions down the line. Assuming you don't already know what I did. Assuming you're not here, a faint fragment of your living self, *because* of what I did.

Let's not get ahead of ourselves though. I was almost halfway through the month Nikolai had given me, two days before my next sparring match, with another beating staring me in the face, when it finally happened. Call it a breakthrough. Call it an epiphany. Call it pure dumb luck. Just whatever you do, please don't give that fucker Emery any credit.

Even if it did happen in his class.

* * *

Perception was my least favorite class as a first-year. Ethics had twenty-one other first years to distract Ms. Ferra. Projection had people hurling fire and lightning and shit. Sometimes *literal* shit when Silt got pissed. Control… well, at least the new building still had a giant window I could people-watch through. But Perception? All it had was three of us kneeling in a circle in a dark room in complete silence, while Emery sat at his desk, doing fuck-all.

Or so I thought. Vibe told me later that Emery gave her assignments every class; to identify the emotions he was pushing her way—increasingly complicated shit like regret, guilt, and stress—and to separate them from whatever emotions Muse was putting out at the same time. Freddy had his own assignments, although I never learned what they were. Truth is, I wasn't entirely sure why the Switch had been placed in both P's, given that his powers seemed based entirely on Projection instead of Perception.

Anyway, those two had assignments and exercises to complete in Perception, but all I had was time to kill. Normally, that would've sucked. Most of the time, it did. But with Nikolai's ultimatum hanging over my head, it meant Perception was the one class other than Control where I was not only free to meditate and beat my head against the wall of my own power… I was actually encouraged to do just that.

And I did. Eyes clothed, breathing steady, mind scratching away at the layers of emotion and hard-earned shell that I'd peeled away so easily in Sally's presence. None of it did any good. Trying to reach that emptiness meant thinking about the emptiness and thinking about the emptiness made me think about the reason it was there to begin with and that… well, that was just another path to anger and starting the whole fucking cycle all over again.

We still had a half-hour left to go, but my knees were killing me, and my focus was shot. With a sigh, I shifted position and opened my eyes. I wasn't admitting defeat… not really. I was just acknowledging reality; victory wasn't happening any time soon.

Kayleigh was across the small circle from me. I watched her breathe—eyes twitching back and forth under closed eyelids like she was dreaming—and wondered for the first time exactly what her empathy was showing her. I knew she could track emotion to its source, but were other people one-sized blobs of sensation or could she perceive more than just distance? Could she see shape or color? And was I an empty hole in the middle of that space or did I not register at all? Was I just background noise, like a tree or a stone?

There's a saying you may have heard. God knows Emery said it more than a few times during class, because he was exactly the sort of asshole that liked to hear himself talk and didn't mind if we'd heard it all before.

Perception is reality.

Pretty sure the saying's got nothing to do with Crows, given that it predates the Break by at least a few decades. But the thing is, as I was thinking about Vibe and how her power didn't see me, about the possibility that I was nothing to her senses but void and vacuum, I felt the empty space inside of me respond. Instead of digging for that emptiness, I sat outside myself, and the emptiness rose up of its own accord, filling me until nothing, not even the pain in my knees, remained.

It lasted a handful of seconds before the realization of what I'd done hit me, and with it, an elation that promptly swept the emptiness away. For a moment I just knelt there, part of me already questioning what I'd done and felt.

Then I did it again.

And again.

And again and again all the way until class was over.

For the first time in weeks, I had hope.

My breakthrough happened in Perception, sure enough, but that doesn't mean Emery Goldstein deserves any credit. If you want to credit anyone, credit Vibe.

Credit the power that can't even see me.

CHAPTER 54

After eight months, the pits were familiar territory. I could even tell them apart by the patterns of stains across their cement floors. This was pit number two, where Silt had splattered Santiago's nose right after kicking the druid in the balls, and where Prince had vomited up his breakfast for at least the sixth time.

Eight months of bloody history layered on top of all the classes that had come before us… it should have bothered me, I guess. Instead, it felt like home.

The man across the pit from me though? He fucking bothered me.

Alan Jackson was a nightmare even in human shape. Shifted into his animal form, he was far worse; arms dangling to the ground, overly long, multi-jointed fingers ending in claws that could pierce even the Viking's skin. Instead of a nose and mouth, Alan had a wide snout filled with sharp teeth, and the shaved pate of his skull had been replaced by a thick coat of black fur.

Only the eyes stayed the same… but then, there'd always been something inhuman about Alan Jackson's golden eyes.

"Just roll over and play dead, Crow." The words were distorted, forced out through a mouth more suited for carnage than communication. "Sooner this is over, the sooner you can leave this class to those who belong."

Maybe he was trying to be nice, in his own way. Maybe he was taking pity on the poor little useless Crow.

But you already know how I feel about pity.

I bared my teeth at the monster. "It's time someone taught you to sit up and beg."

I stepped outside of myself and waited for the emptiness to come.

Nothing happened.

Alan Jackson was already in motion.

"Fuck."

* * *

I had plenty of time in the med ward to think about what had gone wrong.

First, I'd pissed off Alan Jackson.

Second, I'd failed to call on my power when it mattered. Maybe it was the difference between combat and a quiet classroom. Maybe it was a question of adrenaline or the irritation and fear I'd been dealing with.

Whatever the reason, I was that much closer to getting kicked out of Combat. I only had one more sparring session before Nikolai's deadline was up.

At least it wouldn't be against Alan.

My healing had finished a while earlier, but when I went to push myself up and off the table, Gladys was there with a crooked finger in my face. "You're not going anywhere, young man, until we can be certain the internal bleeding has stopped."

"How long will that take?"

"As long as it takes. Now lie your bony ass back down."

There was no arguing with Gladys when she used that tone of voice.

"I'm not sure pissing off Alan Jackson was the best decision, tactically speaking," said the med ward's other patient, flat on his back on the far gurney.

"Yeah, well." I couldn't shrug, because they'd taped one arm across my chest, but I rolled my eyes at Paladin. "That was just phase one of my plan."

"When is phase two?"

"I'm still working on it. But it sure as hell won't involve Alan—" I scowled. "And when is he going to pick a codename anyway? I'm getting damn tired of saying Alan-fucking-Jackson all the time."

"I hear he wants to be called The Manimal."

"Seriously? That's—"

"Almost as bad as Baron Boner? Yeah."

I scowled again, but Matthew wasn't looking my way, his eyes focused on the ceiling as the other Healer rebuilt the bones in his leg.

"What happened to you?" Almost nine months in, and I was no longer convinced Paladin was my arch-nemesis, but part of me was still glad to see he'd gotten his overly pretty ass handed to him.

"Orca happened. I made a mistake and she capitalized." He shook his blonde head, voice tight with pain and frustration. "It won't happen again."

"You sure about that? That's three in a row."

"Laugh it up while you can, Skeletor," he told me. "You're fighting her next."

That killed my amusement. One fight left to prove I belonged in Combat, and it was going to be against Nadia, almost as deadly as Alan and twice as fast.

I needed to figure out how to use my power when it actually mattered.

I needed a miracle.

Most of all, I needed help.

CHAPTER 55

"You want me to do *what?*" Silt folded her arms across her sizable chest and frowned.

"I told you already. I want you to spar with me." I swung my arms back and forth to get the blood moving. "I know how to fight and I know how to summon my power, but I can't seem to put the two together. If I'm going to beat Nadia…"

"You're not going to beat Orca, Boneboy. Not now, not ever."

I swallowed my protest, knowing she was right. "I need to at least not look totally pathetic against her… and that means using my power in a fight."

"And me knocking you around is going to help with that?"

"If it doesn't, I'm kind of fucked."

Sofia shook her head. "If we take our powers out of the equation, you're a better fighter than I am. And if you go full-Walker on me, what the fuck am *I* supposed to do? These legs aren't made for sprinting."

"That's why we're out here, and not in the Pits." I'd brought Silt to the clearing behind Bard's office, the same place where Shane's memorial service had been held, and where Caleb had smacked me down with a lucky shot. "I want you to use your powers."

"I'm still not following. I can just have the earth swallow you up to your knees, then go get a tree branch and hit you in the face until you stop moving. What exactly would that accomplish?"

"It would piss off Gladys, if nothing else, but that's not what I was thinking of either. Did you ever see the vid where Evan Earthquake fought King Rex?"

It took a moment. For all Silt's mastery of pre-Break pop culture, she was far less knowledgeable when it came to Cape vids, but eventually I saw the light dawn in her eyes.

"Do you think you could manage a smaller version of that?" I asked.

"That's… a bit advanced for a first-year."

"It's that or I ask Jeremiah to help instead."

"Wouldn't help," she muttered. "In his flesh form, you'd kick his ass. In his stone form, he might just kill you."

That pretty much mirrored my thoughts, which is why I'd sought her out in the first place. "I know, but I don't have any other options. I don't want to push you outside your comfort—"

A heavy blow blasted me from behind, picking me up off my feet and tossing me a full five feet past the squat Earthshaker. I spread my arms in front of me as I fell to lessen the impact, and tucked into a roll. When I'd made it back to my feet, I found my attacker standing next to Sofia; a featureless simulacrum of mud and dirt with four roughly hewn limbs.

"It's okay," said Silt, her grin wide and wild. "I think I've got it figured out."

* * *

Mama Rawlins once described karma as *someone doing the shit to you that you did to someone else.* Not sure if that's the official definition. Not sure I even believe in karma, but training with Silt sure felt like some kind of payback for how I'd trained Stonewall.

Only difference was, when Jeremiah and I were training, we'd *both* gotten tired. We'd both gotten bruised and battered in the process. Silt's golem didn't have that problem. It didn't tire, it didn't ache, and it sure as fuck didn't stop.

"I think you almost had something that last time."

I was bent over with my forearms resting on my thighs, sucking wind, and wondering how I was going to explain to Gladys my latest round of injuries, but I still managed to shoot the Earthshaker a surprised look. "How could you tell?"

"You were moving differently. Less like someone who wanted to puke their balls out." She spat to the side, and yawned. "Is this really helping?"

"I think so," I wheezed. "I'm getting the hang of calling my power in mid-fight. It's just holding onto it that's difficult."

"You didn't have that trouble when you fought Paladin."

"I was mostly unconscious by the time my power kicked in. There wasn't much in the way of thought or emotion left." I swallowed and forced myself upright. "That's not an approach I want to rely on."

"Makes sense. Can we hurry this up a bit though?"

"Why? You have plans tonight?"

"I have a date."

"Seriously? Am I the only one at this school who doesn't have a love life?"

"Probably. It's not like you talk to anyone but me and Vibe and, on very rare occasions, Evie."

"That last part is Wormhole's decision, not mine. She still thinks I'm going to eat her, I think."

"She'll come around. Maybe." Silt frowned. "Speaking of Vibe… where is she?"

"No clue. I haven't seen much of her recently."

Light dawned in Sofia's broad brown face. "Since the Ethics class where you and Isabel almost threw down?"

I frowned and reviewed the past week. "I guess so. Why?"

"You told the whole class that Kayleigh's life meant more to you than the rest of the world. That's the sort of thing that'll give a girl pause, Skeletor."

"Isabel was trying to trap me with some ethics bullshit, Sofia."

"So you were lying?"

I gave the question more thought than it deserved… mostly because I was too damn tired to go back to fighting just yet. "I don't know. Truth is, there aren't a lot of people left in the world that matter to me. Kayleigh. You. Maybe a few others. I'm not going to let anyone mess with people I care about… even in a hypothetical."

"Well, half the first-year women thought it was kind of sweet, while the other half are waiting for you to murder us all as part of some sort of weird romantic gesture."

"I'm not Lady Valentine, for fuck's sake." It was my turn to frown. "Which side was Orca on?"

Silt sighed, and muttered something under her breath. After a moment, her grin came back. "The side that's going to kick your ass in just a few days if you don't figure this shit out. Ready for more?"

"Do you have the time? I don't want to interfere with your date."

"I've got a half hour or so left. Plenty of time to pile-drive you into the dirt some more."

* * *

As I'd said, the tricky part wasn't calling on my power. It wasn't even calling on it during a fight. The tricky part was staying out of my head as the fight progressed. The moment I started worrying about what my opponent was doing, or what I was doing, or even about how my power was functioning at all, I'd be right back at square one, getting my ass kicked.

I guess it was a good thing I'd been spending the past eight months learning how to stay out of my own head. All those hours meditating, seeking inner peace and all that shit, and it turned out *existing in the moment* was the whole fucking key to using my power.

Pretty sure Gabriella Stein would've been horrified to realize it. Alexa though? She'd have just smiled that little smile of hers.

Kind of makes you wonder if she knew something all along, doesn't it?

* * *

I could tell I'd found a zone when my aches faded away. Silt's golem slowed in mid-strike; not snail-slow like the world seems to a Jitterbug, but slower than it had been moving all evening. I slipped one punch, then another without even thinking about it. My answering blows tore through tightly packed dirt and soil.

Part of me heard Silt's sudden intake of breath and the corresponding exhalation as she fought to keep her golem intact, but both noises were faint and indistinct. My body was already moving, one hand's fingers extending like a spear to drive through the golem's shoulder, while the other hand tore at the crease that appeared as if by magic. Then I was past the dirt creature, its severed arm crumbling in my bare hands.

I pivoted inhumanly fast, that same distant part of me watching my planted knee buckle under the strain, and then I was coming back at the golem. My other knee went up into the creature's core, followed by two open palm-strikes at the same spot. For all of Silt's power, her creation was really just a walking dirt pile; it exploded into hundreds of smaller fragments, spraying the clearing with dirt.

When the dust settled, I turned towards the Earthshaker. She was on her feet a good ten feet away, brown eyes serious. One thickly muscled arm was extended towards me, palm-down, and the ground between us quivered like it was made of pudding. "You still in there, Boneboy?"

I let my mouth fall open, hiding a wince as the pain my power had been blocking suddenly lit up my knee and both hands. "Braaaaaaaaaaaains."

Silt rolled her eyes and let the earth go quiet. "Brains?"

"Supposedly, pre-Break Walkers hungered for human brains."

"Have we not met? *I* know that. I'm just surprised you do."

"I did some research a few months back when I was trying to figure out my power."

She looked at the scattered fragments of her creation. "I'd say you've figured it out. Nadia may finally get that fight from you she's been looking for."

"Yeah."

"Thought you'd be happier." Silt shrugged. "At least you're not smiling. Is there anything else or can I go get pretty for my date?"

I took a halting step and my knee collapsed under me, dropping me onto the loose clumps of dirt.

"Actually," I managed, looking up at the stocky Earthshaker, "I could use some help getting to the med ward."

CHAPTER 56

On the far side of the pit, Nadia went through her warmups, every movement slow and precise. I'd seen her fight dozens of times—including the many occasions where she'd kicked my ass—and her routine never changed; one motion flowing smoothly into the second as if she was practicing katas in the mirror instead of getting ready for carnage. Her blonde hair was in braids, tight to the scalp, and the sleeves of her grey Academy sweatshirt were rolled up to the elbow, exposing deceptively slim forearms.

I probably should have been doing some stretching of my own. Gladys had patched me up after my sessions with Silt, but I was tight and sore all the way from my hamstrings to my neck. My shoulders were the stiffest of all, but that was just tension. This was my last chance to prove I belonged in Combat class.

I couldn't see Nikolai or the other first-years in the observation room, but I gave a nod to one of the three cameras trained on us from above. I took a long breath, drinking in the familiar smells of blood and dust and sweat and fear. I held the air until my head was swimming and my lungs felt ready to burst, and then I exhaled.

When the oxygen left my body, all my fear, stress and doubt went with it, replaced by the empty void of my power.

Nikolai's call to start the match had barely sounded before the grey-clad Stalwart was coming forward in a blur. In our first few fights, Orca had used her speed to analyze my movements and measure my response time. After so many easy victories, she no longer bothered.

Guess I'm not the only one who falls victim to expectations.

Nadia's movement was still too fast to see, but with my brain disengaged, my body translated impulse to action instantaneously. I twisted to one side, feeling a blast of wind as her lead jab slid past me. Her second fist was already on its way, but an angled step forward took me inside the arc, robbing her blow of any real force.

From there, I unleashed my own punch, all triceps and bad intentions, and for one sweet moment, time seemed to come to a halt. I had what felt like years to watch my hand rocketing toward Nadia's face, to see the widening of ocean-colored eyes as she strained to avoid a strike she'd thought me incapable of throwing. Then time caught up with itself, and my fist impacted right above the cheekbone, the blow resonating all the way up to my shoulder. Her head spun, just a shade faster than the rest of her, and the Stalwart staggered and fell.

I pressed my advantage, but Orca somehow turned her fall into a crouched, spinning leg sweep, the bone of her shin blasting into the meat of my calf. I watched my leg buckle—part of me noting that it was the same one I'd injured fighting Silt's pet—but pain was distant and hollow, locked away like emotion itself. My weight shifted automatically to the other leg, and I brought my damaged knee forward and up, straight into the crouching Stalwart's face.

Impossibly, she got one hand up fast enough to brush my knee aside. A breath later, her second hand struck like a spear to my extended thigh, staggering me again. She used the moment to break away, throwing herself backwards almost the full length of the pit.

When she rolled to her feet, she was smiling.

I almost lost my carefully crafted bubble of stillness then and there. Eight months of school, eight months of sparring, and that was the very first time Nadia had ever smiled at me.

It was one of the most beautiful things I'd ever seen.

She spat out a mouthful of blood, promptly killing the moment, but her pale eyes were sparkling, like ocean waves in the mid-day sun. Her voice vibrated with excitement.

"Finally!"

* * *

This time, Orca's approach was measured, displaying none of her earlier recklessness. She circled slowly, testing my defenses with lightning-quick attacks, but I had little difficulty spinning with her and avoiding the blows. With my power flooding my body, banishing exhaustion and pain, Nadia had as much chance of wearing me down as I did Dominion. The small part of my mind that retained conscious thought was happy to declare a stalemate.

Which is when she finally went back on the attack.

I spun away from Orca's punch as she danced forward, but my answering elbow found nothing but air. She had already ducked down to hammer her open palm into the side of my injured leg. The knee-cap popped grotesquely to one side, but I completed my spin anyway, driving my off-hand down towards Nadia's face.

By the time that punch arrived, she was gone yet again, springing smoothly past me and back to her feet. Ligaments in my arm stretched and strained as I pulled it back into position at a speed no merely human body was built to support, but as fast as I was, the Stalwart was even faster. Long-fingered hands clasped onto my wrist and shoulder like steel manacles, stopping the motion dead. With a quiet grunt of effort, Orca rotated my arm and pulled.

I didn't feel a thing, but the pop as my shoulder dislocated must have been audible even on the observation deck.

Orca threw three hammer-like blows to my midsection, but despite the sharp snaps that heralded cracked or broken ribs, I was still moving. I saw that realization enter Nadia's lovely eyes as she again stepped smoothly away. Then, those same eyes darted from my misshapen leg to my dislocated shoulder and the arm that dangled limply at my side.

Her smile widened.

A smarter man would have seen that smile for the danger sign it was.

A less desperate man might have just tapped out then and there.

I moved forward, one leg unsteady beneath me, my only working arm raised.

And then Orca showed the first-years of Combat class exactly how to stop someone who doesn't feel pain.

You take them apart. One limb at a time.

I almost wish she'd followed Alan's months-old advice, and just decapitated me instead.

* * *

It was afternoon by the time Gladys let me leave the med ward. I was used to missing Control on sparring days, but for the second time in a month, I'd missed Perception too. I could have caught the last half of Projection if I really wanted to, but every part of me hurt and none of me wanted to deal with Emery Goldstein. In fact, skipping *all* of my remaining classes sounded like a pretty phenomenal fucking plan.

November was on its way out, but the Los Angeles sky remained bright and blue, the weather mild enough that the grassy hill called the beach was still dotted with students in shorts and tees. I thought about heading out to join them, but my Academy sweats identified me as a Power, and I wasn't feeling up to the usual whispers and stares.

I got enough of those just limping my way across campus to the first-year dorms.

As I passed into the relative darkness of the common room, Kayleigh bounded up off of a couch, and rushed over to me. My eyes were still too busy adjusting for me to see her expression, but her voice sounded worried.

"Damian! You look terrible!" One small hand wrapped around my bruised wrist, she guided me to the couch. I'd barely seen Vibe over the past few weeks, but she seemed as casual as ever. If Sofia was right, and Kayleigh *had* taken my argument with Ms. Ferra the wrong way, she'd already gotten over it.

Either that or she just needed another break from her Empathy.

I settled into the couch next to her, trying not to groan. Gladys was taking this *only heal the first-years to 80%* thing a little too far. "You should see the other guy."

"We *did* see her. In Control, this morning." Kayleigh's voice was quiet.

"Oh. Please tell me they didn't heal the bruise?"

"First black eye she's had in months," she confirmed. "Was it worth it?"

"Ask me again in a few days, when I find out whether or not I'm still part of Combat class." I shook out the fingers of my right hand and gingerly formed a fist. It wasn't until after the fight that I realized I'd cracked two knuckles with my first punch. They were healed now, of course, but throbbed like a motherfucker. "After eight months, it was nice to at least land a hit."

"You like hitting women, Crow?"

Don't ask me how I'd managed to miss the silver-eyed Lightbringer on the far couch. Maybe Orca had broken my eyes too. I glanced past Vibe to Olympia and frowned.

"Shouldn't you be in Projection, Spectra?"

"Mind your own business," she shot back.

"I will if you will." I rolled my eyes. "But since you asked so nicely, no, I don't like hitting women. Even obnoxious ones who treat me like shit. But *hitting people* is kind of the whole point of the class. Besides, Nadia's dismantled me every single time we've fought… it was nice to turn the tide this once."

"I heard she still kicked your ass." Olympia's eyes were still fixed on the far vid screen, but I could hear the spiteful satisfaction in her voice.

"She kicked yours too, back in first semester, Olympia," shot back Kayleigh.

"She's kicked everyone's asses except for Alan's, and even there, she holds her own." I shrugged, wincing as pain radiated through my recently dislocated shoulder. "I *know* she's better than me. I wasn't trying to win… just to show that I could survive."

"And did you?"

I looked down into Kayleigh's concerned eyes. "I'll find out from Nikolai soon enough. For now, I just want to relax and not think." I kicked my feet up on the nearby table, and leaned back into the couch's cushions, turning my eyes to the vid screen on the far wall.

After a few moments of blessed non-conversation, I frowned. I'd seen pretty much every Cape vid ever made, but I didn't recognize this one. It didn't seem to feature any Capes at all. In fact…

"Are you two watching the *news*?"

"Yeah, why?"

"It's just… kind of boring."

"It's the world we'll be defending when we graduate," said Vibe.

"*If* we gradua—" I started to say.

"Besides, you've heard Amos. The better we understand current events, the better we'll be able to respond to, or even predict, future crises."

"I think he slept through that class, Kayleigh," said Olympia, her tone still snide, "but here's a little something that just might grab his interest." She waved a hand to engage the vid screen's volume control, and the smooth, cultured voice of the anchorman rolled through the common room.

"…And that concludes today's address. As you've just heard, President Weatherly, in his first major policy change since taking office, has declared next February's Remembrance Day to also be a national day of reconciliation. For the first time in the Hole's thirty-year history, family members of the prisoners will be permitted carefully supervised visitations." He paused, letting that statement sink in and then nodded to the camera. "It's a bold step, and one that supporters are already saying could define the president's legacy. For more on the administration's decision, let's go to noted sociologist and criminal reform advocate, Dr. Heinrich Wass. Are you with us, Dr. Wass?"

Kayleigh muted the vid screen and turned back to me. "Isn't your—"

"Yeah." Olympia had been part of the group that researched me, so she knew all about my dad. I'd told Kayleigh and Silt the story when they came back for the new semester.

If I'd ever questioned Vibe's claim that she couldn't read my emotions, her next question banished those doubts forever. "Are you going to go see him?"

I shook my head. Even if leaving campus hadn't been strictly forbidden, there was no way I was going to blow off the last few days of school to make a trip out into the desert. Not for him. Not ever.

"That asshole killed my mom. If I ever see him again, it'll be to return the fucking favor."

CHAPTER 57

The good news is that Orca kicking my ass—yet again—wasn't enough for Nikolai to drop me from Combat class. The better news is that he decided to give me one more shot, and the best news of all is that the next opponent ended up being my very own roommate, aka the worst fighter in class not named Damian.

Turns out that was *also* the bad news. It's one thing to lose to Alan Jackson or Nadia; pretty much everyone does, and the fact that I'd scored a hit on Orca had to count in my favor. But when you lose to Stonewall? When you end up breaking every bone in both of your hands because his skin is solid rock and your power doesn't give you the strength or durability to match up?

That's when you find yourself back in Nikolai's office.

* * *

This time, I didn't bother taking a seat. Partly because I knew what was coming, partly because I was pissed, and partly because my ass was bruised to hell and back after the fight with Stonewall. Instead, I rested my puffy, swollen hands on the back of the chair and waited.

Nikolai didn't mince words. "I'm sorry, Banach. You're out."

Even knowing the words were coming, I felt the bottom of my stomach drop. "It's been less than three weeks since I learned how to trigger my powers, Nikolai. Give me more time."

"I gave you long enough. Much more of this and I have a feeling I'll be explaining to Bard why he has another dead first-year on his hands." Nikolai shook his massive head, jaw clenched. "Part of my job is knowing who's suited for close combat and who isn't. Like it or not, you're in that second group."

"That's bullshit, man!" After all that work channeling the emptiness that was my power, it was almost nice to indulge in some genuine anger.

"That's life, kid. Of all people, you should already know that." He leaned back in his badly undersized chair and fixed me with a glare. "I was part of the Cape team that took down Lord Bone. Did your study group uncover that little bit of information when you were researching faculty?"

"Not that I know of."

"Crimson Death gets all the press these days, but Lord Bone was the real deal. Absolute nightmare in a top hat and white tuxedo. It took seven of us to take him down. Our Shadecaster got his ticket punched and most of the rest still bear scars."

I wasn't sure where he was going with all this ancient history, but I saw my opportunity. "Now imagine having a Crow on *your* side for once!"

Nikolai continued as if I hadn't said a word. "I've heard some of your classmates call what you do going full-Walker. But do you know what makes a real Walker dangerous?"

"They don't feel pain and they don't stop?"

"Nah. That just makes them a pain in the ass. What makes them dangerous," he explained, "is that they come in packs. For every walking corpse you take down, the damn Crow will be killing normals and raising another three or five to replace it. An endless supply of expendable soldiers, every one of them tireless, fearless puppets."

"I don't get tired—" I began.

"That's not the fucking point, Banach. When you use your power, it's impressive, I'll grant, but there's only one of you. Even worse, you're not raising Walkers, you're turning yourself into one. So what happens when someone decides to put you down?"

There didn't seem to be a great answer to that.

"You die," he concluded. "Not feeling pain is a long way from being invulnerable. A Crow's power lies in sending the dead to do their bidding while staying safe themselves."

"But my power doesn't work that way."

"Yeah. That's why we're here."

I smacked the back of the chair with one hand and did my best not to howl at the pain that raced through my recently healed fingers. "So what the fuck does that mean for me?"

"It means you need to leave Close Combat to those built for it." If I didn't know better, I'd have sworn the old Titan was trying to be kind. "Maybe you'll have better luck with one of the other Cape paths."

"No doubt. I'm sure I'll kick some serious fucking ass at Perception," I growled. "Come on, Nikolai. I've taken History of Powers. Everyone knows powers manifest internally or externally. Never both. The other Crows were externals, but I'm clearly not. Combat's the only thing my power's good for."

"Then you need to give serious thought to another career," the big man growled back. "I've got enough dead kids on my conscience without sending another one to his grave."

I wasn't going to beg, not to Nikolai, and not to anyone else. But still… "Give me until the new year. Maybe there's something more I can—"

"Sorry, kid. I told Bard my decision while you were being healed at the med ward. Just thought you deserved to hear the news straight from me." Nikolai rose to his feet, massive bulk blocking the light of the single lamp, and nodded to the door behind me. "For what it's worth, I wish you luck."

Like most wishes, his was worth nothing at all.

* * *

It took less than an hour for the news to spread among the first-years. Their reactions were about what you'd expect. Kayleigh was all outrage and sympathy, Silt was gruffly supportive, and Wormhole was… still convinced I was going to murder her, I guess. Caleb spent the next week walking around with a victorious smirk on his face as if he'd had a damn thing to do with my failure. Paladin's expression was perfectly calibrated between appropriately sympathetic and aloof, and Jeremiah…

Turned out my roommate was all marshmallow beneath that dark chocolate shell.

"I'm *so* sorry," he said for the second time that day, and the seventh in the past week and a half.

"Stop apologizing." I was flat on my back on my bed, Glass face-down on my chest, as I stared up at our dorm ceiling. "It's not your fault."

"You went straight from our fight to the med ward to being kicked out of Combat. How is that not my fault?"

"It just isn't. Was it Alan Jackson's fault—" I was *not* calling the guy The Manimal. "—when he tore you a new one?"

"Sort of, yeah."

"Wrong. He did what he's supposed to do. Just like you did."

"But now you're—"

"I'm not out of Combat because you won. I'm out of it because I *couldn't* win." That truth had been weighing on me for almost nine days. I didn't agree with Nikolai's decision—because fuck that sadistic bastard—but he was right that temporary immunity to pain didn't mean shit against super strength, super speed, or—as my roommate had unfortunately demonstrated—rock-hard skin. I might as well be a One or Two for all the good my power did me.

"But if it weren't for you, I'd be getting kicked out of Combat myself any day now."

Truth was, I *had* been pissed at Jeremiah at first. I'd spent a lot of my free time teaching the big fucker how to fight, and then he'd turned around and used what I'd taught him to ruin any hope I had of being a Cape. But it was hard to hold on to all that righteous anger when the guy seemed as upset about it as I was.

"Nikolai wasn't going to kick you out, Stonewall. He was just waiting for—" I cut off as an all-too-familiar rhythmic banging started in one of our neighboring rooms, followed almost immediately by paired moans. "Oh for fuck's sake!" I got out of bed, walked over, and banged on Jeremiah's wall. "It's eleven in the morning, El Bosque! Can't you and your girlfriend fuck somewhere else for a change?"

Shockingly, neither Santiago nor London took my advice. I rolled my eyes. "A building full of horny, eighteen-year-old Powers, and they give us dorms with inch-thick walls. This is one fucking thing I'm not going to miss." I tossed myself back onto my bed and tried not to listen as the Druid and Pyro went at it.

"No shit. Anyway, what were you saying—" Jeremiah cut off with a frown as a particularly loud moan interrupted him. "Okay, this *is* getting ridiculous."

"There's only one thing we can do," I agreed. "Retaliate in-kind."

"I'm sorry?"

"You need to bring a nice girl home and bang her brains out. Preferably when I'm on the other side of campus, thanks all the same."

"Wait… what?!?"

"I'd do it, but…" But Orca wasn't interested, as she'd made abundantly clear. "Look, Paladin may be keeping himself pure, but almost every other guy in the class has managed a one-night-stand… except for you and me. And that's just fucking embarrassing."

"Actually…" Jeremiah coughed. If he'd been any less dark-skinned, I was pretty sure I'd have seen a blush. "I've been kind of seeing someone."

"Seriously? Who?" I waited as he stammered out something entirely unintelligible. "Just promise me it's not Winter, okay?"

He gave me an odd look. "It's *not* Winter."

"Or Tessa the Pube-Hunter."

"Tessa the what?"

"Never mind." In the other room, London and Santiago finally fell quiet. "What was that? Three minutes? El Bosque's improving."

"This was not how I expected Sunday morning to go," grumbled my roommate. "Why are you here anyway? Don't you have counseling?"

"Not this week. Bard decided to give me the week off for good behavior." Actually, Alexa was away on some sort of work emergency. Someone in the world was in critical need of dispassionate diagnosis.

"So what are you planning to do with your free time?"

I shrugged. I'd been wondering the same thing for almost a week. There didn't seem much point in putting that time into my powers classes—let alone the *academic* ones—when I was now all but guaranteed to wash out of the Academy as a first-year. "I don't know. Try and find a non-powered woman who doesn't know—or care—what I am, I guess."

"Christmas break's coming up. You could always come meet my family. My sister—"

"Are you seriously trying to set me up with your sister?"

"—has plenty of friends," he continued with an ominous glower. "Maybe one of *them* wouldn't hate you."

"It's a nice thought, but like I told you before summer break, I'm not allowed off campus. Looks like it will be another week of me having the whole place to myself." Part of me almost hoped Sally would make another appearance… but I wasn't sure if that was the insanity talking.

We both looked to the door as someone slid a crisp white envelope into our room. Jeremiah picked it up with a frown. "It's addressed to you."

The envelope contained a card with a green wreath embossed on the front, below the words *Season's Greetings*. On the inside, the pre-printed message read *'Tis the season for merriness. Come join us for a night of celebration…* except the words *us* and *a night* had been crossed out and replaced with *me* and *an hour or* so, respectively. The sender had added another message below in that same uneven scrawl:

Banach. A little bird told me I'm not the only fart staying on campus for Christmas. Come on by and have some food. There will be booze.

"Bard?"

I shook my head, and nodded to the signature. It was almost entirely unreadable, but I'd seen it on my History of Powers exams. "Amos."

"I forgot he lived on campus."

"Yeah. Looks like I have plans after all."

Truth be told, I wasn't sure I wanted to spend a few hours with Amos. I only understood half of what the old fucker said, after all, and he wasn't shy about enumerating my faults. But he'd promised food and booze, and hadn't said one word about me having to pay for it.

Maybe it would be a merry fucking Christmas after all.

CHAPTER 58

Christmas Eve at the Academy is weird. The weather is mild, the campus' many trees still green and leafy. The sun goes down early, like it does everywhere else during winter, but out there on the coast, it takes forever to fall into the ocean, and the shadows it casts across campus seem to stretch for miles. Weirdest of all is the silence. Every student and teacher with a place to go has left days earlier, and college grounds that were built to house thousands seem almost desolate and abandoned.

No doubt, it had been like that during our two-week summer break too, but between the hordes of ghosts swarming me at every opportunity and my still-unexplained three-day talk with Sally Cemetery, I hadn't been in the frame of mind to notice. Now, a part of me almost missed the bustle. Having only one roommate was something I was still getting used to. An entire dorm building to myself was a long fucking way from comfortable.

A single sliver of sun was poking above the western woods as I walked the empty paths between equally empty buildings to Amos' house. In honor of the occasion, I'd pulled out the fancy, not-so-new suit Jeremiah had given me. The legs were a little short, and the sleeves a little long, but the black went well enough with my too-pale skin, and after a shower and quick shave, I felt mostly presentable.

Not sure who I was trying to impress. Amos didn't have a daughter that I knew of… and if he did, she'd be over a hundred. Even *her* hypothetical daughters would be too damn old. Mostly, I think I was just enjoying wearing something other than Academy sweats for once.

Amos' home was a little cottage on the southeast side of campus, tucked behind the regular students' dorms, and surrounded by apple trees and a white wooden fence that was at least as old as I was. Warm light poured out through the two windows that flanked the front door, and the door itself was partially open. I smelled real turkey—free of that oily, slightly artificial odor that synth-meat never quite managed to hide—and something that my nose enthusiastically identified as pie.

"I can hear your stomach growling all the way from the door, Banach. Don't just stand there like some sort of Salt Lake missionary; come on in and lend a hand."

I followed Amos' voice into the cottage. The crusty old professor was in his kitchen, a blue and white striped apron over his own slightly worn suit. He picked up a bowl of steaming vegetables and nodded to the stove where a platter of freshly sliced turkey had been set aside. "Grab the bird, if you please. Getting it out of the oven almost did me in."

"You could've just waited for me."

"And let it burn? For all I knew, you'd fallen asleep on your way over. Or is it just my voice that has that effect on you?" He put the vegetables down on a dining table in the other room, and came back, gesturing imperiously. "Come on, young man! That turkey's not going to move itself."

I picked the wooden platter up with a grunt. There had to be twenty pounds of meat. "How many people did you invite tonight anyway?"

"Invite? Half a dozen… but they all had other plans, as usual. It'll just be us."

I looked from the large turkey in my hands to the smaller—if equally appetizing—ham on the counter, next to two pies and a basket of fresh rolls. "Amos, how the hell are we going to eat all of this?"

"One fork at a time. Or two forks at a time, if you've got the dexterity for it." He gingerly shook the gnarled fingers of his left hand. "When I was your age, I'd have looked at a meal like this and asked where the rest was!"

"I'm not sure you were ever my age." I carried the turkey out to the table. A plain white tablecloth sat beneath the dishes the old professor had already carried out, and two candles brightened the small room.

"One-hundred-fifty years old and I still can't get no respect. Eat your heart out, Dangerfield."

"Who?"

"Just another guy who died before you were born," he muttered, placing the rolls on the table, and heading back to the kitchen. "Water or beer?"

I opted for water.

I know; I don't know what the fuck I was thinking either.

* * *

I don't know how people ate before the Break, but either Amos had been lying or they'd all been as big as King Rex. Two heaping plates of food later, we'd barely managed to make a dent.

I eyed the piles of sliced turkey still on the platter. "I think there's more now than when we started."

"It's possible I overdid it," he admitted. "But you know what that means? Leftovers all the way to Remembrance Day."

"It was too much, but it was good." I looked the old man in his slightly rheumy eyes. "Thanks for going through all the trouble."

"My pleasure. It gets a little spooky around here during the break. Figured you might appreciate the company as much as me."

"How'd you even know I would be around?" I shook my head and answered my own question. "Bard."

"I've been a professor almost a century, Banach, and there's one thing that's never changed during that time."

"What's that?"

"Nobody gossips like teachers. Like it or not, you're a topic of conversation around these parts."

"Fantastic." I eyed the apple pie, and debated having another slice. "Glad to hear I'm keeping everyone entertained."

"Make no mistake; if it were just about entertainment, there's plenty to be had from all you first-years. That Mikkazi boy, for instance… Anyway, you've got your detractors, sure enough, but a fair number of us are pulling for you." He made a face. "Now, if you go crazy and start raising Walkers to attack the campus… that'll change things a bit."

"I don't think there's much chance of that… the *raising Walkers* part, anyway."

"So I've heard. Sorry to hear your power's a bust." His eyes were almost kind. "So are you still moping about it, or have you started thinking about what's next?"

"What do you mean?"

"See, moping is when you get bad news and, instead of doing something about it, you sulk like a—"

"I know what moping is," I interrupted.

"Oh. Well… good. I swear, feels like half the words I use fell out of the vernacular decades ago, only nobody ever bothered to tell me." He frowned, and lowered his bushy eyebrows as he shot me a mild glare. "But if you know what moping is, why'd you ask?"

I couldn't tell if he was doing this on purpose or not, but I shot back my own glare. "I was asking about the second part."

"Ah." Amos cut a thin slice of pie, and slowly levered it onto his plate. "Well, you're a Low-Three who's been kicked out of Combat class. What's your best shot for making it to another year at the Academy?"

I'd given it plenty of thought already, and the real, brutally honest answer was that I didn't have a shot at all, but that's not the sort of thing you say to a teacher, even if he's just fed you pie. "Weapons, I guess. Perception and Projection are pointless, and nothing about my power lends itself to Mobility."

"So what… you're going to carry a big stick around with you, and then do that Walker thing you do?"

"A club's not going to keep me from getting murdered as soon as a Shifter or Titan gets their hands on me. I was thinking something ranged. Maybe a rocket launcher."

"Which doesn't make use of your power at all."

"As far as I can tell, my power's useless against anyone Low-Three or higher. You wanted to know my best shot at making Cape. That's Weapons."

"I asked for your best shot at sticking around at the Academy. Who says you have to be a Cape?"

"I'm a Power."

"So am I. So what? College is about more than just making Capes. Hell, most of the students here are studying to be something else."

"What are you suggesting then? That I become a History teacher?"

"Oh God, no! I'm just saying that there's plenty of non-Power things you can do with your life."

"Oh yeah? You have a career in mind where it's okay if I go nuts and start killing people?"

"There's always the postal service. They're used to that sort of thing."

I didn't bother to ask what a postal service was. It didn't sound all that useful, regardless.

* * *

An hour or so later, we'd moved to a couch in the small room Amos had designated *the den*. The old man was on his third beer of the night, and I was basking in the unfamiliar sensation of being uncomfortably full. I was halfway to sleep when he finally spoke again.

"I love this house. Hundred-plus years of history in its walls."

"A hundred years?" I cracked one eye. "It was here before the Academy?"

That prompted a loud cackle. "Hell no! A century ago, these grounds were prime real estate, Banach. It was a place for millionaires' mansions, not a humble little cottage like mine. After Jonathan started the Academy, I talked the young man into moving my cottage down from Santa Barbara. That was before half the town slid into the sea." He chewed on his lower lip, eyes distant in memory, then shook his head. "Anyway, he wanted to just build me a new house, but hell if I was going to let this baby go."

"Why?" It was a nice enough place… and a whole lot cozier than Mama Rawlins' had been, but if Bard had offered to build *me* a new house…

"I told you already! History!" Amos scowled at me, then waved his beer to gesture at the space around us. "I've had to replace a lot of the furniture over the years, but this is the house my wife picked for us to retire in. Damned if I'm going to let it go."

"You're married?"

"Forty-seven years together when the Break happened." He took another long pull of his beer bottle. "Funny thing is, we both survived it, up there in Santa Barbara. Two geezers making it through an apocalypse that claimed millions."

"What happened?"

"Dr. Nowhere happened. Time happened. It took a while before we realized I wasn't aging. I mean, at sixty-nine, who can tell, right? But after ten years? The truth got a little harder to ignore. She was getting older, and I was stuck where I'd been at the Break. Four years after that, and she was gone."

As someone who still didn't expect to make it to twenty, it was hard for me to imagine even knowing someone for sixty-plus years, let alone living with them, but the sorrow in his voice was impossible to ignore. "I'm sorry, Amos."

"She's been gone for decades now, and I still expect Alicia to walk through that door every morning." He sighed into his beer. "She even liked my jokes. Woman like that's a national treasure, young man."

I didn't say anything, but something in my silence caught his attention. He peered at me from his end of the couch. "Cat got your tongue? Tired of an old man's ramblings?"

"Your wife's name was Alicia?"

"Yeah. Pretty name for the prettiest damn woman you've ever laid eyes on. A real lady too. Why?"

"I just knew an Alicia once."

"Knew?"

"She and her parents moved up to Palo Alto less than a year before Scarlet's attack."

Amos set his beer bottle down on the table in front of us with a thump. "She mean something to you, this Alicia?"

I shrugged. "I don't know. Maybe."

"Then we're doing this right." With a creaking of joints, he pulled himself back to his feet and tottered down the hall past the kitchen. When he came back, he held two short glasses in one hand and a small bottle in the other.

"That's not beer."

"Hell no, it isn't. This here is a sample of the Dalmore 50." He placed the bottle almost lovingly on the table. It was an odd shape, with a square base and rounded corners that persisted even as the bottle tapered up to the round cap and cork. The bottle's interior was a lot smaller than the exterior, like a test tube suspended in crystal, and only half-full with a light, amber liquid. He poured an inch or so of alcohol into each glass.

"What is it?"

"One of the few benefits of outliving everybody I ever knew." He raised the glass to his nose and breathed in, like he was sniffing a flower. "It's whisky, Banach. Bottled pre-Break, 1978 on the old calendar."

I took a whiff of my own glass, but all I got from it was an almost overpowering smell of strong alcohol. "Is it expensive?"

"Before the world fell apart, I'd never have been able to afford it. Now? Considering that the country it came from doesn't exist anymore?" He rolled the glass around in his hand, watching as the whisky caught the light. "I'd say it's damn near priceless."

Oh. I took another careful sniff. When I looked up, Amos was watching me, his own glass raised high.

"To Alicia," he said.

"To Alicia."

The whisky burned all the way down.

CHAPTER 59

It was close to midnight by the time I started back to the dorm, the campus swimming unsteadily around me. First time I'd ever been totally sloshed. First time I'd let myself be, to be honest. Guess that was one upside of being the least impressive Low-Three Crow in existence; self-control no longer seemed all that necessary.

After twenty minutes of searching for the dorm, I gave up and found the nearest bench. The night was far warmer than it would have been in Bakersfield, but the aged concrete was cool even through my suit. I lay back and watched the stars slowly spin above me.

At the orphanage, Christmas had been some kids' favorite holiday. While Remembrance Day had involved Cape vids and presents, Christmas was Mama Rawlins' one attempt at making us feel like a family. Ten to twenty of us down in the living room, sitting in a circle on the floor and eating a double portion of synth-meat, the older among us telling bullshit stories about the good life, about the sort of foster parents we'd all end up with. One year, Mama Rawlins even put aside enough of her money to buy a bottle of sparkling cider. Another year, I talked Alicia into pouring out a big bucket of strawberry slushy, and before you knew it, there were twelve little kids—Nyah among them—with bright pink lips and tongues, every one of them sprinting around the house like Jitterbugs.

Maybe it was the whisky, or maybe it was Amos' talk about his own Alicia, but for the first time in a while, I found myself missing those little shits, some of whom I'd actively bled for. Even found myself missing Mama Rawlins and her eye-watering perfume that was at least half tobacco and stim-weed. At least in Bakersfield, I'd belonged. It was hard to feel that way at the Academy, where I was useless as tits on a bull. Hard to feel like I *wasn't* alone when the only other person on campus was snoring on his couch. Dinner had been nice, but all the whisky in the world couldn't change reality.

Maybe I used my power as I was lying there, feeling sorry for myself. Maybe I didn't. Given how drunk I was, it's hard to say for sure. All I know is that when I finally dragged my eyes away from the night sky, Mom's ghost was standing next to the bench.

I hadn't seen her since that summer night with Sally, but Mom didn't look any different for her absence. Same faded sundress. Same blissful smile under empty eyes. Sally had told me ghosts like Mom and Shane weren't people anymore… that they were just empty shells of energy that my power animated like puppets. Sally had told me a lot of things, but given that she was a ghost herself, at least some of it had to be bullshit. I focused my blurry vision on Mom, and for the first time in years, spoke to her directly.

"Why are you here, Mom? Why did you come back when I was nine? There's no way *I* could have called you, not at that age. I didn't even know how my power worked!"

She stayed silent, still smiling, and a little bit of the old anger got me to my feet.

"Why won't you answer me? What do you want? Are you just here to see how I'm doing, with you gone and dad rotting in the Hole? Because the answer is *not fucking great!* That's what happens to orphans in this shit-stained world!" I clenched my fists and spun away. "You had to know what Dad was. Why the fuck didn't you run?"

When I turned back, Mom was right in front of me, and for just a moment, for one fraction of a heartbeat, that smile was gone, and those eyes were dark and filled with something halfway between sorrow and rage.

Then her ghostly hand swept up through my chest, and the world fell away.

* * *

I had just put the third and final pie into the oven when the front door banged open. "Damian, sweetie, is that you? I thought you were going to play with Mary a little bit longer?"

It was David, not Damian, who came through the door, his tie loose and dark hair a mess. If his coming home at two in the afternoon on a work day hadn't told me something was wrong, the wild look in his grey eyes would have.

"Is everything okay, dear? Did something happen at the office?"

He brushed past me without answering, marching through the kitchen and into our master bedroom. I wiped my hands on my World's Greatest Mom apron and followed him in to find his head and arms buried in the closet, pulling out boxes and tossing them aside.

"David? Love?" I took a careful step closer. "You're scaring me. What's going on?"

His frenzied motions stopped suddenly, like a switch had been thrown, and I watched the tension drain from his shoulders. When his head came into sight, he was smiling that dopey, slightly crooked smile I'd fallen in love with on our very first date, so many years ago. "It's alright, Elora," he said, "Everything is going to be fine."

That's when I saw the knife.

"David, where did you get that?" The blade was six inches long and sharp along a single edge that tapered to a point. I'd never seen it before.

"I've always had it, packed away in a box." He shook his head, as if in wonderment. "Only I somehow forgot it was there. Can you imagine?"

"Not really." I swallowed hard and did my best to keep my voice level. "But what do you need it for? You're not… you're not going to hurt yourself, are you?"

"Me?" He rolled his eyes and laughed. "Of course not, silly. That wouldn't help at all."

"Help what?" I shrank back as he took two steps across the room, but then he was past me, heading back into the kitchen. "Why do you need a knife?"

"It's for Damian," he called back over one shoulder, that same smile still on his face. "Our boy needs to die. You said he was over at the Smiths'?"

He was two feet from leaving the kitchen, ten feet from the front door, and at most a hundred from the Smiths' house next door—Tom, Casey and little Mary—but somehow I got in front of him before he'd taken another step.

"What in God's name are you talking about, David? Why would you want to hurt our son?"

He looked down at me in confusion. "It's not about hurting him. Nobody wants that. It's about ending him."

I didn't know what had happened at work, or what it was that had pushed my husband of six years over the edge, but I felt my fists clench. "You listen to me, David Theodore Jameson. Put that knife down. Right. Now. We're going to talk about this like adults or I'm calling the police and that will be the last you see of your son or me."

He looked down at the knife in his hand and then back over at me, the confusion spreading. "You don't understand, Elora. I'm doing this for you. I don't know how I forgot, and I don't know how she made me remember, but our son is meant for horrible things. If you knew what he was—"

"Put the knife down," I said again, "and tell me." I waved to the breakfast nook on the far side of the kitchen, conveniently close to the rolling pin I hadn't gotten around to putting away. "If it's as bad as you say, I'll help. We can do it together. As husband and wife."

"Together? I'd like that." He started to lower the hand that held the knife when I heard it; a sound I'd heard thousands of times over the past few years; a young boy's shoes flapping carelessly against the pavement as he ran up the driveway to our house.

"Mom! I'm hungry! Did you make pie?"

The light went out in David's eyes. The knife came up and he took another step towards the door.

"Mooooooooom?"

"Damian, run!" I lunged for the hand that held the knife, and even though I was half the size of my husband, the impact staggered him. He turned from the open door, and something silver flashed between us.

I didn't feel the blade the first time it entered, but as it slid back out from under my ribs, my legs turned to water. It was all I could do to hold on to that arm, trying to stay upright, trying to use my body weight to keep my husband from turning on our son, as the knife kept darting in and out.

"Dad? Mom?" Damian skidded to a halt on the red-splattered tile, eyes going wide as he took in the scene.

I tried to yell at him, tried to tell him again to run, but there was no breath left in me, just blood bubbling up past my lips even as it gushed down my stomach and legs.

My fingers went numb. I watched them slide free of David's arm, watched the kitchen spin around me as I dropped helplessly to the floor.

In the doorway, little Damian opened his mouth to scream, but I couldn't hear a thing. My head bounced off something hard, and blackness crept in from all sides until the only thing left was a blurred view of the man I'd loved, his grey eyes widening with the realization of what he'd done.

The world shrank even further. Pain. Confusion. Fear.

And finally, silence.

* * *

I came to on my hands and knees in the grass next to the bench. I hadn't remembered Mom telling me to run. For thirteen years, all I'd remembered was the sight of her and the smell of blood and apple pie. Now, my own memory merged with Mom's vision; the vacant look on my father's face, the cold ice of the steel blade perforating her flesh, and the worst revelation of all… the thing I had never known:

Mom had died because of me.

I vomited up every bit of Christmas Eve dinner and Amos' prized whisky, puking until there was nothing left in me and my body was wracked with dry heaves. I wiped my mouth with one hand, brushed my too-dry eyes with the other, and rose unsteadily to my feet.

Mom was still there, back to smiling like she didn't have a care in the world.

I staggered away from her, bumped into the bench, and fell heavily to the concrete pathway, saved from another concussion only by my teachers' many, many lessons in how to fall.

"That was real, wasn't it? How did you do that?"

Mom's ghost stayed silent.

* * *

I still don't know if it was my power that kept Mom from leaving for all those years, that kept that one memory alive in her hollow shell for me to access when I was an adult… or if it was Mom herself that somehow held on; some tiny spark of left-over consciousness that allowed her to stick around to show me the truth of her final moments.

It's one of the questions that troubles me on nights like this, when the dreams drive me from sleep, when there's no one and nothing around except for ghosts like you. I can't count the hours I've spent thinking about it, wondering. If it was Mom's doing, *why* had she done it? If it was instead my power at work, how had I even known there was more to see?

Some questions don't ever get answered. Some questions haunt you forever.

But at eighteen, still a little bit drunk somehow, those questions hadn't occurred to me yet. My mind had space for one thought and only one thought, repeated again and again and again until the echoes sounded like thunder.

My father needed to die.

CHAPTER 60

You might think patricide's the sort of thing that seems less attractive sober, but by the end of Christmas break, I was more committed than ever. I was never going to be a Cape and whatever Amos might say, I was never going to be a well-adjusted, salary-earning member of his postal service either. The Academy was free to members of the Cape program, but it was a long way from free for normal students, and I had fuck-all in the way of money or ways to generate it. After almost a year of school, I was right back where I'd been before Mr. Grey found me; no prospects and no future beyond the still looming and unavoidable descent into madness.

About the only thing I *could* do was make sure my father got what was coming to him.

Father kills mother so son kills father.

Now there's a post-Break fairy tale for you.

***

By the time students started trickling back onto campus, bright-eyed and eager for the last two months of school, I had a plan. Funnily enough, it was the government that made the whole thing possible. The Hole was as much a fortress as it was a prison, buried deep below the earth and entirely impregnable… but President Weatherly's recent announcement changed that. On Remembrance Day, I would be able to meet with my dad, ask why he'd wanted to kill me, and send his homicidal ass to hell where it belonged.

Assuming I could get *to* the Hole, anyway. That was my first problem. I wasn't concerned with Bard's rules about leaving campus anymore—when it was all over, I sure as fuck wouldn't be allowed back as a student, even if I survived killing my dad—but the Hole was way the hell out in the desert, and I didn't have any transportation other than my own two feet and badly worn sneakers.

My second problem was even bigger. A day of quick research had told me that the prisoner meetings would take place in the Hole itself, in a subterranean space set aside for the event. Given the nature of the inmates, it was a sure bet that dampeners would be in place and running at full strength, preventing me from calling on my power. Worse, the whole place would be teeming with guards ready to put down anyone—inmate or visitor—who got out of line… and I was pretty sure trying to murder my dad qualified.

I needed a weapon, and it needed to be a guaranteed kill-shot, because I'd only get the one opportunity.

Planning a murder in one of the most heavily guarded buildings in the Free States would've been a challenge for anyone, let alone an eighteen-year-old who'd slept through a good portion of his first year at college, but like I said, I had a plan.

More importantly, I had someone I could ask for help.

* * *

The one positive about not having much shit is that what shit you do have is always easy to find. I waited for Jeremiah to head out for a New Year's party at The Liquid Hero, and retrieved what I needed from my underwear drawer. The card Her Majesty had given me was as glossy as ever, the seventeen digits on its surface glittering silver. Those numbers took me to a net page with a single text box on my Glass' browser. I tapped in my request and watched the whole page go dark.

There was no telling when Her Majesty would get my message or how she'd respond, once she did. I needed to stay put at the Academy and wait for a reply.

Less than two months to Remembrance Day.

I found myself counting the hours.

* * *

One thing nobody tells you about life-changing decisions is how little the rest of the world seems to care. There is no personal epiphany that can stop the world from spinning, not unless you're Dr. Nowhere in disguise. Toss in the fact that I couldn't tell *anyone* my plan—given the likelihood that they'd not only object to pre-meditated murder, but tell someone who could do something about it—and I found myself having to pretend interest in stuff that no longer mattered in the slightest.

Like the Remembrance Day dance, for example.

"Oh *that* one's cute!"

"I don't know." Vibe frowned down at the Glass in Wormhole's hands. "I knew a girl who wore a dress just like that back at high school Prom. She was a major jerk." She tapped the screen and her face lit up. "Now that's more my speed."

"It's just so… blue."

Kayleigh arched an eyebrow and tucked a strand of dyed hair behind her ear. "What's wrong with blue?"

On the far side of the bench, Silt sighed loudly and looked across the clearing to me. "Be glad you live in the guys' wing, Skeletor. This is the twentieth variation on this topic I've heard since we got back from break."

"It's the *only* dance we get this year, Sofia," Evelyn reminded her roommate. "And it won't just be us, but also second and third-years."

"And faculty and representatives from some of the premier Cape teams in the country," Silt finished. "I know. I'm just saying it's a lot of effort and energy to spend on an outfit you'll wear once."

"We could all be dead in two years." Vibe rolled her eyes and tapped Wormhole's Glass a second time. "I say we enjoy ourselves in the meantime. Just because *you* don't want to buy a dress…"

"The one I have is good enough." Silt yawned. "It's black, shows off a ridiculous amount of skin, and—with the right pair of heels—might almost give me long enough legs to get Boneboy drooling."

"I don't know." I faked a frown. "I mean… we've already slept together. Taking you to a dance seems like a step backwards."

"Because there isn't an ounce of romance in your coal-black heart," she shot back, her grin spoiling the fake outrage. "Besides, I already have a date."

"Seriously? I thought London, Santi, and our two Hydromancers were the only first-year couples so far. Who's the no-doubt-secretly-terrified guy?" I frowned. "Please tell me it's not Paladin."

"Matthew? Please. I'd break his skinny ass in two."

"I'm not sure skinny is the right word," said Vibe thoughtfully.

"Mmhmm, more like perfectly chewable," agreed Wormhole.

"*Anyway*," said Silt, pausing to toss a glare at the other two women, "my date's not a first-year. Debbie's a normal."

"Oh." I wasn't sure if I was more surprised that Sofia's date was female or that she wasn't even a Power.

"Oh?" Silt's glare switched to me.

"Is she cute? And does she know about… *us*?"

"You're an asshole, Skeletor." She grinned, and the awkward moment passed. "Somehow, I don't think she's threatened at all."

"What about you, Damian?" asked Kayleigh.

I shrugged. "I *am* kind of threatened, but if Silt thinks we can make it work…" A motion of Silt's thickly muscled arm sent a piece of dirt flying across the clearing at me.

"No, I meant what are your plans for the dance?"

Since I'd be hundreds of miles away that day, doing my best to commit murder under the eyes of a dozen prison guards, I hadn't given the dance any thought. But that was one of the things I couldn't say. "I don't know. Some of the guys are renting tuxedos, but I've got a suit from Jeremiah that should do just fine."

"I think she was asking who you were going with, Boneboy."

"With all the women actively campaigning to date me, I'm still trying to narrow down the applicant pool," I said drily. "Maybe I should run background checks. I want to make sure whoever I select doesn't somehow tarnish my spotless reputation."

"I'm surprised you haven't asked Nadia yet," said Silt.

"Orca has a date." That was Evelyn, who'd continued to browse dresses on her Glass.

"She does?" I frowned again. "Please tell me it's not—"

"It's not Paladin." It was Wormhole's turn to frown. "I swear… you're obsessed with the poor guy."

"Who is it then? Alan Jackson?"

"Seriously? Can you see Alan Jackson at a dance?" Vibe shuddered.

"She's going with Prince," said Evelyn.

"Wait… *what?*" It was hard to think of a first-year more different from Nadia than still-chubby, unathletic Johannes "Prince" Callum. "But he *fainted* the one time they sparred!"

"From what I hear, he dances almost as well as he sings. And nobody sings like a Siren."

I tried to remind myself that I wasn't even going to the dance, so I shouldn't care who Nadia went with, but after nine months of trying—and failing—to impress her in the sparring pits, her choice still hurt.

"Do you really have a bunch of girls in mind for the dance, Damian?" I was so used to Kayleigh sitting next to me that it was strange seeing her on the bench with Silt and Wormhole for once. Or maybe it was the fact that she was wearing a dark blouse and long, pleated skirt instead of her usual Academy greys.

"Shockingly, no. It turns out necromancy isn't the turn-on everyone told me it would be." Getting kicked out of Combat class *had* lessened the amount of terror I inspired in the other first-years, but they still seemed fully capable of resisting my immense sex appeal. "I was thinking of asking Gladys."

"You know… *we* could always go together."

"You and me?"

Somehow, the blush showed even through her naturally golden skin. "As friends, I mean."

Under her breath, Silt muttered something that sounded weirdly like "*…two steps back.*"

"All those people," continued Vibe, her words almost tripping over each other, "and all their emotions…"

Somehow, that made things harder, not easier. I didn't want to promise something I knew I couldn't do—especially if Vibe would be relying on me to block her Empathy—but telling her I wasn't going to the dance would leave her wondering why. The last thing I needed was someone as smart as Kayleigh digging into my plans. "Sure," I found myself saying, "I'd be happy to go with you."

For some reason, Silt looked even more troubled. Maybe she wasn't as confident about her date with Debbie as she'd been pretending.

CHAPTER 61

By the time I finally heard back from Her Majesty, I'd solved my transportation problem. More accurately, it had been solved for me, and once again, I had the government to thank. Because the Hole was way out in the middle of the fucking desert, and the vast majority of the Free States' population didn't have cars, shuttles had been arranged from the major cities. The Los Angeles shuttle was scheduled to leave two days before Remembrance Day from an old and unused bus terminal several miles south of the Academy. With all the running we'd been doing for the past year, I could manage three miles in my sleep.

With transportation solved, all I needed was a weapon.

I came back from another Ethics class where Isabel Ferra and I had spent long minutes glaring at each other to find my Glass blinking with a received communication. There was no header data at all… just a five word message:

Outside west wall. Midnight. Tonight.

Finally.

* * *

The west wall was the one our clearing overlooked, although I'd never gone all the way down the hill to the wall itself. Trying to climb an unfamiliar wall in the dead of night seemed like a horrible idea, but I had three things working in my favor. First, because of the hill, the wall was only ten or so feet high from the Academy side, instead of the fifteen to twenty feet it was everywhere else. Second, security was mostly about keeping people out, not keeping people in.

And third, I'd spent the last month reliving my Mom's dying moments every time I closed my eyes. I'd hop off a forty-five-fucking-foot wall if it got me even an inch closer to killing my murderous asshole of a dad.

Climbing the wall was easier than I'd expected. Los Angeles didn't get earthquakes anymore—not natural ones, anyway—but the ground had settled since the wall's original construction, and small cracks in the stone made for usable finger holds. Summoning my power gave me both the strength to cling to those tiny holds, and the ability to block out the pain of the rough stone shredding my fingertips.

Getting down the other side was more of a challenge. The hill kept sloping to the west, which turned my ten foot climb into a twenty-five foot descent. Cracks and fissures still existed, but I didn't have the luxury of reaching up and feeling around for them. Instead, I found myself clinging to increasingly small holds while my sneaker-clad feet brushed the wall below me in search of something new to cling to.

I was working my way down, hanging from one hand while I extended the other one out for the next handhold, when I finally slipped. Maybe it was my power giving out. Maybe it was the blood from my torn fingers making the rough stone slick and slippery. Maybe Madame Fate is just every bit as merciless a bitch as the stories say. Either way, I was still fifteen feet up when I went airborne.

A fall like that's probably not going to kill you unless you land on your head but it can still fuck you up. I had just a moment to send Dr. Nowhere a mental *fuck you, asshole* before I impacted… hitting something firmer than dirt that nevertheless gave way beneath me with an almost-metallic grunt.

The smell of leather was the first thing that penetrated my daze. Next was the impossibly firm and fine body pressed against me from below. Last, but not least, was the glint of pale moonlight off the reflective visor of a motorcycle helmet.

"What did I say about reaching out to me for a booty call, kid?" As much time as I'd spent thinking of Her Majesty—how she looked in her leather riding outfit or the way she'd absolutely shredded that Pyro on the road down from Bakersfield—I'd somehow forgotten her raspy voice and the discordant sound of razor blades and barbed wire that seemed to follow her about.

"Funny. Thanks for the catch." I rolled to the side and off of her with something close to regret. As hot as Nadia and London and a handful of the other first-years were, they were still teenagers, like me. Her Majesty was all woman, and built like a template of voluptuous, badass perfection. "And for coming."

"Felt like you were only a few seconds away from coming yourself just now," she mocked. "Don't tell me you've spent ten months saving yourself for me?"

"Something like that." Some physical reactions really *were* involuntary. I glanced up at the wall I'd fallen from. In the moon's pale light, it looked hundreds of feet high. "Should we get out of here before the guards come?"

"Assuming you can walk with that thing." The humor vanished from her voice like it had never existed. "The further away from this place, the better."

I climbed to my feet, adjusting myself with one hand. With a soft creak of leather, Her Majesty was back on her own two feet. I followed her for several blocks and then into a side street.

"What's that?"

"That's my bike." The visor turned my way, its smiley face decal barely visible in the darkness. "You know, the one we rode for half the trip here? Shit, school really does rot the brain, doesn't it?"

"I recognize your motorcycle. Glad to see you got it repaired too. But I was talking about *that.* Actually, *those.*" I motioned to the still lumps around the bike, visible in the overhead street lamps' circle of light.

"Ah." I heard as much as saw her shrug. "Turns out one of the city's gangs claims this turf. I had to remind them not to touch what wasn't theirs."

I looked at the shredded remains that had once been three… or maybe four… people, and swallowed.

"It's a dog-eat-dog world, kid," she continued, kicking away a machete that had been twisted in half. "This particular bitch was just more than they could handle."

I told myself that whoever the dead men were, they'd gotten what was coming to them. They'd been out here looking to cause harm, and the city was probably safer with them gone, but even so… I was the reason Her Majesty was even in the city. I was the catalyst that had unknowingly engineered their meeting tonight.

Their deaths were on me.

Seems a bit weird, I know, to spare even a moment's remorse on strangers I didn't know—strangers who'd have probably hurt and robbed other normals if they hadn't run across the storm of shrapnel that was my ever-smiling companion. Seems especially weird, since I was planning a cold-blooded murder of my own, but the truth is, I carry every death with me; both the ones I was present for, and the ones that I caused. Mom and the crying boy at Mama Rawlins'. The four bandits on the mountain road towards Los Angeles. Unicorn. And now these nameless, faceless strangers.

My death count was in double-figures, and I was only eighteen. It's the sort of thing that would have given most people pause. Hell, it gave *me* pause, but I had one more person to add to the list, and I had to know if Her Majesty had brought what I needed to make that happen.

I put the freshly dead bodies out of mind and turned back to the leather-clad Shifter.

"Do you have it?"

"Just like that, huh? Quick grind and grope and then straight to business?" Her voice went smooth and liquid, reminding me of that night by the fire almost ten months earlier. "Maybe you really are my kind of guy." The laughter that followed buzzed like a swarm of angry bees. She went to her bike, stepping casually through a small pool of gore, and pulled something from the saddlebags.

"What is it?" It was shaped vaguely like a gun, with a grip and a barrel, but it was thin, smaller than my palm and too light to be metal. Even stranger, it was warm to the touch.

"What you asked for. Small. Single shot. Guaranteed kill. Just don't feed it after midnight."

"Feed it?" For just a second, I felt the weapon twitch in my hand. "This is *alive?*"

"It was a joke, kid. Sort of." She shrugged. "Fuck if I know. I figured you wouldn't want something that security could spot, and there's not a scanner in this country that will pick that up. Something to do with it being part organic, I guess. Don't worry though; it's not sentient. Not this far out of his range anyway."

"Whose range?"

The motorcycle helmet cocked to one side, as if Her Majesty was studying me, but the yellow smiley face decal made her face impossible to make out. "Legion, obviously."

"How did you get *Legion tech*?"

"The same way I get most shit. I stole it when I was in Old Baltimore. Was a pain in the ass, especially while I was still in the fifty-mile radius of his power, but now I guess I'm glad I took it."

"I didn't know you'd been to Old Baltimore." I'd never met someone who'd gone further east than the Badlands. Hell, I'd never even *heard* of someone doing it.

"I've been almost everywhere on this continent. Wherever the job takes me. That city's a cake walk compared to some towns. You think Legion's a horror, you should meet his brother."

I'd also never heard that the lord of Old Baltimore had a brother. "What about West Virginia? Have you been there?"

For a moment, she went quiet. "No jobs in West Virginia, little Crow. No people. Nothing at all except for the one house and the woman sitting on its front porch."

"You've seen Grannypocalyse? With your own eyes?"

"Such as they are… and from a distance." The helmet swiveled back and forth for a moment. "Eighty years old if she's a day, drinking from a cup that never runs out of tea, in front of a house that was old and decrepit when the Break hit. And nothing around her and that house for miles and miles but radiated wasteland. Like I said, there's worse places than Baltimore."

"Damn." I looked down at the weapon in my hand just in time to see it twitch a second time, like a muscle's involuntary contraction. "Still, this has got to be priceless."

She shrugged with another soft creak of leather. "I left you my card for a reason. Can't turn around and complain when you use it, can I?"

"Yeah. About that…" I wasn't going to look a gift horse in the mouth, whatever the hell that meant, but I had to know. "Why *did* you give me the card?"

As she spoke, the ever-present rasp in her voice strengthened, harsh and grating. "The world's a toilet, but some people get shit on more than others. Seems to me you're in line to get more than your share." Before I could ask what that meant, she continued. "Speaking of, how's the whole Crow thing treating you?"

It was my turn to shrug. "Turns out it's a bust. Strong enough to ruin my life, but too weak to make it as a Cape."

"That's… unexpected."

"That's why I need this."

"Going out on your own terms? I can appreciate that." Before I could say more, she raised a gauntleted hand. "I don't want to know the details. Figure I'll hear about it on a vid or something; you and your sweet little ass going down in a blaze of glory. Just make sure whoever you aim that at is someone you want dead, because once you squeeze the trigger, there are no takebacks."

In my mind, I saw Mom die—*felt* her die—all over again. "That's not a problem."

"A man of conviction. In this day and age, that might be even rarer than the toy I brought you." She swung one impossibly long leg up and over the body of her bike and brought the electric engine to life with the flick of a switch. "Guess this is it then. I'd tell you to look me up in a few years, once your balls have finished dropping and you're ready for some grown-up fun, but I'm pretty sure you'll be dead long before that happens."

"I'm pretty sure you're right." I watched as she pulled away through the carnage that had been some of L.A.'s finest gangbangers. Within moments, her bike's tail light had faded into the night.

"Goodbye, Your Majesty."

* * *

I didn't have a chance in hell of climbing the wall I'd fallen from, let alone doing it in the dark. Luckily, I didn't have to. I followed the wall around to one of the main gates. There, I flashed my student ID to the guards on duty. The Academy scanners didn't emit so much as a warble as I carried the gun through, and within ten minutes, I was back in my dorm room.

I had both transportation and a weapon.

One month to go.

Nothing was going to stop me now.

CHAPTER 62

"What would you like to talk about in today's session, Damian?" Alexa was all in black, as usual, and as still as a screenshot behind Dr. Gibbings' wooden desk.

"I don't know. The Graduation Games, maybe? That and the dance are the only things anyone wants to talk about these days."

The former-Cape studied me for a minute or so, and I wondered what it was she saw. The distance between us—a distance that had started to narrow after summer break—now seemed like an un-crossable chasm. I hadn't told her about my mom's vision, and I sure as fuck wasn't going to tell her how I intended to celebrate Remembrance Day, and that had left me feeling like I was going through the motions, session after session, searching for something meaningless to discuss.

Midnight wasn't dumb—far from it—and I knew she'd picked up on the slow disintegration of our relationship, even if she didn't understand the reason for it. I wasn't surprised at all when she finally decided to call me on it.

I was, however, surprised with how she broached the subject.

"I suppose we could talk about the games, as if you cared even the smallest bit about them, but I think I'd rather talk about you leaving campus Friday night."

"How did you…?" I stiffened, part of me unconsciously reaching for my power even as the truth hit me. "The gate guards."

"The guards," she agreed. "They record every individual that passes through their gates. Imagine my surprise when I received an alert that you had been one of them."

"What do you want me to say?"

"I want to know why you left. And given that the guards only have record of you coming back in, I'd like to know how too."

"I hopped the wall by the forest's edge," I told her, figuring a little bit of truth might help the rest of my lies go down. "As for why? You try being cooped up on this campus for a full year, let alone sleeping in the same room with The Human Snore. For one night at least, I wanted some space."

"You jumped the west wall?" Alexa's voice sharpened. "Fascinating. Did you know that the police found several dead members of the Blood out in that direction yesterday morning?"

"I don't watch the news, so no."

Black eyes met mine from across the room, and I felt the light in the room dim almost imperceptibly. "I will ask you this once and only once. Did you have anything to do with those bodies?"

I shook my head and told the literal truth. "I didn't kill anyone, Alexa."

She waited for a long moment, still studying me, then nodded. "Good. Now let's get back to you leaving campus in the first place. That's the second of Bard's rules that you've broken. Are you *trying* to get kicked out of the Academy?"

"No." If I'd been smart, I would have just left it there, but the anger inside of me surged back up. "But let's be honest. It's just a matter of time now."

"Meaning what, exactly?"

"Don't bullshit me, Alexa! I know the teachers talk. You know *exactly* what I mean. Combat was my best shot at becoming a Cape, and that's gone to hell now."

"And that's why you've started paying even less attention in class than usual? Why even Macy has publicly wondered why you're still showing up to Mobility?" She caught my surprised look. "As you said, teachers *do* talk. And I have ears in place to hear when they do."

"The end of the school year—and my time at the Academy—is less than a month away," I told her. "They should be happy I'm showing up to class at all."

Alexa shook her head. "I would have sworn you were the sort of person who would die before he quit. Clearly, I was wrong."

That stung, as it was no doubt intended to. "What did you want me to do? Become a postal service employee?"

"A what?" She frowned, but moved on. "I told you not so long ago that there were other ways for a Power to serve than as a Cape."

"For a first-year dropout who's doomed to go crazy? I bet the recruiters are just lining up." They could join the non-existent line of women other than Vibe who wanted to go to the dance with me.

"You've been here a year, and you're still sane. You don't know—"

"Sally told me—"

"Sally Cemetery said a lot of things," she interrupted, eyes flashing, "most of them contradictory. And that's assuming her ghost was even real!"

"If it wasn't, then I've *already* gone crazy." I smiled the smile that Silt still said gave her nightmares. "Either way, I'd say I'm fucked."

For just a moment, Midnight's careful mask slipped, and I saw something that looked suspiciously like weariness and very real concern.

"Hold it together for three more weeks, Damian. I'll have answers for you by Remembrance Day. I promise."

That brief moment of naked compassion almost did me in. I almost told Alexa everything; the truth about Christmas, about what I'd seen of my mom's death, and what I was planning to do. Part of me wanted to know what alternatives she had in mind. Part of me wanted to imagine a future where I didn't die, insane and alone.

Ironically, it was Gabriella Stein's lessons in Control and Alexa's own instruction over the past year that helped me choke down that part of me. There was a shuttle leaving Los Angeles two days before Remembrance Day, and I was going to be on it. Everything else was just a dream.

I met her eyes and lied. "Okay."

Felt almost as bad about that lie as the one I'd told Kayleigh, weeks earlier.

* * *

I was in a weird mood as I trudged back across campus. Some of it was guilt, of course. Whatever our differences, Alexa had spent months trying to help me, and necessary as it had been, lying to her didn't feel good. But mixed in with the guilt was a whole lot of other stuff. Anger. Exhaustion. Impatience. Even sadness and regret that nobody would know what had happened to me until the vids hit. That I wouldn't get to say a real goodbye to the handful of people I called friends.

Like I said, a weird mood. Maybe that explains what happened next.

* * *

On a Sunday afternoon, the common room was normally packed, so I was surprised to find only two people there when I entered. Olympia and Tessa. Spectra and Poltergeist. Could've been worse. Could've been Winter. The Weather Witch was still lacking a date for the dance, and she was taking out that frustration on everyone she saw. But that was Penelope to a T; you'd almost feel bad for her if she wasn't such a raging pain in all of our asses.

Anyway, Olympia and Tessa weren't the worst two people who could've been there in the common room, but they were a long way from friendly, so I headed straight for the men's dorm. Halfway across the room though, I stopped. Felt almost like I was standing outside my body, even though I hadn't summoned a shred of power. Finally, I turned and made for the nearest couch.

Whatever conversation the two women had been engaged in came to a screeching halt as I took a seat one couch over.

"Can we *help* you, Damian?"

By all accounts, Poltergeist had found a date almost as fast as Silt. Great tits notwithstanding, I pitied whoever she'd chosen. It was a sure thing that he'd end up regretting it before the night was done. It'd be a minor miracle if he escaped with his pubic hair and dignity intact. For once, I didn't say that though. Instead, I just looked over at her and nodded.

"I was hoping to talk to Spectra, Tessa. Do you mind?"

Where Tessa's tone had been a flawless blend of needle-sharp sarcasm and contempt, mine was… almost as polite as the words themselves.

Maybe *weird mood* didn't cover it. Maybe I had finally gone insane.

Tessa seemed almost as taken aback by my tone as I was. She blinked her green eyes, stopped a moment before she was going to say something, and threw an exasperated look in Olympia's direction. "Spectra?"

"It's fine, Tess." Olympia's voice was firm. "I'll talk to him. You've got your fitting anyway."

"If you're sure…" At the answering nod, Tessa rose to her feet, still looking puzzled, and headed outside.

"Fitting?"

"For her dress. I had mine this morning."

"Oh. I didn't realize you had a date—"

"What do you want, Crow?" Olympia interrupted. "You asked for a moment, and you've got it. But I want you to know," she continued, her hands glowing with a light almost as silver as her eyes, "that I'm not scared of you. If you try anything, I will burn you down where you sit."

"Ishmae already tried that," I shot back. "I'm still here."

"Not for much longer, from what I hear."

That took the wind right out of my sails. "Yeah. That's why I wanted to talk to you."

"If you're looking for someone to help you cheat, you can just…" Her voice trailed off. "Actually, I don't see how that would even work."

"It wouldn't. I'm gone in less than a month, and we all know it."

"Oh." For the first time, she budged slightly from her defensive position on the couch. "What do you want then? Money?"

Honestly, it wasn't until that very moment that I knew the answer, although some part of me must have known long before I sat down. Maybe that guilt I'd mentioned was stirring up trouble, the way guilt so often does. Or maybe I just wanted to accomplish one decent thing before I headed off to commit murder. Either way, I thought of Bard and the impossible mission he'd given me after Shane's funeral.

"I wanted to apologize," I finally told her.

I'm not sure which of us was more surprised.

* * *

"Apologize? For what?" Just like that, she got suspicious. "What did you do…?"

"Nothing." Not yet anyway. "I just know what it's like to lose family to a Crow. I'm sorry that happened to you, and I'm sorry me being here this year has made things worse."

"Oh." Olympia had gotten better control of her power as the year progressed, and no longer broadcast her emotions in light form for everyone to see, so when the glow around her hands dimmed, I took it as a good sign. "Did you know I was born with silver eyes?"

Fucking Lightbringers. Work up to an apology and they just change the subject on you.

"It's not a Power thing, I mean," she continued. "At least I don't think so. My little sister had them too. You wouldn't believe the amount of teasing we got growing up."

"One of the kids at the orphanage had horrible gas."

"What?!?"

"Fat Joey. Sometimes I wonder if he was such an asshole because he didn't want people making fun of his farts." When her confusion showed no signs of clearing, I shrugged. "We're talking about embarrassing qualities, right?"

For just a moment, I thought Spectra was going to carry through on her threat to liquefy me. "What I was *saying*," she continued, perfect nose now wrinkled in disgust, "is that we can't always help what we are. It's not your fault that you were born a Crow. It's not your fault that a Crow murdered my family and most of a city. It's maybe not even your fault that you've been an asshole this whole year, considering that we were assholes to you first."

Mission accomplished, Bard, I thought to myself. If I survived killing Dad and somehow escaped afterward, maybe I could tour the country and show the people that Crows weren't all bad.

"What *is* your fault," Olympia continued, voice going hard, "is whatever you do after you leave the Academy."

For one terrifying moment, I thought she *knew* somehow, but before I could say anything to incriminate myself, she was speaking again.

"Crows go crazy. That's a fact. It sucks for you, but it's still a fact. So what are you going to do to keep from hurting people when you do?"

"It won't be a problem."

"Oh really? How can you know for sure?"

The short answer was that I'd be dead or in the Hole, but I obviously couldn't say that. So I went with the answer I'd have given three months earlier, back when I thought I still had a future.

"I have the word of someone I trust that they'll take me out before I get that far."

Olympia scowled. "Silt may talk a big game, but—"

"It's not Sofia. It's not a first-year at all." As I spoke, I realized for the first time that maybe I had an idea what Alexa's *other* job entailed… and exactly what sort of work a Power who *wasn't* a Cape could do. "They'll put me down when it becomes necessary."

"Oh. Well… good." Spectra rose to her feet and, after a moment's hesitation, extended her hand. "I can't say I'm going to miss you, but… good luck wherever you end up."

Her skin was just about the softest thing I'd ever touched. "Good luck being a Cape."

"And if you're not the perfect gentleman with Kayleigh at the dance," she continued, still holding my hand, "neither you nor this mysterious watcher will need to worry about you going insane." Silver eyes sparked for just a moment, and then she was past me, heading for the women's dorm.

Sometimes you just can't win.

CHAPTER 63

If the Remembrance Day dance was the first topic on my classmates' lips, the Graduation Games were a close second. Everyone was busy dredging up tales of past games and vids of some of the more notable contests. One of the second-years had even set up betting pools on how this year's crop of third-years would perform. By the time the games had arrived, I was almost as sick of hearing about them as I was the dance.

That didn't keep me from piling into the stands with everyone else for opening day. With finals *and* Power examinations behind us—all of which I'd happily flunked, since that shit didn't matter at all anymore—the chance to watch someone else sweat had a certain appeal.

Most of you have probably seen the Graduation Games on vid; third-years competing against each other in power-related competitions. After three years at the Academy, the graduating Capes had been ranked first to last, and that week of competition was their last chance to show that they deserved the rank they'd been given… or one even higher.

What the vids didn't capture is what a madhouse the whole thing was.

At any given time, there were multiple events happening concurrently. The field had been divided into a dozen smaller arenas; obstacle courses on one end and open sparring circles on the other. Some of the action didn't even take place *on* the field, but above it;

Flyboys and Wind Dancers making sure their contests occurred within visual range of the bleachers holding the Cape team recruiters.

In those same stands were the families of both third-years and graduating normals. From what little I could see, only the latter group was having much fun; the parents of future Capes were white-knuckled and tense as they watched their children perform.

As first-years, we'd been relegated to bleachers at the very far end of the field, wedged in with the freshman normals. For that one week, the shortage of space and the excitement of the games combined to erase the invisible barrier between our two groups. Silt and her Remembrance Day date, Debbie—a blonde almost as slim and small as Vibe—sat on one side of me, with Kayleigh on the other. I was busy watching Paladin's hulking laundromat buddy, WarChild, battle a Stalwart who was as thin as she was tall, but no less deadly for that fact.

Seeing those two third-years fight drove home the massive gulf in skill between their class and even the best of the first-years. It also reinforced Nikolai's words the day he'd kicked me out of his class. If the other first-years in Combat kept improving like these two third-years clearly had, I really *would* have ended up dead sooner or later. Skill is all well and good, but skill *and* power wins every time.

Vibe's excited shout pulled my attention from the bout, just moments after the unnamed Stalwart vaulted over WarChild's head, avoiding a charge that might very well have flattened her. The Empath was pointing to the recruiter stands.

"There's Aspen! Supersonic said she'd be here!"

Sure enough, a slender woman in a glittering silver costume had swooped down from the sky to take her seat with the other recruiters. From this far away, I couldn't make out her features, but there wasn't a person in the Free States who didn't know what Aspen looked like.

Dominion was the Free States' most powerful Cape and Paladin was its most popular, but nobody was as famous—or at least as recognizable—as Aspen. A lot of people make headlines when their powers first emerge, but few do it on national vid like she had. Major Disaster had been laying waste to San Diego, having already disposed of that small city's unofficial Cape squad, when he made the mistake of picking up a bus and throwing it through two downtown skyscrapers.

One of the passengers on that bus? Sixteen-year-old Aspen, who'd been in town with her high school team for a volleyball tournament. She hadn't just walked away from the wreckage, she'd flown… right back through the smoke and the destruction. As the nation watched, she traded blows with the infamous Black Hat, delaying him just long enough for the Los Angeles Defenders to arrive.

She'd saved a city at sixteen. I'd lost my cherry to Alicia. As far as I was concerned, I'd gotten the better end of the deal.

"I guess the Defenders sent her as their representative instead of Paladin," I said, slightly disappointed.

"I think you're the only straight man I've ever met who didn't get heart palpitations just from being in the same city as Aspen." Silt frowned.

"I'm not saying she isn't awesome. Low-Four in three different power classes? That's hard to beat." I shrugged. "But I like Tempest best."

"Whatever floats your boat, Skeletor. Whatever floats your boat."

"I wonder if the Defenders need an Empath," mused Vibe. Moments later, she sent me an apologetic look. "Sorry, Damian."

"It's okay. I may not end up becoming a Cape, but I've had plenty of suggestions for other careers I could try instead."

I think the worst part of those two months had been pretending that I had a future that measured in years instead of days. Fake optimism is fucking tiring.

"They'll figure something out, Boneboy," insisted Silt.

"And if Bard doesn't, *we* will," agreed Vibe.

"Could you all keep it down?" asked Winter, two rows behind us and seated with the normal she'd somehow blackmailed into being her date to the dance. "I'm trying to listen to the announcer."

Of course she was.

* * *

The Graduation Games run for a full week. The first three days are all individual events, while the next three are team-oriented, but it's the seventh day that everyone loses their minds over. That's when they hold the finals for every contest from the preceding week. More than eight straight hours of the very best third-years demonstrating their skills. If the Academy sold tickets, they could make a fortune.

I wouldn't be there to see the finals. The shuttle to the Hole left at noon on the sixth day, one day before the finals, and two days before the Remembrance Day dance. Maybe I should've been pissed about that, too, but the allure of the games had faded quickly. Turns out watching an event you know you'll never get to participate in is its own kind of torture, especially for a first-year, and *especially* with every one of your classmates watching the field in rapt fascination, their hopes and dreams almost literally painted across their faces.

I blew off day four. Spent some of it rehearsing what I was going to say when I finally saw my asshole dad. Spent the rest of it out on that hill-side bench in the woods, watching the ocean. The ocean doesn't give a fuck about people. The ocean's going to be there long after we're dust. Not sure why, but I found that comforting.

I blew off day five too, but this time I spent it in bed with my Glass. That turned out to be a tactical mistake, as it made it all the easier for Jeremiah to track me down.

"Hey Damian, the second-years are having an end-of-year party over at The Liquid Hero. Feel like coming?"

The shuttle to the Hole was leaving in just over sixteen hours. The absolute last thing I needed to do was go drinking.

On the other hand, it was quite possibly the last time I'd *get* to go drinking.

"What the hell," I decided, "I'm in."

Still eighteen.

Still an idiot.

CHAPTER 64

Parties at The Liquid Hero weren't all that uncommon, especially with classes over for the semester. What made this one special was that it was Capes-only; adults, first-years, second-years, and the handful of third-years who were either done with the Graduation Games or willing to be hungover for the championship round. For only the second time all year, drinks were on the house.

Hektor was working the bar instead of the door, and as we entered, Jeremiah peeled off to say hello. I nodded to Olympia, out on the dance floor with London, Santi, and an over-muscled second-year, and went looking for my classmates. The second-years who weren't working the bar had taken over the upstairs tables and the booths along the far wall were occupied by third-years and adults. That left us first-years making do with the tall tables between the booths and the stairs. Poltergeist, Cyclone, and the Viking barely fit around one, and Supersonic, Wormhole, and Paladin crowded around another. The last two tables each had open spaces, but since Winter stood alone at one of them and Orca and Prince were together at the other—holding hands and sharing a beer, for fuck's sake—neither option was appealing.

I went back to the bar and ordered a screwdriver, a drink I only knew from vids. The vodka was cheap and the orange juice was synthesized, but at least it wasn't beer. Or whisky. After Amos' priceless bottle, and Mom's subsequent visitation, even the thought of the stuff turned my stomach.

I tossed back one glass, ordered another, and waited for a minute or two for salvation to appear. Silt, maybe, or even Vibe, as unlikely as that would be. No luck. Finally, I gave in to the inevitable, and headed to the table with Orca and Prince.

I was still ten feet away when Freddy "Muse" Ficus, our Low-Three Switch, took the final spot.

That should have been my first clue that the night was destined for disaster, but the vodka was already working its magic, warming me from the inside, and I wasn't looking for portents or signs. With a shrug, I changed direction, and headed for Winter's table.

If Penelope had ever worn heels, she would have been close to my height, and I was the tallest of the first-year men not named Alan Jackson, Eric Thorsson, or Jeremiah Jones. In flats, she was still a head taller than most of the other women, but tonight, she seemed smaller somehow, gazing wistfully into the depths of the empty wine glass on the table in front of her.

"Winter." I put my screwdriver on the table next to her glass, already resolved to ignore the obnoxious Weather Witch until space opened up at a different table.

"What do *you* want, Damian?" Our table was on the far side of the bar, right next to the booths, and some careful trick of architecture or engineering helped reduce the deafening music to background noise. It was one of the few places on the ground floor where conversation *didn't* require yelling back and forth. Just my luck.

"Does it matter?"

"No." She spared me a glance. "Do you *ever* wear anything other than Academy greys?"

"Not often," I answered honestly. "I'm pretty sure grey is my color."

"Grey isn't anyone's color." She rolled her eyes, and raised her wine glass to her lips, grimacing when she realized it was empty. "I can't believe Kayleigh agreed to go to the dance with you."

There was a reason Winter had been the only one at her table.

"And old what's-his-name is going with you." I shrugged. "There's no accounting for taste."

"His name is Benjamin, he's an asshole, and if I ever see him again, I'm going to shove a lightning bolt up his ass," she told me bitterly.

What was it with the first-year women and guy's asses?

"He canceled on me," she continued, as if I'd asked for further details. "Three days before the dance, and I'm suddenly dateless. Me! A High-Three! How does a *Crow* have a date to the Remembrance Day dance when I don't?" Without even looking, she grabbed my screwdriver off the table and drained it in one long gulp.

I shrugged. "It helps that I'm hung like a horse."

Maybe it was a lie, maybe it wasn't. It *definitely* wasn't the reason Kayleigh wanted me there, but since I was going to be dead or in prison by the time the dance rolled around, I figured some creative storytelling couldn't hurt.

Also, watching Penelope Von Pell, High-Three Weather Witch and Full-Five pain in the ass, spit vodka and orange juice across the table was entertaining as hell.

* * *

When trouble finally came, it wasn't a first-year who started it, no matter what you might have read about that night. It sure as fuck wasn't me, though I seem to get the blame in at least a few of the stories. Truth was, it wasn't a student at all. It was one of the adults I'd barely noticed when we first came in. Most were seated with third-years, making them either parents or over-eager Cape recruiters, but there were two booths that consisted of nothing but adults, all men. They'd gotten noisier as the night dragged on, but I guess that was true for all of us. Free alcohol has that effect.

Anyway, one of the men—short as Prince, wide as the Viking, and clothed in black denim with a red bandana skullcap—was passing our tables, two mugs of beer in each hand, when a visibly drunk Muse, coming back from his sixth trip to the bathroom, stumbled into his path. The man was either Stalwart or Jitterbug, and that was the only thing that allowed him to avoid the otherwise inevitable collision. Even so, he lost about a quarter of the beer in each mug. He threw the Switch a dirty look and kept that glare going all the way back to his booth. After he dropped off the mugs, he came right back at Freddy, one large paw catching the first-year's shoulder.

"Hey dickhead! How about you look where you're going before you get your ass beat?"

Muse's eyes were rolling so hard I wasn't sure he could see a thing, but I saw him swallow a couple of times, mouth gaping open like a fish trying to breathe air.

"He's drunk, man. He didn't mean anything by it." Caleb was there, as fast as only a Jitterbug could be, to help the drunk Switch back to his seat.

"Of course he didn't." Captain Denim shook his head. "Just one more reject from baby school, isn't he?"

There were only a few tables close enough to hear him, all of them populated by first-years, and that little comment got our attention.

"You have an issue with the Academy?" asked Tessa, her hard voice undercut slightly by the fact that she was clinging onto the table with both one hand *and* her telekinesis.

"Bunch of failed ex-Capes ruining the next generation? Damn right I do."

"The Academy has a spotless reputation," began Winter, in that haughty, instructional voice most of us knew far too well.

"Founded entirely on bullshit." He eyed Winter from under bushy eyebrows, and snorted. "Surprised you can't smell it with a beak like yours. What do they call you? The Incredible Nose?"

"We call her Winter." If you'd have told me I'd be speaking up on Penelope's behalf, I'd have said you were even crazier than I was, but there I was. I blame the vodka. "She's an obnoxious pain in the ass, but she's *our* obnoxious pain in the ass."

"Shut up, Damian. I want to hear what this cretin's problem is with the Academy."

Guess gratitude was too much to expect.

"I told you, girl. It's bullshit. All your little classes. All your games on the field. How many of you fuckers even know what death is?" He cut the Weather Witch off angrily. "And I know about the Healer you morons got killed. I'm talking *real* death, not a dumb-ass accident. How many of you have seen someone die in blood and pain? Raise a fucking hand or shut up and leave the real Capes to their beer."

I stepped forward, mostly steady even after four screwdrivers. "You want to talk death, I'm your man."

I saw realization hit. "You're the Crow kid, aren't you? Black Hat pretending he can be something else."

Before I could respond, Paladin was there. Because of course he was. Matthew-fucking-Strich, only person left in the bar who *wasn't* at least a little bit drunk. He placed a cautionary hand on the older man's shoulder. "Sir, I think maybe you've had enough. Nobody's trying to start—"

The other man shrugged off Paladin's hand. "You don't get to touch me, kid. You haven't earned the *right* to touch me. Do you know who I am?"

"I'm guessing you're Backstreet, and you and those *fine* gentlemen over there are members of the Bay Area Brawlers." Poltergeist paused, and sent the man a smile so sweet even Paladin looked worried. "San Francisco's junior Cape team."

One of the other Brawlers pounded a fist into the table and started to rise.

"Tessa!" That was one of the few occasions that year that I saw Matthew lose his calm. Not the *best* one, mind you… that one was still a few seconds away. "On second thought, I think we've *all* had enough. Why don't we just call it a night?"

Tessa started to nod, but Backstreet wasn't done yet. "And you're Paladin's kid, aren't you? Now there's a real man's Cape! Not sure if I'm more impressed by his performance on the battlefield or in bedrooms around the country. How does your mom feel about the old man stepping out on her—"

He didn't get to finish the sentence. They say it's impossible to surprise a Stalwart, but a full night of drinking proved that story wrong: Backstreet never saw Paladin's punch coming.

If the older Cape had just gone down, it might still have been the end of things, but he tried to return fire. Problem was, Matthew's punch had spun Backstreet around. The other man's drunken swing didn't come anywhere near Paladin. Instead, it smacked squarely into the face of a Titan seated one booth over. The Titan pushed back—hard—and Backstreet flew through the air to take out a couple of second-years making out on the dance floor.

All three went down, and the next thing we knew, second-years were vaulting over the balcony from upstairs, even as the remaining Brawlers erupted out of their own booth.

They call it the Bar Fight of 74. By the time it was done, there were thirteen concussions, three times as many broken bones, and so many other injuries that Bard had to ask one of the visiting recruiters—a Mid-Two who'd nevertheless earned a spot on a Cape Team by virtue of being a Healer—to pitch in at the Med Ward. In a lot of ways, that fight was the Class of 76's public introduction to the world.

Wish I remembered any of it.

CHAPTER 65

It says something about my first year of college that when I woke up, I felt the cold metal gurney beneath me, instantly knew where I was, and rolled right over and went back to sleep. Not sure when the med ward had become as much a home as my actual dorm room, but there was something comforting in the loud whir of the industrial fans and Gladys' grumbling as she moved from patient to patient.

The next time I woke, the fans were as loud as ever, but Gladys was nowhere to be seen. Every gurney in the med ward was occupied, and someone had wheeled in half a dozen more tables, creating a makeshift second row in front of the first. Those tables were also mostly full, although as I watched, a second-year, her party dress spattered with what looked suspiciously like vomit and blood, was helped down by another second-year in pristine Academy greys.

My own greys had been cut off of me, yet again, which was more than a little weird, as I was pretty sure I'd avoided the melee for once. Gladys was taking this whole infatuation thing too far. Tessa was bundled up two gurneys over, still unconscious. Aware that the cold might disprove all my claims of horse-sized appendages, I scanned the room to make sure Winter was nowhere to be seen, then dropped to the tile floor and hurried to grab a fresh set of greys.

A few of the less unconscious patients got an eyeful of bony Crow ass, but embarrassment was a secondary concern at that point. Whatever healing I'd gotten had washed out my hangover, and I had no difficulty seeing the clock above the med ward sink.

10:15 A.M.

I had less than two hours to get dressed, retrieve my weapon, and get my ass over to the shuttle station.

The campus was empty, but I could hear the crackle of the announcer from the Graduation Games field, almost drowned out by the ensuing roar of the crowd. Even on the far side of campus, the crowd's noise dwarfed that of previous days. Whatever team competition was going on had to be an exciting one.

Ten minutes later, I was in my dorm room, and twenty minutes after that, I was showered and clothed in my ill-fitting suit, my one-shot weapon tucked into the suit coat's interior pocket. I was hustling down the hallway when the common room dorm opened, and Paladin came in from the other direction. He stopped, took a look at me, and shook his head. "You might as well go back to your room. None of us are allowed at the Graduation Games today. Bard's orders."

That seemed like a shitty thing for Bard to do. Luckily, it didn't affect me at all. "Fuck the games."

Matthew looked tired, uncombed hair and dark circles under his eyes ruining the usual vid star prettiness. He shrugged. "Whatever."

As he started to walk past, it was my turn to stop him. "Hey Paladin."

"Yeah?"

"That was a pretty sweet punch. Didn't know you had it in you."

He shook his head. "It was stupid. I should've known better."

"Sometimes, it's okay to be stupid."

"Good to know." He started to move past me again, but my hand on his shoulder stopped him a second time. "What do you want, Damian? It's been a rough few days, and I'd like to spend some time meditating. Alone."

I checked the internal clock in my head. Still over an hour to go. I could knock out three miles in as little as twenty-two minutes. That left me time to tie up one last loose end.

No, I didn't punch him. Fuck knows, I'd already tried—and failed—that plenty in Combat class. Wouldn't do to get blood all over my only nice set of clothes, especially if that blood was mine. No, this loose end was something else altogether.

"You're not taking anyone to the dance, are you?"

He frowned. "I'm not going at all. Why?"

I swallowed and reminded myself that it was too late for anyone to stop me. "Because I need you to take Kayleigh."

"Vibe?" His blue eyes went wide then sharpened. "I thought *you* were taking her?"

"Nah. I'm leaving. Today."

"You're what?"

I shrugged. "No point in waiting for them to kick me out, is there?"

"Do you *always* have to do everything on your own terms?"

"Fuck yes. We can't all grow up rich."

"You think my life is so great." Paladin shook his head. "You of all people should know better than to blindly believe what you hear."

"Unless you spent your sixth birthday dreaming about your mom bleeding all over the kitchen floor, I don't want to hear how fucking tough your life has been."

"Fine. Whatever. Goodbye and good riddance. But why ask me to take Kayleigh to the dance?"

"So she's not alone? Jesus, did they forget to program in compassion when they were upgrading your firmware?"

Honest truth; I didn't know exactly what firmware was back then.

"I meant *why me*?"

Every time I shrugged, my too-big suit jacket flapped open. I made a mental note to be aware of that fact when I passed through the Hole's security. Legion's gun might not show up on scanners, but it was plenty visible to the human eye. "She thinks you're cute," I said absently. "I guess some idiots still have a thing for vid star looks and muscles. Also…"

"Also?"

I frowned. "You're never drunk, and outside of last night's truly awesome exception—" He started to say something, but I talked right over him. "—you're never out of control. Maybe that'll help mitigate the whole Empath thing… maybe it won't… but I know one thing for sure."

"And what's that?"

"You'll be a gentleman. Only dance of the year… I'd say Kayleigh deserves that."

There was a long silence as Paladin just stared at me. Finally, he shook his head. "I don't get you at all."

"If you did, I'd be worried. So you'll do it?"

"Yeah."

"Good." I left him there with a confused look on his face.

Goodbye, Paladin. Turns out you weren't my arch-nemesis after all.

Too bad. We could've had some epic wars.

* * *

Still fifty minutes left, even after that little conversation. Plenty of time, really, but not so much that I could afford additional distractions.

Like Silt waiting for me in the common room, for instance.

For the third time in as many months, that room was almost empty. Nobody but Silt, and with the vid screen off, it was the quietest it had ever been.

Guess that's how she'd overheard my conversation with Paladin.

"What're you doing, Skeletor?" Her muscular arms were folded across her broad chest, and she stood like a small boulder, directly in my path.

"What I can to make sure Kayleigh has a good time at the dance. Paladin's self-control might help with Vibe's Empath—"

"Kayleigh's been in control of her power for almost two months now, you dumbass!"

"She… what?"

"Did you think you were the only one learning to control their power? That's what being a first-year is about!"

"But…" I frowned. "Then why did she ask me to the dance?"

"I guess it doesn't matter." She looked me up and down and shook her head. "You never had any intention of going with her, did you?"

"I can't." I met Silt's angry gaze. "I've got unfinished business elsewhere, Sofia."

She blinked, recognizing the phrasing. "And it couldn't wait until *after* the dance?"

"It can't even wait until the last day of the Graduation Games," I told her. "There's a shuttle leaving Los Angeles in less than an hour, and I need to be on it."

Her frown deepened. "Damian… today *is* the last day."

"No it isn't. The fight at The Liquid Hero was last night, so this—"

She was shaking her head. "There were so many injured that the Healers kept you all asleep until you could be treated. It's been more than a day."

Details I'd been ignoring started to seep in. Paladin's odd comment: *It's been a rough few days.* The look he'd given me when I said his punch had happened just last night. Even the unusually loud Graduation Games crowd.

It was the final day of competition. Day seven, not day six.

I'd missed my shuttle by almost twenty-three hours.

I was completely fucked.

* * *

I stood there for almost a minute, my thoughts running wild. Assuming President Weatherly's so-called *Reconciliation Day* became an annual thing, I'd have another shot at seeing my dad the following year, but only if I found a job or some form of income. Maybe I could swallow my pride long enough to beg some cash from one of the well-off first years—Kayleigh, Evelyn, or even Matthew—but even then…

I stopped as a thought hit me.

"Sofia, where's Wormhole?"

"In our room, last I checked. She made it back from the med ward a few hours ago. Why?"

"Because I need her help."

CHAPTER 66

After almost a year, I still knew nothing about Wormhole's power. The only time I'd seen her use it was in Control class, popping back and forth from one end of the narrow mat to the other. If that was the full extent of her capabilities, I remained totally fucked; it would take at least a million two-foot hops to reach the Hole, and I'd be crazy or dead of old age long before we got there.

But if that was all she could do, Evelyn would never make second-year, and from what I'd heard, her future at the Academy had never been in doubt. And she'd once told Silt she might be able to teleport her to Texas by graduation. My geography was pretty damn shaky for anything east of the Free States, but I knew Texas was a hell of a lot further away than the Hole.

As for *why* she'd help me, and how much I'd have to tell her first… well, I had almost sixty steps to figure all that out before we reached her room.

* * *

Evelyn was on her bed in Academy greys, browsing her Glass when Silt and I marched inside. I watched her face transition from welcome—when Sofia appeared—to suspicion—when I followed—to something approaching alarm as we crossed to her side of the room.

"Sofia? What's *he* doing here?"

"Given that he just realized that the brawl fucked up his escape plan, and that whatever ride he'd arranged left almost twenty-four hours ago…" Silt shrugged. "I'm guessing he's here about your power.

Just don't expect him to tell you any of the details. Turns out Boneboy's not big on trust."

I winced. Maybe it was a good thing my trip to the Hole was going to be one-way. I seemed to be burning bridges behind me everywhere I went.

"Escape plan?" Evelyn looked confused, then horrified. "You were going to leave the Academy yesterday? *What about the dance?*"

"If I never fucking hear about the fucking dance again…" I cut myself off in mid-tirade. "The dance is fine. I just won't be here for it."

"But Kayleigh…"

"Is going to learn shortly that she's been set up on a date with Matthew Strich," interjected Silt, "courtesy of Skeletor himself."

"What?!?"

"That's beside the point," I said, shooting Sofia a glare. I'd done what I could to make the dance better for Vibe. What the fuck did she want from me?

"Right." Wormhole folded her arms across her chest in an eerie reproduction of Silt's usual gesture. "Because all that matters is what *you* care about. You're leaving, and you want me to help you get wherever you're going."

I swallowed. "Yeah."

"And why exactly would I do that?"

Turned out sixty steps hadn't been nearly enough.

"I don't know."

"Fucking hell, Boneboy. That's your sales pitch?"

"Until ten minutes ago, I was taking a shuttle. *This* wasn't part of the plan!" I turned back to Evelyn. "I don't have any carefully thought-out arguments to convince you with. I don't even know if you *can* help me, but the only other person I could ask is Caleb and he—"

"Hates you," chimed both women.

"—can't fly while carrying anything bigger than his own ego," I finished. "But I'm not going to beg…" I paused. "Unless you think that will make a difference?"

"Where do you need to go?"

"Seriously? You'll take me?"

She put her Glass aside and gave me a slow nod. "I won't lie… I'm very okay with the thought of you not being here anymore."

"Evelyn!" For someone still pissed at me, Silt was weirdly quick to come to my defense.

"He's your friend, Sofia, not mine."

Maybe that should've hurt, but even after all these months, I didn't feel very close to Wormhole either. Having friends in common is a long way from actually being friends.

The Teleporter looked back to me. "Where do you want me to take you? It does matter."

This was the moment I'd been dreading. I looked to the still-open dorm room door and lowered my voice. "The Hole."

"The *Hole*? Why the fuck would you—" Silt turned to me, confusion vanishing from her broad face to be replaced by… something else. "Remembrance Day?"

"Or Reconciliation Day, as President Weatherly's calling it. Yeah."

"Your father?"

I nodded sharply, trying not to show the anger that rose up even at his mention. "Haven't spoken to him in almost fourteen years. I've got some fucking questions."

"Shit, Damian. I'm sorry."

I didn't know what she was apologizing for, but it didn't matter, because Evelyn was already shaking her head.

"I can't take you to the Hole."

"Why not?"

"I can only teleport to places I've been. I've never been there."

"But… you told Silt you'd take her to Texas."

"After *graduation*, and I said I'd *try*. We don't know if this is one more limitation baked into my power or if it's just some sort of mental block. Either way, I can't help you. Not yet, anyway." She hesitated and then added, almost as an afterthought. "I'm sorry."

There were no second-year Teleporters—third-years either, for that matter—but I was pretty sure there was a Flyboy or two. Maybe I could track one of them down and… convince them to fly a perfect stranger with a shit reputation all the way out to Black Hat prison…

Yeah, that plan had success written all over it.

"Fuck."

"Hold on a second." Silt had her own Glass out and was tapping its screen, a look of concentration on her face. "You and your family came from Flagstaff, didn't you, Evie?"

"Yeah, when I was a kid. That was the longest week and a half of my life. Until this year's exams, anyway. I swear the highway was more rubble than road. Why?"

"Because it looks like there's a little town along what's left of I-40 called Ludlow that you must've come through. It's only forty-five miles from the Hole."

For just a moment, I let myself feel optimistic. Then reality seeped in.

"Forty-five miles through the desert, Sofia. I'm not sure I could even survive that trip. I sure as hell couldn't do it in a day."

"Then it's a good thing you won't have to." With a broad smile, Silt spun her Glass around and showed me what she'd found.

It was the route for the shuttle from Los Angeles. It would be making a brief pit stop in Ludlow the next morning.

"I could kiss you right now," I told her.

"I'll pass, not that you don't look nice in your suit and all." The smile morphed into the grin I was used to. "And freshly showered and blood-free, for once. What a catch!"

We both turned to Evelyn. This time, she was nodding.

"Ludlow. Yeah, I think I can do that. But it's going to have to be soon, and I'll need to come right back."

I didn't have a problem with either part of that, but curiosity pushed me to ask. "How come?"

"Because the dance is only thirty hours away, and with a jump that far, I'll need every minute of it to—" She broke off with a blush, then shrugged. "You'll see, soon enough."

* * *

After that, things went quickly. Wormhole procured a water bottle from the depths of her over-stuffed closet, pulled out a pair of oversized pink sneakers that clashed horribly with her Academy greys, and excused herself for a trip to the restroom.

At first, neither Silt nor I spoke. I glanced around the dorm room she and Evelyn shared, learning more about them both in that minute than I had all year. Wormhole's side of the room was pink. All of it, from the sheets and comforter she'd brought from home to replace the Academy bedding, to the flower paintings she had framed and hanging above her bed. Silt's side of the room was almost shockingly stark by comparison. The only wall decoration was a black and white brush painting.

"What's that?"

She glanced at the painting and then away. "The Rio Grande. Only thing between Brownsville and what used to be Mexico."

I squinted. "Are there *people* in the water?"

"Yeah." Her voice was quiet. "You're not coming back, are you?"

"So they can kick me out? Why bother?"

"Were you even listening when Kayleigh and I said we'd figure out a way—?"

"To keep me here? The fact that anyone would even bother to try means a lot, but if I'm not part of the Cape program, I have to pay tuition, and I have no money."

"How much money is no money?"

I gritted my teeth. "Six dollars and thirty-nine cents." And I'd stolen all but a dollar of that from the slushy store's cash register back in the day. "You think I wear Academy greys all the time by choice?"

"But…" she nodded to my suit.

"A hand-me-down from Jeremiah, in exchange for teaching him how to fight. Didn't realize at the time it would come back and bite me in the ass." I shrugged. "Anyway, no money means no tuition, and no tuition means I can't be a student here, regardless of what anyone does."

"Do they not teach Bakersfield kids about scholarships? You could—"

I almost let myself consider it, the possibility of a few more years at the Academy. Not as a Cape, sure, but still in the general vicinity of the handful of people I privately called friends. Then I remembered that this whole conversation was just a smokescreen. In less than a day, I'd be dead or taking my father's place in the Hole, and all the scholarships in the world wouldn't change that.

I forced myself to look amused and shook my head. "I've had tutoring every weekend since I got here, and I *still* think I failed my exams. Does that sound like scholarship material to you?"

Some truths are more evident than others. She blinked and looked away, broad shoulders sagging. "So this is it then."

"Yeah." I swallowed past the sudden lump in my throat. No tears—still no fucking tears—but something inside of me squeezed down like it was caught in a vise. "I guess so. Sorry I won't be around to help in Brownsville. Thanks for everything, Sofia Black."

"You're a shitty friend, Damian Banach," she retorted, wiping her own eyes, "but you are my friend. Take care of yourself."

"I'll try. Tell Debbie that if she doesn't treat you right, I might just come back and sweep you off your feet."

Silt snorted, but before things could get even more maudlin, Evelyn returned.

The Teleporter had pulled her dark hair back into a bun, and her face was scrubbed clean, but the first thing I noticed was that she'd changed into a fresh set of Academy greys… a set that could have easily fit the Viking. On someone as small as Evelyn, it was a ludicrous amount of extra fabric.

"What the hell?"

She scooped up her water bottle, dropped it into a messenger bag, and swung that bag over one shoulder, extending her other hand to me. "You'll see, soon enough. Shall we?"

I nodded and took her hand. It wasn't as soft as Olympia's, but in my limited experience, nothing was.

"You're sure you can do this, Evie?" asked Silt.

"Yeah. I don't even remember the town, but my power sees Ludlow just fine. It's not going to be fun, but I can do it. See you in a bit, roomie."

And just like that, the world faded around us.

CHAPTER 67

Every Power is different. That's what the Academy says about us, and as far as I can tell, it's true. Two Weather Witches of the same rank will interact with the world in different ways, with different strengths, limitations, and even methodologies. Flyboys all fly, of course, but some do so by pushing against the earth, some do so by nullifying gravity's effect, and some, like Rocket, just do it through a combination of forward propulsion and vast quantities of speed.

So I can't tell you what teleportation is like. I can only tell you what teleporting with Wormhole was like.

It sucked.

Imagine a pit where no light has ever penetrated, where the very concept of light has never even existed. Strip away oxygen, strip away form and shape and weight and sound and every other sense you've taken for granted all your life. Then, make it really fucking cold, because heat, like light, is just an illusion from another world.

Finally, give time a kick in the ass right out the door. I don't know how long we were there, in that place. In the real world, only a few seconds passed, if that, but in that dark pit, it felt like days, or even years. When I realized I couldn't breathe, I started grasping for my power. Was still grasping for it, months later, before I'd even started to exhale.

And then we were through, out into a desert sun that seemed impossibly bright, dry arid soil rough against one of my palms, and Wormhole's hand feeling grossly distorted in the other.

"Shit. There's no way in *hell* I'm going to be able to get Silt to Texas in one hop." Even Evelyn's voice seemed different after that long silence. Usually borderline melodic—though I'd never tell her so—now it was almost as rough as Her Majesty's.

It wasn't until I looked over at her that I realized why.

The sweats that had hung on Wormhole's slim frame now struggled to contain her girth. The hand I held was well past pudgy, each finger as thick around as two of mine put together. Even her features were almost unrecognizable under a thick layer of fat.

"What the fuck?"

"Stare a bit longer, asshole." She shook free of my hand, her body quaking even with that slight movement.

"Sorry, I just…" I coughed. "Is this normal?"

"You mean do I swell up like a blimp every time I teleport?" She wobbled her head. "No. It's a factor of distance."

"I don't understand. Are you… some kind of Shifter?"

"As if." She shrugged. "I don't know how real wormholes work, but I fix two locations in my mind, and… sort of burrow between them. But I absorb some of the excess energy along the way and convert it to mass. On short trips, it's almost unnoticeable. A few hundred miles, and you get…" She waved an obese arm. "…this."

A thought occurred to me. "Did I just completely ruin your chances of going to the dance?"

Her smile was tight. "I'd say you pushing Paladin and Vibe together already did that, but it's not like Matthew didn't have months to ask me if he was going to. *This* won't make it any worse. My body starts dumping the excess mass as soon as we emerge. Shouldn't be more than an hour or two until I'm back to normal." She looked down at herself and frowned. "Maybe three. This is the farthest I've ever traveled. But at least I did it."

As I looked around us, I saw that she was right. Less than twenty feet away, a battered green sign, so desolate that not even a Druid had bothered to transform it, welcomed one and all to the town of Ludlow.

We'd made it.

* * *

I don't know what Ludlow was like pre-Break. Maybe it was a thriving metropolis or something. If so, the desert had spent the last eighty-plus years swallowing its pre-Break magnificence, because what remained made Bakersfield seem like Los Angeles. Hell, it made that nameless little town where I'd been tested seem like a real fucking city.

Ludlow had five buildings. One was an old gas station that had been converted to electricity at some point. One was a dilapidated convenience store that I was convinced was older than our country. The other three were residences, and only one of those still had a roof.

"You take me to the nicest places, Evelyn."

"No wonder I don't remember it."

"Here I thought Bakersfield was the ass crack of society." I turned to the Teleporter and extended the hand she'd shaken free of moments earlier. "Thank you. Have a safe trip back to the dorm. Tell Kayleigh—"

"I'm not going anywhere yet," Wormhole interrupted. "I have no idea if there's a limit to what my body can absorb, and I don't want to chance it, if so. Until I'm somewhere closer to normal, I'm staying right here."

"Oh." A few hours alone with Evelyn wasn't quite how I'd expected to spend my last day of freedom, but at least she wasn't Winter. "Then let's head over to the charging station and find some shade."

We were still twenty paces away when the long barrel of an ancient rifle extended from one of the open windows. A weathered voice called out. "That's close enough. Not sure where you two came from, but I don't have any cash on the premises, so you can just keep right on walking."

"I'd be happy to do so," I shouted back, watching the rifle weave back and forth, "but my ride's coming through Ludlow tomorrow, and I need to be here to meet it."

If the cracked voice and unsteady rifle barrel hadn't already told me the unseen speaker was old, his loud cackle would have done so. "Ain't been a ride through here for more than a month, young man. What makes you think one's coming tomorrow?"

"Tomorrow's Remembrance Day. President Weatherly arranged shuttles to the Hole."

"President Weatherly can kiss my wrinkled ass," I heard the old man mutter. "Are you sure that's tomorrow?"

"Pretty sure, yeah."

"Well, shit. I better make sure the charging station's powered up then." The long barrel slowly withdrew out of sight, and the next thing we saw was an old man stomping his way out from the convenience store.

"Ah hell, you're just kids." He slowed as he reached us, eyes darting from Wormhole's temporarily hulking form to me. After almost a year at the Academy, my ribs no longer showed, but I was still on the skinny side. "I'm not here to tell young people how to live their lives, but maybe the two of you should renegotiate your portion sizes?"

"This isn't what I normally look like!" protested Wormhole.

"Not that it would matter if it was," I put in. Wrecking Ball, one of the original Ten who'd come to Dominion's call, had been wider than she was tall, and she wasn't any less venerated than the other nine.

"Easy for you to say, Skeletor," Evelyn muttered.

"It's a Power thing," I explained to the old man.

"Didn't mean nothing by it," he muttered, taking a closer look at the Teleporter. Rheumy eyes dropped to her grey sweats and widened. "You both go to the Academy?"

"Yeah."

"Had a grand-nephew that graduated a decade or so ago. Druid who went by the name of Bramble. You folks hear of him?" He frowned as we both shook our heads, then shrugged. "Joined the Hammers of God out in Salt Lake City. Died a few years later."

"The Hammers do good work," said Wormhole. "I'm sure he saved a lot of lives."

"Could be." He shrugged again, shoulders as bony as mine poking through his light cotton shirt like the exposed scaffolding of a building. "Anyways, y'all can wait in the store if you want. Don't have no vid screen working or nothing, but it's got air conditioning and it's a shit-ton nicer than out in the sun."

"Thank you…"

"Randy." He puffed out his chest. "Randal S. Thurston. Happy to be of service to the Free States' finest."

* * *

It took Wormhole four hours to return to her usual weight, and she got ready to go immediately after, swaddled in the clothes that would be skintight again when she re-appeared in Los Angeles. She filled her water bottle at the pump near the charging station and turned to me.

"I think you'll agree that I went above and beyond to help you out today."

They were the first words she'd said to me in almost two hours.

"You did."

"Good. Because I have a favor to ask in return." She slid the water bottle back into her bag. "Don't come back."

My own plans notwithstanding, that kind of hurt.

"I'm sorry?"

"It's not that I think you're a bad person. I just… there are a lot of *good* people in our class, and I don't want—"

"Me dragging them down," I finished, feeling that old, familiar pain.

"Yeah." She swallowed and looked away. "Do whatever you have to do. Just… don't come back."

"I wasn't planning on it," I said, but she was already gone.

* * *

Over the past year, I'd grown used to sunsets in Los Angeles. Grown used to watching the distant ball of fire drop down into the ocean, to twilights that seemed to last as long as the nights themselves. My stay in Ludlow reminded me just how different the desert was. Night came fast and once it did, there was nothing but darkness for miles in every direction, darkness that the two electric lanterns outside Randy's convenience store did nothing at all to lessen.

The storekeeper had wandered off to his house some hours earlier—muttering something about an early morning and what a pain in the ass it was going to be to have actual customers—but I'd decided to stay out by the store for the night. It was just as well that I did; the ramshackle walls of the old man's home helped muffle the loud snores emerging from within.

With the sun down, the weather cooled quickly, and I moved from inside the store to its front step, my back resting against the old wooden door. I hadn't missed Bakersfield often during my time at the Academy, but being in the desert felt a bit like coming home. A year at school had changed me, and the few friends I'd somehow managed to find had changed me even more, but that was another life, another me. For tomorrow's meeting, for my father, I needed the old me, the one who'd never tricked himself into thinking he could be a Cape, the one who always did what needed to be done because he had no future to worry about.

I looked from Mom's ghost, barely visible in the middle of the empty road, to the cold stars that littered the desert sky, and I scrubbed at those new parts of me, the places where Alexa and Unicorn, Vibe and Silt, even Stonewall and fucking Paladin had managed to reach me. I scraped it all away until there was nothing left but the raw nerve underneath.

"One more day, Mom."

I fell asleep with one hand on the moist warmth of my stolen weapon.

CHAPTER 68

Randy was up way too early for comfort. I'd left my Glass back in the dorm room, so I didn't know what time it was, exactly, but the sun was barely peeking over the eastern horizon when the old man tottered out to the charging station, joints creaking. I sat up and gingerly rolled my head from side to side, feeling every day of my almost-nineteen years. I still didn't remember much of the brawl at The Liquid Hero, but I must've seen *some* action because I kept finding bruises in interesting places.

This once, it would have been nice if Gladys and the other Healers had brought me up to one-hundred-percent.

Randy was over by the charging station, frowning at a squat grey box partially buried in the dirt next to one of the coils. With a grumble, he hauled back and kicked it, the sole of his shoe flapping in the wind.

"Is everything okay?"

"Yup. This old girl just gets temperamental in the morning." He grinned, exposing several empty sockets where teeth had once been. "Kind of like my two ex-wives! But she should be warmed up and ready to go by the time the shuttle gets here."

I took a closer look at the box he'd kicked. "Is that a generator?"

"Nah. We're on solar out here, but after you store that excess energy., you need to be able to get it back out to actually use it. That's what this does." He checked the readings on the nearest charger and nodded in satisfaction before turning back to me. "So why's a kid like you going to a place like the Hole? And without your pretty friend?"

"Same as everyone else, I guess. I've got a relative down there. My father."

"Sorry to hear that." He ran one hand through the strands of white hair that were already plastered to his scalp. "Guess the apple fell pretty far from the tree though, you being in the Academy and all."

"Yeah." Against my ribs, the Legion tech gun pulsed like a heartbeat. "Guess so."

* * *

Pre-Break buses were weird things. Gas burning, smoke belching, and noisy as fuck, with too many windows, too few wheels, and no armor whatsoever to speak of. No shock that public transportation had died out everywhere but the major cities, I guess. If Aspen had been riding in one of those old school death traps when Major Disaster threw it through a building, the Free States would have been one Cape poorer.

Modern buses still aren't all that common. I'd never seen one up close, but they've made it into enough vids that I knew what to look for; low-to-the-ground, heavily armored, and slow-as-hell.

The shuttle that showed up in Ludlow was all of those things, and yet it still bore almost no resemblance to a bus. If anything, it looked like some sort of wheeled centipede, multiple armored segments attached to each other in a long line that stretched almost seventy feet down the road. There were no windows to speak of and every segment of the centipede sported a round turret on its roof and side walls.

It wasn't the array of armaments that had my attention though—the security at the Academy put even a shuttle like this to shame, after all—it was the figures soaring overhead.

The shuttle was escorted by Capes.

It made sense, in retrospect. The information on the shuttles had been freely available on the net, as Silt had already demonstrated, which raised the likelihood of Black Hat intervention. The army was all well and good, but where Black Hats were concerned, you needed Capes to fight them. If every shuttle had an escort like this one, it meant a significant number of the Free States' heroes were working escort duty instead of their usual patrols.

It also meant my margin of error was smaller than I'd anticipated. It was one thing to smuggle a weapon past normal soldiers, and even to use that weapon before the Hole's guards could take me down. It was another thing entirely to do so under the watchful eyes of the country's finest.

The lead Cape swooped down from the sky. Her crimson and silver costume identified her as Mistral, a long-time member of the Society, the other Los Angeles super-team. Unlike the Bay Area Brawlers, who Tessa had accurately labeled as San Francisco's "B" team, the Society Capes were just as well regarded as their counterparts in the Defenders.

The Society also believed that there was no such thing as *too much* firepower, which is why the Wind Dancer held a cannon that was everything Randy's old rifle hadn't been; sleek, modern, and capable of spitting out over a thousand rounds a minute.

Mistral came to a halt ten feet in the air above us, her crimson sash streaming in the breeze that kept her afloat. An armored helmet hid her features, including a nose that I knew had been broken at least a dozen times. "Names and occupations, citizens."

"Randal S. Thurston, ma'am." Randy gave the Cape a little bow that didn't look nearly as ridiculous as it should have. "Proprietor and, as of about two years ago, sole resident of this here town."

"And you?" That visor rotated in my direction, the cannon in her hands as steady as a rock.

"Damian Banach," I told her, mindful of the other Capes that had spread out to encircle us from above.

"The boy's a student at the Academy," Randy filled in helpfully. "Here to catch a ride to the Hole."

I couldn't see Mistral's frown, but I could hear it. "This was supposed to just be a charging stop. I wasn't told anything about additional passengers. How did you even get out here?"

"I had a classmate from the Academy teleport me over." I shrugged. "Meant to board back in Los Angeles, but I kind of overslept in the medical ward."

"In the med ward, huh…" For the first time, something like humor entered the other woman's voice. "You wouldn't happen to have been part of the little brawl that went down at The Liquid Hero?"

"You've heard of it?"

"The bar?" She laughed. "I graduated in 61. We practically helped build that place. As for the fight, it's all anyone's talking about. I hear Paladin's kid put Backstreet right on his ass?"

Jesus. Word really did travel, considering the shuttle had left the very next morning.

"Yeah. First time I've ever seen Matthew lose his temper."

"Good for him. Wasn't sure the boy had it in him." Mistral descended the rest of the way to the ground, touching down in a brief swirl of dirt and wind. Up close, she was shorter than I'd expected, the gleaming costume emphasizing her broad shoulders and narrow waist. She was dark-skinned and remarkably stacked, one of the few details I *did* remember from her vids.

Growing up without much in the way of an outlet for my hormones… was it any surprise I'd gravitated to Cape vids? Now that I'd spent a year at the Academy, I understood just how much sweat and tears went into maintaining the physiques I'd seen on all those vids. Frankly, that just made me appreciate it even more. And a little bit relieved I wasn't going to live long enough to wear a costume of my own

"You're going to have to wait here for just a few minutes, Mr. Banach. Like I said, we weren't expecting new passengers, so all of the equipment is packed away."

"Equipment?"

"President Weatherly's order grants access only to blood relatives or spouses of the inmates interred within the Hole. We need to verify your identity and that you meet the criteria." A few armed soldiers had left the shuttle's lead car, carrying something heavy between them. "You don't mind a little blood, do you?"

"I'm a first-year," I reminded her. "If I did, I'd be screwed."

"True enough." She had a nice laugh. "Mr. Thurston, is there an external outlet we can hook up to?"

"Sure enough," said Randy. "Also have a suggestion for you young folk. Given the size of that behemoth on wheels over there, recharging's going to take a while. You might want to get that started first."

"Not a bad idea." Mistral said something into her short-wave radio—one of the multi-band versions only Cape teams had access to—and the shuttle inched its way up to the charging station.

By the time it had arrived, the soldiers were there with their own burden. While the scale didn't compare, it had a lot of similarities to the machine used for the powers test. Perhaps unsurprisingly, it also reminded me of the Maze.

"It's a modification of the testing machine's design," Mistral confirmed.

"And the Maze?"

"Different Technomancer, I think, although the testing machine may have been his starting point." She paused. "How do you know about the Maze? I didn't think they'd brought it out for this year's Graduation Games."

"They didn't." I swallowed. "I saw it up close and personal during the year. Unfortunately."

"The High-Three Healer boy?"

"Unicorn. Yeah." Guess I shouldn't have been surprised she'd heard about that too.

"That was a dark day for the Free States. Lost both a Healer and a High-Four Pyro. Minor miracle we didn't lose the other two on the scene, from what I hear." She paused again, but this time, the silence lasted for a good ten seconds. "Wait… Damian, you said?"

"Yeah."

"You're the baby Crow."

I knew what was coming, but fuck if I was going to act ashamed of who I was. I squared my shoulders. "Yeah."

"Good for you, kid."

"I'm sorry?"

"It takes stones to walk the path you've chosen." She shook her head. "Century or so before the Break, half the world wanted to believe my people were nothing but animals. Sometimes, all it takes is one individual to show the world what it can do with its stereotypes."

I ducked my head. If she hadn't been almost old enough to be my mom, and if I hadn't been less than twelve hours away from proving her wrong, I would have proposed to her then and there.

Probably should have anyway. Could've at least given her a funny story to tell when I was gone.

Instead, I just cleared my throat and nodded. "Thank you."

* * *

When the machine was plugged into Randy's outlet, and I'd been plugged into the machine, Mistral flipped a few switches to bring the device to life. A padded cuff wrapped itself around my upper arm and slowly squeezed. Moments later, the machine extended a long, silvered needle. Before I could even make a size joke, that needle flashed forward and buried itself in the vein of my arm. I watched blood trickle down into the tube at the needle's end.

"Name of the prisoner you're visiting, please." Mistral was all business again, checking the screen built into the machine.

"David Jameson."

She nodded at something I couldn't see. "Affirmative. I've verified that he remains an inmate at the Hole."

"I thought all sentences at the Hole were for life?"

"Yeah." She cocked her head and I could feel her studying me. "Life tends to be a bit shorter down there though, even with military-grade dampeners. Relation to the prisoner?"

"I'm his son."

"And he's *also* a Crow, I see, albeit only a Two." She shook her head. "Maybe the eggheads are right about genetics playing a role in the powers we get." The machine beeped three times, and she paused to read something new that had appeared on the screen. "Verified. Welcome aboard, Mr. Banach."

As the soldiers bundled away the machine, I stuck out my hand. "Damian."

"What's your Cape name, Damian?" She shook my hand, her grip firm.

"Still working on it," I admitted. Somehow, Baron Boner didn't seem appropriate.

"Take your time. Once it gets out, you'll never be able to change it." I couldn't see her grin, but again, I could almost hear it. "Looks like we have space in car C if you'll go take a seat." She gave both Randy and I a nod, and then the winds swirled around her, lifting her back into the air.

Mistral. Second nicest Cape I ever met. Smoking hot too.

She'd die a few years later, when some asshole raised King Rex as a Walker and went on a rampage through New Mexico.

Wasn't me.

I promise.

CHAPTER 69

Car C was the fourth of the five segments that made up the shuttle, and one of only three that was accessible to passengers. As Mistral had said, there was ample seating available, and I made my way down the aisle until I found an empty row. Some of the other passengers had personal Glass devices with them—even older models than the one I'd left behind—and a few had actual books, but the rest of us just sat in silence as the shuttle shuddered back to life and started moving.

As we crept toward the Hole, conversations started to crop up around me. The old man with bushy eyebrows and a belly-length beard was here to see his son for the first time in nineteen years. The tired-eyed woman two seats ahead of me was bringing pictures of her one-year-old twins to the father who had been imprisoned before their birth. Brothers, sisters, children and parents… everyone had a story. Some were looking for answers. Some were looking for closure. Some just missed the inmate in question, illegal deeds notwithstanding.

By the sound of it, I was the only one there with murder on his mind.

The miles fell away behind us. I spent those hours in silence, watching my mind's replay of Mom's death. Wasn't the same as feeling it, but the images were enough to keep my anger at a boil. I thought of everything that might have been if Mom had lived, thought of what my life might have been like. Most of all, I thought of that look on my dad's face as he drove his knife into Mom's body again and again and again.

You don't understand, Elora. This is for you as much as it is for me.

Fair enough, because *this* was going to be for Mom and me.

* * *

Finally, we reached the Hole, the end of a journey that had been, for me, almost two months in the making. I could hear soldiers disembarking from the rear car, coming up past the passenger sections to listen to orders being relayed from the front. Finally, our own exterior door disengaged with a metallic whine, and we stepped out into the blinding sun of the Mojave.

The Hole wasn't much to look at from topside; just a huge reinforced bunker with a single door leading in. According to my research, that bunker held nothing but armed guards and an elevator. The prisoner meetings would be somewhere in the cavernous installation underground, past the barracks for the guards who lived on premises, but far above the actual cell blocks.

A line of people stretched from the bunker into the desert, and we joined the end of that line. Noon in the Mojave wasn't anyone's idea of a great place to hang out—even in February—but an Earthshaker had fashioned temporary structures of iron and steel to provide shade to those who waited.

I turned to a nearby soldier who couldn't have been more than a year or two older than me. "Are we the first city to arrive?"

"Third, sir." He nodded to the other side of our shuttle, where two others were parked. "By far the largest though. I think the administration expected a better turnout."

"Guess so." I was still debating whether that was a good or bad thing—fewer people meant I'd get in more quickly, but also meant scrutiny might be higher—when the unnamed soldier excused himself and hurried forward to join an older man in fatigues. At the same time, one of the Capes who had escorted our shuttle—the Baron, judging by his costume—took to the air and headed south at full speed. Around us, other Capes did the same; Mistral and Breeze transporting not only themselves but the bulky forms of Incredible Ivan and Captain Crush. Moments later, they were gone.

When the soldier came back to take his position next to the line, his face was pale, his features slightly pinched.

"What's going on?"

He glanced at me, then back at the older man who was clearly his superior officer, and finally shrugged. "It looks like our neighbor to the south got wind that our Capes would be occupied today. His forces are attacking across the border. The Thunderbirds and Red Flight are already in the field, but they've put out a call for reinforcements."

"What about them?" I nodded to another handful of Capes now speeding off in the opposite direction.

"That wildfire up north just jumped the fire break. North Star needs help with evacuations." He scowled, unconsciously stroking the butt of his assault rifle. "Of all the days for everything to go wrong."

"Are we in danger?" That was the man who was here to see his son. He looked one or two revelations away from total panic.

"No, sir, we're going to be just fine." The soldier flashed a reassuring smile down the line. "In addition to the Hole's own guards, you have the finest of the 184th Regiment's First Battalion protecting you folks. We've also still got plenty of Cape firepower here, on loan from the Emerald Legion and Stormwatch."

That got my attention. The Emerald Legion wasn't in the same league as North Star or the Defenders, but they were still a big name. Stormwatch was a smaller operation, but it was my favorite Cape team in the entire Free States, for one reason and one reason only.

I scanned the skies above for almost a minute before I saw her.

Tempest.

Almost every straight man in the Free States—and at least half the gay women—had a crush on Aspen, but Tempest had been my favorite from the moment I hit puberty. And there she was, as long-limbed and beautiful as she'd been in that very first vid, simply clad in the sleeveless top and leggings she'd chosen for her costume. She was too far up for me to see the golden ribbons tied into her dark hair, but I knew they were there, could picture them streaming out behind her as she brought down lightning on her enemies.

Even if Winter lived to be a thousand and turned out to be a Full-Five in disguise, she'd never be half the Weather Witch that Tempest was.

I shook my head. My first time in Tempest's presence, the *only* time I'd ever be, and I was there to break the law she'd fought for more than a decade to uphold. In a better world, maybe we'd have ended up as teammates. In a perfect world, there wouldn't have been a need for teams at all, or Capes, or even soldiers.

But I didn't break the world. And I sure as hell wasn't going to survive it.

I took one last look at the Cape soaring high above us, then followed the line of people into the Hole.

* * *

We filed past another large scanner, then between sets of armed and armored checkpoints whose bristling gun mounts covered both the exterior door and the elevator at the far side of the room. Sandwiched between those checkpoints were the surface-level dampeners, enormous machines that dwarfed even those at the Academy gates. I wasn't sure if the size discrepancy suggested an increase in power output or if the Hole simply used an older model, but Mom's ghost faded before we'd gotten within twenty feet of the machines.

The line snaked back and forth, ending at another set of checkpoints and the massive titanium-alloy elevator door. Standing by that door was a thin, older man in a uniform of all-black. He wore the same insignia—a circle of red around a smaller black circle—that I'd seen on the other Hole guards.

As we came to a stop, his voice rang out, sharp and quick like the crack of a whip. "Ladies and gentlemen, welcome to the Hole. I am William Maroney, the warden of this facility. Before we get to the reason you are all here today, there are some ground rules we need to go over." He paced in front of the line, arms clasped behind his back, looking for all the world like a character from a vid. "You will obey myself and my guards at all times. Each of you will be permitted only the time allotted to meet with your inmate. When that time is up, you will promptly leave the meeting room to return groundside for future instructions."

"You will not touch the prisoners," he continued. "Nor will you give them anything, no matter how innocuous that item may be. Any attempt to do so will result in the confiscation of that item and the removal of the inmate in question."

He scanned the crowd, eyes hard as nails. "Failure to follow these rules will, at best, result in your immediate ejection from these premises. At worst, you could face federal charges of your own. My guards and I are here for your protection, but our primary duty is to see that our prisoners remain incarcerated. I strongly suggest that you do not test our commitment to that duty. Are there any questions?"

Amazingly, there were none, although the tired-eyed woman from my shuttle car had a coughing fit that still managed to delay the proceedings.

"Very well," said Warden Maroney. "With that out of the way, let me explain how this is going to work. You will be rotated down in groups of twenty to a room we've converted for visitations. Each of you will be assigned a table in that room, and you will sit at your table with your hands in plain sight for the duration of your visit. Once your group is in place, we will bring your relations up from the cell blocks, and you will be given thirty minutes to converse with them. If you finish earlier, you may signal one of my guards, and they will return your relation to their cell. However, you will remain with the rest of your group for the duration. You will enter and leave as a group."

I did the math. I was near the end of the line, which meant I'd be part of either the fourth or fifth group. That gave me a wait time between ninety minutes and two hours. After the months of anticipation, it felt like an eternity.

The Warden wasn't quite done. "And now, ladies and gentlemen, allow me to repeat my earlier greeting. Welcome to the Hole. You stand above the Free States' premiere facility for incarcerated Powers. The security elevator behind me leads to the housing for the two-hundred men and women who work at this prison—guards, doctors, technicians, and support staff—as well as the space that has been converted to a meeting area for today."

"The cell blocks themselves are located five miles below the surface, accessible only by a secondary elevator. At any time, either of those elevators can be disabled, preventing access to the surface. As those few of you who possess powers yourself will have already noticed, our dampeners run at maximum power at all times. Both you and our inmates are effectively normals while on these premises. We apologize for the inconvenience, but I hope you all understand why it is necessary."

Around me, heads nodded.

"Excellent. Then let's begin with group one."

The elevator door was at least a foot thick, but it slid open with little more than a whisper. Accompanied by a dozen guards, the first twenty visitors stepped inside and were whisked out of sight.

CHAPTER 70

When you factored in the additional time it took to travel down to the meeting room, get everyone seated, and bring the requisite prisoners up from their cell blocks, thirty minutes of visitation ended up translating into more than an hour of real time. A little bit after noon, guards passed out sandwiches and water to those of us who had yet to make it down. It was synth-meat and stale bread, and a hell of a long way from what the Academy cafeteria provided, but I was hungry enough not to care. I'd drunk plenty of water, but the only thing I'd eaten in the past twenty-four hours had been a candy bar from Randy's convenience store.

I know what you're thinking, but I didn't steal it. Randy had been asleep at the time, but I'd paid anyway. Overpaid, really. That may well have been the first and only $6.39 candy bar in history. But what the fuck, right? Life savings or not, you can't take that shit with you.

By the time we'd finished our sandwiches and the guards had come by to collect our trash, the second group was finally on its way back up. I was already sick of waiting. I'd had ample time to make a more accurate recount, and it had showed that I was in the fifth group, not the fourth. That meant I had yet *another* hour of standing in the bunker with my thumb up my ass and an illegal weapon barely hidden under my clothes. I just wanted to get this shit over with.

From the grumblings around me, I was pretty sure everyone else felt the same way, which is why I was stunned to see a guy at the tail-end of group four swap places with the older woman directly ahead of me in line.

"Thought that lady was going to collapse if she had to stand up much longer," the newcomer told me cheerfully. He was half again my age, but bone-skinny and ragged in a white tank. "Not everyone's built for this sort of thing, you know?"

"Not sure I'm built for it either."

His laugh was sharp, there and gone in an instant. "Wait until you're almost thirty, and mortality's starting to close in on you. Who are you here to see?"

"My father." The last thing I wanted to do right then was talk, but something—maybe it was the limited manners the Academy had tried to drill into me, or maybe it was the multiple hours I'd already spent doing nothing—compelled me to ask. "How about you?"

"Older brother." He eyed me speculatively. "You ever hear of Firewall?" I shook my head, and his expression fell. "Figured, but it never hurts to ask. That's my bro. High-Two Technomancer. Somehow, he got the brains *and* the power in our family."

Can't remember if I've spoken about Technomancers yet. Didn't have one in the Class of 76, so I might have skipped right over them. Most famous one is probably Legion himself, way out in Baltimore, but there's a bunch in the Free States too. Technomancers interface with electronics. Not to power them—that'd be Sparks—but to make them do new stuff. Guy who created the testing machine was a Technomancer. Not much call for them in the Cape world, but the commercial and military sectors just love them.

Criminals too, I suppose. Bank robbery's a hell of a lot easier when one of your crew can scramble the cameras and unlock the vault with a wave of their hand.

"I don't know," I finally replied. "Maybe he got the power, but you're the one who's still free."

"Huh. Never thought of it quite like that." He slapped me on one shoulder with a grin. "Guess maybe *I* got the brains!"

* * *

Two hours later, it was our turn. *Finally.* We crowded into the elevator with the same dozen guards, men and women who'd gone from the very pinnacle of paranoid awareness to something like resigned boredom over the course of the day. The door whisked shut and the elevator started down.

It was hard to gauge distance from inside the elevator, but we didn't seem to go as far as I'd expected. Four or five floors down, maybe, and then the elevator was opening onto a room every bit as large as the entryway above. We exited to the sounds of the one woman's ever-present coughing and were directed to our seats. Between the guards who had taken the elevator with us, and the ones already in the room, we were outnumbered significantly.

There were exactly twenty tables, arranged in neat rows of five. Across the room was the second elevator, the one that went down to the cell blocks. A green light above its closed door indicated that it remained operational. I took my seat—fourth row from the elevator, furthest to the left, if you care—and placed my hands on the table as the warden had instructed. The people who'd been at the table before me had clearly done the same; there were sweaty prints on the cold metal surface.

Two guards, one on each side of the room, waved to their respective security cameras, giving the all-clear before pivoting to face the cell block elevator with the rest of us. There were no numbers above the doors like you see sometimes in vids, nothing at all to indicate that the elevator was moving at all. As the minutes crept by, I could feel as much as hear both the guards and other visitors shifting restlessly.

Fifteen minutes later, the doors slid open. A line of inmates in orange jumpsuits, arms and legs shackled in front of them, shuffled into the meeting room, escorted by even more guards.

The lead prisoner was fucking enormous, a big black guy whose beard put my former roommate's to shame. His faded jumpsuit strained across broad, muscular shoulders, and he was a head taller than anyone else in the room.

Titan, I decided, before my mind conjured up images of Alan Jackson and Stonewall. *Or Shifter.*

Three tables away, the tired-eyed woman who'd brought pictures of her twins managed to stop coughing long enough to flash a brilliant smile at the big man. His answering smile was almost lost in the darkness of his tangled beard.

"You see where to go, Jaws," the lead escort rumbled. "No funny business or this visit ends early."

After Jaws, there came a succession of inmates, some of them almost as imposing, many of them… not. Bushy Eyebrows Guy's son was the spitting image of his old man, if taller and in considerably better shape. At the other end of the spectrum was Firewall, the aforementioned Technomancer, whose hairline had receded well past his ears, and who looked like a stiff wind would blow him over.

He wasn't the most pathetic of the inmates though. Nor was it the trembling, shivering kid with the enormous nose and prominent Adam's apple who the guards named Pusher—a Telekinetic, I assumed. Instead, that honor went to the last inmate off the elevator. He didn't have a Black Hat name because he'd been caught after his very first murder. Almost fourteen years later, he was a misshapen bundle of skin and bones, with wide, staring eyes, and the same beak of a nose I saw whenever I looked in the mirror.

David-fucking-Jameson.

Crow. Murderer. Father.

* * *

My father tripped twice on the way over to my table, and each time, he had to be reoriented after getting back to his feet. When he arrived, he stood there staring blankly at the wall behind me. Finally, the nearest guard pushed him into his chair.

Dad had never been a great looking guy, even in Mom's one memory, but now he looked like someone you'd find sleeping by a dumpster. His dark hair stuck up in every direction and his long, crooked nose dripped rivers of snot right past the corners of his half-open mouth. All the fat had been boiled away from his features, leaving too-prominent cheekbones and weathered pale skin.

We both had grey eyes, but mine were the color of old concrete, while his were paler. I'd have called them silver before I met Olympia and learned what real silver eyes looked like. I watched those eyes wander haphazardly around the room, like they were following a mosquito in flight. It was ten long seconds before he even noticed me. When he did, his eyes widened.

"Damian?"

I'd rehearsed what I was going to say. I'd even practiced my speech, just so I could maximize whatever time I got, but now that the moment had arrived, I couldn't say a word. All I could see was his face as it had been, years earlier—to me as a five year old coming home to his mom's murder, and to Mom when she'd fought to save my life—overlaid atop the desiccated figure sitting in front of me.

My plans went right out the window, taking those carefully rehearsed words with them. I was sliding one hand to the edge of the table, preparing to reach for Her Majesty's gun, and questions and interrogation tactics be damned, when my father did something wholly unexpected.

He smiled.

The one thing I *didn't* have was his smile. Sofia said I didn't have a smile at all—just a threat of impending violence, dressed up in exposed ivory—but even as a child, my smile had been quieter, more private. My mom's smile.

My dad's smile was wide and jolly and heartfelt and he had no business making it, sitting across from the son he'd tried to kill, the son he *had* orphaned.

"Damian!" He blinked away tears, and beamed even more brightly. "Look at you, all grown up big and strong! Your mother must be so proud!" He looked around the room. "Where is she?"

And that's when I realized my father didn't know.

* * *

I sat there for a moment in stunned silence as my father's voice rose to a whine.

"Where is she? Elora? Elora?!?!" He pulled his hands from the table and started to rise, but a guard was there in an instant, pushing him back down into his seat. The disgust on that guard's face turned to pity as he looked my way.

He wasn't the only one looking. Half the visitors were watching us, and at least as many of the inmates, although Jaws was focused on the two photos his wife was holding up even as she continued to cough.

With so many eyes on me, I had no chance of pulling the gun before someone stopped me, but there was no fucking way I was going to let this man cling to a fantasy where he hadn't stabbed my mother eleven times, hadn't stood over her as she bled out, as the cops and the paramedics came, far too late to do any good.

I leaned over the cold metal surface and caught his grey eyes with mine.

"She's not coming, asshole. You killed her."

He paused in mid-yell, and gave me a confused look. "Killed who?"

"Elora Banach. My mother. Your wife. Her blood. Your knife. Don't you fucking sit there and tell me you don't remember! You don't get to do that!"

This time, the guard's hand was on my shoulder, though I didn't remember having risen from my seat. "Sir, I'm going to have to ask you to sit down and lower your voice, or this visit is over."

"I'm sorry. It won't happen again." I dropped back down into the chair and made a show of unclenching my hands, and laying them, palms-down, on the table. Twenty-some minutes left, and I'd already managed to get a guard's personal attention. This was going all wrong.

I lowered my voice, and spoke to my dad. "I need you to remember. Not just what you did but why. It's important."

"What I did?"

I gritted my teeth and tried again. "You came home from work early that day. You went to your closet, and you dug out a knife that Mom had never seen."

His eyes sharpened, and for just a moment, I thought I had him.

There was more coughing from the woman with the photo… the longest and loudest bout yet. She brought a handkerchief to her mouth, and hacked into it like a smoker on her last lung. My father's eyes danced away to focus on the new distraction. "Why did I want a knife?" he finally asked.

"This isn't a story," I told him. "This is what happened. This is why you're here. I need you to think. Think about Elora."

"Yes, Elora." He nodded slowly, and I watched his face go even paler. "So much blood."

Those three words almost did me in.

"Yes," I finally managed. "There was blood everywhere."

"On her dress. Her pretty yellow dress." For the second time, tears glittered in my father's eyes. He started to rock back and forth in his seat.

"Yes. You told her that you were going to kill me. You said—"

"You don't understand, Elora," he interrupted, eyes drifting away from my face again. "I'm doing this for you. I don't know how I forgot, and I don't know how she made me remember, but our son is meant for horrible things."

I swallowed, but before I could ask the questions I'd come to ask, he kept going.

"I'm so sorry, my love. I should have told you about the visions. I should have told you about the headaches, but I thought I was going crazy. Then she came, and it was like a fog had been lifted. I remembered what he'd done to me. I remembered why. I knew what I had to do." Tears streamed down his gaunt face in dirty rivulets. "But it wasn't supposed to be you. I swear it wasn't!" He reached out with both manacled hands, not to me, but to someone past me.

I turned and saw Mom's ghost standing behind me. For only the second time ever, she wasn't smiling.

When I turned back, that same guard was back, pinning my father to his seat. I made sure my own hands were where they were supposed to be, and tried to catch my father's attention.

"Who are you talking about? She came? She who? What he did to you? He who? Tell me why. Please…!"

"I'm sorry, Elora," he said again, voice low but desperate, "I don't know how she found me. One moment I was alone, the next she was there."

"*Who?*" I hissed. "Who was there?"

For the first time in minutes, he looked in my direction, his eyes wide and empty. "Sally Jenkins, pale and wary, seems to be so ordinary."

My blood went ice cold. "What did you just say?"

"But all the bodies she could bury," he moaned, "would fill the whole world's cemetery."

My mind went blank and still, but before I could even begin to grapple with the enormity of what he had just said, I came to another realization… one that had nothing to do with my father's words.

We were in the Hole, with its military grade dampeners.

There was no way my mother's ghost could be present.

I looked to the guard behind my father, my own eyes suddenly wide. "Something's wrong—"

A low snarl echoed through the room and Jaws sprang out of his chair. Thick coarse fur sprouted from his exposed skin, his jaw lengthening into a snout. Manacles snapped like they'd been crafted of tissue, and in one long, loping stride he was on top of the closest guard, tearing out the man's throat with teeth that had become razor sharp.

For a moment, time came to a halt. I watched the dead guard's body start to fall, as Jaws turned towards the next guard on the perimeter. I watched a second prisoner surge to his feet, fire issuing from his fingertips. Most of all, I saw Jaws' wife, still seated, and the handkerchief that held the round object she'd just coughed up.

If it wasn't Legion tech, it was one hell of a knock-off.

Then things *really* went to shit.

CHAPTER 71

I'd spent the last year training at the Academy. No matter what Backstreet said, everyone else knew it was the best place in the Free States for a Cape to learn. Our instructors were all top-notch, and from day one, they'd worked to train us for battle.

None of it prepared me for how quick and brutal a fight with Powers could be.

The guard at my table went up like a torch, one of many as a ribbon of white-hot fire lashed out across the room. Screams mixed with gunfire and bodies hitting the floor, and then just like that, it was over.

Thirty guards, eleven visitors, and nine inmates, dead in the time it took to draw a breath.

On the far side of the room, Jaws straightened out of his crouch, blood dripping from clawed hands. "Firewall. What've we got?"

The Technomancer held up an index finger. A few seconds later, he nodded. "I'm in."

"Both elevators?"

"Yeah. Give me one more second, and..." Sweat beaded on the inmate's scalp, then he smiled. Around us, I felt the dampeners go offline. "That'll do it for the dampeners, too."

"What about the cameras?"

"Overrode them as soon as the device came into play. No alarms registered on the network. We should be golden. I can hold this all as long as it takes."

"You've got twenty-five minutes before we're supposed to head up, hon," called the tired-eyed woman who'd smuggled in the Legion device. "It's going to be tight."

"We knew it would be from the start," Jaws growled, turning back to the Technomancer. "What about the dampeners in Cell Block F? Can you shut them down?"

"No dice. Every block's on a different network, and all of them are out of my range. If I came down with you, I might be able to…"

"Nah, we need you up here, keeping the cameras looped and the elevators running. Red?"

"Yeah?" replied the Pyro who'd just killed a good thirty-five people. He was heavyset and blunt-featured, his smile almost as greasy as his hair.

"You're on crowd control. I'm going to get the VIPs."

"You sure you don't want any backup down there?"

The Shifter took the bloody device from his wife, his clawed paw dwarfing her human hand. "The VIPs know we're coming. This little thing should be all the backup I need."

Moments later, he was on the second elevator and out of sight.

* * *

"Listen up, all you fine, law-abiding motherfuckers," drawled Red, swaggering around the room like he owned it, "if you do *exactly* as I say, some of you just might make it out of here alive. Do otherwise, and you'll share *his* fate." He gestured, and one of the remaining prisoners was engulfed by a column of fire, the flames so hot the man barely even managed a scream.

"What the fuck, Red?" complained Firewall.

"Guy narced on me to the guards back in 69." He scanned the room, and just that quickly, a second orange-clad inmate went up in flames. "And that one looked at me funny last week. As for the rest of you shackle-wearing assholes," he continued, addressing the last six inmates, "I don't know you, and I don't give a fuck who you were before this. This is your shot at freedom. Join the cause if you want a place in the new world order. Stay out of our way otherwise."

"You're insane if you think you're getting out of here alive," declared the old man with the bushy eyebrows. "Just give up before you make things worse on yourselves."

"Funny thing about life in the Hole, old man," said Red, his grin going dangerous. "Ain't much left to scare us with. And we've got a few surprises ready for the assholes upstairs. Too bad you won't be around to see it—" He cut off as the imposing figure that had been seated across from the old man rose to his feet. "The fuck you think you're doing, Stalwart?"

With Jaws gone, the Stalwart was the biggest guy left in the room. He looked across the table at the old man, and then back at the Pyro. "He's my dad. I'm not going to let you hurt him."

"Your dad's got a big mouth. Someone his age should have learned better by now." Red cocked his head. "How long has is it been since you saw daylight, Stalwart?"

"Nineteen years."

"Nineteen years? *God damn*! That's a whole fucking life already. How old were you when they sentenced you? Twelve?"

"Sixteen."

"Ain't that the way it goes. Just a kid but one mistake costs you the rest of your life. And here's your old man, still kissing Cape ass. Maybe *you* should be the one killing him, not me."

"Killing people is what got me here in the first place" The Stalwart shook his head. "Three dead in an armed robbery. All of them innocent. Nineteen years is less than I deserve."

The Pyro spat to the side and looked past the Stalwart to his father. "Hold your head up, old man. You should be proud. It takes a special kind of stupid to spend nineteen years here and *still* feel guilty." His hands came up and fire spat across the room at both of them.

Apparently, nobody had told Red that alcohol was the only way to surprise a Stalwart. As quick as the Pyro's flames were, the other man was even quicker, rolling across the surface of the table to knock his father out of his chair and to the ground. A moment later, the Stalwart was back on his feet, the chains that shackled his arms and legs tearing apart with a noise that echoed through the room. He ducked another ball of fire and charged.

Every eye was fixed on the two dueling Powers. I reached into my suit coat and let the Legion gun fall into my hand. My father hadn't even reacted to the mayhem around him. He was still in his chair, lost in his own world, pale lips flapping open and closed like a fish out of water.

I raised the gun and placed its oddly shaped barrel directly between his eyes.

"This is for Mom, you piece of shit."

Even then, he didn't look at me, pale grey eyes still fixed over my shoulder on my mother's unsmiling ghost. I watched his mouth form unvoiced words, watched something like a smile spread back across his face.

I pulled the trigger.

* * *

In Weapons class, Jessica Strich taught us that every gun had a different trigger pull. The Legion weapon's trigger was smooth as silk, sliding back with the tiniest bit of pressure. On some guns, that would have been the end of it. On this gun, I hit a point where resistance built in the trigger.

Single-stage trigger vs. double-stage. Usually, the difference between them is just a matter of knowing exactly when the gun will fire. This one time, it was the difference between being a cold-blooded murderer and… I don't know. Something else.

I hit that point of resistance and stopped. Held it there for an impossibly long moment and then finally let my finger fall away. I wasn't a Cape. I'd never be a fucking Cape. But I wasn't the kind of asshole who just sat back and let innocent people die either.

Gun still extended, I turned to the action.

The Stalwart charged through a conjured wall of fire. His orange jumpsuit ignited, and exposed skin went black and smoking, but his extended hand caught the fleeing Pyro's arm, and the crack of a snapping bone joined the roar of the flames.

Red scrambled backward, one arm hanging loosely at his side, the other reaching behind him for balance. The Stalwart bounced off the wall, changed direction and came right back in.

He was within arm's reach when Red opened his mouth and spat fire.

Somehow, the Stalwart dodged most of the blast, but he staggered and went to one knee.

I rose to my feet sighted along the Legion gun's short barrel.

"Red, look out!" Somehow, I'd forgotten Jaws' wife. Maybe I'd discounted her because she wasn't a Power. Maybe I'd gotten that tunnel vision Nikolai had always warned us about. It was a rookie mistake, the sort of thing the Academy trained us to avoid.

She screamed her warning and Red was already ducking aside as I finished pulling the trigger.

I guess it's a good thing the Pyro hadn't been my target.

Across the room, Firewall stiffened as my round struck him. I'd been aiming center mass, as Jessica taught, but an almost supernatural lack of recoil and my own unfamiliarity with the weapon meant I'd shot him in the right hip instead.

It didn't matter.

Something spread outward from the point of impact like a ripple on a pond, something recognizable only by the carnage it left behind. It chewed through the Technomancer's jumpsuit, skin and bones, consuming as it spread. He was dead long before that ripple reached his heart, but it kept on going anyway, even as the last few bits of him crumbled to the floor. In less than a second, there was nothing left to suggest a man had ever stood there.

I'd asked Her Majesty for a guaranteed kill, and I'd sure as fuck gotten it.

The Stalwart used my distraction to get back to his feet. The right side of his face and body was a mass of blood and burns, but he loped forward like a savage on the hunt. First one step, then another, dodging Red's increasingly panicked blasts.

That should've been the end of it. In Cape vids, that *would've* been the end of it, a reformed Black Hat finding his way to the light, finding redemption even as he stopped a jail break before it could truly start. One more example of truth and justice triumphing even over the darkness of one man's heart.

Problem is, this wasn't a Cape vid.

Three tables away from me, one of the remaining inmates raised his still-shackled hands. Darkness pooled in his open eyes.

The Stalwart's own shadow reached up and wrapped itself around him, pinning him to the nearby wall.

Red stopped on a dime and reversed course. His good hand extended in front of him like he was pushing a wall, and fire poured into the Stalwart's struggling body. When the Pyro's flames finally cut off, there was nothing left behind but scorch marks on the wall, and a blackened, shriveled corpse that fell to the floor and exploded into fragments of ash.

I recognized the sound that came out of the Stalwart's father's throat. I'd made a sound just like it when I was five.

Red spared a moment to spit in the direction of the Stalwart's ashes and then turned to me, his expression ugly. "If you'd shot me instead of Firewall, you might have had a chance." Flames gathered again around his open hand.

"Probably should have," I admitted. What I *really* should have done was ask Her Majesty for a gun with more than one round. The weapon had gone cold and lifeless the moment I fired it, as if whatever powered it had left with the bullet. I tossed the gun aside and reached for my power instead. "But he was the one controlling the cameras."

Lights above both elevators went from green to red. Somewhere above us, an alarm began to sound.

CHAPTER 72

I had a split-second to appreciate—even enjoy—the look of shock on the Pyro's face, and then fire was coming at me like hell's own fury. There was no dodging that, not entirely, but with the cold emptiness of my power filling my body, I rolled away from the worst of it, taking cover behind a metal interview table that went red, then white, then melted into slag, leaving two half-torched table legs behind. I scooped up one of those legs, ignoring the hot metal that seared my flesh, and dodged from table to table. All the while, I was expecting the Shadecaster to pin me like he had the Stalwart, but the expected attack never came. One quick peek showed me why; the Power was slumped down in his chair, smoke coming out of empty, sightless eyes, as if Red's flames had burned him through the shadow he'd controlled.

Two down and only Red to go… assuming none of the other inmates were in on the jailbreak… assuming all of them stayed put.

I might actually have a chance.

If you're ever a Cape—hell, even if you come back as a normal, and go through life never facing danger at all—do me a favor; don't even think those words.

It's just asking to be fucked.

The doors to the cell block elevator exploded outward in a cloud of steel shrapnel. More bodies hit the floor, but I can't tell you if they were inmates or civilians. I can't even tell you how many people died in that one instant.

I was too busy staring at the fragment of steel embedded in my chest.

* * *

It didn't hit my heart.

You hear that sort of shit on vids sometimes, as if the heart is the only organ that matters in the body. But in the real world, when a twisted metal shard flies across the room and drives itself into your chest, it doesn't matter if it hit your heart or not. Fact of the matter is, you're still beyond screwed.

I watched blood well up around the steel shard, watched as it started to soak through the front of my one and only suit. I watched smoke drift from the arm and hip that hadn't escaped Red's initial blast, looked down at the hand I couldn't feel, the hand that was practically welded to the table leg I'd hoped to use as a weapon.

Twenty seconds in, and I was already a wreck.

Jaws stepped through the remains of the elevator doors, back in human form, and calling out even as he came through the smoke. "What the hell's going on, Firewall? The elevator locked down almost a hundred feet below. If we'd been any further down, the gas would have—" He stopped and looked around, mouth falling open. "What the fuck happened here?"

I couldn't see Red from where I was slumped on the ground, but I could hear him well enough. "Had ourselves a couple of would-be heroes, Jaws. They took out Firewall, but I put them both down."

"And now the entire facility knows what is going on." There was no humanity in the whisper that slithered from the depths of the elevator.

"Not to worry," said Red, his voice going wobbly. "We still got this—"

I barely saw the sliver of shadow that shot from the elevator like a spear, but I heard Red's voice cut off, mid-sentence, followed by a body hitting the floor in several pieces.

"We're going to have a fight on our hands, getting out of here." Jaw's voice was oddly diffident. "We could've used him."

"Incompetence is a cancer," answered the cold voice. "It must be excised lest the entire organism be compromised." The speaker stepped from the darkness of the elevator's interior, followed closely by two others.

I knew all three of them, even out of costume.

The owner of that terrifying voice, a whip-thin man with black hair to his waist, was Fallout, a Mid-Four Shadecaster who had assassinated one President, two senators, and more than a dozen Capes.

Behind him was Tremor—squat, hunchbacked and grotesquely muscular—a Low-Four Earthshaker and the villain who had sank Santa Barbara into the Pacific.

Last but not least was Maul, larger even than Nikolai, leathery brown skin so covered in tattoos that his features were almost impossible to discern. A High-Three Titan, he was infamous for eating the people he killed. His favorite entrée: elementary school children.

They were three of the four founding members of the Legion of Blood, three of the worst Black Hats taken alive in the past decade.

And they were all free.

* * *

Almost free.

A loud noise sounded from the elevator to the surface, and the light above its door—which had previously switched from green to red—went out entirely.

"Shit," said Jaws. "They must have just collapsed the shaft."

"And flooded it with gas," agreed Tremor. "Nice fucking escape plan, Shifter."

"It's not *my* plan," protested Jaws. "If you want to take it up with the big man, that's your call."

"I ain't afraid of Carnage," growled Maul.

"That's because you're an idiot, dear boy," whispered Fallout. "Carnage would tear you into pieces the size of your shrunken testicles. Besides, as I have informed you on multiple occasions, our former leader no longer sits at the top of this villainous pyramid." The Shadecaster turned back to Jaws. "There were three individuals of note specified in this allotment of civilians. Your oh-so-lovely wife—shockingly still with us, I see—Firewall's brother, dearly departed, much like the Technomancer himself, and one other."

"Yeah." Jaws cleared his throat. "Looks like she died in the initial attack."

"*She?*" Fallout hissed. "I don't care about an unpowered gutter trash civilian. That's one less fool we will have to reward or dispose of. I care only about her specific relation, the reason she was selected to be part of this group!"

"Oh. Right." Jaws raised his voice. "You still with us, Pusher?"

"No thanks to that idiot Pyro." The twitching inmate with the enormous nose staggered into view. "First I have to augment his power just so he can take care of one dumbass Stalwart… then he nearly kills me taking out a teenager." He stopped and eyed Fallout. "As for my sister, I'm more than happy to accept the reward on her behalf. Cash is preferable."

I didn't have the oxygen to curse out loud, but I was doing plenty of it in my head right then.

Pusher wasn't a Telekinetic like I'd assumed.

Pusher was a Switch.

Three insanely powerful Black Hats, and they had an Amplifier.

* * *

"You'll have your reward, as well as your freedom," said Fallout.

"In that case, what do you need me to do, boss?" asked Pusher, rubbing his still-dripping nose with the back of one hand.

"The warden has deprived us of one elevator," said Fallout. "Tremor will provide us with another." He scanned the room. "I'd say twenty or so feet in diameter should suffice."

"You sure?" asked Tremor. The Earthshaker didn't have much of a neck, but his head sort of wobbled. "Ceilings above us are titanium, Fallout. That's gonna take a lot of power, even with Pusher here. Do we really need to bring so much shit up with us?"

"Six remaining civilians, not counting Mr. Jaws' doe-eyed darling. That's six hostages should we need them… and six distractions if we do not."

"And the unaligned inmates?"

"They had their opportunity to help, yet did nothing. Given the loathsome nature of the Pyro in question, their cowardice would be forgivable," Fallout spread his hands out, palms upward, "were I in a forgiving mood."

Spears of shadow streaked from his spread fingers, every one of them striking a target.

I was a long way from being able to stand up, but turning my head was feasible, if barely. I looked behind me, already suspecting what I'd find.

The route I'd taken trying to evade Red's attacks was a mess of melted tables, scorched walls and toppled chairs, but in the middle of all that destruction, one chair had somehow remained unscathed, not just whole, but pristine. My father sat upon that chair, hands resting on a table that didn't exist anymore, the biggest smile I'd ever seen spread across his face.

Above that smile was the long, crooked nose we shared, but above that was nothing but empty space, a gaping hole that had been drilled straight through the back of his skull, a hole that dripped shadow instead of blood.

The ground began to shake as Tremor summoned his power. Without a sound, without fanfare or ceremony, my father's corpse sagged to one side, then slipped out of the chair and onto the floor.

* * *

I don't know what to feel sometimes. Some nights, I set my power loose just to avoid feeling anything at all.

Truth is, my father deserved to die for what he did, deserved to die for the murder of an innocent woman, for blood spread all over a white-tiled kitchen. If fate hadn't put me in that particular visitor group, if Firewall's brother had swapped places with me instead of the anonymous old woman… I'm pretty sure I *would* have killed him down there in the Hole. I'd have reached the trigger's point of resistance and kept on squeezing, would have gone to my grave feeling justified, if not proud.

But truth doesn't always tell the whole story. Sometimes, there isn't just one story to tell. My father was a murderer, but he was also a victim, a victim of whatever had been done to him before he met Mom, and whatever had been said to him on the day he killed her. He was a pawn in a game I didn't know anything about, a game whose players included Sally Cemetery and this still-mysterious *he*.

Maybe one day I'll learn to pity my father as much as I hate him. Maybe one day I'll even learn to forgive him.

But I wouldn't hold your fucking breath.

Even if you *are* already dead.

CHAPTER 73

There was a brief time when Evan Earthquake was every bit as popular a vid star as Paladin and Tempest. He was a little shrimp of a guy, lacking the usual Earthshaker build, and known as much for his coke-bottle spectacles as the three-piece suit he called a costume. His time at the top of the charts lasted less than a year. Three episodes and a shitty catchphrase that never caught on, and then just like that, he was gone from the vids like he'd never existed.

Turns out earthquakes only make for great vid until the casualty counts start rolling in.

Anyway, I saw all three Evan Earthquake episodes. Wasn't my favorite Cape, but what the fuck else was I going to do at Mama Rawlins' before I met Alicia? I saw every one of his vids and that's why I can tell you something beyond a shadow of a doubt:

Evan could never have managed the shit Tremor pulled that day.

The edges of the floor curled upward around us like a bowl with a flat center. The ceiling—the *titanium* ceiling—curled down to meet the floor's edges, forming a crude sphere of metal and stone that shunted aside dislodged debris from above. Then, we were rocketing upwards, propelled by an unbelievable force, blasting up through a hundred feet of reinforced levels.

After twenty seconds or so, our momentum started to slow, and I had a moment of hope that, even with Pusher's aid, Tremor had reached his limits. One glance upward killed that dream. The floor of our makeshift elevator had slowed, but the ceiling hadn't. The sphere separated back out into two hemisphere, with the space between top and bottom halves widening with every passing second. The top half seemed to hesitate for a fraction of a second, as it impacted the thickest barrier of all—the bunker that sat just above us—and then it blew the roof off and kept going a hundred feet into the air. It spun a few dozen feet to one side before gravity reasserted itself. When the mass of titanium, steel, and stone came back down, it was a good fifty feet away, striking one of the idle shuttles with the force of a medium-sized bomb.

Pusher collapsed where he stood, blood dripping from his nose and ears, a vein in his head throbbing like he'd just mainlined stim-weed. Even Tremor dropped to one knee, but he had enough juice left that our elevator rose to merge seamlessly with the floor of what had been, moments earlier, a heavily guarded bunker.

In thirty years, the Hole had never suffered a jailbreak. Those sent to the Hole were doomed to die in the dirt, in darkness and despair.

Fallout, Maul, and Tremor stood beneath a sun they were never supposed to see again, and Tempest swooped down to meet them.

* * *

Clouds formed out of nowhere above the descending Cape. Wind swept in from the west to swirl around the Black Hats, kicking up a cloud of dust and dirt. This close, I could see the ribbons in Tempest's hair and even the red bindi between her eyebrows. She hovered, fifty feet up in the air, the winds carrying her voice to everyone below.

"The law requires that I give you this one opportunity to surrender, but I really hope you don't take it."

"Surrender?" Fallout's whisper floated just as easily on the wind. "To you?"

"To us." Tempest kept her voice even, but the clouds swirled above her as additional Capes appeared. Rocket from the Defenders, Typhoon from the Watchmen, and at least three other faces I recognized from Stormwatch and the Emerald Legion. The walls of the former bunker had collapsed, and I saw a dozen other Capes around us at ground-level, mixed in with the troops of the First Battalion and the few Hole guards who had survived our explosive emergence. "There are five of you, Fallout, and almost twenty of us. We all know you don't like those odds."

"True enough." He looked up at the Weather Witch, his long, dark hair whipping about in the manufactured breeze. "Perhaps you should go find reinforcements."

"Funny you should mention that." Her smile was hard-edged and mocking. "When the alarms triggered, Lucian flew off to do just that."

"The Morning Star himself goes to summon aid? Perhaps we *should* consider surrender." Fallout cocked his head, considering. "What are your terms?"

Still unseen, tucked in between rubble and the remains of a table, I frowned. Too much had gone into this escape plan for Fallout to just give up. So what the fuck was going on?

"No terms, murderer," answered Tempest. "You go back to your cells. The individuals who aided in your escape go before a judge and jury. I'm offering you your lives, nothing more."

"So very tempting," said Fallout, his whisper oozing contempt, "but perhaps I can make a counter-offer."

If I hadn't still been on my back, I would never have seen it. High in the sky, far above the circling Capes, the clouds parted, letting a ray of sunlight slip through.

No, not a ray of sunlight, I realized, as it moved. It was Lucian, the Morning Star, leader of the Emerald Legion. But… hadn't Tempest said he'd left to get reinforcements?

Without knowing exactly why… without even knowing I was going to do it, I opened my mouth and shouted.

"Tempest, look out above you!"

I don't know how she heard me. Maybe the wind carried my voice like it had hers and Fallout's. Even harder to explain was why she acted on my warning, but she did… immediately and without even pausing to see who had said it.

A beam of light tore through the sky where she'd been hovering, moments earlier.

Moth, one of the Flyboys from Stormwatch, was less quick on the uptake. A second beam of light caught him as he turned to see where the first had come from. It lanced right through him, and sent him careening from the sky.

"Lucian? What are you doing?" Tempest looked to the distant figure high above, but the Cape's only response was another blast of light, crackling through the air. This one exploded into the military troops clustered on the ground, launching broken and blackened bodies into the air.

"Joining the winning side, it would seem. So much for your reinforcements," whispered Fallout, shadows collecting around his long, slender fingers. "It's time I showed you mine."

I couldn't see what was happening from my place on the ground, but the front lines of Capes and army suddenly stiffened and turned, spinning to react as some unseen force struck them from the rear.

* * *

"Be a fellow of good cheer and kill the young spoilsport, Maul," hissed Fallout, still audible even over the cacophony of screams, battle cries, and chattering assault rifles. "The rest of you, form up on me."

The good thing about having a table leg practically welded to your hand is that it makes for a convenient means of levering yourself to your feet. My power did the rest, quiet and empty, keeping the pain distant, controlling my body like I was a Walker in truth.

With every step in my direction, Maul got larger. Ten feet away, he scooped up the twisted remains of one of the meeting room tables, holding the entire thing in one hand like it was a giant club. Five feet away, he roared and swung his weapon.

I was already moving. If I'd dodged backwards or to the side, like the Titan had clearly expected, I'd have ended up a man-sized smear out there in the Mojave.

Instead, I charged forward.

The first lesson in fighting someone bigger than you is to nullify their reach advantage. Maul was large and terrifyingly strong, but he wasn't any faster than a normal. I let my power push my body to its limits, eking out an extra bit of speed. If I somehow survived, I'd pay a price for that… but it got me inside and under the arc of the Titan's swing.

The second lesson in fighting someone bigger than you is to not let them touch you. Thanks to my fights with the Viking, I knew punching Maul would be a terrible idea. I also knew not to try scaling his back and choking him out, no matter how cool it might look in vids. This time, I kept things simple; I thrust the sharp end of my half-melted table leg into the vulnerable skin at the back of the big man's knee.

The metal table leg, as battered as it was, was a hell of a lot tougher than my fist… just not tough enough. The sharp point hit the Titan's skin, and glanced off, leaving little more than a narrow scratch behind. Even worse, the jarring impact tore the table leg right out of my hand, taking with it multiple layers of skin.

My power kept me on my feet somehow, but when Maul's club came swinging back through, the only option for avoiding it was to drop down. I hit the ground hard, and the shard in my chest slid even deeper. I could hear the audible wheeze that meant I'd finally punctured a lung. It was all I could do to roll onto my back.

Maul was standing above me, blocking out the dark and stormy sky. I watched a foot the size of a trash can lift up then drop toward me like a meteor falling from the sky. I gritted my teeth, snarled soundless, bloody-lipped defiance into the air, and braced for the impact.

It never came. Something white streaked in from my periphery to strike Maul's leg with an audible ring of metal and a storm of sparks. When my vision cleared, a tall man in silver chainmail and a white surcoat stood above me, a shield strapped to one arm, and a bloody sword held in the other.

They called him the White Knight. One-time leader of the Los Angeles Defenders, he'd retired a decade earlier to take an advisory role with the Hammers of God. He had to be pushing seventy, but his movements were as fluid as ever.

Maul howled in anger, his club whistling through the air. It was the sort of blow that would have obliterated a tank, and the White

Knight didn't try to take it head-on, but instead swayed to one side, letting it whistle harmlessly past. He slid back in at an angle, leading with his shield, pushing Maul's arm and weapon out wide. Then his other hand thrust forward, driving his famous sword right through the Titan's torso.

Maul grunted, but his free hand punched the White Knight in the chest. The old Cape lost his helm and flew back a dozen feet. As hard as he went down, he was back on his feet almost immediately, white mustache and beard slick with sweat and sticking to a gaunt, wrinkled face.

"Come and die, old man," taunted Maul.

"I think I'll stay right here," said the White Knight, breathing heavily, "but thanks all the same."

"Coward!" Maul raised his club and charged the Cape.

"I call it prudence." On the third step, Maul slowed. On the fourth, he dropped to one knee, his free hand clutching at his chest. "That was your heart I hit," continued the White Knight. "Every step you took just tore the hole open further."

The last shreds of strength evaporated from Maul's arms. Still five feet from his opponent, he fell to the earth and died.

The White Knight hurried over, still breathing heavily. A seasoned eye looked me over, taking note of my wounds, and the old man shook his head. "Stay still, lad, and keep pressure on that wound. When this is over, the paramedics will—"

I never got to hear what the paramedics would do, as something hit the Knight from behind, tossing him twice the distance Maul had already sent him.

One of Fallout's reinforcements had broken through the army's line. That was bad enough on its own, but when I saw who it was, all hope of victory fled.

He was the leader of the Legion of Blood and the one Black Hat even Fallout feared. Unofficially ranked as a Mid-Four Titan *and* a Mid-Four Stalwart, he'd fought the adult Paladin and several members of the Defenders to a stalemate on multiple occasions.

Carnage was here, and we were all going to die.

* * *

The infamous Black Hat didn't spare me a glance as he stepped forward. Even at nine feet tall, he moved with that grace unique to Stalwarts, his long, powerful legs crossing the distance at inhuman speeds.

The White Knight barely got to his feet in time. Blood poured down the right side of his face, but he'd held on to both shield and sword somehow. Pale eyes widened as he saw who was coming toward him, and then a sort of resigned determination set in. He raised his shield and his sword. "So be it. Let's see what you have."

I'd seen Orca and Matthew fight more than a dozen times, and I'd seen WarChild and that anonymous Stalwart compete in the Graduation Games, but nothing prepared me for seeing two Cat Four Stalwarts in battle. It wasn't just that they were fast and skilled… even the first-years were like that. It was like they were communicating in a language I couldn't even comprehend. Every strike was a puzzle instantly divined and solved by the opponent. For almost thirty seconds—a lifetime at that speed—not a single blow landed.

Carnage's gruesome smile widened. "Tiring already, old man?"

"Come and find out, monster." Sweat mingled with blood, but the White Knight blinked both away.

Carnage was already in motion, gliding past the Cape's defensive sword thrust. The other man lashed out with his shield but Carnage stopped it dead with one giant hand. With a low growl, the Black Hat ripped the shield up and to the side.

I don't know what the old man had done to try and brace himself, but it didn't work. The shield went flying and his arm went with it, torn from its socket in a spray of blood, shredded tendons and splintered bone.

The old Cape's scream was lost in the sounds of dying men all around us, but as I watched, something like triumph entered his eyes. The sword strike Carnage had dodged on his way in had been one last, risky feint, pulled back at the very last moment. The Black Hat was too close to dodge, too far out of position to block.

The White Knight drove his sword forward, all of his remaining bodyweight behind the blow.

Still on my ass, still struggling to rise without even a table leg to support me, I watched the Titan's body heave up and down, as if trying to dislodge the sword I couldn't quite see. Then I heard the sound, drowning out even the roar of machine guns firing in unison.

Carnage was *laughing*.

He hoisted the White Knight into the air. In the Cape's left hand—now his only hand—was a golden hilt, and the three-inch fragment of blade which was all that remained of his legendary sword.

"I hear you used to be something back in the day," Carnage said, leaning forward to let the other man's blood cascade down over his face. "You should've stayed retired."

The hand holding the White Knight came down like a hammer, smashing the old Stalwart into the earth again and again. By the third impact, there was nothing left but a broken body in shredded chainmail.

CHAPTER 74

Carnage tossed the White Knight's corpse aside and headed for the ridge where Fallout and the others were making their stand.

A costumed Flyboy came crashing down out of the sky twenty feet to my left, hitting the earth like a missile of blood and bone. Above me, the sky crackled with lightning and thunder as Tempest brought the storm's fury to bear on the Morning Star. The traitorous Cape was on the defensive—building shields of solid light as he was tossed about by hurricane strength winds and sheets of rain—but that was the only good news I saw. Over half the original Capes were missing, and the handful who remained with Tempest were being overwhelmed as additional Black Hats took to the sky.

On the ground, the situation was somehow even worse. The staccato crackle of gunfire mixed with the crash of thunder, but the First Battalion's lines had broken, and what had once been a strong, if hastily assembled, perimeter had fractured into chaos. Pyros, Lightbringers and Telekinetics rained down death on each other from a distance as Titans, Stalwarts and Jitterbugs waded through the sea of soldiers and civilians like earthbound Gods.

I sucked air into my one working lung, spat out blood from the other, and lay there, useless and injured, as people died around me.

Maybe Nikolai had been right all along. Maybe if I'd taken Amos' advice and worked toward an academic scholarship, I wouldn't have ended up in the desert, bleeding out while multiple teams of

Capes fought and died. Hell, maybe I even *deserved* to have it end like this.

But you know what?

Fuck going out on my back.

Fuck going out easy.

Never lived easy. Wasn't going to die that way either. Not even if the world ended around me.

I rolled to one side and slowly, painfully, pushed myself back to my feet.

* * *

There wasn't any part of the White Knight that remained recognizable, just a hunk of meat and bone, discarded in Carnage's wake. I was staggering past the corpse, too worried that stopping would make it impossible to start again, when something caught my eye.

The hilt and broken blade of the Knight's sword.

I shouldn't have been able to bend down to grab it, but I did anyway, scooping it out of the dirt without slowing. More pain, but it blended in with the rest, still distant if no longer possible to ignore.

I passed Maul's body next and then, not much further on, found Tremor. The Black Hat was on his back, eyes wide open, with a strangely neat bullet hole through his forehead, and what remained of his brains spread across the desert beneath him.

Score one for the men and women of the First Battalion.

As I reached the ridge, I found Carnage and Jaws in a field of broken bodies. The Shifter was limping badly, his natural regeneration overwhelmed by the sheer number of injuries he'd suffered. Carnage was covered in gore, but otherwise untouched. As I watched, he scooped up a dead Cape with one enormous hand and threw her twenty feet through the air into a cluster of soldiers.

At the center of the space they'd cleared, Fallout was at work. The Black Hat was turned to the sky, his long hair streaming out behind him. Spindly fingers wove invisible patterns in the air, and high above us, shadows stretched from the clouds to grasp one of the last few soaring Capes. The unknown Wind Dancer faltered, his mouth opening in a silent scream, and shadows poured in through that mouth, through his eyes, his nose and his ears.

Moments later, the Cape's wind deserted him, and he dropped from the sky like a stone.

A fresh storm of bullets came down from the far side of the ridge, where soldiers had formed a knot of resistance around a handful of Capes and the wreckage of another shuttle. Jaws staggered yet again, then he and Carnage turned to crush the opposition. For a moment, there was nobody looking in my direction.

I staggered through the bodies toward Fallout.

I wasn't quiet. There's no such thing as being quiet with a punctured lung and four barely functional limbs. But with Tempest's storm raging around us, with soldiers screaming and dying, and Capes and Black Hats sounding their battle cries, the sounds of my passage almost went unnoticed.

Almost.

I was three feet from Fallout, creeping up behind him, when the cry went out.

"Fallout! Look out!"

Somehow, I'd missed Jaws' wife in the sea of corpses.

I didn't have time to kick myself for making the same mistake twice in a row. I didn't have time to even think. Instead, I lunged forward, the White Knight's broken blade fully extended in front of me.

Fallout's own shadow reached up and stopped me cold, one tendril wrapped around my outstretched wrist like a steel manacle, even as another twined itself around my feet. The Shadecaster didn't bother to turn in my direction. His sight was fixed on Tempest, long fingers momentarily paused, as if he was waiting for something.

High above us, the Weather Witch brought her arms together. The hurricane winds Lucian had been fighting suddenly reversed, and the Morning Star soared forward.

Right into a storm of lightning the likes of which I'd never seen before.

Struck hundreds of times in less than a second, the Lightbringer plummeted from the sky like a fiery comet.

Tempest paused to watch him fall.

Fallout's fingers began to dance.

I'd been straining to reach the Black Hat from the moment he caught me, but his shadowy grip was as strong as any Titan's. I watched darkness gather around his spindly fingers, seconds from lashing out with lethal force.

I thought of the low-level Shadecaster that Red had inadvertently killed down in the Hole.

And then I reached up with the bloody mess that was my free hand. I tore the metal shard out of my chest, and I stabbed down into the shadow that held me.

For just a moment, Fallout staggered, and the grip around my wrist and feet loosened. I took that final, all-important step, and drove the White Knight's broken blade into the Black Hat's back.

* * *

If there's one thing I'd learned in the Academy, it's that there is no such thing as unnecessary overkill. I twisted the broken sword, pulled it out, and stabbed again.

The hand that stopped me this time was flesh and blood and as large as my head. With a flick of his wrist, Carnage threw me backwards all the way across the ridge.

I landed hard in a pile of dead or dying soldiers, and felt something in my spine give way. My legs splayed uselessly to the side and blood fountained from where I'd removed the metal shard, but my eyes still worked.

I saw Fallout on one knee, both hands still extended upward.

I saw shadows stab down from Tempest's own thunderclouds like the negative images of lightning strikes. I saw her obliterate some with lightning of her own, saw her build a wall of wind and rain against the others.

And I saw the shadows slide right through that defensive wall to strike her.

I saw Tempest die.

And two hundred feet below her, I saw Carnage turn and start to come my way.

Fuck this fucking shit.

* * *

I couldn't feel my legs. I could barely move my arms, and darkness was starting to creep into the edges of my vision, but what I remember more than all of that was the emptiness of my power spreading from my core. I felt it reach my heart, felt my heart skip one beat, then a second. Felt it reach my mouth, making my tongue go numb. I felt it reach my eyes, felt them flutter shut.

Some people say there's a great tunnel of light when you die, and an uncontrollable urge to travel toward it. Some people say you see your own life flashing before you, every decision made, every mistake, every blessing.

I opened my eyes and saw ocean.

It wasn't the Pacific, not really. There wasn't any water and there wasn't any sky. There was just darkness, like an ocean's waves, tiny pinpricks of light reflecting off the surface. Except even that was wrong, because it wasn't darkness; it was emptiness, and it wasn't light, it was something else, something that pooled in increasingly shallow puddles in the dead bodies about me, something that barely glimmered in the imperceptible forms of ghosts across the battlefield.

For the first time, I saw with my own eyes that balance of life and death of which Sally had spoken.

Even in this strange perspective, Carnage was a giant; a bonfire of energy twenty feet tall. I watched him come as the last bits of life trickled out of me, as my emptiness spilled over into the earth and the corpses around me. He stood there and said nothing, content to watch me bleed out on my own.

I've said it once, and I'll say it again,

Fuck going out like that.

I pulled on that dark-watered ocean around me, the dead and the almost-dead, even the pockets of buried decay in the desert beneath me. I pulled that death back into me, kept pulling until metaphysical seams started to tear, as my core struggled to contain the emptiness I'd taken.

Then my right hand, my good hand, reached up of its own accord. Fingertips brushed the exposed skin of the Black Hat's thick ankle.

I let all that emptiness go. Out of me and into him.

Fuck you, asshole.

They weren't the greatest last words ever spoken—or thought, since I lacked the breath to speak them—but they were mine.

Sometimes you just have to take what you can get.

CHAPTER 75

That's how it was supposed to go anyway. Orphan Crow, Academy dropout, and would-be murderer giving his life to take the big bad down with him.

Problem is, it didn't quite work like that.

Oh, I killed the fucker; make no mistake about that. All the death that had pooled in a hundred soldiers and I don't know how many Capes flooded through me into Carnage like a tidal wave he couldn't see. Asshole never knew what hit him.

What I didn't expect was that the emptiness I'd forced into him didn't consume his energy so much as displace it. As black waters filled his nine-foot-tall, unstoppable frame, drowning every molecule of his existence, all the energy that had previously occupied that space was pushed out along the path of least resistance.

Into me.

For a brief, horrifying moment, I thought *that* was going to kill me, wild energy running roughshod through my broken body, but what my shell couldn't hold spilled right back out of it. I pulled my hand away from Carnage's ankle and the excess energy splashed into the bloody earth beneath me, soaking into the soil until it was lost from sight.

When it was over, I took a breath and it didn't hurt. Stretched my legs out and watched them move. Every part of me felt vibrant and energetic, whole and unharmed, and the emptiness at my center was silent and still for the first time in months, curled in about itself like a seed waiting for spring to sprout once more.

I rose to my feet, and watched Carnage's body crumble into dust. Looked from that swiftly decaying body to the wide eyes of the half-dozen Capes who had just arrived, their bright costumes scorched and pitted by what looked like magma.

"You're too fucking late," I told them. "We already lost."

"Look again," said the lead Cape, a pale-skinned woman in the Society's colors.

I turned and stared.

A single man floated in the sky, the sun a halo around him as the last vestiges of Tempest's storm dissipated.

Dominion had arrived.

* * *

Thirty minutes after that, it was over. The Black Hats who didn't scatter or surrender died where they stood, most of them swatted like insects by the Free States' only Full-Five. Twenty minutes later, a rescue operation was in full swing. Fliers from the Society and Red Flight brought in paramedics from the 184th Regiment as well as both Academy Healers *and* the recruiter who'd been visiting campus.

I stood in the middle of the chaos and tried not to be in the way.

I stayed there for almost an hour. Mistral had just returned from taking some of the critically injured to the nearest hospital when she caught sight of me. I watched her land and make a beeline toward the open circle of space and silence that seemed to follow wherever I went. Someone intercepted her; a Cape I didn't know. I couldn't hear their words, but the way that other Cape kept glancing in my direction told me exactly who they were talking about.

Mistral listened for a few seconds, then shook her head. She stepped around the other Cape, ignored whatever it was they were still saying, and continued in my direction.

We stood together in silence for a long while before she spoke. "Hi, Damian," she finally said. "Are you okay?"

"My father is dead." I'm not sure why I said it. I'm not sure that I even cared, but the words slipped out anyway.

"I'm sorry."

"I don't know if I am." I frowned into the distance.

"Maybe you should sleep on it?" she suggested. "There's a kind of shock we all experience after even minor battles… and this one was anything but minor."

"Tempest died." Maybe she was onto something. Maybe battle shock why I kept saying things she already knew.

"I know," said Mistral. "Rocket too. And Moth and far too many other good men and women, Powers and normals alike."

"Where *was* he?" She followed my gaze to where Dominion stood in his own circle of space and silence. "If he'd been here—"

"Then we'd have lost all of Arizona and New Mexico to our southern neighbor," said Mistral, her own voice going hard. "Tezcatlipoca took the field today for the first time in decades. Dominion spent seven hours battling him, giving the rest of us time to destroy the monster's foot soldiers."

"Oh."

"There are no easy days, Damian. No easy days and no easy decisions." For just a moment, she hesitated, then she reached out, patted me on the shoulder, and walked away.

I watched her go, watched until she took to the sky with the next handful of injured victims, and then I turned and looked again at Dominion, still standing in his bubble of silence.

* * *

Any other day, a teenager drenched in blood would be the kind of thing that people took notice of… but this wasn't any other day. As I walked through the crowd, I could tell who knew what I had done and who didn't. The ones who did skittered out of my path like scared animals. The others ignored me entirely.

It was almost a relief when I reached Dominion's pocket of quiet.

Maybe it was because he predated the Cape generation or maybe it was because he didn't need to worry about things like public relations or sponsorship deals, but Dominion had never been featured in a single Cape vid. Even when people told stories about him, it was about what he'd done or said and not what he looked like. I think most of the country had built up a certain image in our minds. Taller than Paladin, stronger than Atlas, square-jawed and handsome, with eyes that blazed like miniature suns.

Turns out Dominion was kind of short, with broad shoulders and a noticeable paunch pushing against his classic red and gold costume. His hair was cropped, but the stubble was steel-grey, and his skin, dark brown like the Bakersfield mud after a rainfall, was thick with wrinkles. He didn't look his age—he had to be pushing at least a hundred, given that he'd been in his twenties during the Break—but he was a thousand miles of bad road from looking young. His eyes, an unremarkable brown, were locked on the corpse at his feet.

In death, Tempest was older than she'd looked in the vids, white strands of hair mixed in with dark, and crow's feet and lines around her eyes and mouth. Someone had wrapped her body in a blanket, hiding most of the damage she'd taken, and her eyes were shut. I'd love to say she looked peaceful, lying there, but that's just not how death works.

"Are you okay?"

No clue why I, of all people, thought it was a good idea to check on Dominion. Maybe it was that battle shock again. Maybe sucking down Carnage's life energy had fucked with my head. Only thing I knew for sure was nobody else had seemed willing to do it.

Dominion kept his eyes on Tempest's body, his reply a slow rumble that I had to strain to hear.

"Some people see a light and all they want to do is snuff it out. It's always been like that, even before Dr. Nowhere." He bent over and picked up a ribbon that had come free from Tempest's hair, clenched it tightly in broad, weathered hands that could shatter mountains. "But me, I wasn't satisfied with just a light. I had to build a bonfire that our enemies could see from orbit. And what did it get us?"

I wasn't sure the question was meant for me. I wasn't even sure what he was talking about, but I took my best shot at answering anyway. "A country where everyone can be free. Even normals."

"And what happens to this country when I'm gone?"

After a moment's thought, I shook my head and shrugged.

"I guess whoever's left will do what we can to hold the line."

He didn't say anything for a long moment, staring off into the distance, standing over the body of a dead heroine young enough to be his great-granddaughter.

Eventually, he nodded.

"Good man." He spared me a second glance. "What's your Cape name, son?"

I discarded a half-dozen options, including—sadly enough—Baron Boner. Somehow, after a year of not knowing the answer to that question, only one name seemed to fit.

"Walker."

CHAPTER 76

Now *that* would be a good way to end the story.

Problem is, that's not how the story ends. Not even this little piece of it.

You already *know* how it ends.

I told you back at the very beginning.

CHAPTER 77

My expulsion hearing was held in a conference room near the Academy's administrative offices. There were no lawyers or audience members. There wasn't even a judge to bang his gold-plated gavel, like you see sometimes in old vids. It was just the review board and the defendant aka the accused aka me.

This being the Academy, the review board was mostly Capes. Bard was the lone normal, flanked by Macy Johnson, Isabel Ferra, the adult Paladin, and Dominion himself. I didn't know how my Ethics professor had made the cut, but I was pretty sure she was the only one of the bunch who actively hated me.

By the fourth hour, I was considerably less confident.

By the second day, I was wondering how I'd survive on the streets when they were done.

It's kind of funny… I'd spent the whole damn semester worrying about getting kicked out because I was too weak to be a Cape. The battle at the Hole had proved I belonged… yet it was my presence at that battle that might end up getting me expelled.

Shit's just never easy, is it?

"I think we've spent enough time on the specifics," said Bard, a very long time after I'd come to the same conclusion. "Mr. Banach left campus without permission, breaking one of the stipulations of his continued enrollment, and he did so by convincing his classmate to engage in a potentially dangerous overreach of her abilities. There's also the question of his woeful academic performance, several reported incidences of physical violence, and a multitude of vehement complaints from at least one of his professors."

Isabel Ferra didn't even have the grace to look ashamed about that last bit.

"Do you have any words you'd like to offer in your defense, Damian?" finished Bard.

I frowned. "I *had* to leave campus if I was going to see my father. Maybe the timing sucked, but that was President Weatherly's fault, not mine. And if I hadn't been there—"

"Your actions at the Hole are irrelevant to these proceedings," snapped Isabel.

"Well, that's pretty convenient for that one *anonymous* professor who's had it in for me from the moment she heard a Crow was coming to school," I shot back.

"Damian…" warned Bard.

"Sorry." It'd been almost two weeks since the battle, but I was still sleeping even worse than normal. I pinched the bridge of my nose and tried to muster up a usable defense. "I only asked Wormhole for help because the brawl made me miss my shuttle. She didn't seem concerned about the distance of the jump." I paused to hedge that statement just a bit. "Outside of being able to fit into her dress for the dance when all was said and done."

"As for my grades…" I shrugged. "I was passing most of my classes until it became obvious I wasn't going to make it to second-year. And I did pass the first semester. Right?"

"Somehow," muttered Isabel.

I nodded. "Well, there you go. Is there anything I missed?"

"I'm pretty sure there was something about violence," Macy said helpfully, tossing in a wink and a grin.

That was one accusation I felt no guilt over. "Violence is part of what we do, isn't it? Half our classes are about training us to fight. I'm not saying I'm a model student," I admitted, "and maybe I could have handled some things better—like when that dickhead accused me of killing Unicorn—"

"Mr. Banach," warned Bard.

"Right." I winced. "Anyway, Capes need people that will run toward the action instead of away from it. If nothing else, I'd say I meet that criteria."

"Courage is part of what makes a Cape, but self-control is an even greater necessity," said Dominion, speaking for the first time in hours.

"I'm not the first-year who punched Backstreet in the face—"

Matthew's father scowled.

"—but yeah, self-control is something I should work on," I admitted.

"Mr. Banach is not the first student to get in a fight on campus, and he'll be far from the last," said Paladin dismissively. "Unlike Isabel, I *am* interested in his exploits at the Hole." He leaned forward in his chair, pinning me to mine with a hard-eyed stare. "In particular the fact that he used a piece of Legion tech to kill Firewall."

I hid another wince. The revelation that they knew about the gun had been an unpleasant surprise. Of the six civilians that Fallout had spared for hostage usage, two others had actually survived... and one had not only witnessed my shooting of Firewall but reported it during his debriefing. The only reason I wasn't on trial for possessing contraband technology was that the witness *only* remembered me shooting it. Nobody knew I'd been the one to smuggle it in, which meant I'd been able to keep my plot to kill my dad—and Her Majesty's involvement in that plot—secret.

"It's like I told you," I said, lying through my little Crow teeth, "I saw it on the ground after the initial attack and grabbed it. I knew a gun when I saw one."

"Care to hazard a guess on where it might have come from?" That was from Dominion, who was a hell of a lot harder to lie to than Paladin.

I shook my head. "All I can think is that one of the other conspirators smuggled it in, like Jaws' wife did the dampener override. Maybe they dropped it when Red went ballistic?"

"That seems far-fetched," said Paladin.

"Does it?" Macy shook her head. "The alternative explanation is that some unrelated third party *also* smuggled in Legion tech. Who?

Why? And what are the chances that this individual was, by pure coincidence, in the same group of twenty that was down there when the escape attempt occurred?"

"All good questions," said Bard, rubbing his eyes tiredly, "and ones which I suspect the Security Council will be grappling with over the next several months. However, as Isabel pointed out, Mr. Banach's actions at the Hole are not on trial here. Is there anything else you'd like to say, Damian?"

I'd had two days to think about what I wanted to say. I straightened up in my chair and met his gaze. "Yeah. Whether you all want to talk about it or not, what happened at the Hole proves I have some power. All I want is the opportunity to use that power."

For a terrifying moment, I thought nobody would ask, but finally, Dominion spoke.

"For what purpose?"

"To protect the people who don't have any. Isn't that why Capes exist?"

***

I thought I'd scored some points by paraphrasing Dominion's own quote about power, but ten minutes later, I was back out in the hall, sitting in an uncomfortable, slightly wobbly chair while the review board debated my fate within.

It had been a tiring two weeks and I was still a long way from processing everything that had gone down out in the desert. As horrific as the battle had been, it was the stuff before it that was keeping me up at nights. My father. Sally Cemetery. The mysterious third party and whatever it was he had done. I'd gone to the Hole for answers and revenge. In some ways, I'd gotten both, but they had only made things worse.

Stifling a yawn, I watched a student amble down the hall in my direction, Glass in one hand and a manila folder in the other. He was about my age, but short, and soft around the edges. Either he was a normal student—working as an office aide through the year-end break—or an incoming first-year, with no clue whatsoever about the hell Nikolai had in store for him.

With his head buried in his Glass, he'd almost reached me before he realized someone else was there. He shrieked and threw up his hands.

I plucked his Glass out of the air, but the manila folder went everywhere, spilling out type-written pages and a handful of black and white photographs.

"You okay?" I passed the Glass back over.

"You're him, aren't you?" His eyes were wide and glued to my face.

"Him who?"

"The Crow who killed Carnage."

Got to admit it; I really loved the sound of that. The little bit of awe in his voice didn't hurt either.

"Call me Walker." The first thing I'd done with my own Glass was verify that the name hadn't already been claimed. For once, luck had been on my side.

"What was it like?"

In my mind, I watched Tempest fall from the sky. Just like that, the conversation stopped being fun.

"A lot of good people died," I finally said. "I'm pretty sure it wasn't worth it."

"Oh." He dropped his eyes, and started stuffing photos and pages back into his manila folder.

"Wait." I peered over his shoulder. "What are those?"

"Black Hat files," he told me, opening the folder wide. At the top of the loose stack was the picture that had gotten my attention.

Her Majesty was instantly recognizable in the figure-hugging leather outfit and ever-present motorcycle helmet. The helmet's visor was down, as usual, showing that same smiley face decal, and she had one gloved hand raised toward the camera, middle finger extended.

"That's—"

"The Queen of Smiles," the student supplied helpfully. "Now *there's* someone worth going bad for, am I right?"

I tucked that name away for future research. "I heard she was more mercenary than Black Hat."

He shrugged. "I guess so. I don't put the files together… I'm just sorting through them for the board." He saw my confused look and nodded to a corkboard that hung further down the wall. "The Most Wanted board?"

I followed him down the hall to see for myself. The board held photos, aliases, and other details for ten of the worst Black Hats to operate in the Free States.

"The Security Council has a digital version, of course, but Dean Bard likes to do some things the old-fashioned way. Carnage *was* number six. With him dead, we'll add someone new to the board. Not the Queen," he added. "She's barely top twenty-five, unfortunately. I wouldn't mind walking past *her* photo every day."

Any other time, I might have kicked his ass for objectifying the subject of my own unrequited lust. This once, not even the Queen's fantastic figure could hold my attention. I was too busy staring at the board.

With Carnage gone, there were only nine Black Hats posted. Eight had a wealth of details next to their names, along with images that captured their likenesses from every angle. The ninth one was different, represented by a single photo and an index card. The picture had been taken at night and from far away, but it showed a man of average height, average build, and thoroughly average appearance. There was only one thing that kept him from being completely forgettable.

He had eyes like copper pennies.

Even in the grainy photo, they glittered in the dim light of the street lamp above him. I'd seen those eyes before. They belonged to the man who had taken me from Mama Rawlins, the Finder who had set me on my path to joining the Academy.

I stared up at the photo of the man I knew as Mr. Grey, and looked at the index card pinned next to it. No powers, no aliases, no known associates.

Just a single name:

Tyrant.

EPILOGUE

In the conference room, Isabel, Macy, and Paladin debated the fate of Damian Banach, each of them making their cases to Jonathan Bard. The dean listened attentively, but his gaze couldn't help but stray to the final member of the review board, the most powerful person in the room—if not the world—and the only one who wasn't speaking.

At last, Dominion stepped forward. "I know you have your reasons for everything that you do, Jonathan, but I would love to hear why we're having this trial."

"What do you mean?" asked Isabel Ferra. "The boy's presence at the Academy was contingent upon adherence to certain rules. He failed to—"

"Between sounding the alarm at the Hole and killing Carnage, the boy saved innumerable lives, Isabel. As terrible as our losses were, they would have been far worse if he had not been there."

"And that justifies breaking the rules? And his word?"

"It does." Dominion glanced at Bard. "But you already knew that, didn't you?"

"I did." The dean cleared his throat. "This university exists to train Capes and those of us who support them. Damian proved he has the makings of a Cape, and he did so in the middle of a battle that claimed the lives of vastly more experienced Powers. I'm not going to expel someone like that simply because he broke a rule. Even if it was *my* rule."

"Then I'm going to repeat Dominion's question. Why have the trial?" asked Paladin. "Some of us have lives that don't revolve around your facility."

"This was for Damian's benefit, wasn't it?" realized Macy. "The hearing, the judgement… it's all just another lesson."

"Exactly. The fact that I have no intention of expelling him isn't the point. What matters is that he's spent two days thinking about what he did and sweating our judgement." Bard looked at the Powers arrayed around him. "The Academy isn't just about training someone to use their abilities. It's about teaching them to behave like a Cape. Damian needs to learn that he'll be held responsible for his actions."

"And how will he learn that when you've just dismissed any consequences for his action?"

"Did I say there wouldn't be consequences?" Bard shook his head, smiling. "All I said was that I'm not expelling him. By the time I'm through with young Mr. Banach, he might very well wish I had."

"Meaning what?" demanded Isabel Ferra. "You're going to cut his food rations for a week? Maybe limit his Glass privileges? Or force him to spend *more* time bloodying his knuckles on our students' faces?"

"Even worse." Bard's smile sharpened. "I'm going to give him a job."

* * *

Much later, after Damian had been informed of both his reprieve and his punishment, after Isabel had departed, fury disrupting her usual graceful strides, and after Macy had gone for her nightly ultra-marathon sprint, Dominion, Paladin and Bard remained.

Bard looked to Dominion. "With everything that's happened, we haven't had the opportunity to talk. How are you holding up, old friend? I know how close you and Tempest were."

"Everyone I know dies," said Dominion, his voice a quiet rumble. "That's just the way of the world… but it shouldn't have been her time. Not yet."

"The whole tragedy should never have occurred," said Paladin. "I'm told the Security Council wants to take a closer look at everything that happened. Up to and including the president's decision to open the Hole in the first place."

Bard shook his head. "President Weatherly and I are far from friendly, but I find it hard to believe he intended any of this to happen. There's already been talk of impeachment. What if the escape plan had actually succeeded?"

"It wasn't a total success," said Dominion, "but it wasn't a total failure either… and it cost us far too much either way."

"Has there been any sign of Fallout?"

"None," said Bard. "But a certain department whose name we're not supposed to say has dispatched their agents to hunt him down. I hear Midnight is among them."

"Good hunting to her," said Paladin, voice firm. "The sooner that whispering bastard is put down, the better."

"As dangerous as Fallout is—and in some ways, he is a greater threat than Carnage ever was—I think he is the least of our concerns," said Dominion. He shook his head slowly, a great sigh buffeting the furniture in the room. "I keep returning to the escape plan and all the work that went into it. Someone with access to inmate records was not only able to identify the perfect blend of low-security prisoners to spring the real targets… they were able to track down the relatives of those inmates, bribe them to participate, and supply them with Legion tech. They were able to locate Carnage, persuade him to join a larger assault force, and then somehow bring that entire army to the doorstep of the Hole without anyone noticing."

"We made that last part easy," said Paladin with a frown. "Most of the Capes that would have been scouting the area had been dispatched to deal with the other crises."

"Which is the element that concerns me most," said the old Cape. "Two large-scale disasters occurred on Remembrance Day, a thousand miles apart, each requiring widespread Cape intervention… intervention that resulted in security being pulled from the Hole."

Paladin went as white as his costume. "The wildfire is one thing, but… Tezcatlipoca's attack must have been a coincidence. That creature doesn't have allies; he has minions or enemies."

"And yet his attack came at the worst possible time." Dominion shook his head. "I don't believe in coincidences like that."

"Which means someone out there," said Bard, voice quiet, "was not only able to engineer the bloodiest battle in recent Cape history… they were also able to forge an alliance with our neighbor to the south."

"And we have no idea who they are."

Bard shivered. "That puts this little trial of mine in perspective, doesn't it? Suddenly, I'm far more worried about our country than I am about whatever Damian might do next to make my life difficult."

"I'd worry less about what Walker does next, and more about what he's already done," said Paladin.

Dominion nodded. "You see it too."

"See what, exactly?" asked Bard.

Paladin shook his head, his expression troubled. "I've fought Carnage three times. Every time, I had other Defenders with me, and every time, Carnage escaped. Twice, we were the ones who ran. And your eighteen-year-old Crow kills him? With a *touch*?"

Dominion nodded again, his face pensive. When he finally spoke, his words were soft.

"There is no way that boy is just a Three."

ABOUT THE AUTHOR

Chris began life as a gleam in someone's eye, but birth and childhood were quick to follow. He's been fortunate enough to live in Spain, Germany, and all over the United States of America, and is busy planning a tour of the distilleries of Scotland.

A graduate of the Johns Hopkins University's Writing Seminars program, he put that degree to ill use for twenty years as a software engineer, but has finally circled back around to the idea of writing for a living.

Chris currently lives in Nevada with his angelic wife and ever-expanding whisky collection and occasionally ventures outside to peer upwards, mutter to himself about 'day stars', and then scurry back into the house.

See These Bones is his first novel and the beginning of the Murder of Crows trilogy. Chris frequently shares new content, including some complete short stories, on his author website at https://christullbane.com.

Made in United States
North Haven, CT
29 July 2022